GIRL SEX 101

Written by Allison Moon

Designed and illustrated by kd diamond

Lunatic Ink

To all the girls I've loved before.

— Allison

To Jennie,
who taught me
what girl sex
really is.

— kd

Adapt what is useful,
reject what is useless,
and add what is
specifically your own.

Bruce Lee

TABLE OF CONTENTS

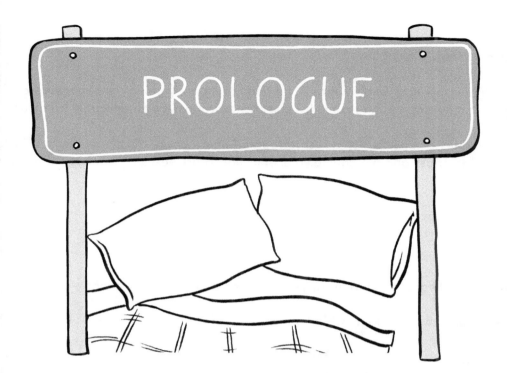

PROLOGUE

DAY 0

Jamie sits naked at her laptop, sweating into her sofa's itchy upholstery. A little horny and a little bored, she types into the search bar: media jobs, Oakland. Nothing. She sighs and clicks over to her favorite porn site. No updates there either. She selects her camera, and her bluish face stares back at her, blinking just out of sync with her real eyes. She fills her cheeks with air, a chipmunk pufferfish kind of face. She hits 'record' and makes the face into the camera, watching the seconds tick by on the screen with increasing anxiety. Her cell phone rings. The screen glows with the name "Layla." Jamie lifts her phone and hovers her thumb over the "Reject" button. She releases the air from her cheeks and answers.

"What are you wearing?" Layla purrs from the receiver, not even waiting for Jamie to say hello.

Jamie snickers. "Nothing but sweat and a smile."

"Sweat. I remember sweat."

"How's Vancouver?"

"Overcast. And expired. I'm going to San Diego."

"Why?"

"I sold Olive to my brother."

"You're giving up the Ovlov of Love?"

Layla makes a tiny sound of ambivalence. "She and I are merely going our separate ways. She's a Swedish van. I'm a Korean girl. We come from separate worlds. It's an amicable break up."

A flood of memories of Layla's Volvo rush through Jamie's brain. Mostly sex in the back, a few romantic camping trips, and, of course, the epic fight and ensuing breakup, all in that boxy behemoth.

"Fancy a roadtrip?" Layla says, interrupting Jamie's reverie.

"Roadtrip?"

"Vancouver to San Diego. Ten glorious days. I need some adventure. A change of scenery."

Jamie holds her breath and fidgets with the torn seam of her pillow.

"C'mon! Olive's getting old, and I'd rather not drive that distance alone. My playlists are only so long," Layla says. "I mean it's not like you have a job to leave."

"Hey," Jamie says.

"It'll be like old times. You, me, and Olive. A bag of sex toys in the back and a bag of jerky in the front. Forget about your Cali troubles for a while."

Jamie chews on her lip.

"Come on, Jamie. Wanna go for a ride?"

AUTHOR'S NOTE

I believe most sex educators (myself included) have a sincere, magnanimous desire to help people discover and understand their bodies and how pleasure moves through them. But anyone who asserts they have written the definitive guide to any kind of sex is either lying or fooling themselves.

It is from this place, of consideration of bodies, understanding of difference, and respect for individual journeys, that I have written Girl Sex 101. I have no doubt that eventually some words will be woefully out of date and some concepts will require reassessment. The multitudinous experience of sexual bodies is too vast to pin down in any one way for any length of time.

Sex will progress, integrating technology, medical advances, social justice concepts, and shifting interpersonal relationships and interpretation. Thus, I suggest reading Girl Sex 101 with an open and flexible mind. It doesn't claim to encompass all bodies, all expressions, and all identities. It does attempt to give credence to difference when relevant, and simple, straightforward advice where necessary.

Girl Sex 101 is neither definitive nor complete. To that end, I charge those who find incompletions in this book to fill in the blanks in their own way. If you feel there is something lacking that demands to be shared, I recommend you make and share it, in whatever way suits you. Sex is a cocreation, and so is the creative process. Share your voice with the world, and help complete the story.

Allison Moon
February, 2015

BEFORE WE HIT THE ROAD

The bulk of this book is written by me, Allison Moon. I've been teaching sex ed to adults since I was barely one of them. This book represents a step in the evolution of the class Girl Sex 101 which I first taught at Burning Man in 2007 to a group of eight women. I've since taught that class or variations of it to thousands of people across North America.

You may have noticed that I am one person. This means, while I attempt to represent a wide degree of points of view, I am still one person and I have my own opinions. To combat this whole "one person, one brain" impediment, I've enlisted the help of 16 other sex educators who represent a variety of orientations and interests.

I've also surveyed readers like you. The content of this book represents the points of view of roughly 127 different people who enjoy some variation of sex between women.

But still, we're only roughly 140 people. You, I hope, are more. You may read some things you agree with, and some things that challenge or provoke you. Sex is not a monolith, and in the following pages you'll find many conflicting opinions. I strive to present the few immutable facts about sex as facts, and allow the rest of the information to be taken or left as it suits you.

I also encourage you to keep notes. If I use a word you don't like to use, go ahead and cross it out and replace it with your own. If there's something you want to try, highlight it and leave the book lying around where your partner might find it. Or, better yet, read it together.

Girl Sex 101 is organized to build upon concepts. You can skip around, but you may find yourself lost when I mention a concept you missed, especially as things heat up between Jamie and Layla.

Speaking of those two, you'll notice that this book includes a story. The purpose of this story is to help elucidate the concepts presented in the book, while adding a bit more sexy fun. All the pages with a stripe down the edge are the story. You needn't read them to understand the book, but they may help get the juices flowing, if you catch my drift. And even if you think you know everything there is to know about girl sex, at least you'll have some sexy stories to enjoy.

Overall, I strove to create the book I would have wanted when I was coming out 17 years ago. I hope it can help you gain confidence to discover your own roadmap of sexual pleasure, identity, and connection.

GIRL SEX 101: RULES OF THE ROAD

1) **Not all girls have vulvas, and not all vulvas have girls.** Girl Sex 101 is about honoring the sexuality of the girl you were, the girl you are, or the girl you are becoming. We've taken pains to provide inclusive examples and language to help illuminate sex with all kinds of girls. Not everything you read will be what you expected from a book about lesbian sex. This is by design. Not everything you *experience* with lesbian sex is always expected. We also acknowledge that many readers may indeed not identify as girls, and we think that's awesome, too.

2) **When I say women, I mean women, which means you, if that's you.** It doesn't matter what you're packing, most of this book will be equally accessible to you. If there are any anatomy-specific parts of this book that are different for factory-installed versus user-upgraded bodies, I'll mention it. Otherwise, you can assume that when I'm talking about clits, etc., I'm talking about *your* clit, etc., whether or not mainstream society would call it something else.

3) **A note on pronouns:** While I support the use of the singular "they" and acknowledge the increasing prevalence of non-binary pronouns, I use to the pronoun "she" for clarity's sake. Unfortunately, the singular they—especially in print, especially when talking about sex—can get very confusing very quickly. Blame the English language. I know "she" may not be your pronoun or your partner's, and I know it's not a perfect solution, but I encourage you to do what women have had to do for thousands of years, and treat "she" as neutral and universal.

4) **Some of the words used in this book may be challenging to you** (like "bits," "girl," "clit," "pussy," "fucking," "holes," etc.) Some words I like to use may gross you out, confuse you, or make you angry. The words we prefer to use for sex are as unique and individual as our personalities. This makes talking about sex very challenging. For this reason, I use 2 tactics:

   • When anatomical specificity isn't necessary, I defer to the vernacular (i.e. "fucking" for whatever you like to do with a partner, "pussy" for the part you consider a pussy, "eating out" for oral sex on a female-identified person, etc.).

   • When anatomical specificity is necessary, such as the Anatomy chapter, I use the words you'd use with a doctor, which are usually most easily understood by the largest population. If these words don't work for you or squick you out, cross them out and write in your own.

5) **BODY SHOP Sections:** Most chapters end with a Body Shop section. This is where you'll find information specific to certain kinds of bodies that weren't covered in the bulk of the preceding chapter, like pregnancy, menstruation, trans bodies, disability, and more. Of course, these sections can't be exhaustive, but hopefully they'll help round out your understanding of each chapter's topic.

6) See the title? **This is Girl Sex 101, which means introduction.** There are some topics that are undoubtedly part of girl sex (like fisting, muffing, and kink), that we don't spend much time talking about. If you want to dive deeper for more comprehensive exploration of any of the topics in this books please see the Recommended Reading section, where we list a ton of great books, blogs, and resources.

7) **"Woman" is not a monolith.** We all have different constellations of pleasure, so I invite you to disagree with my assertions. Just as our bodies respond differently to different things, so do our minds.

8) **The opinions of the educators included in this book belong to those individuals who wrote them.** Their inclusion in this book doesn't necessarily indicate an endorsement of such opinions. Nor does their sharing of content indicate an endorsement of all the content in Girl Sex 101. We're all artists and individuals with our own outlooks on life. Your reading of this book doesn't mean you have to believe every word in it, nor are we liable for what naughty adventures you get into because you read this book.

One last note on language

Labels can mean different things to different people. What one person finds offensive may be another person's preferred identity label. That doesn't mean you have to use, or even like, the words I'm using. Just be aware that there's variability that is informed by age, region, community, and more.

I am not a gatekeeper to your labels or preferences. You can choose to identify however you want and I'm not going to tell you you're wrong.

None of the language I use here is perfect, not even for cis people. What's radical now may be passé or even offensive in five years. The conversation about sex and gender is moving faster than language we have for it. I consider this a good thing, but it does create serious challenges when trying to eke out some Truths from the information we have.

Much of this book is my attempt at negotiating these challenges while offering some concrete tips to improve the pleasure for all girl-loving girls. I hope I can help.

BECOME A CUNNING LINGUIST

**There may be some words that are used in these pages that are new to you.
Some of them are becoming increasingly common and others are unique to this book.
Check it!**

AFAB & AMAB
"Assigned female at birth" & "assigned male at birth" respectively. They're an upgrade from the previously used terms FTM (female to male) and MTF (male to female). Variations include DFAB ("designated female at birth") and CAFAB ("coercively assigned female at birth").

Why not just use "trans"? Well, AFAB/AMAB are useful when talking about the factory-installed equipment that often goes along with that "It's a girl!" or "It's a boy!" designation. For clarity's sake, in Girl Sex 101, I use **female-assigned** and **male-assigned** when speaking about anatomy.

BISEXUAL
The sexual attraction to people of your own sex and different sexes. See also "Pansexual."

BOTTOM SURGERY
Genital reconstruction surgery.

CIS
An adjective to describe someone who feels generally in alignment with their assigned gender. For example, a person who happily identifies as a woman now and was greeted into the world with "It's a girl!" is cis.

FACTORY-INSTALLED
The kind of equipment we're born with.

GENDER ESSENTIALISM
Stereotypes that suggest that certain genders must include certain traits. For instance: girls like dolls and boys like sports. Gender essentialism is lazy and often completely incorrect. The implication is that if someone doesn't fit the mold for their gender they are somehow wrong or broken.

GIRL/WOMAN

Should be obvious, no? Well, not really. I use the terms girl and woman interchangeably, knowing full well that might get some panties in a bunch. But I also use the term to describe identity, not genitals. When I use "she," "girl," or "woman," I'm making zero claims about what someone is packing in their panties. Unless it's necessary for me to draw a distinction by using the terms cis, trans, female-assigned, or male-assigned, a girl is a girl is a girl.

GIRL DICK

There are a lot of terms trans girls use to describe their genitals, including "outie," "strapless" & "clit." I'm not about to tell anyone what to call their parts, and you're allowed to use whatever words you want. In trying to decide what word to use to describe what is what is commonly called a penis in male-assigned people, I polled 15 trans girls. The answer was almost unanimously "girl dick." I fully realize as a quasi-cis person, any term I use can be loaded, and that time may send "girl dick" and other terms out of fashion, but I want to be both accurate and inclusive, which is a pretty tough tightrope to walk. I hope that comes across in the following pages.

Note: I do use the word "penis" sometimes when not referring specifically to trans women, as in the Anatomy and Safer Sex chapters. Plenty of girl-sex-having girls have sex with penises, too, so I want to be clear about risks.

GROUNDED

Not what your parents do to you when you miss curfew. In this context, it's kind of a woo-woo way of saying feeling calm, present, and in one's body.

LESBIAN

As an adjective, it describes sex between two women. As a noun, it usually describes a woman who has sex only with other women.

NON-OP and POST-OP

In Girl Sex 101, non-op means a trans woman who hasn't had bottom surgery. (Whether she ever will or not is beside the point). Post-op means a trans woman who has had surgery and is now the proud owner of a vulva.

NORMATIVE or NON-NORMATIVE

Normative means rules based on what's considered "normal" in our society, aka "cultural norms." It's important to understand that cultural norms reflect mainstream values, NOT scientific truths. "Heteronormative" is a popular derivation, meaning the rules of society based on heterosexual mating rules: the whole "one man with one woman with babies" thing. If that's "normative" (not normal) then anything that doesn't fit this picture is, by definition, Non-Normative. The fact is, when it comes to sex nothing—and everything—is normal.

P/V, P/A, or P/V(A)
Short for Penis-in-Vagina, Penis-in-Ass, or Penis-inVagina-or-Anus penetrative sex, respectively.

PANSEXUAL
Sexual attraction to people regardless of gender or sex.

QUEER
A catch-all term for any non-normative sexual attraction or identity. Some people identify as Queer or use it as an adjective for a kind of sex or act. As a verb, means to skew or remove from the norm. Throughout the book I'll use queer as shorthand for bi, lesbian, and pan-oriented folks.

TRANS
Trans is a term used to designate a person who doesn't identify with their assigned-at-birth gender. Some people identify themselves with the term trans, others consider it a term only used when drawing comparisons between cis and trans people. I use the word trans in the book only when it's important to draw such a distinction. Otherwise, everyone is just a "girl" or "woman" with no special adjective.

TRANS CLIT
Another variation on what trans girls might call their bits.

SEX
Okay, so this one's obvious, right? No way! Sex is waaaay more than the penis-in-vagina story we've been told ad nauseum. Sure, it can be p-in-v, but that's just one specific flavor in a world with 1001 varieties of sex. In these pages, we'll explore some of the other delicious flavors you can enjoy.

TOP SURGERY
Most often used to describe breast removal for a trans masculine person. Can also imply breast implants.

USER-UPGRADED
This is the word I use to describe post-op genitals. I use this in a "car" kind of way, not a value statement kind of way. It's designed to draw a distinction between "factory-installed" (i.e. genitals we're born with) and surgically-modified.

VULVA-OWNERS
Another way of saying cis women AND post-op trans women AND trans masculine folks who kept their factory-installed genitals.

There may be other words that you don't understand in this book.
You can find a bigger, searchable glossary online at GirlSex101.com.

DAY 1

Layla stares at the monitor, where flight 690 from Oakland blinks "ARRIVED." She sips her coffee and people-watches to pass the time. She envies the travelers on their way to or from various adventures, making up exotic stories for all of them. She fingers the keys in her pocket, eager to start the journey.

Jamie would have checked at least one bag. That bag would be filled with gear; Jamie loved her toys. If customs were to get too interested, Jamie would either be late or angry, probably both. Layla takes another sip and continues watching the crowd. She glances down at her clothes and tugs the hem of her shirt. She scratches at what looks like a crusty spot of hot sauce. Dammit. But maybe that's okay. Make her look like she's not trying too hard. Layla adjusts in her seat and takes another sip of coffee.

Someone catches her eye. The woman struts through the lobby in three-inch heels and a purple A-line dress that emphasizes her big hips and makes her cleavage look like it should be registered as a national monument. She turns heads with every hip sway. Layla slips her aviators down from her forehead to hide her curious eyes, tracking the curvy, brown-skinned femme as she traverses the floor.

The woman glances in Layla's direction. Layla fights the urge to look away. Instead she holds steady, and cracks a sly smile. The woman's mauve-painted lips spread to reveal a gleaming, gap-toothed smile. She changes her vector ever-so-slightly, swerving those hips past Layla's table to arrive at the cafe counter. With a sultry alto, she tells the barista she wants something sweet. That's Layla's cue. Her heart thuds in her chest, but that's all part of the game.

She arrives at the counter just as the woman snatches her wallet out of her snakeskin purse.

"I'll get that," Layla says.

"Oh you will?" the woman replies, a challenge.

Does Layla push back? Recant? This is the part of flirting she hates, where feminism and chivalry stare each other down. But the woman is smiling and the barista is waiting. Layla lays a five on the counter and the woman lets it be. The barista takes it and leaves the change on the counter as the two women size each other up.

"You coming or going, sweet thing?" the woman asks.

"Hopefully both, in that order."

The woman chuckles and places the straw between her lips for a slow and deliberate sip. "How much time does that give me?" she asks.

"Depends on how good you are," Layla replies.

The woman holds out a perfectly manicured hand for a shake. "I'm Dixie."

"Layla."

The woman fishes a pen from her purse and writes her number on a napkin. "I'm headed to Victoria tonight. Call me if you're in the area, and I'll give you a proper bon voyage."

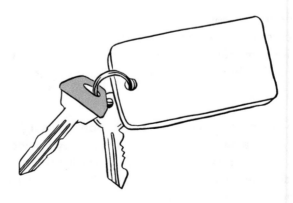

FLAGGING, FLIRTING, & FINDING

So, you wanna sleep with ladies. Welcome to the club.

Until pretty recently, lady-lovin' ladies had to rely on a carefully curated looks and cues to let people know they were "friends of Sappho." Luckily the cultural closet is becoming an unpleasant memory, and we have things like OkCupid profiles and Craigslist ads to help us find each other.

Queer women are realizing that we don't have to look specific ways in order to read as gay. But that doesn't mean that the flagging has stopped. Of course there is still some queer invisibility for the femme-inclined or transmasculine folks who "pass," but it's becoming more acceptable for a woman to, say, wear heels and nail polish and still want to sleep with girls. And that legit desire to be both expressed in one's appearance *and* read as queer has inspired some elaborate forms of flagging.

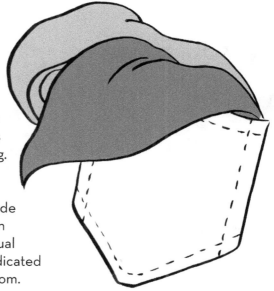

Flagging is a technique most popularly demonstrated by the "Hanky Code." The Hanky Code is a color code for handkerchiefs that some gay men put in their back pockets to communicate their sexual interest. (*Ah, if only ladies had it so easy!*) Color indicated activities and pocket placement indicated top/bottom.

According to the Hanky Code, for instance, wearing a navy blue handkerchief in your left back pocket meant you were into anal sex as a top, whereas wearing a light blue handkerchief in your right back pocket meant you liked to perform oral sex.

The code has become increasingly elaborate over the years, now including things like mosquito netting, gold lamé, and five different shades of blue. Queers of all genders have adopted the hanky code, too. The only real problem is that you need to rely on other people knowing the code to get good results. A secondary problem is that queer women still don't have nearly the kind of hookup culture gay men have, so there's less anonymous bathroom groping to be had (not none, mind you, just less).

Queer women have instead used other cultural signifiers like haircuts, tattoos and fashion choices to broadcast their penchant for puss. (There's a reason one of the most formative coming-out gestures for many women is the "dyke haircut.") These cues vary by region, ethnicity, community, generation, and subculture (e.g. leather dyke vs. sporty dyke).

HOW YOU FLAG

I try to keep a queerdo haircut just to make things simpler for everyone ;)

MY EXPRESSION IS VERY FLUID. ONE DAY I MIGHT WEAR A DRESS AND MAKEUP, OTHER TIMES I MAY WEAR A LEATHER VEST, AN LGBT T-SHIRT AND BIKER BOOTS.

It frustrates me that the only way to be visible as queer as a female-bodied person is to make oneself look more masculine. I wish I knew ways to look queer while presenting as female.

AS A FEMME I STRUGGLE WITH THIS A LOT. I WANT OTHER QUEER INDIVIDUALS TO KNOW I'M FAMILY! BUT THEY CAN'T TELL SOMETIMES BECAUSE I'M STRAIGHT PASSING. THAT MAKES ME SAD SOMETIMES, BUT I RECOGNIZE THE PRIVILEGE I HAVE IN SOCIETY BECAUSE OF IT.

I CAREFULLY CURATE ALL ASPECTS OF MY PRESENTATION AND APPEARANCE SO THAT MY OUTSIDES MORE CLEARLY REFLECT MY INSIDES, WHICH ARE QUEER, STRONG, POWERFUL, AND FEMININE. I DO THAT THROUGH POSTURE, GROOMING, SPEECH, AND CLOTHING CHOICE.

Wearing rainbow jewelry. Tattoos.

DYING MY HAIR. DRESSING IN MASCULINE CLOTHING. BINDING MY CHEST. NOT WEARING MAKE-UP.

FLIRTING

Flirting is hard. In fact, I think it's the hardest part of dating women. Flirting with a hottie you're pining for can make cunnilingus with a pillow queen feel like a freakin' cake walk.

If you're shy, trust me, I understand. There's a reason why I write books instead of, I don't know, meeting people. I hit on my first adult girlfriend by asking a friend to do it for me. Seriously. Then when I got her number, I didn't have a pen so she wrote it in lip gloss on my valet ticket.

The next day I had to decode pink glittery hieroglyphs to get the chance to see her again. It wasn't my proudest moment.

I've gotten better since then. Years of fucking women has a way of building one's confidence. But before you can be the super stud you were meant to be, sometimes you have to be a little awkward.

So yeah, flirting is scary. But it doesn't have to be. **Flirting is just getting to know someone, and being playful at the same time.**

When you flirt with someone, you're learning if your style of playfulness is compatible.

For instance, have you ever playfully teased someone and had them take it the wrong way? Or, have you ever been teased and got super hurt about it?

That's usually not because either of you is a jerk, but because you have different styles of play. Some people require a foundation of trust to be able to kid with each other. Some people can't learn to trust someone unless they get teased.

I was at a wine shop in New York City and saw a woman who was 100% my type and yet way out of my league. She was wearing designer glasses and an expensive suit and was filling a cart with bottles of nice Bordeaux.

I would have kicked myself for a lifetime if I didn't say something to her. I wanted to know who she was, at least a little bit, before our lives diverged. I was, in a word, attracted.

Since I was feeling playful I said, "I want to go wherever you're going," and gestured to her cart.

She laughed and said the party was at her place. I told her she had lucky friends. I smiled and wandered away. I didn't want to be creepy, just wanted to make a connection. Later I was in line behind her and she showed me the bottle. "Do you like Bordeaux?" she asked.

I said yes, which I do, but frankly, I was starting to feel a little outclassed. Instead of asking more about the wine she chose, I asked her what the party was for. She said it was because this amazing wine was on sale and she wanted to share it.

What I should've done was ask more about the wine. I could have asked why she liked it, or where she had it first. Clearly she was a wine geek and she was giving me an easy in. I could have learned a lot about her and maybe created some affinity.

Shoulda coulda woulda.

I left feeling grateful I got to connect with such a woman at all, but also feeling like I missed an opportunity to get to know her (and get invited to her party!).

What happened at the wine store was what I call "Geek Calls." Geek Calls are folks' ways of talking about what they're into. And if you learn to listen for them, they make flirting a breeze.

The word "Geek" used to be a slur, but it's being reclaimed in a big way to mean people who are just really into something. Most people are geeks about something. Hiking, lacrosse, fashion, travel, sex, books, photography, physics, makeup, art, poetry, basketball, Twitter, camping, cocktails, social justice, video games, comics, philosophy and on and on and on. Geekery can be your hobby, or what you want to do when you have some time off. It's what you google when you're bored. Or what you like to talk about with strangers and friends alike.

Being out about your geekery will help you meet other people into the same thing (this is the essence of dating profiles, after all). And it will help you have conversations with people you've just met.

1) BE A GEEK. I MEAN, NO PRESSURE, BUT...

You know that saying, "Life is what happens to us when we're busy making other plans"? **Well, girls are what happen to us when we're busy doing awesome things.**

Kayaking, banjo-playing, dog sitting, music festivals, museum docent-ing, grad school, the Coast Guard or whatever. People are attracted to people who are passionate about something. You are most attractive when you are engaged in something you love. You could put on clothes you don't particularly like, go to a bar you've never been to before, and not know what to talk about. Or you could spend your weekends doing something that is soul-filling-ly fun. If you love hiking, where are you more likely to meet girls who like hiking too? A bar? Or a LGBT hiking club?

Hi, I'm Allison. And I'm a talent slut. I've dated five opera singers, four musicians, three actors, two power-lifters, and two entrepreneurs. You could say I have a type. And that type is PASSIONATE. Passion is sexy. Watching a lover fully-engaged in their full self-expression is one of the hottest things I can imagine. Cultivate your own creative fires, and don't be surprised if cuties show up wanting to feel a little of your heat.

2) BE YOURSELF.

I know this is obnoxious advice because it's such a cliché. But your mom was right. Be yourself. Why? Because you're more likely to meet people who are into people like you by being, well, you. If you pretend to be into swing dancing because the girls are cute, but you really prefer German speed metal, stop hanging out in the swing clubs and get thee to a metal club! Sure, you may end up sifting through a sea of dudes and/or duds. But it's better than dating a girl whose hobby annoys the crap out of you.

WHAT ARE YOU GEEKY ABOUT?

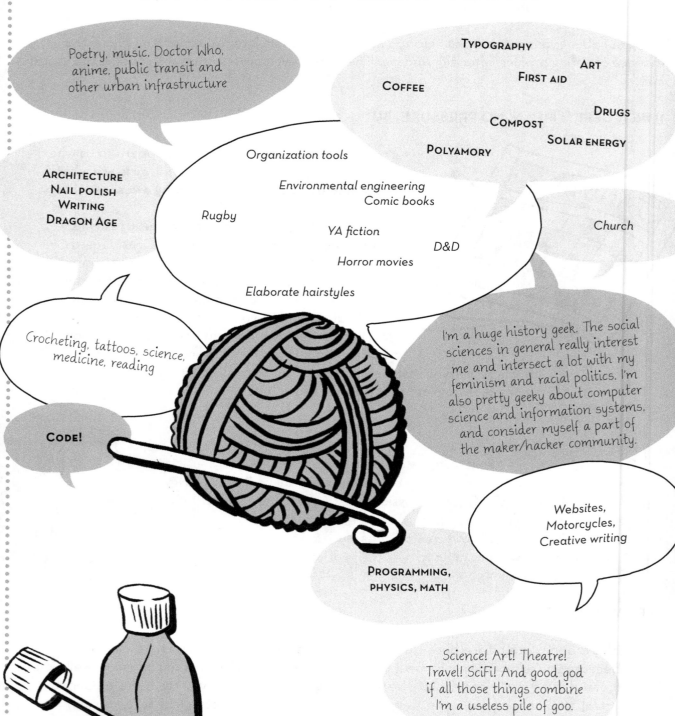

Poetry, music, Doctor Who, anime, public transit and other urban infrastructure

TYPOGRAPHY

ART

FIRST AID

COFFEE

DRUGS

COMPOST

SOLAR ENERGY

POLYAMORY

ARCHITECTURE
NAIL POLISH
WRITING
DRAGON AGE

Organization tools

Environmental engineering
Comic books

Rugby

YA fiction

D&D

Church

Horror movies

Elaborate hairstyles

Crocheting, tattoos, science, medicine, reading

I'm a huge history geek. The social sciences in general really interest me and intersect a lot with my feminism and racial politics. I'm also pretty geeky about computer science and information systems, and consider myself a part of the maker/hacker community.

CODE!

Websites,
Motorcycles,
Creative writing

PROGRAMMING,
PHYSICS, MATH

Science! Art! Theatre! Travel! SciFi! And good god if all those things combine I'm a useless pile of goo.

WHAT IS "CREEPY?"

The word "creepy" is often used to describe people (usually dudes) who approach people (usually women) in an off-putting or vaguely threatening manner. The stigma of the term has made many folks terrified of being called creepy. But what is creepy? **And how can you avoid being That Guy?**

CREEPY is being attached to an outcome. If you approach someone with the goal of sex, and then find things not going in that direction, you may try to steer things back to sex. This is creepy. If you get butthurt when things go in a different direction and then start to resent the object of your affection because they aren't behaving the way you want them to, this is creepy. Being attached to an outcome means that you want to have ultimate control of someone else's experience. You want to move them around like a videogame character instead of giving them free choice to opt in or opt out.

INSTEAD, do as our Buddhist friends do and Practice Non-attachment. Learn to be okay with another person's preferences and proclivities, even if they don't stack up to your hopes. Let people have their autonomy and choice, even if that choice is to not hang out with you.

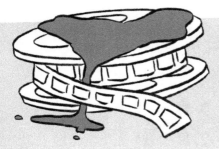

CREEPY is not taking "no" for an answer. Here in America, we have a weird attachment to tenacity. I blame Hollywood. Romantic comedies constantly reward creepy behavior. Whether it's stalking, inappropriate declarations of love, or wearing someone down until their "no" turns into a "yes"—those things are creepy.

INSTEAD, let no mean no. If you're gracious, generous, and kind when hearing no, sometimes people will change their minds. But only if you've listened, heard, and honored them to begin with.

CREEPY is hiding your intentions. "Do you need a ride?" "Want to come up for a nightcap?" If your intention is to get laid, using subterfuge to get what you want is creepy.

INSTEAD, talk about it. If you suspect the person you're grooving on is sweet for you too, ask them on a date, or say you'd really like to make out. If you don't know if they're attracted to you, find out first. Say something like, "I think you're cute. Would you like to hang out one on one sometime?" If they don't reciprocate, then back off. Don't try to trick or coerce them into taking off their panties for you.

CREEPY is needing to lower someone's status to feel good about yourself. "Negging" isn't sexy or flirtatious; it's preying on someone's insecurities to force them to try to win your approval. It basically makes you everyone's crappy, disapproving stepdad. I don't know many people who find that dynamic alluring, just triggering and crazy-making.

BE NICE. This doesn't mean you have to use cheap flattery. Just be sincere and treat people with respect. You catch more flies with honey. And more honeys with honey.

CREEPY is thinking if you were better looking you'd get away with bad behavior.

MMMMAYBE. But you can look like Portia de Rossi and still be creepy. And using good looks to be a creeper is just shitty.

Realize that even the most classically gorgeous among us have their crosses to bear. And being charming and kind will get you much farther with women than you might think. As queers, we tend to have a much broader idea of attractiveness, with more openness to gender expression and the many ways people can be hot. Of course, we can be just as shallow as anyone, but there's more in your favor if you're a queer and not Kerry Washington-level hot.

CHEMISTRY VS ATTRACTION

How will I know if she really loves me? I try the phone but I'm too shy, can't speak. Falling in love whenever we meet. I'm asking you cuz you know about these things!

Oh, Whitney, I know that feel, girl. What Ms. Houston sang about is a pretty universal feeling. We like someone, but we can't tell if she likes us back. We want to reach out, but we get flustered. We prepare a statement only to forget our perfect lines as soon as she's listening. We don't know how to figure out if she even cares.

Before you get all discombobulated with passion, let's take a moment to examine what's happening. It's called **Attraction**. Thumper called it "twitterpated." Odds are, you know what that's like. You feel heat, energy, a little nervous tickle inside. You want to touch her, to smell her hair, to learn all about her.

Attraction can be purely physical (something about her pheromones gets you all worked up). Or it can be physical plus a little intellectual/emotional excitement (pheromones plus "What's your favorite color?"). Or it can be heavy on the emotions and intellect, with just a dash of physical attraction. This is what we usually call a "crush."

I'M NOT A PLAYER, I JUST CRUSH A LOT

Crushes are awesome. They energize you. Excite you. Bring a glow to your cheeks.

Carol Queen says that a crush is to love as masturbation is to sex: it can keep you on your game, get the blood pumping, help you learn more about yourself and what turns your crank, and see you through some dry spells.

Crushing is healthy. You can have crushes while you're single, in a monogamous relationship, or playing the field. Crushes don't have to hurt anyone, and they aren't cheating.

A defining aspect of Crushing is that it's a one-way street. It's something you feel for another person, whether or not that person reciprocates. Often the object of your affection won't

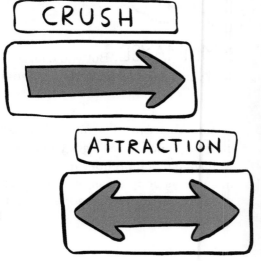

reciprocate. Unrequited crushes can be delightfully painful, or just plain painful, but they still help exercise your lust muscles. When a person does reciprocate your crush (lucky you), we enter into the land of Chemistry.

CHEMISTRY

Chemistry is when two people have mutual attraction. It's a conversation, a dance, a shared energy. I think of it as a sonar ping. You send out the ping, and you wait for another ping to come back. Chemistry is when stuff starts to get really interesting. If crushing is the masturbation of love, chemistry is the sex of it. It's when they not only make you blush, but you make them blush too. Or giggle, or flirt, or scoot a little bit closer. Chemistry doesn't have to mean anything. You can have crazy chemistry with people you never plan on dating or sleeping with. You can have crazy chemistry with people that end up becoming your bffs, painting buddies, bandmates, or best friend's partner. Or you can explore dating, sex, friends-with-benefits, or romance. It's all gravy, as long as everyone is on the same page.

If you're nervous about rejection, a good step might be to stop pursuing attraction and instead seek out chemistry. If you crush a lot and hit on everyone you crush on, you'll probably get rejected a lot. There's nothing wrong with getting rejected, but if you want to improve your odds, seek out chemistry instead.

If you wait to see if you have chemistry with people you're attracted to, when you make a move, you may find your odds of success improve.

What does this look like in practice?

Chemistry can look like:
Reciprocal flirting
Mutual casual touch
Lingering eye contact
Creating excuses to spend more time together
Eager exchange of information
Asking questions about each other
"What are you up to now? Wanna come along?"

In short, chemistry is a two-way street.

PRO TIP: Chemistry does NOT negate verbal consent. You still need to ask and get permission before you touch or escalate any sort of chemistry into the sensual or sexual realm. Chemistry is simply an indicator light—a temperature gauge, if you will—as to whether you wanna try to get that car on the road.

HOW DO YOU FLIRT?

I'm a bit of a joker so I would probably act stupid or try to get them to laugh.

Eye contact, small gestures, laughing, engaging in conversation.

I suck at all of that. You have to hit me with a 2x4 for me to even notice someone is flirting with me.

Humor, suggestiveness, geeky awkwardness. The line I used most recently was a Star Wars pickup line: "I must be from Alderaan, because you just blew up my world."

I TRY TO BE SUPER WARM AND OPEN WITH A PERSON.

Flirty talk. Random touching (with lots of attention paid to whether it's appreciated).

Shamelessly stating intentions and waiting for the blush.

I'M AUTISTIC AND DON'T DO SUBTLE WELL, SO MY FAVORITE WAY TO FLIRT IS USUALLY TERRIBLY BLUNT AND TO THE POINT.

SPEAKING IN NERDISH (THE HOTTEST LANGUAGE OF ALL!).

I strike up a good conversation and hope it goes my way.

I'm a big fan of showing how good of a listener I am. People honestly love to talk about themselves, which is fantastic because everyone has a story to tell. My best pick up lines are when I can remember a small fact about them that I can say the next time I see them. It really works.

I usually get to know people as friends first and then segue into a romantic relationship from there.

I'm petite, very femme, and present fairly vanilla. People are often very surprised at how sexually confident, experienced, and assertive I am. I really enjoy playing with gender expectations and getting the element of surprise.

Be curious and give compliments. Ask questions and listen consciously. Be open. Find moments of connection and elevate the discussion. Be direct, but not pushy.

FINDING

Looking for love and building community look pretty similar. Your job for both is to be as *you* as you can be and then seek out people who dig you for it.

Sometimes this means throwing meetup groups or potlucks or joining sports teams or teaching workshops or assembling an all-dyke World of Warcraft guild.

Places like bars can work too, but they don't always foster connection as much as they do sloppiness. Your results may vary.

If you're looking for attention from the womenz, here are two ways to start:

I call it the **Hunter** method and the **Broadcaster** method.

The Hunter is what we usually picture when we think of a classic suitor/seductress. She's the person scanning the club for someone who catches her eye. She moves in with a line, and tries to land a number or a date. There are plenty of ways to hunt that aren't this cliché, but you get the picture. Hunters often "collect" people, whether for romance, sex, or friendship. They can be highly selective or generally amiable. They're usually extroverts and they like to have a tribe of friends. They're often in relationships, and they're usually relationships that wouldn't have happened unless the Hunter did the approaching. Hunters have a better time when there are plenty of people to meet and talk to. It doesn't matter if they end up talking to someone who they're not sexually interested in, as long as they made a nice connection with a new person. Hunters can be super slutty or super selective. They like to throw parties or events, and they always want to know who's who.

Broadcasters are usually introverts. They prefer going home alone instead of spending time with a dud. They usually have a strong sense of self and are fine being the one at the bar reading a book instead of scoping the scene. The strong suit of Broadcasters is that you can get a good sense of them by just looking at them—the way they dress, carry themselves, and speak are all indicative of who they are. It's not necessarily artifice, but a careful understanding of how people read them. Broadcasters do "them" loud and clear and attract people in the process. Some broadcasters are the life of the party, and some hang back and let the party happen around them. The key is that they're projecting a signal. Like a game of Battleship, Broadcasters are just themselves in a space and let Hunters find them.

My partner is a Hunter. I'm a Broadcaster. When people ask me how I met my partner, I usually say because I wasn't looking for anyone. I was happily living my life, filling my time with things that brought me joy, and I ended up attracting someone who loved me specifically for those things. My partner likes to collect people, and I was one of them.

Most people are a mixture of both traits, depending on how shy you are, if you're surrounded by friends, if you're already partnered and just looking for friends, and so on.

CULTIVATING YOUR HUNTER

Learn to approach people (see GIRLS & FEAR).

Cultivate a curiosity about people.

Be out in the world. It's easy to meet people virtually, but then you only get to know them that way—virtually. Log out every once in a while and get out on the scene.

Do things. My dating life was the most active when I was a theater reviewer in LA. I got comps to every show in town, so it'd be easy to dazzle my date with a night at the theater. Free dance classes, donation-based yoga, bike rides, or whatever. Get out and find your enthusiasm.

CULTIVATING YOUR BROADCASTER

Discover your personal style: Hunt for hair and fashion styles that make you feel good, that make you feel YOU. Try to make yourself look like the person you want to look like. This can also influence things like your name and pronouns. Being a Broadcaster means being YOU loud and clear.

Find friends who share your interests. Good friends are the best wing women a girl can get. They have the dirt, they aren't afraid to share your opinions, and they'll make sure beer-goggles don't lead you astray. Sure, they may have slept with that one girl once but it was no big deal. Being a broadcaster is easier with friends, just make sure they don't clit-block you.

Be patient. The problem with broadcasting is that women aren't taught to be aggressors. There's all sorts of negative messaging telling girls to be passive and polite instead of active and interested. So as a broadcaster you might have to deal with some hot—but reserved—ladies.

GIRLS AND FEAR

"I will not be afraid of women..."
- Dar Williams

I had a crush on a girl I used to see at a lesbian club about once a month. She was tall, beautiful, and always smiled when she danced—a rare quality among the Los Angeles lesbian scene. She illuminated the space. Her eyes were bright, she wore her black hair cropped short, and her style with simple but classy.

And that's all I know about her. Because I never talked to her, never asked her name, never said hello. Once, after six months of not seeing her, she reappeared, and I screwed up the courage to approach her at the bar. But I hesitated, and in that lost moment, her friend wedged herself between us, not noticing me and my clumsy attempts at connection.

I saw this woman one more time after that. I was at Dinah Shore, the big lesbian party in Palm Springs. We were in a crowded hotel hallway. I was being pulled through the crowd by a friend. As I was dragged through the dense crowd, I spied her. She, too, was being dragged through the crowd, in the opposite direction. When I saw her my heart leapt. I tried to move to her, willing to fight my fear but struggling to fight the mass of bodies. For those of you old enough to get the reference, it felt like the opening sequence of *Empire of the Sun*, when Christian Bale is torn from his mother in the exodus of Shanghai during World War II. The crowd swept us away from each other, and unlike kid Bale, I never saw her again.

You'd think I'd have learned my lesson. But you'd be wrong.

Around the same time, I had a monster crush on a slightly famous woman who was on the board of the nonprofit where I worked. Whenever she came into my workplace, my pulse pounded and I would stammer or hide.

My boss knew about the crush and nudged me like a fawn, giving me tasks that got me close to her.

Despite her being friendly, single, and super gay, I could never bring myself to ask her for coffee. Oh, and did I mention we lived in the same neighborhood? I'd see her at cafes, the supermarket and yogurt shops (yogurt was big in LA at the time), but despite having tons of things to talk about, I could never say anything.

Finally, after *years* of that nonsense, I resolved to ask her for coffee. Unrequited love is for suckers, I convinced myself. Can you guess what happened next?

The night before the event where I would see her and propose (coffee), I learned she was performing on stage in New York, and thus wouldn't be at the event. A month later I heard she was engaged. Soon after, she landed a big role and her celebrity status shot out of the stratosphere. The next time I saw her she was married and famous. Opportunity blown. Window closed. Cue sad trombone.

So what is there to learn from my tales of woe?

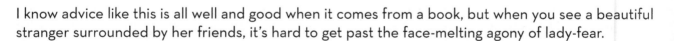

When it comes to hitting on girls, one night of awkward conversation is less horrible than years of regret. Both these incidents happened nearly 10 years ago now, but I still cringe at my ineptitude.

What would have happened if I simply complimented the dancing girl on her haircut or asked my celebrity crush for coffee? Ugh, I still wonder. Worst case, they'd look at me weird and avoid me. Best case, I'd be dancing with the woman of my dreams.

I know advice like this is all well and good when it comes from a book, but when you see a beautiful stranger surrounded by her friends, it's hard to get past the face-melting agony of lady-fear.

HERE'S HOW TO DEAL:

1) **BE SINCERE.** Compliment her on something that you genuinely appreciate. Like her style? Her hair? Her smile? Her taste in coffee beverages? Just say so. It's always about breaking the ice, and it doesn't have to look like some sleazy pickup line. Women usually learn to put up walls around men, for obvious reasons. But rarely do women behave the same way when approached by other women. If you're sincere and not just emulating the worst of dudebros, odds are she'll

be polite back, especially if you're offering a sincere compliment. If they're jerks, whatever, they've probably cured you of your crush. Be a good person, be sincere, be kind. Women could use more kind people who ask without taking, and give without expecting reciprocation.

2) **BE FRIENDLY.** If the object of your affection is with friends, be friendly to everyone. Approaching like a lion to try and take down the weakest member of the herd is just another shitty tactic. Most women will see right through that. Lead with the possibility of connection, not just the possibility of sex.

3) **DON'T GET ATTACHED TO OUTCOMES.** I've met some excellent friends at clubs and bars. Some of them I was hoping to hook up with but didn't. A few of them I was hoping to hook up with and totally did. The reason why this works is that sex wasn't the point. It can be an excellent cherry on top, but if you approach a woman with the singular goal to get into her crotch, you're a dick (see what I did there?). Being attached to a preconceived outcome is what makes the creepy vibe happen. You're allowed to flirt, use innuendo, and let her know you'd like to take her home. But if she says no, you have to be okay with that and back off. That's what separates the creeps from the cool kids. Have you ever watched a single creepster roam a bar, hitting on anything with tits? When he's shot down, he gets butthurt, makes it about her, and then moves on to another woman where he repeats the same steps. This is what being attached to outcomes looks like. It makes a person think that having sex on one specific night is what defines the night as a success or a loss. If you're not attached to outcomes, success can look like a myriad of things from having a nice conversation, making a bunch of new friends, or just breaking through your anxiety and asking a pretty girl to dance.

Lesbian communities tend to be more intricate and intimate than other communities because of this lack of attachment to outcomes. You might hit on a girl and find out she's monogamously partnered, but you end up falling in love with her ex, who's also the nanny of her kids. This kind of thing isn't weird at all in many queer communities. So embrace the possibility of nuance in relationships. Flirt and play with the intention of connection in its myriad ways, and odds are, you'll find something that works for both/all of you.

4) **JUST FREAKIN' SAY SOMETHING.** It doesn't have to be brilliant, clever, or even cogent. You just have to break the seal. Getting shot down is an opportunity for closure. Instead of the big weeping wound of "What could have been?!" You'll get the "Eh, nothing will be. Alright, moving on..."

Flirting may not be revolutionary, but the way you do it can be. Mainstream culture teaches women to envy and distrust each other. As a woman-loving woman, you have the opportunity to undo a tiny bit of shit that we ladies have to deal with in this world. You can be attracted to a woman without it only being about what she can do for you. Use flirting as an opportunity to practice listening, compassion, connection, and respect. You may end up with new friends!

TOBI'S TRANS-MISSION

THEY CAME FROM WITHIN:
TRANSPHOBIA IN OUR COMMUNITIES

The queer community is not immune to transphobia. I know a lot of trans women who avoid queer events because they've had bad experiences. Some of the most aggressive and hurtful transphobes use their queer identities to dodge scrutiny for their actions by making it seem like "infighting" rather than straight up anti-trans oppression.

It can be difficult for trans women and their partners to navigate the social dynamics of larger queer community spaces. Several cis women I've dated have been accused of not being "real" lesbians— even by friends. Cis women may be encouraged to hide or reject attractions they have to trans woman for fear of how others would respond if they acted on them. At the same time, a lot of trans women get the message that they are un-dateable. I've lost track of how many times I've heard a trans woman lament that she'll never find a partner because anyone attracted to men wouldn't be attracted to her as a woman but no one attracted to women will see her as enough of a woman.

It's tempting to fall into this line of thinking, and a lot of trans folks pick it up. But it's not true. First off, did you notice how this line of thinking ignores the existence of bisexual and pansexual people? That should tell you something about this argument right there. It's true that things can be difficult, but there are always possibilities. Trans women are women, and so it should not be surprising that many folks attracted to women in general will find themselves attracted to a trans woman now and then. The problem is not so much a lack of attraction, but messages that tell people to hide it, feel shame for it, or reject it. Luckily, there are plenty of people out there willing to reject societal messages when it comes to matters of the heart. It's one thing queers, in particular, seem to be really good at.

Tobi Hill-Meyer is a multiracial trans woman with over a decade experience working with feminist and LGBTQ organizations on a local, state, and federal level, having served on several boards and offering support as a strategic consultant.

VANCOUVER

"Fucking customs," Jamie says, her first words upon their reunion. She puts down her bag and steps into Layla's open arms. Layla feels thinner than Jamie remembers, her ribs meeting Jamie's fingertips through the cotton of Layla's t-shirt.

"They give you a hard time?" Layla asks.

"They thought I was carrying dynamite. I told them the only things I'm planning on blowing up with these," she shakes her suitcase, "are clits."

Layla laughs. "And maybe some customs agents' minds."

Layla takes Jamie's bag and they walk to the parking garage. "You look good," Layla says.

Jamie runs her fingers through her hair. "Really? I feel...rumpled."

"Yeah, but rumpled sexy. The whole torn jeans and sex hair thing. You look like an incognito rock star."

Jamie flashes the devil horns sign. "Well party on, Lay."

"Party on, Jay."

Layla drapes her arm around Jamie and leads her to the garage.

"Here she is!" Layla shouts, gesturing to the army green van parked in the corner of the garage.

"Olive!" Jamie smiles.

"The Ovlov of Love," Layla responds.

Layla opens the back and throws Jamie's bags in. Jamie peers inside. "She looks like she hasn't aged a mile."

"She's gonna," Layla says. "We're gonna make this girl *werk*."

Jamie jumps into the passenger seat, landing with a crunch and crack. "Ouch!"

"Up! Up! Up!" Layla shouts.

Jamie rises from the seat and finds a crumpled sweatshirt draped atop a pile of CDs.

"Mp3s too modern for you?" she asks, rubbing her ass.

Layla grabs the stack of music, dropping a cracked CD onto the van's floor. "Dammit, I really liked this mix."

Jamie examines the broken CD case and sits back down. "Wow, it's college all over again."

"I've been feeling nostalgic." Layla turns the ignition and pulls onto the road. "When do you need to be back in the Bay?"

Jamie shrugs. "Any time before the 13th. I have a job interview then."

"What kind of job?"

Jamie screws up her lips. "Receptionist at a non-profit."

"Sounds like a dream!" Layla snarks.

"More like a nightmare. But income will at least help me sleep at night."

"Well we got twelve days before you have to think about it."

"Ayup," Jamie says. She rifles through her backpack and retrieves her iPod and portable speakers.

She fiddles with the iPod, its Geiger-counter click underscoring Layla's voice.

"We can swing that," Layla says. "First stop, Victoria."

"The island?"

"Not just an island, the capital of British Columbia!"

"What about Olive?"

"We'll take her on the ferry."

"That makes zero sense," Jamie says.

"It'll be easier to get into the States."

"I promised Barbara and her wife we'd meet them for dinner in Seattle tomorrow."

"No problem. We'll spend a day in Victoria and then take the ferry to Seattle and do customs there."

"Instead of just driving straight there."

Layla pulls onto the highway. The silver-green of the city takes shape. Gray clouds cling to dark mountains in the north. "It'll be fun."

Jamie narrows her eyes, the catalogue of Layla's past subterfuges rushing through her brain. "Why?"

"Why what? I just told you."

"Why really?" Jamie asks.

"Jesus, do you have to be such a buzzkill?"

"I knew you'd change plans before we even got started," Jamie says.

"This is a roadtrip; we're not supposed to have any plans."

"You said you wanted your van in San Diego in ten days. How is that not having a plan?"

"There's wiggle room."

Jamie blinks as realization dawns. "Oh."

"What?"

"You're getting laid." She returns her attention to the iPod.

"No," Layla says. "What? So?"

Jamie mutters, "For fuck's sake."

"What do you care? It'll be a pretty ferry ride. You'll get to see our province capital. I'll buy you some poutine. It'll be fun."

Jamie groans. "Oh come on."

Layla laughs. "She's real fierce, Jay," she says. "Curves like whoa. If you saw her, you'd sympathize."

"I can't believe I'm blowing my meager savings for this."

"Hey." Layla grabs Jamie's hand. "We're having an adventure, escaping our lives for a little while. Getting laid in Victoria—or wherever—is the point. If you're lucky, I may even give you a second chance at all this hotness." She gestures to her body like a spokesmodel.

"Because that always went so great when we dated."

"It was one of the things we were good at."

"One of the few things," Jamie says. She squeezes Layla's hand and presses play on the iPod. A clean guitar riff carries the vocals in. *There's a war inside of me...*

Layla laughs as the song rolls on. "Is this my broken CD?"

"I've got all the same music." Jamie holds up her iPod. "I just remade the playlist."

Layla smiles and Jamie returns it.

"So, Victoria, huh?" Jamie says.

Layla nods. "This is gonna be a good trip."

VICTORIA

DAY 1

Dixie's house smells of cooking rice, roasted peppers, and red wine.

Dixie breezes through her kitchen in a summer dress and sandals. Layla looks down at herself and smooths the front of her stained t-shirt.

They rush through dinner, sharing nervous glances and small talk. Dixie opens a second bottle of wine and suggests they move to the couch.

Layla scans the living room. An altered paint-by-numbers hangs over the sofa: a gothic mermaid and kinky gnomes decorate the otherwise bland landscape. Half-finished knitting projects fill a basket at Layla's feet, topped by a pornographic cross-stitch waiting to be framed. Layla looks at Dixie's sly smile; even her orange lipstick fits the bold and kitschy aesthetic.

Their tense shared smile says it all. But Layla sits still. Dixie's confidence is immobilizing. The moment passes, and Dixie shows her disappointment with a simple downward glance and sigh. She takes Layla's wine glass away, setting it on the coffee table, and peers into Layla's eyes. Layla struggles to hold her gaze, seeking the glass of wine in her periphery. She pins her hand between her knees to prevent herself from reaching for it as a prop to hide behind.

Dixie holds the moment so long that Layla's face grows hot. Then, finally, Dixie cups Layla's cheek. Her touch is blessedly cool against Layla's burning cheek. Dixie runs her crimson-painted thumbnail against Layla's lower lip.

"Can I kiss you?"

Layla nods.

Dixie's lips are dry but plump, consuming Layla's small mouth with heavenly softness. Dixie releases a little moan, and Layla finds her confidence. She presses into Dixie and their mouths open, tongues tumbling over each other. Layla smiles as their kisses grow fervent, finding delight in their compatible styles: mostly lips, gentle flicks of tongue, softness, and shared—but limited—moisture.

Dixie reaches for the hem of Layla's shirt and pulls it over her head, exposing Layla's bare chest and small breasts.

Layla relaxes onto the purple velvet of the sofa, letting Dixie's full bosom sink onto her chest. She is consumed by Dixie's curves.

"I want to put my hands on your tight little body," Dixie purrs into Layla's ear. "Tell me what you want me to do to you."

Layla freezes and then squirms.

Dixie leans back and removes her hands. "You don't like being touched?" Dixie asks. "It's alright, baby, you can be stone."

"I'm not stone though. I like being touched—all over. I guess people just think that because..."

"You're butch?"

Layla laughs nervously and blushes. "Sorry. My face gets hot when I drink." She reaches for a glass of water and drinks it down. Dixie watches and waits. Layla sets the empty glass on the table with a clink. "I want you to do me. I do. I'm just so used to topping, I don't know what to say."

Dixie traces a fingertip from Layla's ear, along her neck and chest, to circle her nipple. "You mean you have a hard time asking for what you want?"

Layla shakes her head. "No, I mean, no one even usually asks. So I guess I don't know the answer."

Dixie leans in and kisses the path her finger traced, whispering into Layla's clavicle, "Oh that's easy. Lay back and relax. We're going to play a game."

Layla's heart beats hard against her ribs. Dixie leans over her and strokes her face with light touch. Layla shivers.

"You like that?" Dixie asks.

Layla grins. "Is this the game?" Dixie glides her light fingered touch down Layla's cheek to her neck and chest.

"How do you like your nipples played with?"
Layla shrugs and mumbles, "You know, the usual way."

"Oh honey." Dixie chuckles. "All the ways are the usual ways." Dixie licks the tip of Layla's nipple and says, "I'm going to gently bite your nipple. I want you to slowly count up from one, and as you do, I'm going to increase the pressure on your nipple. Stop counting when it stops feeling good, okay?"

Layla smiles. "One..." she says.

"Two..."

"Three..." she sighs.

"Four...Five..." she moans.

"Six—Yeowch!"

Dixie relaxes and kisses Layla's breast. "Five-and-a-half then?" Dixie purrs. "I can work with that."

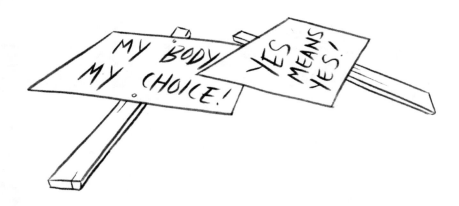

COMMUNICATION & CONSENT

Like it or not, when you get it on with people, you're going to have to talk about it. This is especially true if there are quirks or nuances about things you like or don't like. This is especially *especially* true if you have any triggers that could cause the hotness to derail.

Part of being a responsible sex-positive person is knowing that no one is going to read your mind. No one is going to "just know" that you like something or not, even if you have all the same equipment. It's your job to speak up and share the stuff your partners need to know. This applies to STIs just as much as it does to things you really like.

YOU 101

Before you can tell someone what you like, you have to *know* what you like.

At the very least, these are things you need to be able to communicate succinctly and straightforwardly:

Anatomical terms turn me on. Talk Latin to me, baby!

Call it my junk, not my pussy!

This is my outie, and this is my cunt.

"No" zones. Some people don't like being touched in certain places on their bodies or in certain ways. If there's a part of your body you don't want touched, tell your partner up front.

Words to use/avoid. What do you call your stuff? If there's a word that would freak you out or turn you off, let your partner know. This is especially important if using a certain word would be akin to misgendering you.

Bottom lines. If there's a kind of touch that shuts you down or freaks you out, communicate that up front. Feet are a huge erogenous zone for some people and anathema to others. Likewise, spanking can seem innocuous to some folks, but it can be annoying, painful, or freaky for others. Know what you hate, and be ready to talk about it. But be careful not to judge other people's likes. Don't squick her squee!

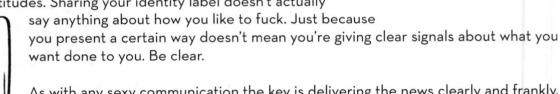

STI status and protocols. You should share anything about your health that will directly affect you partner. This means communicable STIs. You also want to share any rules for safer sex you have.

Turn ons/Turn offs. Will dirty talk make you giggle? Will hair pulling rev your engine? Let 'em know. It's just as important to share turn-ons as it is bottom lines.

Your identity is not a recipe. Butch bottoms exist. So do stone femmes, trans guy pillow queens, trans women who like getting blow jobs, dykes who sleep with cis dudes, monogamous kinksters, and on and on and on. Humans contain multitudes. Sharing your identity label doesn't actually say anything about how you like to fuck. Just because you present a certain way doesn't mean you're giving clear signals about what you want done to you. Be clear.

> I only have oral sex with dental dams, okay? Cool!

As with any sexy communication the key is delivering the news clearly and frankly. You're not telling your partner you have a month to live. You're telling them what will make sex fun. Your partner probably doesn't want to annoy you, trigger you, or turn you off. You both win if you're upfront with this stuff.

If your partner reacts poorly when you say "Call it a cock, not a clit, please," then you may want to reassess if this is someone you want near your genitals at all.

It's fair for you to feel annoyed sometimes by having to teach an intro class on your body. This is often true if you sleep with people for whom you are a "first" of any kind. (The number of bi-curious but inexperienced girls I've slept with...Oof.) You get to decide if that particular person is worth the You 101 class. But getting the intro class out of the way is often the only way you can enjoy spring break.

And remember, you can't teach a class if you don't know the material. Explore, masturbate, experiment. Then give the your sweetie the map.

BUILDING YOUR OWN ROADMAP

Sometimes it's hard to figure out what feels good. Because most of us aren't encouraged to self-pleasure (i.e. masturbate), many of us never spend much time mapping our own pleasure response. Sometimes we don't know that we like clitoral stimulation more than penetration, or a little bit of anal in combination with g-spot pressure. Figuring out what you like takes time, energy, and most of all, curiosity.

MASTURBATE

If you already masturbate regularly, next time give yourself twice the time you usually take. If your usual routine is hammering or vibing your clit for three minutes before you run out the door, try giving yourself five minutes of exploratory time before you bring it in for a landing. If you like to spend 15 minutes before bed, try 30 minutes of something new. Try moves on yourself you've never done. Try to emulate moves lovers have used on you that you liked.

If you don't masturbate already, there's no time like the present. Put this book down (or better yet, flip to a picture or story that turns your crank) and start blazing a trail. There are very few sensations a partner can generate for you that you can't generate yourself. So if you like partner sex, you can certainly like masturbation.

If porn's your thing, consider yourself a winner for being alive in this day and age. The Internet is for porn, after all, so start googling and diddling. (See the Appendix for our suggestions.)

Overall, try things. Flick, twist, tug, and rub in a bunch of different ways. Buy a new toy on the internet and take it for a spin. Watch instructional DVDs and try it that way. Rent Black Swan and try to channel Natalie Portman (without the whole *masturbatus interruptus* part).

When you're exploring, stay present with your body. It's natural to want to lose yourself in the fantasy. That's awesome. No problem there. But! When you're doing pleasure recon, take the time to notice the sensations. Your nipple likes it when you flick it that certain way? Noted. The Magic Wand is way too buzzy for you? Into the giveaway pile it goes. This information is gold when it comes to sex. It gives you the chance to make your current and future lovers into sexual rock stars.

Everyone likes feeling like a rock star in bed. Help them help you. It is literally a no-lose scenario: **Step 1:** Learn what you like. **Step 2:** Communicate what you like. **Step 3:** Your partner gives you what you like. Everyone wins. But the first step is that you have to know what you like. So get yer lube and get to it.

So you know you like it when your taint is tickled with a feather while you finger your own ear. Awesome. How do you communicate that to a lover?

This is a tough one for a lot of folks. I've been teaching sex ed for over 10 years, and I still have a hard time speaking up sometimes. So, I know that feel, bro.

Here are some ways to get better at it:

Practice saying what's on your mind right away. The longer you hold onto it, the weirder it'll feel. It's like needing to pee when you're at the movies. You could try to hold it, but then you end up spending the entire movie distracted by the intensely increasing agony of needing to pee. Instead, just get up, go pee, and miss 2 minutes of a 2 hour movie that your friend can fill in for you in 2 seconds. It's a no-brainer. Same with speaking up during sex. Do it fast, do it right away, and enjoy instant satisfaction.

Yummy noises are your friend. Worried about being articulate? Worry no more. It's a scientifically-proven fact that sexy sounds are sexy to hear. Moans, grunts, purrs, and sighs serve the delightfully double duty of sounding hot and letting your partner know they're doing things right.

BONUS: Sexy sounds aren't just sexy for your partner to hear, they help keep the sexy going for you, too. Seriously, next time you're jacking off, try making all the porno sounds you can. (Preferably if the kids/roommates are out.) It might feel a little silly, but, hey, jacking off can feel a little silly. Just go for it. Hit the high notes, growl like a tigress, moan like Belladonna. Stay authentic, just amplified.

Ask Either/Or questions. If you're topping and need to get more info from a reticent partner, the best way to get better answers is by asking better questions. "Faster or slower?" "More pressure or less?" "Stay here or move up a bit?" "More lube?" Anything your partner can answer clearly with a shake/nod of the head or a simple one-word response is a good question.

BONUS TIP: This is a question I want you to eradicate from your lexicon: "Is this okay?" Any answer to this question gives you exactly 0% constructive information. It's the sexy time equivalent of "How are you? Fine, thanks." Don't do it. Instead, ask "Do you like this?" That question is easily answered with a yes or no. And with either answer, the next question can be "What would make it better?"

Schedule "Do Dates." If you're in a relationship, or just sleeping with the same person on a semi-regular basis, schedule a "Do Date." This is an opportunity for you to practice receiving pleasure, while your partner learns to navigate your body (and vice versa).

RULES FOR A DO DATE:

1) One person is the receiver, one is the giver. This may be challenging for both of you, especially if one of you is more accustomed to being the top than the other, or one of you feels weird being the center of attention. Work through it.

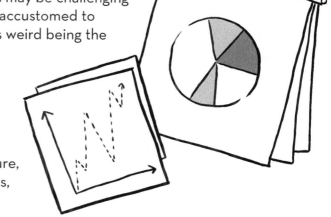

2) Let go of goals. The only goals of a Do Date are to start building a map of pleasure and to practice communicating. Don't make it about orgasm. You should spend the majority of your time meandering, playing with sensation, pressure, rhythm, energy, and requests. If orgasm happens, awesome. If it doesn't, awesome.

3) No reciprocity in the moment. A lot of lesbian sex is "I do you, you do me." This is great, but not the point of the Do Date. Do Dates are to practice giving separately from receiving.

Do Dates are great for new relationships, but they can be even more amazing for long-term lovers. You can learn new things about your lover's body that you never figured out together before.

Play the Number Game. Pussy got your tongue? If you, like lots of folks, get a little pre-verbal when you get turned on, it's hard to articulate what you want. Try this game as a workaround:

Have your partner stimulate you in some way she knows you like. Let's say it's stroking your outer labia. She can ask, "On a scale of 1 to 10, where's this?"

All you have to do is come up with a number. Let's say you say "4."

Then, she can ask, "What would make it a 5?"

Appreciate. Don't underestimate the power of positive reinforcement. Now's the time to use your yummy sounds. Do you like the way she's licking you? Say so! Or, at the very least, moan so. Consider this the "positive reinforcement" part of training your lover to do things you like. Same thing if you're topping. Does she look sexy? Tell her! Are you happy she said yes to your invitation for a date? That's a sweet thing to whisper into her ear when you're nibbling on her neck.

Making Upgrades. Generally happy with the way things are going but need to make a small shift? Use the Appreciation Sandwich, a technique I learned from relationship educator LiYana Silver.

The Appreciation Sandwich is composed of three parts:

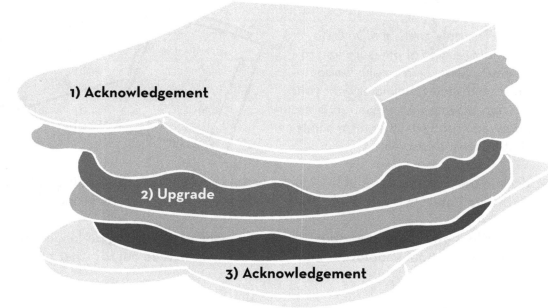

1) Acknowledgement

2) Upgrade

3) Acknowledgement

(See? It's like a sandwich!)

Let's see it in action:

Or (this one I've used a lot):

Reciprocate. It doesn't have to be at the same time, or in the same way. Reciprocation means you should show up with the same amount of presence and awareness as your partner. You should be willing to offer them something they'd like, even if it's later on. All relationships are a two-way street, so figure out how you can meet your partner heading in her direction. Even if your partner is stone and you're a pillow queen, there's an exchange of reciprocal energy possible. Check in and see what she'd like from you.

Need to have a bigger talk than just "move this there"? Try having the conversation not in the bedroom. Over dinner, on a walk, or on a long drive, these can all be great times to broach the subject.

I like to do it when I'm driving. It helps me stay calm (since I have to focus on the road), it allows for easy escapes of eye-contact, and the movement of motion can be soothing.

You might like to have "the conversation" when surrounded by other people (like at a cafe) or when the two of you are alone.

DISCLOSURE

If you have something big to share but don't know how to do it, here's an excellent formula to try. This was invented by relationship genius Reid Mihalko of ReidAboutSex.com. I've used this a bunch, and I even use it in the book! Check it out:

REIDABOUTSEX'S DIFFICULT CONVERSATION FORMULA

1) I have something to tell you.

2) Here's what I'm afraid will happen when I tell you...

3) Here's what I want to have happen...

4) Here's what I have to tell you...

This formula can work for all sorts of challenging situations:

The formula works for all sorts of situations. I use it for big and small things in my relationships—everything from coming clean about a white lie to having a Serious Talk about the Future of Us.

If you're afraid of sharing something with your partner or potential partner, consider why. If you're actually concerned for your safety if you disclose something, consider if you feel safe going to bed with this person at all. How much fun do you really expect to have if you're nervous for your safety? It is likely best for you to not even go there if you don't think this person can handle you non-aggressively.

If you're afraid of rejection or your partner freaking out, there are ways to deal.

First, try the Difficult Conversation Formula.

Second, have the talk when you both aren't naked and entwined.

Third, accept the possibility that your partner may indeed freak out a little bit. Most people don't handle new information well, and few of us love hearing the words "Can we talk?" So allow your partner to have the freak-out if they need to.

Fourth, if you being honest and straightforward about something important to you freaks out your partner, consider the fact that they just saved you a lot of emotional baggage down the road. Do you really want to date/fall in love with/commit to someone who can't handle something true and real for you? Sure, it may not make it any less sucky, and you may have really liked that person. But in the long run, you're better off scaring off the people who don't get you so that you have more room in your life for the people who totally *do* get you.

WHAT ABOUT WHEN YOU DON'T KNOW WHAT YOU WANT?

All of us know the feeling of searching for an answer and coming up blank. Sometimes it's because the answer is something we didn't know exists.

Sometimes it's because the thing we want feels so shameful or embarrassing, we bury it from even ourselves. And sometimes it's because we genuinely don't know what we want. The answer to all these conundrums is education, the Internet, experimentation and maybe some therapy.

Experimentation can look pretty simple:

> HARDER OR SOFTER?

> I DON'T KNOW. TRY SOFTER. HMMM....

or fairly complicated

> So then you finger me as we both sing 'Closer to Fine' and spank each other with these tambourines. Did you bring condoms?

If you don't know what you want:

1) Take a breath and think into the space posed by the question. Anxiety over not knowing usually happens when you feel pressured to have the answer right away. *Don't rush this part.* Give yourself time to think it over.

> 3 Mississippi, 4 Mississippi, ...

2) If you know the answer after breath and thought, answer. If you don't, think of what you might like that wasn't even part of the question.

3) If you're still coming up blank, ask them to try one of the options, with the caveat that if you don't like it, you'll say so. Sometimes we don't know what we want because we don't know what the result will be. Co-create a result and then decide if you like it or not.

> DO YOU WANT FASTER OR SLOWER?

> PANCAKES!

4) When in doubt, back up the action to the last thing you remember liking. Or...

5) Cuddle and reassess. Cuddling is your neutral zone. It's intimate and sensual, and it feels good. If you get overwhelmed or anxious, go to the cuddle zone and ground.

> Ack, slow tickles! Faster, faster!

CONSENT

Consent can feel like a scary word. It's so often associated with non-consent that it's hard to talk about in any way that feels remotely sexy. But it's a skill you can learn, just like cunnilingus, and it's a necessary concept to grok. When it's done right, it's super sexy.

Consent is making sure you and your partner are on the same road trip.

The bar for consent is actually set pretty low. All it means is everyone is agreeing to the activity. You can get basic consent by simply asking if someone wants to do something and waiting for them to say "yes."

This low bar is a start, but for high-quality consent, we need to make two upgrades:

- **Informed consent**
- **Enthusiastic consent**

Informed consent means everyone's on the same page and crystal clear. It means deconstructing euphemisms and discussing expectations. For example, if you consent to watersports with me, you might be really disappointed when I don't show up with a jet ski.

Do you want to go on a walk?

YES!

Enthusiastic consent means not only agreement, but genuine enthusiasm for the proposed activity. Enthusiasm mitigates issues of bullying, coercion, intoxication, and peer pressure.

If negotiating sex is like choosing a restaurant, enthusiastic, informed consent is "China Grove? I love that place!" or "I've been meaning to try that place!" or "Yes, but I'm allergic to shrimp, so please don't order that." Enthusiastic, informed consent is **not**, "If it's really important to you" or "I don't know what the food is."

If the concept is still daunting to you, let's take it back to the root of the word. "Consent" shares a lot with "Consensus." Essentially, consent is the practice of consensus. It means everyone gets a vote, and everyone's vote matters equally. A lack of consensus means the proposition won't move forward.

In the restaurant example, consensus is:

Consensus is not:

Nor is it:

CONSENT IS...

1) **Consensus.** All parties must agree on the activity.

2) **Instantly revocable.** You are allowed to change your mind at any point, even midway into an activity.

3) **A way to make everyone feel safe, respected, honored, and appreciated.**

4) **An opportunity to use your voice and discuss likes and dislikes.**

5) **An opportunity to learn about your partner.** You may have no problem speaking up in the moment, or getting yourself out of a situation you don't want to be in. But not everyone's like that.

6) **Revolutionary.** Women's bodies are treated as public property. People are constantly telling us how to look and how to act. People touch us without asking all the time. They shout lewd comments at us and trick us into responding to them. Men, especially, are taught they should "try to get" as much as they can, and women are supposed to tell them when to stop. This dynamic is what people are dealing with daily, and it's the baggage we bring with us when we go to bed with someone, regardless of gender.

You have the power to undo a little bit of this terrible dynamic, simply by asking your partner what she wants, and waiting for her to say yes. It might not change anything in your world, but it can help give her back a little bit of her voice that's been taken away by society at large.

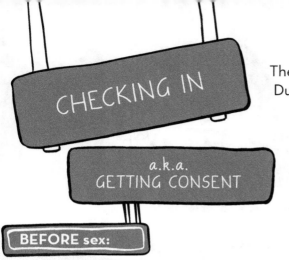

CHECKING IN

a.k.a. GETTING CONSENT

There are three times you want to check in: Before, During, and After Sex.

Before sex, you want to make sure your desires and interests are compatible with your partner's. And you want to make sure you both can say an enthusiastic "yes" to what's proposed.

BEFORE sex:

1) **STI status & protocols** (see Chapter 9 for any easy way to talk about STI's).

2) **Relationship status/agreements.** Are you in a non-monogamous relationship? If you're getting sexy with someone, it's probably a good idea to let them know the deal, lest they feel like "the other woman" or "used" in some unpleasant way.

3) **"No Zones."** Otherwise known as bottom-lines, these are either parts of your body you don't want touched, or a certain kind of touch that would be needle-scratching-the-record bad. No Zones are especially important for some abuse survivors and some gender-variant folks. But they're relevant for all of us. For instance, my partner HATES to be tickled. I risk a knee to the jaw if I accidentally brush an armpit. So armpits are a No Zone. Some folks may freak out if you touch their neck, their breasts, their genitals, and so on, even though everything else is on the menu. Find out what your partner's No Zones are before you trigger them.

4) **Dislikes.** These are less imperative than No Zones, but equally important to assess. Dislikes usually won't trigger you, but they may take you out of the moment. So it's better if you just avoid them altogether.

5) **Likes & Interests.** What's something you can agree on and might want to do together?

6) **Words to use.** Do you cringe when you hear the word "cunt"? How about "junk"? Let your partner know "Don't call it a yoni!" or whatever.

The great part about checking in before sex is that you can do it whenever. If you're on your dinner date, walking home from the movies, or making out at their front door, you can check in. Even if you've been in a relationship with someone for a while, it's never too late to check in about this stuff. You can always learn more about your partner and their body.

What can a consent negotiation look like?

Checking in DURING sex:

I don't know when it became uncool to check in during sex, but that shit's ending right here.

Checking in is SEXY. It means you care about your partner's pleasure, comfort, and emotional state. These are Good Things.

Some people say that isn't "organic" and that's a load of shit. What's not organic is getting stuck in your head because you're lost or triggered or picking up ambiguous signals or no signals at all.

Why checking in works:

1) **It saves you emotional paperwork the next day.** "Just going with it" can feel great in the moment, but in the cold light of day, you may have second thoughts. In my opinion, much of the day-after-drama could be mitigated by checking in before and during sex. Instead of freaking out about STIs after you've done something worrisome, you should have the conversation before.

2) **It ensures you get what you actually want.** Too often we defer to what we think our partner wants instead of asking for what we want. This creates sexy times where two people are doing what they think the other one wants instead of actually talking about it. Sex tends to bring out the insecurities in people. If you have a hard time speaking up when someone cut in line at the bar, it'll likely be hard for you to do the same when your partner is lying on your hair.

3) **It helps you get "repeat business."** If your partner feels respected and heard, she's more likely to want to see you again. If she feels like you took good care of her in bed, she may even recommend you to her friends. That's good customer service in action.

ALLISON'S TIPS
FOR SHORT AND SWEET CHECK-INS

1) **Speak up right away:** or immediately after you notice you should speak up. The longer it waits the longer it festers and the more stuck you're going to get in your head. Nip that shit in the bud.

2) **Ask a simple question:** "Do you like this?" is always a good one. "Feel good?" or even "Yes?" if things are really ramping up.

3) **If you get an affirmative, keep going:** Depending on her excitement level, an affirmation can look like an eager nod, verbal instructions, deeper moans or more vigorous...whatever she's doing.

4) **When in doubt dial it back:** If she's frozen or too quiet to read or is making an ambiguous face or sound, take the energy down a notch or two and try to get a clearer read by asking her a simple question. If you don't get anything from her, stop, get eye contact, and ask again. You're not going to "lose the moment" by pausing. If anything, it'll make things better. You can always ramp it right back up if that's what you both want.

Checking in AFTER sex:

Sometimes you and your partner will be totally compatible during the do, but your post-game differs. There's nothing wrong with that, but it helps to know what you like and be able to communicate it if necessary. Knowing what you like after sex is good. It can help you deal with any awkward post-coital conversations.

Are you a cuddler?

Do you hate feeling "sticky" or "icky" after sex? Do you want to shower right after? Or do you love to luxuriate in the oh-so-sexy funk?

Will you fall asleep immediately after? Will you want to run laps?

Will you want to jack off one more time and then go make snacks?

The answers to these questions can vary depending on your connection to your partner, your mood, or just the time of day. But it helps to know a bit about yourself.

If you like to shower, or read, or sleep, or snack after sex, let your partner know and ask what they'd like.

Remember, your partner doesn't cease to exist after you've had sex with them. They'll have their own needs. If you can find common ground, all the better.

I get pretty energized after sex, so if my partner falls asleep on my chest, I might feel kind of...stuck. So I tell them I'll cuddle until they doze off, then I'll go enjoy some alone time.

AFTER CARE: IT'S NOT JUST FOR TATTOOS!

After care means what you need to feel safe, content and complete. Sex can be an intense experience. It's normal to feel emotional, vulnerable, or activated afterwards. Tears, laughter, chattiness, quietness, alertness, and sleepiness are all natural after-effects of sex. Your job is to make your partner feel just as cared for after the sex as during.

Eye contact and physical contact are usually a good idea. Ask your partner how they are, and listen to their answer. If your partner needs to take some time, or shower alone, or do yoga or whatever, that's great. If they need some connection, cuddles, and conversation, that's great too.

One night stands can be the hardest for aftercare because there can be a bit of that "you saw my O face and now I'm embarrassed" vibe. The best way to handle the awkward is acknowledge the awkward, and just relax. A big part of sexual self-confidence comes from role-modeling that nothing's wrong even when there are emotions involved.

Many of us don't know how to negotiate, because we don't see it role modeled very much. Hollywood doesn't show us that. Porn doesn't show us the negotiation, even though it's an essential part of all good porn sets.

DON'T BELIEVE ME? LET'S ASK THE PROS.

JIZ

"Negotiating sex for porn often depends on the performer, on the co-star, on the company, and on the moment! Negotiations include safer sex and sexual acts, hard limits, personal preferences, desires, and much more.

When I shoot, I often know my co-stars and have a good idea about what they like and what they don't. But even before the scene starts, it's good to go over a general playlist of the things we want to do and state anything we don't. It often takes the form of an 'elevator speech' version of the Yes/No/Maybe/Depends list. People may not realize that the crew on a porn set is just as involved in the negotiations as the performers. At CrashPad, where I work as Production Assistant on shoot days, director Shine Louise Houston goes over what she calls 'the fun stuff' with the performers and crew off camera—so performers feel more comfortable voicing boundaries—and then again a second time while the livestream is on, so that people at home can see what it's like on a set and watch negotiation in action."

NINA

"Here's what I ask every female partner:

'Any injuries I should know about that limit mobility/positioning?'
'What do you hate and that I should never do?'
'What do you love?'
'What words should I never use?'
'What words do you like to hear?'
'May I pull your hair?'
'May I put my hand near/on your neck?'
'Are you allergic to latex?'
'Do you like a smack on the butt?'
'Can you come for real? Do you feel like coming for real today?'
'If so, do you like vibrators? I have a Magic Wand with me.'"

TOBI'S TRANS-MISSION

HOT OR COLD: THE POWER OF WORDS

Language for our bodies is not just a trans issue. Do you find the word "pussy" hot, or is it offputting? Is "cunt" empowering or insulting? Language issues trans women face are pretty much just the same thing. Is it weird or triggering to say "penis"? Is it even weirder to say "clit"? Is it easier to get super technical or is that too clinical? Do you want to get really silly about it or would that feel juvenile? It's such a personal thing and there is no wrong answer, even if you prefer only to call it "that" or make up a new word altogether—I'm quite proud of having come up with the term "strapless" to refer to my own bits. Talking about what language to use and avoid will make sex hotter for everyone.

WORDS TRANS WOMEN (WHO HAVEN'T HAD VAGINOPLASTY) MIGHT USE FOR THEIR BITS

Clit, Queen Sized Clit, Girl Cock, Hen (it's not a cock),
Twat Rod, Joystick, Entertainment Center
Strapless, Penis, The Business, Nub

WHAT DO YOU CALL YOUR GENITALS?

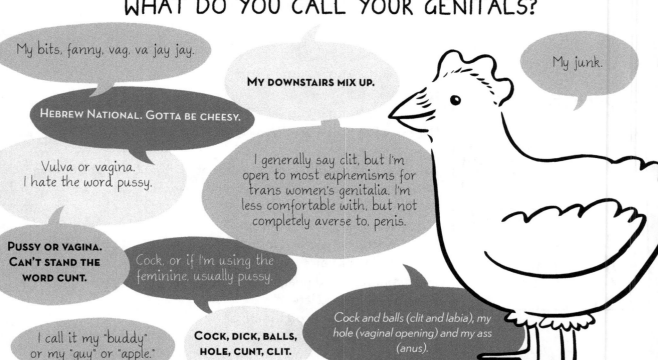

My bits, fanny, vag, va jay jay.

My junk.

MY DOWNSTAIRS MIX UP.

HEBREW NATIONAL. GOTTA BE CHEESY.

Vulva or vagina. I hate the word pussy.

I generally say clit, but I'm open to most euphemisms for trans women's genitalia. I'm less comfortable with, but not completely averse to, penis.

PUSSY OR VAGINA. CAN'T STAND THE WORD CUNT.

Cock, or if I'm using the feminine, usually pussy.

I call it my "buddy" or my "guy" or "apple."

COCK, DICK, BALLS, HOLE, CUNT, CLIT.

Cock and balls (clit and labia), my hole (vaginal opening) and my ass (anus).

EMBODIED YES

Ambiguity is a big part of not speaking up. And that ambiguity can cause a person to process something only after the fact, which is when regret and anger and a whole slew of unpleasant feelings can come in.

Sometimes, as a receiver, it's hard to know the answer to an earnest check-in. It can be hard to know if something is scary-exciting or scary-bad. It can be hard to say when something is just not-great instead of out-and-out bad. If you don't know what a "yes" feels like, it can also be triggering when someone asks you for consent, because you don't know the answer.

As a solo sexual person, practice is paying attention to what "yes" feels like in your body.

I'm going to ask you a few yes or no questions. I want you to answer them aloud and feel into what your yes or no feels like. Give yourself a little time to explore each one before moving on to the next.

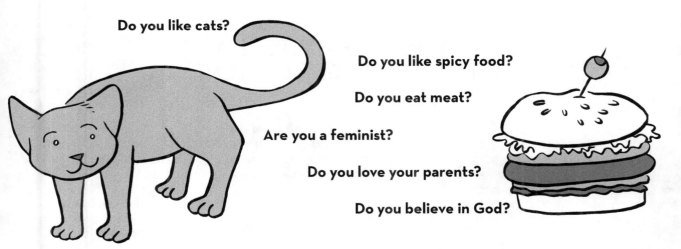

Do you like cats?

Do you like spicy food?

Do you eat meat?

Are you a feminist?

Do you love your parents?

Do you believe in God?

What did your opinions feel like? It's possible some of the answers didn't have an emotional accompaniment, but maybe some of them did. If you answered "no" to any of them, what did it feel like? Is no a slightly repellent feeling? Is there a big energy to it? Does it make you feel alert or gross or tired or activated?

What about "Yes"? What does "yes" feel like? Excited? Energized? Warm? Curious?

Getting a sense of what yes and no feel like in your body can help you along when you're not sure what you're feeling. It can also help you speak up when something doesn't feel right.

The goal is to get to a place where it's as easy to answer a question about sex as it is about whether you like cats or dogs.

Once you pay attention to what a benign yes or no feels like, start exploring what it feels like with touch. Touch yourself in a way you know you don't like. (Whether it's pinchy or feathery or whatever.) Feel how that "no" moves through your body. Does your body tell you to stop doing it? Do you feel ashamed? Or angry?

Now touch yourself in a way you know you like. Does your body scream "More!"? Do you feel happy? Content? Fuzzy?

Then try this with masturbation. Touch yourself in different ways and listen to the voice in your head and body that says "more!" or "no!"

And finally, explore the feelings of yes and no when you're in bed with someone you trust. You can either try the good touch/bad touch game, or just pay attention to the way Yes and No feel while you're playing.

Once you get good at this, it becomes much easier to recognize when these feeling happen in your body, and answers to check-in questions become much, much easier.

WHAT'S YOUR FAVORITE WAY TO CHECK IN AND GET CONSENT?

Look into her eyes, study her face and blush and breathing, just reconnect and ask if she likes it!

"MAY I (straightforward but slightly sexy description of activity)?"

I LIKE HAVING AN AGREED-UPON AHEAD OF TIME PHRASE OR PHYSICAL CHECK-IN —LIKE A SAFE WORD OR EVEN A CERTAIN TYPE OF HANDSQUEEZE OR SOMETHING. JUST A WAY TO STOP AND GET CONSENT EVERY STEP OF THE WAY WITHOUT HAVING TO ALSO MAKE EVERY SINGLE STEP A HUGE ORDEAL.

I LIKE TO MAKE EYE CONTACT AND ASK SOMEONE HOW THEY ARE DOING, IF THEY ARE HAPPY, IF THEY WANT TO CONTINUE DOING WHATEVER IT IS WE ARE DOING.

Consent is something that I think it is good to be really direct about. There are times when it is obvious that you are both excited and enthusiastic, but even when you have had sex together a lot it is still good to just sometimes say, explicitly, 'Is this good? Do you want to do this?'

Usually by explaining that consent is really great and important to me and following on with a straight up 'Where are you at with that right now?'

I don't think there is ANYTHING unsexy about saying 'Can I kiss you?' or 'Can I put my hand here?' I love it!

AS EXPLICITLY AS POSSIBLE. I LIKE TO TURN IT INTO SEXY DIRTY TALK. 'WHAT DO YOU WANT ME TO DO TO YOU? TELL ME.' 'DO YOU LIKE THIS? TELL ME.' 'DO YOU WANT ME TO XYZ? TELL ME.' I WON'T CONTINUE UNTIL I GET A YES OR NO OR OTHER EXPLICIT STATEMENT.

I TRY TO MAKE SURE EVERYONE I AM WITH KNOWS HOW IMPORTANT IT IS TO ME THAT THEY FEEL SAFE TO SAY NO TO ME.

Early and often! I've been with my girlfriend for almost two years and I still check in a lot about how she is feeling when we have sex. I think I always will.

4 PRINCIPLES OF SPEAKING UP*

(*borrowed from CuddleParty.com)

1) **If You're a "Yes" Say "Yes":** This reduces ambiguity and gets you what you want.

2) **If You're a "No" Say "No":** No is a complete sentence. You don't have to explain your "no" or couch it with apologies.

3) **If You're a "Maybe" Say "No":** Maybe keeps people hanging. Say no to give yourself time to figure out what you actually want, because...

4) **You Are Always Free to Change Your Mind:** A "yes" might become a "no" because you don't like the way it feels. A "no" might become a "yes" when you start to feel really comfortable with your partner. A maybe might become either when you have more information. Change your mind as often as you want.

THE 5 PRINCIPLES OF •NO•

"No" is a complete sentence. It's a good word. It's a useful word. It's an important word. But girls are taught that "no" is a bad word. We're taught that the other person's feelings are so fragile our mere "no" can do them irreparable damage. And so we're terrible at saying it.

If you want to get good at everything from flirting to sex to long term relationships, **get okay with hearing "No."** You'll hear it plenty. It won't kill you. Most of the time, "no" isn't about you. It's because the object of your desire is taken, straight, or just not in the mood. It's not personal. And the better you can get at not taking it personally or overanalyzing the exact mosaic of reasons a girl is telling you "no," the happier everyone will be. And when it *is* about you, a person telling you "no" is doing you a favor. A cold "no" is way better than a begrudging "yes" in terms of safety, self-care, and emotional paperwork.

Get good at saying "No." Everything, from flirting to sex, could do with a little more "no's." Especially from the feminine types. We're usually taught to be accommodating, friendly, pliant, and gracious. Some of us take on that messaging more than others. We could all use to say "no" more when we need to.

Learn what "No" *feels* like just as much as what it looks like. Many of us have a good intuition with "no." Something just feels "icky" about it, or flee-worthy, or just anti-fun. The key is to make the connection between the feeling and the voice. When you know what No feels like in your own body, you almost always get better at noticing it in other people. This is a Good Thing.

Know when a No is actually a nervous Yes. Some of us don't have a problem saying no—we're worse at saying yes! Yes can make us feel slutty or anxious or unsure of the next step. If right after you say "No" you're kicking yourself, know that you are allowed to change your mind. From no to yes, yes to no, maybe to yes, maybe to no, later to now, now to later, you are always allowed to change your mind. Sometimes saying No gives you the space to pull yourself together and check in with yourself, and you find the answer is actually Yes. Great! Now go see if the offer is still good.

(Hint: it usually is.)

THE BLANKET YES

A blanket yes is when you're giving consent in advance for your partner to do whatever. This is best used when you really trust your partner and feel empowered about speaking up in the moment should anything change. The Blanket Yes usually becomes most helpful when you're tired of saying "yes" over and over and just want to go with it. If you've already negotiated all your No Zones and Likes/Dislikes, you can give a Blanket Yes that doesn't negate any of the prior negotiations, just gives your partner permission to try things within that framework. Many long term partners give each other a blanket yes after it's clear all of the groundwork is laid and you don't have anything new to negotiate.

HANG-UPS

We all have our hang-ups. Often referred to as "baggage," "sore spots" or "quirks," hang-ups are less specific and less derailing than triggers, but can take the wind out of your sexual sails nonetheless.

Hang-ups can change throughout your life: some issues you had when you were younger just don't matter as you age. Others will appear almost spontaneously. And many will only happen after you've lived through some heartbreak or relationship bullshittery.

Everyone's got hang-ups, and they're nothing to be ashamed of. Like anything, you only have to communicate them to your partner if you think it'll affect them or the sexy times you'll have with them.

So, know what they are and be willing to communicate them as necessary so that hang-ups don't have to hang up the sexy time.

WHAT ARE YOUR HANG-UPS?

I don't like my nipples to be pinched.

No baby talk.

I REALLY, REALLY DON'T LIKE HAIR PULLING.

DON'T SUCK ON MY TOES!

IF SOMEONE IS SUCKING MY COCK AND THEY START TREATING IT LIKE A PUSSY, IT GETS ME IMMEDIATELY OUT OF THE MOOD. IT'S ABOUT HOW THEY WORK THEIR MOUTH THAT MAKES THE DIFFERENCE.

Ear nibbling. I can't handle the sound.

I DON'T ENJOY WHEN PARTS OF MY BODY I DON'T LIKE (LIKE MY BELLY) ARE FOCUSED ON.

I don't like dirty talk or excessive saliva.

Substance use/abuse.

INCORRECT PRONOUNS.

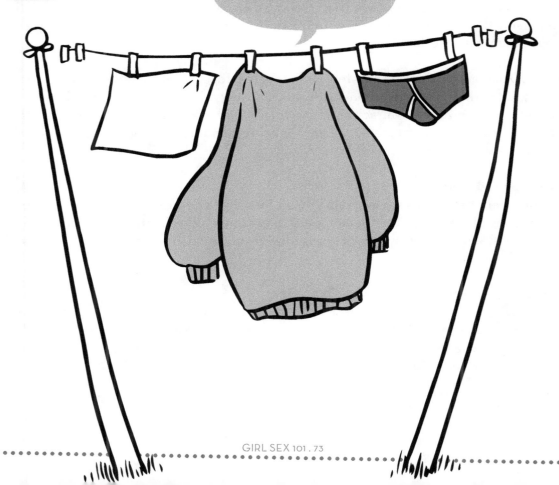

SCENIC VIEWPOINT ↗

SEX FOR SURVIVORS
by Ducky DooLittle

If you have experienced violence, sexual assault or abuse, then you are a survivor. Or maybe an accident, an injury, an illness or a surgery? It could be a childhood experience or something that happened as an adult. It may have been ongoing or a one-time thing. It may have been at the hands of someone you knew casually, someone who was supposed to love you the most or perhaps it was a stranger.

Survivors often thrive despite emotional or physical scars. Survivors can be very proactive people. Nonetheless many survivors face sex and relationship issues.

We may have trouble finding or establishing a relationship. We might feel like our histories are too complex or painful to subject others to. Or perhaps we fear rejection if we share what we have experienced. It can be hard to know when to disclose your history with a new partner. Or sometimes, the more trust and love we experience with a person, the safer we feel to face our traumatic experiences. Unexpected feelings can bubble up to the surface.

In a sexual relationship you may feel disconnected, foggy, or alienated from your own body. Or perhaps you'll feel vulnerable, anxious, angry, afraid or distrusting. Others experience a low sex drive, lack of desire or lack of physical response. If any of these are your experience, you are not alone. These are all normal feelings for survivors. Here are a few ways you may find joy in your body:

Occupy Your Body
If tuning out has been a survival skill for you, learning to be present can sometimes be frustrating or scary. But, to have hot, satisfying, connected sex you must be present in your body. Work to become more engaged with your mind, body, breathing. Tune in with yourself and your lover.

Take Little Steps
Start by turning off the television or whatever distractions provide an escape from your thoughts, body and self. Ride a bike, do yoga, stretch, learn martial arts, eat well, walk your dog, take a shower, get a massage, or masturbate. Take deep breaths, tune in and listen to your body. Do one thing every day just for your physical self.

Be Selfish

It is okay to take time and retreat into yourself. Sometimes it can be very healing to sleep, watch movies, read, bathe or walk alone. Just be conscious of those who love you. Let them know you want some alone time and that you are alright. This will help them to trust you and let go of their sense of worry.

Affection for Affection's Sake

Affection is powerful. It releases happy neuro-chemicals in our brains. Affection with someone you love creates trust and bonds. To have affection with friends, family or your lover can help lift you out of depression. With lovers it is important to establish that not every bout of affection should or will lead to sex. Holding hands, petting, hugging and cuddling are all forms of healing.

Redefine Sex

Sex is not penetration. Penetration is merely one sex act. Sex is something bigger and more profound. It is how you play with your lover in everyday ways. Find fun ways to interact and communicate with your partner. For example, you could make an effort to eat breakfast together, go on walks, dance, sleep in a tent on the lawn for no reason, read erotica to each other, play Scrabble with extra letters and only sexy words, or cook food the two of you love. Sex can also be verbal expressions, love notes, holding hands, cuddling, spooning, massage, eye contact, foreplay, flirting or anything that you find comforting and/or playful. These seemingly unrelated acts really do add up to living more truly in your skin and more orgasms for both of you.

Check Back In to Sex

The fact that you recognize that you are checking out is half the battle. During sex, try to get grounded in your body. Breathe and listen to your breath before, during and after sex play. Flex your pelvis muscles rhythmically as you breathe. Watch for subtle responses in your lover's body, like their breath, sounds and movements. Respond to them. Try sharing a little eye contact with your partner.

Try not to get too frustrated with yourself if you find this process to be difficult. Just don't give up. Being present in your body is a practice that almost always gets easier the more you do it.

Advocate for Yourself

If you need counseling, seek it. If you need medical care, go find it. If you need help of any kind, ask for it. There are organizations and individuals in your life who want to help you. Accept that as a fact.

Often there are free services available for survivors but these organizations can be overwhelmed with requests. Don't let that stop you. If you call an organization and they don't call back, keep calling. There are good people in the world who care about you, but you will almost always be your own best advocate.

Embrace Your History

You may decide to disclose your history to some people; with others you will feel it's none of their business. Some people will be able to accept your history and some will not. Ultimately, it's your history. You never have to disclose any of it to anyone for any reason. You hold that power.

Remember, you survived. By definition you are a badass. Anyone who truly deserves you will love and accept you as you are, even if it is difficult for them to accept the fact that you have experienced trauma.

Ducky DooLittle is a sex educator and author from New York City. She has appeared in the New York Times, HBOs Real Sex, The Morning Show, MTV, NPR, The Howard Stern Show, Playboy TV, to name a few. www.duckydoolittle.com

THE BORDER

DAY 2

Jamie walks along the water, watching people jog and fish off the pier. In the shallows, a group of scuba divers practice for their test. She shivers just watching them.

Her phone buzzes. *Pick you up in ten.*

Second buzz. A text from her cell phone provider reminds her all international texts cost $1.25. Shit. It buzzes again. *I have coffee.* Buck twenty-five.

And again. *You'll be ready?* Buck twenty-five.

Jamie types into her phone, *STOP TEXTING! I'm here. I'm ready. Just stop.*

It buzzes again. *You okay?*

Jamie groans and turns on airplane mode, then opens the video app. She walks down the pier and climbs down to the water, stepping gingerly over the mussels that blanket the concrete. She records the lapping water and two homeless guys feeding fish guts to their dog. She turns the camera to herself silhouetted by the sun. She turns in a circle until she's illuminated, squinting. She considers speaking but has nothing to say. She stops recording.

Layla pulls Olive into the parking beside the beach. "I can't remember how you take it so I brought it black." She hands the paper cup to Jamie.

"Soy milk and sugar."

"Oh. Oops." Layla squints against the sunlight and adjusts her baseball cap. "You ready for Seattle, babycakes? USA! USA!"

Jamie stares at the bitter brew and jumps into the passenger seat. "America or bust."

• •

"Where were you born?" A bald, stone-faced man in a government shirt evaluates Layla.

"Gangwon-do, Korea."

"You're a Canadian citizen?"

Layla nods. "My parents naturalized when I was six."

He punches some keys on the computer. "Says here you overstayed your last visa by fourteen months."

Layla looks at the ceiling tiles. "My brother had some...mental health issues."

"In—" He reads the screen. "San Diego?"

Layla nods.

"Then why was your last address in San Francisco?"

Layla glances at Jamie, sitting on a plastic chair past the X-ray machine, below a grim sign that lists the number of illegal crossings stopped and kilograms of drugs seized so far this year. Layla looks back at the agent and points back to Jamie. "Her."

The officer gestures for his colleague to fetch Jamie. Layla watches the dour woman cross the linoleum floor and gesture with a simple head tilt, not bothering to lift her hand and point.

Jamie jerks her head up, wide-eyed. Layla waves with false cheer.

"Officer, this is Jamie, my fiancée," Layla says upon Jamie's wary approach.

The steel-eyed, border patrolman scans Jamie. "You look surprised," he says.

Jamie glances at Layla and chews her lips. "It's only been a week. I'm still getting used to the word."

"A week?" he says to Layla.

"I wanted her to meet my parents first. I wanted to propose to her in my hometown. We've been together for...what is it hon? Four years?"

Jamie smiles tightly. "Four and a half."

The officer studies their faces then turns back to the paperwork. He types something into the computer next to him and waits for it to load. He reads. He glances back to their faces and then flips through Layla's biographical binder.

"Ms..." the man glances at Jamie.

"Cross," Jamie says.

"Why is Ms. Kwan accompanying you into the United States?"

Layla starts to answer but the officer shushes her. "I'm asking your fiancée. Ms. Cross, why is Ms. Kwan coming into the United States with you?"

Jamie looks at Layla, who attempts to telepathically insert the story in Jamie's brain. "We're driving to San Diego together."

"Why are you driving to San Diego together?"

Layla swallows hard as they're subjected to this most perverse form of the Newlywed Game. She holds her breath, waiting for Jamie to cut and run the same way she did when they broke up. But this time Layla would have no one to blame but herself. She fights nausea as she realizes the depth of her misjudgment.

"To see her brother. He lives there." Jamie says. "He's going to help us plan the wedding since we're both crap at that kind of thing. He's getting his degree in environmental design and has a bunch of connections with nice public spaces. Plus, he has a guest room, so we're going to crash for a few days before we start house-hunting in Oakland. Layla isn't sure about the area, but I think it'll be a good place for us to settle. I mean, it's where we met, I have a job lined up, and I think it's a good place to raise a kid. Although maybe we'll try Minneapolis. That's where my family is from. We could get way more space for our money there, and it's got a pretty good queer community. But I suppose that's farther from her family, so it'd be a conversation—"

The border agent raises his palms. "Okay, that's enough. Thank you, Ms. Cross."

He inks his stamp and flips to the fourth page of Layla's passport. The stamp clunks, and Layla exhales with measured relief.

"What's his name?" the patrolman asks Jamie, casual, almost playful.

"Who?"

"Your soon-to-be brother-in-law."

Jamie grins. "Aaron."

He hands the passport back to Layla. "Congratulations you two."

· ·

Layla and Jamie travel in silence for fifteen minutes. Jamie's gaze chases the scrub brush flying along the side of the van. Finally, they cross some sort of invisible barrier that indicates that they are really, truly safe in the U.S.

"What the fuck?" Jamie says.

Layla shoots back, "I didn't expect them to grill me like that!"

"And so you made up a fiancée?"

Layla chews her lip. "I had that in my back pocket."

"And you didn't think to tell me?!"

"I didn't think it'd go that far! It's never been that hard before!"

"What if I'd answered wrong? You could have been arrested. I could have been arrested!"

"I don't know if that's true."

Jamie kicks the dashboard and turns away to watch the blur of pines through the window. "Why did you even have to lie?"

Layla stares at the road ahead and drums her fingertips against the steering wheel. "Because the truth is always too complicated."

DAY 2

Barbara and Maureen lie in bed, a vibrator in each of their hands. Barbara rubs her vulva with lubed fingers. Maureen adjusts the pillows behind her back.

"Do you want to watch a video?" Maureen asks. "I could use a little something to rev my engine."

Barbara shakes her head, graying twists of hair bouncing against the headboard. She clicks her vibrator on, a purple g-spotter that looks delicious in contrast the deep brown of her skin. Maureen watches her wife's face. She sees part of her reflection in the glare of Barbara's eyeglasses. She turns away, clicking her own vibrator on, a palm-sized toy that looks like an elegant electric razor. She spreads her inner labia and presses the tip against her vestibule.

"Can you pass the lube?" Maureen asks. Barbara reaches for the bottle on the bedside table and passes it to her.

Maureen squeezes the bottle hard. Lube drenches her vibe and puddles on the sheets.

"Yikes," Barbara says, peeking through squinted eyes. "Should I start building an ark?"

"Thank you menopause," Maureen grumbles.

Barbara keeps vibing, squeezing her nipples and licking her lips. Maureen watches Barbara's face and mirrors her movements. Barbara sighs and Maureen repeats it, but her sigh sounds more like boredom than pleasure.

Barbara looks over. "Have you tried putting it inside?"

"I don't like vibrations on my g-spot. It feels weird."

"Hm," Barbara says. "I like it inside."

"Because you have a prostate."

"They seem to register pleasure similarly," Barbara says with a shrug.

"Just because you like something doesn't mean I have to."

Barbara clicks off her vibrator and reaches for Maureen. "We don't have to do this," she says.

"I want to." Maureen turns off her vibrator, too. "I don't like that my sex drive has been in the doldrums. I feel disconnected from you."

Barbara kisses Maureen's shoulder and coos in her soft alto, "How about we both do you, and then if you want to, we can both do me?"

Maureen sighs. "I think that would feel like pressure."

Barbara holds Maureen. "What if we watch that video you like?"

Maureen cocks an eyebrow. "The baseball one?"

Barbara nods beatifically.

"I thought you hated that one."

"I don't hate it. It just doesn't do anything for me. But it works for you." Barbara removes her glasses and places them on the bedside table. "Let's do you together and you don't even have to think about me."

Twenty minutes later, the men on screen are fucking in knee socks and ball caps. Maureen vigorously fingers herself and presses the vibe to her clit. Barbara kisses Maureen's nipples.

"Can you pinch my labia together?" Maureen asks.
Barbara strokes her fingers down her lips and pinches. "Like this?" she asks.

"Lower," she says. "Below my vagina."

Barbara slides her fingers down. "Here?"

Maureen's rolls her hips. "Mmmhmm," she sighs. She clicks to increase the speed on the vibe. Barbara nibbles and kneads Maureen's breasts. Maureen clicks up the vibe one more time, squeezes her eyes shut, grits her teeth, and groans. Her muscles tighten and shiver. Maureen's groan extends into a wail and her body shakes. The men in the porno aren't far behind her. Barbara peeks and then flinches as the screen erupts with ejaculations. She squeezes her wife to her chest. Maureen relaxes and smiles. She clicks off the vibrator. Maureen grasps Barbara's chin and pulls her into a kiss, then reaches for the remote and turns off the TV.

ANATOMY & ORGASM

Ah, health class. The place where, if we were lucky enough to get any sex education at all, it came in the form of ugly diagrams and cautionary tales. Luckily, we get to determine our own sex education now and this time we're focused on PLEASURE.

The first thing to know about genitals is that everyone regardless of gender or sex has more in common than you might think. All genitals morph from the same physiology, and that means that it doesn't really matter what you're packing as long as you can learn what feels good and communicate these things to your partners. For this reason, we're going to take a tour of both vulvas, etc. and penises, etc. If you have a good sense of one set of genitals, you'll have a leg up (so to speak) on learning about the other kinds.

The second thing to know is anatomy is not a monolith. Contrary to those diagrams you saw in health class, there's a lot of variability to genitals. Just as gender isn't a binary, neither are sex organs. Sexual characteristics (genitals, reproductive organs, chromosomes) come in all sorts of shapes and styles. Some men have ovaries, some women have testicles, and some people have a combination of traditionally "male" and "female" characteristics. There are some penises that are smaller than some clits. And there are some ladies with more impressive beards than the dudes.

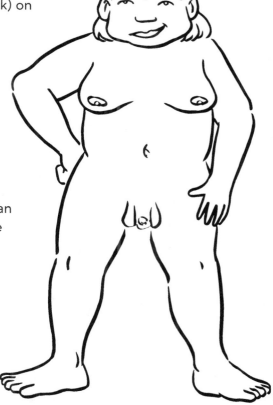

In this chapter I'll be showing you the biomedically-accepted words for parts of our genitals, both vulvas and penises. You don't need to know all the "proper" names of things to have good sex, but it really helps. It's the difference between saying "Take a right at the red octagonal thing on the corner with the tree on it" and "Take a right at the stop sign on Elm Street."

But let's be clear: The only truly "proper" names are the ones you want to use. So, while I'll be giving you some Latin here, you get to decide how for yourself how to refer to your goods and communicate those words to your partners.

In this chapter, I'm telling you how to read a map. I'm not telling you how to get to the Dairy Queen in your town. That's for to you figure out.

So before you go turning at the red octagonal thing, let's take a look at the maps, shall we?

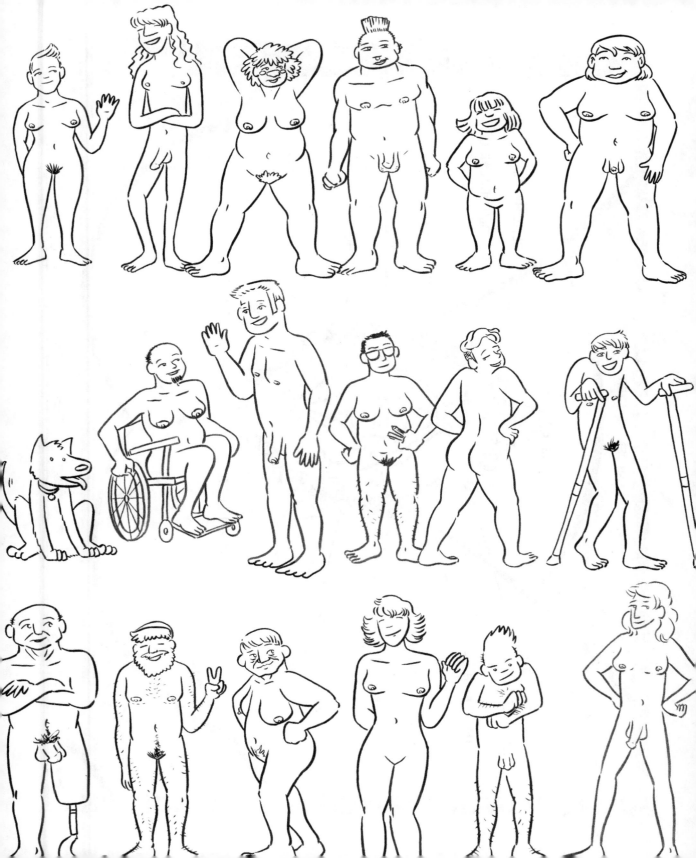

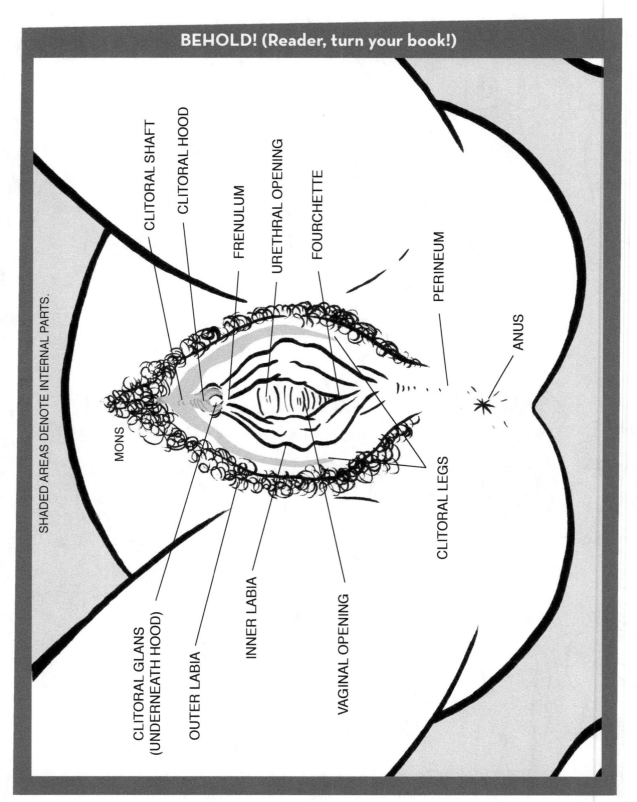

SHADED AREAS DENOTE INTERNAL PARTS.

CLITORAL SHAFT

CLITORAL HOOD

FRENULUM

URETHRAL OPENING

FOURCHETTE

PERINEUM

ANUS

MONS

CLITORAL LEGS

CLITORAL GLANS
(UNDERNEATH HOOD)

OUTER LABIA

INNER LABIA

VAGINAL OPENING

Mons: This is the fleshy pad at the top of the vulvar cleft, over the clitoris. It's usually covered with hair, and is made of mostly fatty tissue. It can handle a lot of pressure and can take a lot of impact.

Outer lips: Sometimes called the "labia majora," these are the big outer lips that usually have hair growing on them. They're fleshy, about as sensitive as normal skin, and can handle a lot of pressure, too.

Inner lips: These are the lips inside the outer lips. Sometimes called the labia minora, they're made of a stretchy kind of flesh that is responsive to delicate touch, but can also be tugged, pinched, and twisted pretty easily without any pain. (Your mileage may vary.) For those of you familiar with AMAB bodies, the tissue resembles scrotal tissue. Mainstream porn tends to show us tiny labia minora that are tucked away completely inside the outer lips. While some people are built like this, plenty of others have inner lips that hang outside the outer ones. Sometimes the inner lips are asymmetrical in that one lip hangs lower than the other.

If you follow the inner lips to where they meet at the top, you'll find the fan favorite—**the Clitoris!** What we commonly refer to as the clit is actually only the tip of the iceberg. In other words, it's the head of the clitoris. The rest of the clitoris extends into the pelvis and isn't visible. But this doesn't mean you should ignore the rest of it. In fact, stimulating the inner clitoris is one of the most powerful techniques for giving pleasure. We'll talk about many ways you can do this in Chapters 4 and 6. In the meantime, just know that the clitoris is bigger than meets the eye. The clitoris is made of erectile tissue and gets bigger when aroused. The size and shape of the clit glans (like, you'll learn, pretty much every part of the vulva) is slightly different on everyone. Sometimes it pokes out. Sometimes it's completely hidden by its hood. Sometimes it pokes out when it's excited and hides when it's not. Some folks have super teensy ones, some have mega honkin clits that look like little dicks. Everyone's different. The clit has more nerve endings than any other part of the body, and sometimes it's so sensitive you can't touch it directly without causing pain. This is why going slow is a good idea. We'll talk more about how to touch it later.

FUN FACT: The clit has an estimated 8000 nerve endings. That's about twice what the penis has (not taking into account foreskin). And pound for pound, inch for inch, the clitoris has the same amount of erectile tissue as a penis. Yes, really.

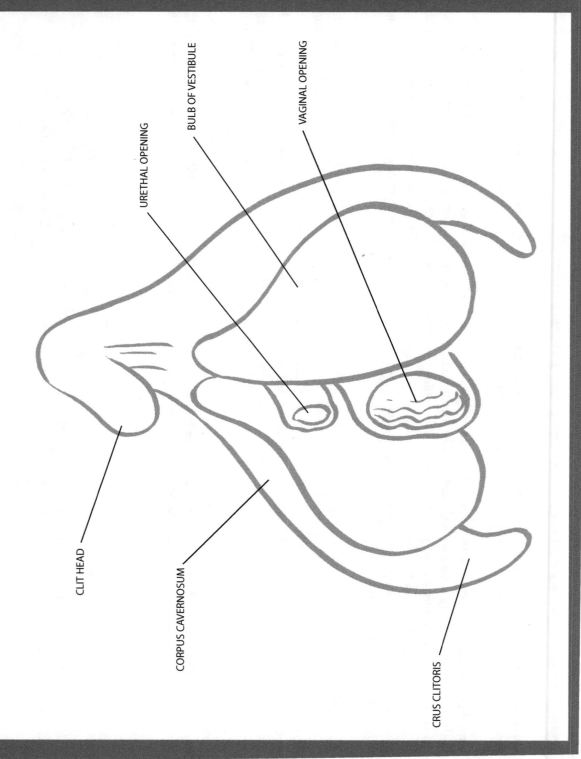

URETHAL OPENING

BULB OF VESTIBULE

VAGINAL OPENING

CLIT HEAD

CORPUS CAVERNOSUM

CRUS CLITORIS

This is what the complete clitoris actually looks like. See that little bean at the top? That's the glans—the only visible part of the clitoris. The rest of it is tucked away inside the pelvis. The wing-shaped parts are the crura (crus: singular, which means "leg" in Latin). The crura run along the inner edge of the pubic bone and respond to gentle pressure. The clitoral bulbs lie on either side of the vaginal opening. When the clit gets engorged, the bulbs swell which make the vagina open and helps the vulva get puffy. (We'll talk about how to stimulate the entirety of the clitoris in chapter 4).

The **clitoral hood** is analogous to foreskin on uncut penises. It usually hangs over the glans (or head) of the clitoris to protect it when it isn't "in use."

As a person gets more turned on, the entire vulva gets engorged with blood and swells. The clitoris, in particular, tends to get bigger, firmer, and more sensitive to touch. It is, quite literally, an erection. Yes, vulva-owners get hard-ons, too.

If you head straight down from the clitoris, you'll see some super-smooth skin that surrounds the vaginal opening. This area is called the **vulvar vestibule.**

In the vestibule, straight down from the clitoris, there's the **urethra.** It's a tiny hole often protected by a little bit of delicate tissue. The urethra is where urine comes out, and ejaculate if you or your sweetie ejaculates during sex. (We'll talk about "squirting" in Chapter 4.) The opening of the urethra is small and usually quite sensitive.

Straight down from the urethra is the **vaginal opening** (aka the introitus).

Below the vaginal opening is the **fourchette**—another delicate, smooth piece of skin. It's called fourchette because that's where the tissue forks into the two inner labia, and French is a sexy language.

Everything above is collectively called the **vulva,** the external part of "female" genitalia. The vagina is only the inside. If you really want to impress a sex geek, knowing the difference between the vagina and the vulva is a great place to start.

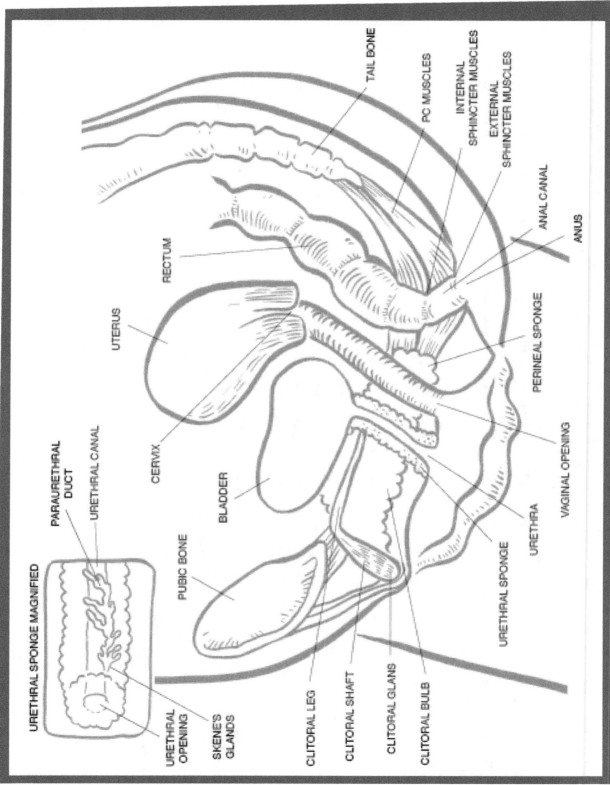

URETHRAL SPONGE MAGNIFIED

PARAURETHRAL DUCT

URETHRAL CANAL

URETHRAL OPENING

SKENE'S GLANDS

PUBIC BONE

CERVIX

BLADDER

UTERUS

RECTUM

TAIL BONE

PC MUSCLES

INTERNAL SPHINCTER MUSCLES

EXTERNAL SPHINCTER MUSCLES

ANAL CANAL

ANUS

PERINEAL SPONGE

VAGINAL OPENING

URETHRA

URETHRAL SPONGE

CLITORAL BULB

CLITORAL GLANS

CLITORAL SHAFT

CLITORAL LEG

The **vagina** is a muscular canal about 2-4 inches (5-10 cm.) long. As with everything, this will vary from body to body. The length and diameter of the vagina increase the more aroused the person gets. The average length of an *aroused vagina* is 4-8 inches. As a person gets more turned on, the vagina will usually start to self-lubricate and clench, creating yummy feelings. Vaginas are built to stretch, so while everyone has a different ability to receive penetration, with practice most people can increase the capacity of what they can receive in their vaginas.

About 1-2" inside the vagina and on the belly side is the **g-spot** (or urethral sponge). It's notable for its unique texture and penchant to swell during arousal.

At the end of the vagina is the **cervix**, which feels like a slick button or disc, with a small dip in the center. This dip is called the **os**, and it's the (very small) path into the uterus. If you have an IUD, the string will often dangle out of the os.

Back outside, below the vulva is the **perineum** (a.k.a. the "taint") and then the **anus.**

And that brings us back to Doh, doh, doh, doh!

Alright, got it? Good! Now we're going to take a tour of penises!

What do penises have to do with girl sex? A lot, actually. First, penises and vulvas are analogues, and like I said before, it can be useful to understand how they both work. If you want to be a good driver, it's helpful to at least have an understanding of how to drive both automatic and manual transmissions, even if you have a strong preference for one of the two.

Second, if you already know your way around one kind of set of genitals, it's easier to understand the other kind. So if you've clocked some cock time, you'll have an easier time understanding vulvas, and vice versa.

Third, a lot of girls have penises. Yep, it's true. Trans women, gender queers, and intersex folks all might have penises. If that's you or your sweetie, it's nice to know your way around their goods. You don't have to like penises, but I suggest keeping an open mind and learning about this stuff anyway. Bodies are cool, and so are people.

For the rest of this section, I'm going to refer to the penis as a phallus. This is because, well, it is one. And so is the clit. Both clits and penises are phalluses. I know it can seem a bit stuffy to use the Latin here, but I think it can also help get rid of some of the stigma associated with the language we use. Remember, a clit is basically a small penis. A penis is basically a big clit. And both of them are phalluses. Both are similar in both in anatomical structure and the way they respond to touch. Keep this in mind when we talk about cunnilingus and hand sex later.

LET'S GO EXPLORING!

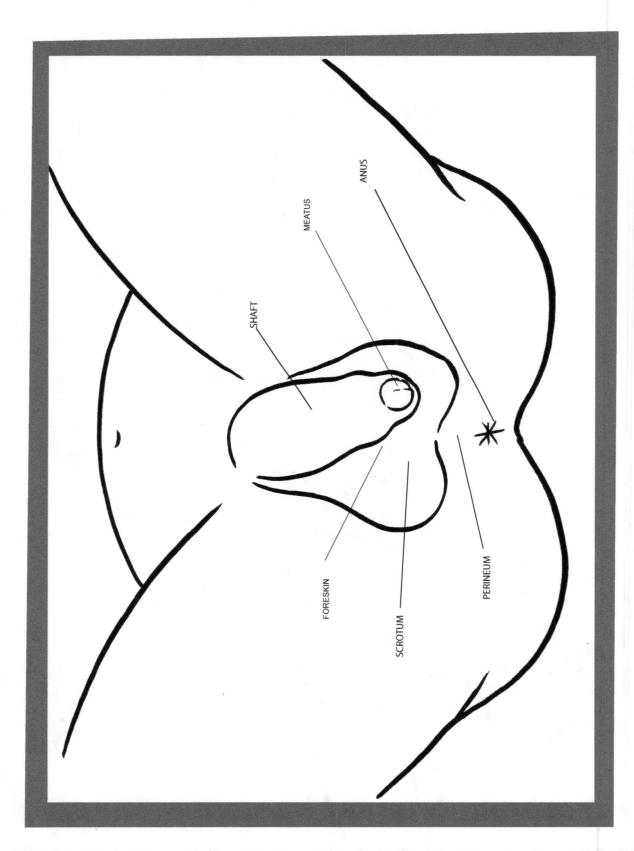

Starting at the top, we have the same mound of soft flesh that protects the genitals from impact. This is where hair often grows.

Then we have the **phallus**. Phallus size is greatly variable. The tip of the phallus is called the glans, and responds to touch much like the clit does.

The **meatus** is the opening of the urethra, through which urine, ejaculate, and precum exit the body. The meatus is usually super sensitive to touch.

Urethra placement is one of the major differences between "male" and "female"-wired bodies. In most vagina-owners, the urethra exits the body just above the vaginal opening, and below the clit (not through the clit). In most penis-owners, the urethra exits at the tip of the phallus. Regardless of placement, the urethra is usually super sensitive. Lubrication is a must if you're going to be stimulating this part of the body. But for those folks who like it, urethra stimulation can feel mighty fine.

Beneath the glans, where the head meets the shaft, is the **frenulum**. The frenulum is another very sensitive part, much like the underside of the clit.

The shaft of the phallus is a homologue to the clitoral shaft. It responds to squeezing and stroking.

On the underside of the penis, you can see the **corpus spongiosum**, which surrounds the urethra. This is erectile tissue, which is responsible for part of an erection. This part is homologus to the vestibular bulbs of the clitoris, which are also erectile tissue, and help open the vagina and make the labia "puff up" during arousal.

 PRO TIP: All genders have erectile tissue, but health issues and hormones can alter the frequency and intensity of erections. People on androgen inhibitors will often not get erections. Happily, there are plenty of yummy things to do with a flaccid phallus, some of which we'll talk about in later chapters.

The **foreskin**, which is preserved on some phalluses and removed on others, is homologous to the clitoral hood. One difference is that the foreskin is often looser than the clitoral hood, and while you'll want to make sure your partner is aroused before you go tugging on it, the foreskin can usually move more easily and pleasurably along the shaft of the phallus than the clitoral hood can.

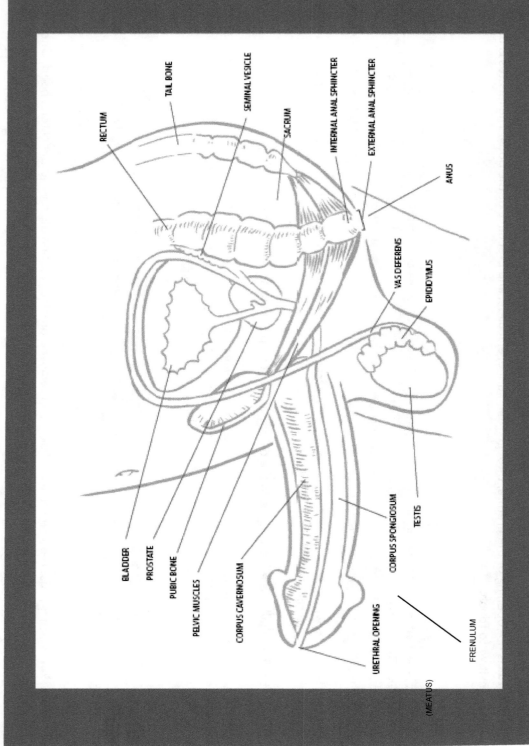

RECTUM

TAIL BONE

SEMINAL VESICLE

SACRUM

INTERNAL ANAL SPHINCTER

EXTERNAL ANAL SPHINCTER

ANUS

VAS DEFERENS

EPIDIDYMIS

BLADDER

PROSTATE

PUBIC BONE

PELVIC MUSCLES

CORPUS CAVERNOSUM

CORPUS SPONGIOSUM

TESTIS

URETHRAL OPENING

(MEATUS)

FRENULUM

Below the phallus is the **scrotum**. The tissue of the scrotum feels a lot like that of the inner labia (even though it's homologus to the outer labia). It feels good to stroke this skin, and even tug on it gently, like you can with the labia (if you or your partner digs it, that is).

Inside the scrotum are the **testicles**, where sperm is made and lives. These are homologous to ovaries (where eggs are stored), which live inside the abdomen alongside the uterus. The **spermatic cord** (containing the vas deferens and other tissue) connect the testicles to the prostate gland inside the body. If you're concerned about hurting your partner by touching her testicles incorrectly, it's good to get a sense of the spermatic cord. Most of the "ouch" that come from testicles happens when the vas deferens get yanked.

Before puberty, the testicles are tucked up inside the pelvis. During puberty, they descend into the scrotum through the **inguinal canal**. Both "male" and "female" anatomies have inguinal canals, though they're larger in male-assigned folks. Some people push their testicles back up into the these canals for "tucking" and some use them for sex. We'll talk more about how to understand and play with the inguinal canals in the Body Shop section of Chapter 4.

Beneath the scrotum we have the **perineum** or "taint" which may be much bigger on non-op "male" bodies.

And then we have the **anus**, which we all have! Yay!

Okay, so why is it important to know all the parts?

Well, a few reasons:

1) **A lot of "female" sexual response hasn't been studied or given the credence it deserves until recently (like 30 years recently).** Until very recently (like, last week), women didn't talk frankly about things so important as their own bodies. So you're being a revolutionary, pleasure-positive badass by knowing these things and helping other people learn them, too.

2) **Knowing the right words can help your lovers give you what you want.** "Bite that fleshy bit down there" becomes a dangerous game of chance when it could mean "outer labia" or "clit." While only a matter of inches and semantics, what feels yummy could quickly become a bad date.

3) **It makes you a better lover.** How many great mechanics don't know the names of all the parts? Knowing what's under the hood is always a good idea.

4) **Pleasure is good for you.** Orgasms are good for you. Getting good at giving them to yourself gives your lovers a better chance of helping give them to you.

In the rest of Girl Sex 101, we're going to talk about stimulation and fun things you can do to these parts. **So get in gear, and let's go!**

SCENIC VIEWPOINT

INTERSEX 101
by Claudia Astorino

Any introduction to girl sex would be incomplete without discussing and celebrating intersex ladies (and the hot, hot sex we have).

Intersex people are individuals born with a mix of biological sex traits traditionally considered "male," "female," or generally atypical. Our society expects bodies to come in one of two flavors: female or male, with the accompanying genitals, gonads, chromosomes, hormones, and so on. With puberty, we can add height, body proportion, chest and nipple form, body hair distribution, and muscle and bone structure.

For people assigned female, we expect that they'll have all the "female" forms of each trait (i.e. breasts, vagina, uterus, clitoris, XX chromosomes, etc); for males, the "male" ones (i.e. penis, testes, chest hair, XY chromosomes, and so on). Intersex people have some "female" traits and some "male" traits, instead of all the female or male ones. For example, I was born with a vulva and vagina, as well as XY chromosomes and testes. Some intersex people also have atypical genital form, where the phalloclitoris (the tissue from where both the clitoris and penis derive) is larger or smaller than usual, gonads with testicular and ovarian tissue (an ovotestis), or more or fewer chromosomes than usual (e.g. XXY).

There's a ton of diversity in what human bodies look like, and they rarely come in two flavors. Societies are beginning to accept that just as there aren't two heights or skin colors, there aren't two ways that sex traits match up, either. Intersex isn't a single category—there are many forms of intersex, and lots of variation within each form, so knowing someone is intersex tells you very little about how their body looks or functions.

Intersex people are just (awesome, awesome) people. So, why is intersex framed as controversial? Basically, because society doesn't have guidelines for how to treat us. Kids assigned female are expected to feel like girls, act like girls, and be sexually attracted to boys; for kids assigned male, vice versa. If one's body isn't easily categorized as male or female, are they a girl or a boy? Will they be gay? Will they be a bearded, tutu-wearing genderfucker? Intersex bodies cause social panic. Although intersex isn't a medical condition, we're routinely medically "treated" without our consent to "fix" our bodies so that we can be "normal" girls and boys. Common "treatments" include cosmetic genital surgery and gonad removal.

So, how does all this relate to having sex with a smokin'-hot intersex lady? I'm glad you asked!

First, treat her with respect. If she discloses her intersex status to you (something she's not obligated to do), thank her for being comfortable enough to share. Ask if it's okay to ask questions, and tell her you're okay with whatever level of detail she is comfortable sharing.

Give her the agency to guide the conversation. Second, be sure not to assume that her body looks or functions a certain way. This is the case for any new sex partner—for intersex people, there are simply a few more questions to ask. Maybe this intersex lady has a phalloclitoris that's larger than the average clitoris, with erectile capabilities. Maybe she has a vulva, but not a vagina. Maybe she has a blind-ended vagina, which has implications for penetration. Maybe she doesn't have much, or any, breast or nipple development. None of these things mean she can't experience pleasure; in fact, you may discover sexy new things to try together! Consider sex with an intersex woman—just like sex with anyone—to be an opportunity to play and co-create something spectacular. Talk to her about how her body informs how she wants to get down, and take it from there.

Finally, be sensitive about issues of consent. Intersex people often experience the medical "treatments" they received as traumatic, and describe this trauma similarly to survivors of sexual abuse. Your intersex sex partner has likely been medicalized, or has had her body medically examined and even cosmetically altered by clinicians without her consent so that her body looks "normal." Consequently, she may have negative feelings surrounding her body and having sex in general. She may need time to establish trust before having sex with you, and may have certain needs during sex. She might not want to have certain kinds of sex. If she feels triggered, she may need to stop having sex. Learn and respect her boundaries. Her medicalization may also affect how her body looks or functions. She may have tissue scars that feel painful (or no) sensation when touched, that she may also feel self-conscious about. Vaginal reconstruction might affect her vagina's stretchiness, smell, or ability to lubricate. While handling consent issues isn't always easy or straightforward, with work and communication, you can have fantastic sex and ensure a good time is had by all.

As an intersex person, there can definitely be weirdness about feeling like your body is okay and desirable. It can be hard to learn where your boundaries are during sex and figure out how to communicate this (and re-assess when necessary). Generally, I always feel safest and sexiest when my partner a) is totally supportive about my boundaries and respects them when I'm triggered, and b) tells me I'm super-hot (I mean, who doesn't like that?)—not in spite of, but because of my intersex body. It's not so much about pressing the right buttons as it is about a willingness have the right conversations. Consent and enthusiasm go a long way in making a sexy time WAY sexier.

Have fun!

Claudia Astorino is an intersex activist living in NYC. Claudia serves as Associate Director of Organization Intersex International's USA chapter (OII-USA), coordinates the Annual Intersex Awareness Day (IAD) events in NYC, and writes for Full-Frontal Activism: Intersex and Awesome (her personal blog) and Autostraddle.com.

ANATOMY BODY SHOP

MENSTRUAL SEX

Sex on your period is a polarizing thing. On the pro side: period sex can ease cramps, some folks are hornier on their cycle, it can be a nice way to feel sexy even when you're not feeling sexy, menstrual fluid can add extra lube, and you're more resistant to pain and eager for sensation. On the other side, some folks just don't want anything near their goods when they're a-flowin' and, yes, it can be a bit of a mess. It's up to you to decide what you want. And it's no one's right to tell you what you should be into. That said, if you want to try period sex, here's how to proceed:

1) **Use barriers.** This is for cleanup and safety. It's easier to throw away a glove than it is to clean under your fingernails.

2) **Avoid cunnilingus unless you've been tested recently.** Hepatitis is spread via blood, which includes menstrual fluid. If you or your partner haven't been tested and/or vaccinated, best to use a dental dam, shower, and/or wear a tampon or menstrual cup to minimize blood exposure, or just play in different ways.

3) **Keep a stash of dark towels by the bed, and use them.** I love using my Liberator Throe for period sex, since it's waterproof, washes clean, and comes in a variety of colors.

4) **Check in.** Yep, as usual. Menstrual sex can feel deeeelightful, but if you or your partner needs to stop or adjust, then stop or adjust.

5) **Affirm.** If this is the first time playing this way, all the same girl-in-society bullshit can kick into overdrive. We can be afraid our bodies are gross or wrong or smelly or offensive. If you're with a menstruating partner, be sure to tell her you think she's the bee's knees.

HORMONE THERAPY

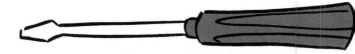

Hormones are powerful things, influencing the way our body behaves, our emotions, and our response to pleasure. Everyone, regardless of sex or gender, has ebbs and flows of different hormones that make us feel different ways. What can come as a surprise, however, is how hormones can specifically affect touch. Hormones can mean that what feels great one day can be annoying the next. Or that what is sometimes a mundane sensation can feel divine. To manage this, expand your repertoire of sensation. Sometimes intimate affection can be as simple as a footrub or a back scratch.

People who take hormones often find their relationship to touch and orgasm shift as well:

I take hormones because of a hysterectomy/single oophorectomy. The hormones lessen my sex drive and make it harder to come when I masturbate.

I GET HORNY EASIER AND MORE FREQUENTLY. SOMETIMES MY COCK GETS HARD FOR NO REASON.

HORMONES HAVE MADE MY BODY MORE COMFORTABLE SEXUALLY. I WENT THROUGH A PERIOD OF INTENSE DYSPHORIA RIGHT BEFORE GETTING ON HORMONES, AND IT WAS SUCH A WONDERFUL DECISION FOR MYSELF, MY EMOTIONS, AND MY BODY TO START TAKING ESTROGEN.

Estrogen gave me the ability to "simmer." Sensation slowly builds, and it can take upwards of an hour for me to climax. It feels great, but sometimes I get impatient and then frustrated.

My penis is now less fun, my nipples are SUPER great to play with.

WHEN I WAS ON THE BIRTH CONTROL PILL, I WANTED SEX LESS AND RESPONDED LESS. LUBRICATION WAS NEARLY NIL NO MATTER HOW MENTALLY HOT I WAS. IT WAS MISERABLE.

I take birth control for period regulation, and it's made my breasts less sensitive. I also get exceptionally horny at the end of my cycle, more intensely and regularly than before I was on the pill.

It's no longer just about the penis. My whole body is a sexual organ now.

ORGASMS ARE MUCH MORE OF A FULL-BODY EXPERIENCE THAT CAN LAST FOR QUITE SOME TIME, BUT AREN'T AS INTENSE OR OVERWHELMING. I REACT TO TOUCH MORE STRONGLY, WHICH NARROWS THE SPACE BETWEEN UNDER- AND OVER-STIMULATION.

POST-SURGICAL BODIES

Sometimes surgery can affect the way pleasure moves through our bodies, and surgeries on the sexual organs can change the way hormones work for us. For some folks who've had hysterectomies, for instance, the vagina will often cease self-lubricating. For cis women, doctors may attempt to preserve as many of the estrogen-producing organs as possible (like the ovaries), to prevent needing HRT (hormone replacement therapy).

POST-OP PUSSY

Genital reconstruction surgery for trans women usually means the creation of a vagina, clitoris, and inner and outer labia. "Post-op" vaginas are usually made from the penis, the penis and scrotum, or rarely, part of the colon. Most modern surgery tries to keep as much of the blood supply and innervation intact to ensure that the woman can still enjoy genitally-focused, sexually pleasurable sensations.

Depending on the details of the surgery, the vagina may or may not self-lubricate, but it's likely that it won't very much. Talk to your partner about what kind of lube she likes (Chapter 8) and make sure to use plenty of it.

The kind of tissue used also influences how "stretchy" the vagina is. Be sure to go slow with penetration (until your partner tells you otherwise) and don't be surprised if your partner doesn't like as much girth as you'd expect, at least to start.

Trans women don't have g-spots, but they do have P-spots (a.k.a. the prostate). The prostate usually shrinks after years of androgen inhibitors, but that doesn't mean it can't still give pleasure. (We'll talk about prostate stimulation in Chapter 4).

A surgically-crafted clitoris is usually made from the glans of the penis. Often this preserves some of the erectile tissue, which can help preserve blood flow and yummy-sensation capabilities.

Trans women don't menstruate, but that doesn't mean they don't have PMS! After hormone injections, many trans women experience the effects of estrogen in a big way. This can mean her body is super sensitive, her orgasms are full-bodied and powerful, and that she's either hella horny or hella not. The rules are always the same: talk to her. See what she's up for. And play (or not) accordingly.

MENOPAUSE

Menopause happens when a woman's body stops producing natural estrogen. This usually happens in middle age and after, though people taking testosterone supplements and people who've had hysterectomies often experience the symptoms earlier. The side effects of menopause are very much like those of using testosterone or removing one's ovaries, cervix and uterus: the vagina stops producing as much natural lubricant, the skin can grow less supple and pliant, sex drive can reduce, orgasm can be harder to reach, and penetrative sex can become less enjoyable. During and after menopause, it becomes more important to use lots of lube, stay hydrated, and take your time. Estrogen creams can be used directly on the vagina to help counteract some of the physiological symptoms of menopause. It can be frustrating for some folks when they begin experiencing these symptoms, since they can change the way they feel about their sexuality. If this is you or your partner, practice kindness, patience, and experiment with new sensations or kinds of play to upgrade your routine.

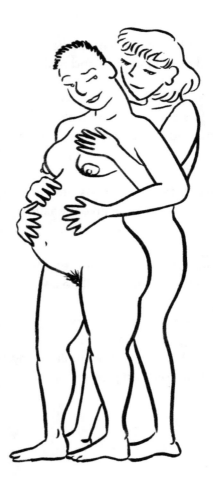

PREGNANCY & SEX

Sex during pregnancy can be hot and fun. The cocktail of hormones, increased groinal blood flow, and shifting and expanding bits can all increase your sex drive AND the way the bits respond to touch. Different trimesters affect what kinds of activities are safe, as does your individual health. The most important thing is to listen to your body and keep things clean, especially when playing with penetration. Talk to your doctor about the kind of sex you have and want to have.

SEX & DISABILITY

Disability and physical impairments can add challenges to sex. Some disabilities can affect the way you respond to sensations or pose logistical issues. The key to dealing with this is being kind, open, and enthusiastic.

Reduced mobility is a common side-effect of disability or chronic pain. This means certain positions may be uncomfortable or impossible, and certain acts may need to be renegotiated. If some positions are challenging for your or your partner, simply explore what works better. This could mean gently reclining during sex instead of lying flat on your back, or making sure to support your body weight instead of giving it all to your partner. Research and development is an important—and hot—part of sex.

Most of the anguish around sex comes from thinking sex has to look one way.

Neither mainstream porn nor Hollywood knows what to do with diverse bodies. Only you know what feels good for your body. So if missionary position with legs wrapped around your partner's neck isn't going to work out, then create something even sexier.

Sometimes disabilities make spontaneous sex unrealistic. Instead, it might require a bit of forethought, planning, and consideration. This isn't a problem, and if you need a bit more forethought, that's nothing to be ashamed of.

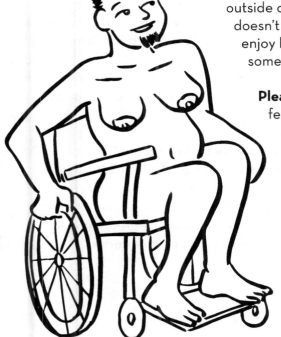

All bodies are valid, and they all have nuances that are invisible to outside observers. Assume nothing. Just because someone's body doesn't work in a way you're used to, doesn't mean she can't enjoy herself. In fact, you might learn a lot about pleasure from someone whose body has different needs.

Pleasure-seek, don't pry. Your job is to make your partner feel safe, cared for, and sexy. Only ask questions that are directly relevant to those goals. You don't necessarily need to know how someone lost their leg in order to know how to make them feel good. If your partner wants to share with you, that's up to them.

No body is broken. Sex is resilient. Pleasure finds a way. Even if your genitals don't register pleasure in the same way as your partner's, that doesn't mean anyone is broken. In fact, folks with various disabilities often find their bodies creating erotic pathways in new and exciting ways. I have a friend who is a quadriplegic who has a fantastic sex life, often incorporating what he calls "Thumb-gasms" into his routine. Explore the possibilities of your bodies together.

Prioritize consent. While we all get touched without our permission, people with disabilities tend to get it even more often. Whether it's getting nonconsensually pushed in your wheelchair, or having someone grab your arm to be "helpful," folks with disabilities are dealing with nonconsent on the regular. Help offset that by getting clear on how and where your partner likes to be touched.

Pain is complicated. Some people are managing pain all the time. Other folks may have quick spasms that come out of nowhere. So the question, "Does this hurt?" can be kind of meaningless in the context of chronic pain and disability. Likewise, for folks managing pain all the time, there are different kinds: a pain that makes you hate everything, and pain that is worth something. For folks with chronic pain, there is often an assessment that happens – whether the pain is worth it or not. It is always up to the person with the pain to decide where their boundaries are. If you're not clear, establish a safeword, so you can tell the difference between "ouchy" and "stop!"

Most people don't handle surprise well. So if you can, give your partner a heads up about what to expect regarding your body. For instance, if arousal makes your face really red, or if sex makes you cough or gasp in a way that could be alarming for a new partner, you may save both of you some anxiety by just saying so beforehand. And as with any new information share, don't say it like you accidentally killed their goldfish. Offer it frankly and kindly, and you'll likely be surprised at how easy it is to roll with.

Bring in Backup. Toys can help asset any sexual relationship, but they can really go the extra mile when dealing with disability. Dildos can help stand in for hand sex, a vibrator can provide a boost to cunnilingus, and thigh harnesses can give a good ride even if you have limited hip mobility. But don't forget about furniture! We live in an era of some pretty fantastic bolsters, pillows, wedges, and benches, all designed for sex. Check out companies like Liberator and Sportsheets to explore options for body support.

Honor the person, not just their ability to "overcome." People with disabilities are often called "brave" but not as often called "sexy," "desirable," and "panty-droppingly hot." If you think your partner is any of these latter terms or more, tell them so. We all need to hear how sexy we are from people who respect and desire us. It's even more important when societal norms aren't in your corner.

ORGASM

At their most basic, orgasms occur when a certain stimulus reaches a critical mass and triggers an involuntary, pleasurable response. For most women, this occurs from stimulation to the clitoris, but it can also originate in the cervix, g-spot, or nipples.

Technically, all female-assigned groin- and ass-oriented orgasms are clitoral orgasms. As we've seen, the clitoral structure is more than meets the eye. It wishbones around the vaginal opening and reaches into the labia. When you stimulate inside the vagina, the clitoral structure gets stimulated, too. And this, boys and girls, is where orgasms come from.

Orgasms can feel vastly different depending on where the stimulation is coming from (we'll talk about g-spots and cervixes in Chapter 4), but that doesn't mean penetrative orgasms are different things, just different routes to the same place.

Most women are most accustomed to orgasming via the glans of the clit. Whether it's double-clicking the mouse, or riding your teddy bear's face, or using that electric toothbrush for an off-label use, clit stimulation usually gets us there faster, harder, and more reliably. Vibrators, fingers, or tongues are usually the best way to stimulate the clit to orgasm.

Orgasms from penetration are a bit harder to come by, but can be delicious and exciting in their own way. Usually g-spot stimulation is key for vaginal/internal orgasms. With g-spot contact, you're stimulating a bunch of nerve endings surrounding the urethra and the internal structure of the clitoris. Pressure on the labia can help achieve internal orgasm, which is why fucking with a strap-on or hand is useful.

THE THREE STEP PATH TO ORGASM

Masturbate

Give yourself different orgasms in as many different ways as you can. Experiment with penetration, glans stimulation, vibrators, hands, dildos, pillow humping, on your back, on your tummy, in the bath, in the shower, on the toilet, anywhere you can get your hands on yourself. Bottom line: try stuff. A lot of us, being human, find one thing that works, and we just keep doing that. This is all well and good when you're on a schedule, but it's not great when you're with a partner. A partner is never going to touch you as efficiently as you touch yourself, what with the whole biofeedback thing. So, try different things, and learn to like different kinds of touch.

Facilitate

Your orgasm is up to you. A partner can help, but you're the captain of the ship, even if someone else is working the rudder. It's your job to put the pieces together to achieve your pleasure. Love candles? Light 'em. Want a towel? Get it. Need a certain kind of vibrator? Bring it. Dig a certain kind of lube? Buy it. Help you help yourself.

Communicate

When your partner is lending a hand (or toy, or tongue, etc.), let them know what you want. You should have a decent grasp of upgrades and pleasant alterations if you've done a good job with the whole 'batin' thing. When it comes to you getting off, be a bossy bottom. Bossy bottoms aren't mean. They're just clear, direct, and in touch with their needs. Be that person.

D.I.Y. ORGASM

If you've never had an orgasm before, it can be tough to figure out what you're trying to "go for."

1) **Touch yourself.** Create a private, comfortable space. Use warm, clean hands. Relax and explore with touch.

2) **When you find something you like, your body will twitch or clench in reflex.** It's a warm, sexy, feel-good kind of clench, not a flinch. When you feel the twitch or clench, go with it. Let your muscles clench more. Feel them relax and contract. This should feel kind of like Kegels, but a more overall warm sensation that encompasses your butt, perineum, vagina and mound, even perhaps your upper thighs. This controlled contraction and relaxation will come in handy. If you have a hard time relaxing after a clench, practice exhaling with the release, pushing out through your vaginal muscles. Like yoga, breathe in when you contract and exhale as you relax.

3) **Ramp up the pleasurable sensation** (usually stroking/rubbing your clit, or grinding up against whatever you're using) and keep clenching and relaxing your pelvic floor muscles.

4) **You should start feeling a echo chamber of sorts between the clenching and the stimulation you're applying to your clit.** You can take it down a notch, or keep ramping up (this is where a vibrator comes in handy).

5) **Keep breathing.**

6) **Explore touching other parts with your free hand**, to increase the pleasure, like your breasts or ass.

7) **Increase both the clenching and stimulation.** You can control it by upping the intensity of the external stimulation (fingers/vibrator/etc.) and internal clenching.

8) **Keep playing until this kind of stimulation reaches a tipping point.** When you notice that tipping point, it's common to tighten many of your muscles and kind of reach for it. I think of it like the high jump. You run and you reach and you kind of throw yourself over the threshold.

9) **If you don't get it at first, don't get frustrated.** The truth is, some people come into coming quite easily, and others struggle with it. But ultimately it's a skill like any other. Sometimes you just need to practice. Luckily orgasmic practice is way more fun than piano lessons.

O, YES!

by Megan Andelloux

SCENIC VIEWPOINT →

The first time I had an orgasm with another person, I was in college. At the time, I didn't understand what had happened. The second week of my freshman year, I walked proudly into my dorm room and exclaimed, "My god, I fell in love last night." My new roommate cocked her head and gently questioned me, because, really, how often does someone actually say that?

Turns out, it wasn't love. What I believed to be love—the magical sensations that had caused me to leave my body while experiencing overwhelming laps of pleasure—was actually an orgasm.

Not exactly a testament to my common sense, but it was an eye-opening experience that led me to start researching sexuality.

The lack of scientific studies regarding orgasms means most of us fumble our way through our sex lives hoping we punch the right button combo to get us that next "level-up."

That fumbling can make it harder to have orgasms, which can be frustrating. So allow me to use my science-loving sex geek mind to give you an orgasm cheat-sheet:

1) You'll make faces, fantastically erotic and fucked up faces.

If you catch a glimpse of yourself in the mirror (or the sunglasses your partner is wearing), you probably are going to think you look weird. This is myotonia...

my·o·to·ni·a [mahy-uh-toh-nee-uh] : tonic muscle spasm or muscular rigidity.

...at work. Embrace it; you do look weird. But don't worry: the person above, in front, or below you (and yes, I'm referencing you if you are getting into it in front of the mirror) is probably thanking their lucky stars that they get to witness such a lovely face.

2) Define what you're looking for in sex.

One of the most COMMON things I hear from folks is this: they masturbate, they have someone go down on them, they play with their butts, etc., etc., but they aren't quite into it. They are going through the motions, they want to play, but it just isn't...awesome.

I bet you've been there—most of us have! Here's the solution: Make a list of all the sexual encounters you want to experience in the next 6 months. It's important, especially within the context of consent, to communicate with ourselves about what we DO want.

Before we can consent to others, we have to consent to ourselves: our desires, our wants and our wishes. It is imperative to have a deep look inwards to communicate with others what experiences can make orgasms possible. Make a list of your fantasies, desires, and curiosities. Get real with yourself about what turns you on! For all you task-master, goal-oriented people, that's a list that you can probably have as much fun making as you can have engaging in.

3) Touch a nerve!

I'm going to geek out here, cause I fucking love science: There are two main nerves that control your orgasms. Think of them like the orange or the white wires during an action movie. Cut the orange wire and the place blows up, cut the white wire and the bomb doesn't go off. Except with these wires, it's a pleasure bomb that goes off, and everyone wins. If you touch the: clitoris, inner or outer lips, penis, scrotum, anus, external junk, etc, you stimulate the pudendal nerve. Stimulation of the pudendal nerve usually causes fast, intense, genitally focused shock waves that go through the butt and genital area.

Awesome, but maybe you want to get in deep and feel all the warmth surround you. Fondle the G-zone or the anterior fornix erogenous zone, or even the prostate. Slowly ease your finger into the rectum and/or on the cervix and stroke away. Touching any of these warm locations in the body stimulates the pelvic nerve. Stimulating the pelvic nerve produces sensations that feel like waves flooding through the entire body. They tend to be slow, crashing, and occur throughout the entire body, whereas pudendal nerve stimulation is genitally focused.

However, you may be thinking, "I want an orgasm without touching the genitals. Can that happen?"

Yes! It could happen, and we can bow down to the body's deep desire to experience pleasure in a portion of your brain called the sensory cortex. The sensory cortex enables all folks to have orgasms. This is one of my absolute favorite facts. ANYBODY is capable of having an orgasm. ANY. BODY. A person who has a spinal cord injury could have an orgasm. A person who has had their clitoris removed could have an orgasm. There are so many non-genitally focused ways people can experience bliss: stimulating the nipples, getting off through thought alone, Coregasms (reaching orgasm by doing abdominal crunches), stimulating the knee(s) or feet, and/or stimulation of the interior portion of the nose, and on and on!

4) Hormones matter.

Hormone levels do matter when it comes to creating sexy feelings and orgasm capability. Illnesses, hiccups in the hormone production department of our bodies and many medications (Hello, anti-depressants and hormonal forms of birth control!) can cause havoc to the sex hormone supply.

If you feel like something is awry, talk to a medical expert, but more specifically, find a sexual medicine specialist. They can order a blood work panel that will look at your hormone levels, specifically testing your sex hormone-binding globulin (SHBG) molecule. With just a little prick, you may get physical evidence that yes, something isn't working the way it should be, and you can be given evidence-based, regulated medications that can increase or decrease the levels that support healthy sexual functioning for you.

5) There has to be tension.

Pelvic tension, that is. In order to have an orgasm, the muscles have to be tight enough to release all the sexy energy you have built up (but not too tight, because that can cause unhappy moments leading to pelvic pain disorders). How can you get tension? Well, before sexy times start, make sure you are exercising your pubococcygeus (PC) muscles.

Strengthening your PC muscles, usually done by doing Kegel exercises, increases your muscle tone and makes for more intense contractions when the power surge happens. The stronger your muscles are, the more noticeable the orgasm will be.

During playtime specifically, you can build pelvic tension by bucking your hips, breathing (don't hold your breath!), and being into the play (meaning you can't just be a passive bunny during masturbation time or with others).

6) Notice the nuance.

You are often not going to have the types of orgasms you see in a movie theater or on your laptop. Orgasms vary: some are delicate little pulses, some make you leave your body, others will make you cry, and some might even be a little bit painful. When people are stating that they aren't sure if they have had an orgasm, I usually tell them to pay attention to their bodies. If they feel a sudden onset of pulses that pop rhythmically through their sexy bits, that is an indicator that they have just experienced an orgasm. Yay! Orgasms change from person to person and experience to experience. That's all normal and healthy.

Remember comparison is the thief of joy. If you keep comparing yourself to others, you might be missing out on the fact that you are actually experiencing your own little perfect blissed out moment. Give yourself over the richness of your own experience of orgasms. Have fun.

Often described as the effervescent sex ed warrior queen, Megan Andelloux is a stubborn New Englander working every day to reduce sexual shame and misinformation.

VIBRATORS

Vibrators are an incredibly reliable way to orgasm. There is a huge array of styles, quality, and motion available now. And thanks to the internet (THANKS, INTERNET!), you can get them delivered to your door, even if you live in a place like Iran or...Texas. Some, like the Magic Wand, have a huge amount of power, and few settings. Some, like the Magic Bullet, are small and have a lighter touch. Most are designed with the clit in mind, but a good many of them are designed for penetration too. The best way to figure out what you like is to try a few. Sometimes this means buying a dud and handing it off to a friend, borrowing one, or buying a cheap one and upgrading to a better version when you know what you like. There are a few sex toy stores that have good return policies, but most online stores are final-sales-only type places. It's hard to blame them.

 PRO TIP: If you have the opportunity to visit a sex toy store that has vibes on display, a good rule of thumb is to test the vibration on the tip of your nose. If it feels painfully intense, try something with a lower setting. If it's annoyingly weak, try something with a bigger motor.

It's a great idea to get good at using vibrators both on yourself (if you like them) and on partners. For many women, vibrators are part and parcel of good sex. Sometimes you'll like having un-assisted sex for a while and then finish off with a vibrator. Sometimes a vibe can be great to add to penetrative sex. (We'll talk more about toys and ways to use them in sex in Chapter 9.)

MULTIPLE ORGASMS

Multiple orgasms usually aren't a BAM!-BAM!-BAM! phenomenon.

More like

... [5 minutes of stimulation] [2 more minutes of stimulation]

 [another 6 minutes of stimulation]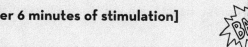

and so on.

The reason they're called "multiple" orgasms, as opposed to, y'know, orgasms, is, once again, because women's pleasure is measured against men's. Whereas most cis men can only have one orgasm per sexual session, many women can have more. This isn't a magical phenomenon. It just is. But when guys are considered to be the standard against which everything else is measured, women's orgasms need the modifier. Instead of us just calling men "singly orgasmic," we call women multiply so. Sexism! You're soaking in it!

Some women can have BAM! BAM! BAM! orgasms, but these are often one orgasm with multiple peaks—kind of the beach-ball at the rock concert kind of orgasm, where it keeps popping up for a while until someone gets distracted. Each peak or "aftershock" can be intensely pleasurable, but they're not necessarily discrete orgasms. The full-come-down full-orgasmo over and over is rarer, but possible as well.

No one is wrong, and no one is broken. If your partner can look at you a certain way and you convulse in joy for fifteen minutes, then bully for you. If it takes you a million years to get to orgasm #1 and you just want a nap afterwards, then nap on, girlfriend! It's all good as long as everyone's having a good time.

The best way to learn how
to orgasm, one or a million times,
is to...

wait for it...

Masturbation is one of the most taboo sexual topics/acts in our culture. We may joke about it, but the sad fact is, you're more likely to share a vivid, detailed description of the mediocre sex you had last night than the totally wholesome orgasm you gave yourself this morning.

When you masturbate, you don't have worry about hurting someone's feelings, making a weird face or sound, or taking too long. So do it often. Do it proudly. And do it for yourself. You don't want to be a chef who can cook a banquet but can't serve herself a bowl of pasta.

A word of warning: If you already know how to get yourself off reliably and quickly, try integrating other techniques into your repertoire. This will make you more likely to respond to the touch of another person.

I learned how to get myself off when I was 12 and then did it as often as possible throughout the rest of my teens. The problem was when I finally started having partnered sex, it was hard to learn how to come from their touch. I never came from cunnilingus, and forget about penetration. It took me many frustrating masturbation sessions of teaching my clit to respond to gentler, more general touch before I could really dig another person's mouth on my goods. So masturbate, but vary it up every once in a while. You don't want to fall into the one-trick-clit chasm.

Okay, so jacking off. That's easy. All it takes is 20 minutes of free time and Netflixing Battlestar Galactica episodes. The hard part comes next...

If you want to teach your partner how to get you off, you're going to have to...*waaaait for it*... masturbate IN FRONT OF THEM.

I know, I know. It can be weird or terrifying to even contemplate (also **hot**—trust us). BUT, the pay off is ENORMOUS. Especially when you're packing the same parts as your partner, it can be fascinating to learn that she jacks off differently from you.

One day after school, I was fooling around with my (sweet but woefully inexperienced) high school boyfriend. He was a virgin and had never seen a woman orgasm before. And he hadn't even gotten close to getting me off. So, I rolled on my tummy, put his fingers on my clit, and moved his fingers against my clit like they were mine. I had a totally organic, non-performative orgasm and blew his fragile sixteen-year-old mind. I could have described it to him verbally or handed him a book, or I could just give him the 2 minute lesson to end all lessons. After that, when I wanted him to get me off, he knew how.

PRO-TIP: When you're going down on your partner, ask her to touch herself. You can do things to her (like penetrate with fingers) while she rubs her clit, all while you get a cinematic view of the way she likes her clit touched. This is a good one to whip out when she's close to cumming but you can't get her over the threshold on your own.

Once you've broken through the "masturbate in front of my partner" threshold, your whole sex life will get an upgrade. Ever been super horny and super tired at the same time? Of course you have. Mutual masturbation is a great technique for nights like those. Cuddle up, jerk off, and drift off to sleep in your yummy place together.

ORGASM FOR TWO

Once you get good at coming on your own, you can try to come with your partner's touch.

1) **Try different things, even if they don't "get you there" as fast.** You need to train your body to respond to different kinds of stimuli, especially if you're used to just rubbing one out real fast. Even if you're a self-pleasure expert, it's helpful to sometimes back up a few steps, and touch yourself as if it's the first time.

2) **Practice reaching.** You can generate pleasure just by clenching your pubic muscles. Practice clenching in response to your partner's touch.

3) **Show them the ropes.** Take their hand and move it how you like, or just talk them through it. Even if you have the same bits, that doesn't mean you both like it the same way. You're going to have to help them out.

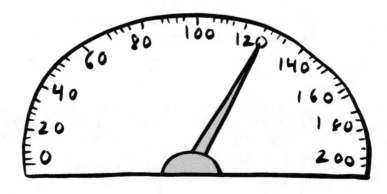

WHAT'S THE MOST RELIABLE WAY FOR YOU TO COME? VIBRATOR? FINGERS? HORSEBACK RIDING?

Vibrator on clit is fastest and most reliable for clitoral orgasms; penetration with a girthy strap-on from behind is less reliable but a close second.

I've never come.

Thrusting a dildo and clit stimulation with fingers or a vibe.

ANAL PLAY.

I can only come while laying on my stomach with a vibrator so that is the most reliable way but also the only way.

Fingers and a bit of pain.

Watching porn and giving myself the rule of using only one finger.

I CAN THINK MYSELF TO ORGASM IF I CONCENTRATE AND BREATHE DEEPLY. THAT'S THE MOST RELIABLE WAY.

TELL US ABOUT YOUR ORGASMS! WHAT DO THEY FEEL LIKE FOR YOU?

Like a river running over, like a waterfall, like all of my insides spreading outward and my outsides curling in all at once, like my bones turn to spaghetti, like a drum beat, like an avalanche, like finally taking your shoes off at the end of a long and exhausting day, like my pelvis is a wild animal set loose, like the big bang starts from my clitoris.

THE BEST EVER. They're super clitoral and then deeply vaginal. the walls of my vagina contract and flex and it feels amazing in my toes and the backs of my eyes and I get sweaty and my heart pounds.

My orgasms feel like a cross between being soaked in liquid metal and being a giant, ringing bell.

LIKE A LITTLE EXPLOSION OF RAINBOWS.

When it's really good...I feel like I have met God. I am one with God.

MINE ARE RARELY BROUGHT ON BY PHYSICAL STIMULATION OF MY GENITALS BY A PARTNER. WHEN HAVING PARTNERED SEX, MY ORGASMS ARE MOSTLY MENTAL AND COME AFTER HAVING MADE HER CUM SEVERAL TIMES, WHICH I FIND INCREDIBLY EROTIC. AFTER THAT, WHILE I'M THRUSTING INTO HER IT FEELS LIKE EVERYTHING FROM MY COCK TO MY HEAD EXPLODES WITH AN ORGASM.

They're really not that fun. I much prefer the bit leading up to them.

Orgasms are my favourite thing about being alive. I've been having orgasms since I was a teenager and since then they've always been an amazing way to know myself, check in with my body, cleanse, feel emotions, get through stuff.

Well, because I'm a geek, as I'm about to orgasm a line graph pops up in my mind to chart my orgasm. It builds up, then peaks super high, then comes down a little bit then peaks again... and so on. Seriously. Is that normal? It's always a red line charted on white graph paper with blue lines. Middle school-style.

THE GIRL SEX 101 PRINCIPLES OF PLEASURE

1) **Be Pleasure-oriented, Not Goal-oriented**: Don't try and "give" her an orgasm right away. This sets you both up for failure. Focus on pleasure. Get a sense of what she likes and follow those breadcrumbs of moans, smiles, and squeezes.

2) **Every Body Is Different**: Treat your girl like she's the unique human being she is. Just because a move works on your ex or on you, doesn't mean she's going to like it. Moreover, a woman's individual body changes day to day. What worked yesterday may not work today. Nobody's broken. Just go back to listening and checking in.

3) **Listen with your whole body**: Relax your mind and listen to her body and voice as it gives you information about what's working for her.

4) **When in doubt, check in:** If you're in your head, odds are she is too. Checking in isn't just good protocol, it can help you both "soft reset" and then get back into the groove.

5) **Keep a sense of humor**: We want all the pressure to be coming from your hand, mouth, and body, not from your brain. This doesn't mean you can't take sex seriously, but sex is about connection, pleasure and play. Bodies are organic and so is sex. This means sometimes there will be funny sounds, smells, or muscle cramps. Go with it.

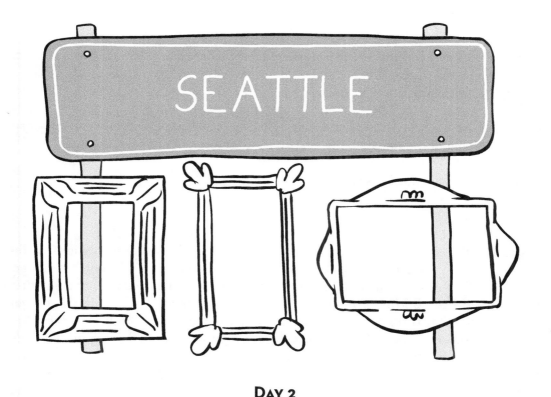

DAY 2

Jamie parks at the curb. Layla pulls on a sweater and asks, "How do you know these people again?"

"Barbara was my media arts professor, back when she was Professor Leonard Burton."

"Oh whoa."

"She made a bunch of art films about her transition. It was pretty awesome. Professor Burton was a mentor of sorts. Introduced me to the work of Bill Viola, Janet Biggs, Valie Export. I've only seen her once since she became Barbara, and that's when I met her wife, Maureen. She's a shrink."

"You ever, y'know—?"

"Professor Burton?" Jamie shakes her head. "Though there was always a bit of weird sexual tension. Her transition really explained that. I've always had a thing for older lesbians."

Layla pulls a face and slides out of the van.

Dinner is simple—grilled chicken and rainbow chard from the Farmer's Market. After supper and small talk, they retire to the balcony to admire the extraordinary view of the Olympic Mountains. Maureen and Jamie sip gin and tonics, and Barbara and Layla drink beers. Jamie and Barbara gossip and reminisce while the others politely listen.

"I was obsessed with that Tap and Touch Cinema piece," Barbara says. "Should have seen it coming."

"What coming?" Layla asks.

"Womanhood," Barbara replies. "The piece is hailed as a hallmark of feminist performance art, shifting the ownership of the female body from male directors onto female creators."

"That was your epiphany?" Layla asks.

"Dude," Jamie scolds.

"Well maybe not the moment," Barbara says, "but I think feminist representations of the body resonated with me. Growing up as a black kid in Georgia, I didn't really have much direct access to the conversation. Film changed that." She holds her fingers in a square around the Seattle skyline, creating a postcard-sized border around the Space Needle. "Because of the frame, it's very easy to assess what a director is trying to tell you. And you often get all of the biases, the internalized bigotry, and the unexamined assumptions just thrown right up there. Film helped me understand the communication potential of an image in context. So that later, when I had my prostate cancer scare, and my doctor put me on antiandrogens, I was able to contextualize my experience of my body better. Otherwise I may just have been ashamed of my penis not 'working' or my muscles not 'looking right.' Instead, I was able to see my body within the frame of my experience of my gender, further contextualized by 53 years of my life as a man. Modern medicine saved my life. But so did cinema."

Maureen smiles and grasps Barbara's hand. They share a tender moment. Layla steals a glance at Jamie.

"How's your work going?" Barbara asks Jamie. "I always hoped you'd expand on your thesis."

Jamie fidgets. "Just getting back into it. Being broke really killed my creativity."

"Put a frame around it."

"That makes more sense when you know what the 'it' is."

"The 'it' is the story. Any story. Like my body, or yours, or yours in concert with another, it's the context that creates the composition."

DAY 3

They arrive in Portland just after dark. Layla glances in the mirrors and flicks her fingertips against the steering wheel. Streetlights cast Jamie's face in ribbons of orange and blue.

"We can drop our stuff at my friend's place and then head out for dinner," Layla says.

Jamie crams her sweatshirt into her backpack. "No, just drop me on Mississippi. I'm meeting a friend."

"Hot. Who is she?"

Jamie pulls a compact out of her bag and checks her face. She applies a layer of lip gloss—the first makeup Layla has seen her apply since Canada—and combs her hair over her forehead with her fingers. "Not telling."

"Then not stopping."

"Ugh. You're the worst."

Layla shrugs.

Jamie sighs. "Remember that gallery owner that sold some of my pieces in the Icara series? Well, his ex-girlfriend. We worked a few events together after they broke up."

"Bi?"

"I assume so."

"You haven't had sex with her yet?"

Jamie shakes her head. "She's partnered. To a girl. It's a casual visit."

"Sure." Layla chews on her lips. "Do you want me to pick you up later?"

"Tomorrow morning," Jamie says, glancing at the screen of her cell phone. "Just text me when you're up." She gestures to a corner bus stop. "Here's fine."

Layla pulls over in front of a closing comic book shop and an opening dive bar. Jamie grabs her bag and jumps out.

"G'night," Jamie says, and trots through Olive's headlight beams and across the street.

• •

The blare of the guitar and bass makes Jamie feel obligated to stand. The boys on stage wail. Jamie is surprised at her nervousness. *Eve's an old friend,* she tells herself. *And she's taken. Don't be stupid.*

Half a beer later, Eve walks in. She scans the club and walks to the bar. Eve relies on her cane more than Jamie remembers. And her bare arm, once smooth, pale skin, now carries a half sleeve of intricate and colorful tattoos. She's still skinny, her shoulder bones jutting out from under her powder blue tank top.

Eve leans over the bar to talk into the bartender's ear. Jamie tries to wade through the crowd to catch her before she orders. Too late. While the bartender pours, Eve looks at the crowd and catches Jamie's gaze. Even from across the club, Jamie remembers why she liked Eve. There's a sharpness in her eyes, combined with an almost feline calm. Eve takes her drink and walks to a table. Jamie catches up with her and sets her beer on the table.

Eve smiles. "Hey!" She leans down for the hug. Enveloped in her arms, Jamie catches a whiff of Eve's hair. It smells like apples.

"Sorry I'm late," Eve says.

"No worries. You're just a drink behind."

"That's good timing, actually. I doubt the bartender will serve me another for a while."

"Why not?"

"It's hard to explain naturally slurred speech to noob bartenders." Eve says. "They always think I'm drunk."

"Are you?"

"Not yet! Let's get a move on!"

Jamie downs the rest of her beer and orders another two for them both.

"You look good," Jamie says, returning to the table. Eve smiles and maybe—hopefully—blushes. In the moment she hides her eyes, Jamie scans her arms, the brilliant tattoos transfixing her gaze. She reaches her hand out, almost, but not quite, touching them.

"Can I?" Jamie asks.

Eve smiles and offers her right arm. "This is a cradle," she says, pointing. "And here's the guillotine." She traces her finger to the top of her shoulder, where a guillotine sits perched above the cradle. "The robot heart controls it all. Because I almost died when I was a baby, and machinery saved my life."

Jamie strokes the picture of the mechanical heart. Eve smiles at her touch.

Jamie drags her finger down to Eve's forearm. "And this?" she asks, tracing a molecular schematic. "Baclofen," Eve says. "To remind me to relax." She offers up her other arm. "I've got THC on this one." She laughs.

"Wow, THC is beautiful," Jamie says, tracing the squiggle of the molecular structure down to Eve's wrist.

"Ain't that the truth."

Jamie holds her fingertips to Eve's wrist and they catch each other's glance. Jamie's chest tingles. She withdraws her hand and takes a thick swig of her beer. "How's Maggie?" she asks.

"Good...I hear," Eve says. "We broke up almost a year ago. She moved to New Zealand. Seeking a hairy-footed hobbit to come home to each night, I guess."

The cacophonous music fills a lull in their conversation. Eve stares at Jamie, her grin sharp and crafty. Her cheek twitches and Jamie notices her lips—pink and full.

"You look different," Jamie says. "What's different?"

"I got a Bac pump."

"A what?"

Eve yanks up the hem of her tank top, exposing her abdomen. A sand dollar-sized mound sits beneath her flesh, a smooth dome emerging from her side. "It doses me with muscle relaxants. It's eased some of the tension in my face, which is why I look a little different. It's great."

"You're bionic," Jamie says.

Eve nods. "You wanna touch it?"

"Really?"

"Go ahead."

Jamie strokes the hard mass beneath Eve's velvety skin. "Wow. That's so wild and—"

"And what?"

"...Sexy."

"You think my Bac pump is sexy?"

"It gets to be inside of you. That's sexy."

Eve drops her shirt. "Hand me my cane."

Jamie withdraws her hand. "I'm sorry. That was stupid."

"Hand me my cane."

Jamie passes the cane to Eve. Eve tosses back the rest of her beer, leans onto her cane, and stands. "Follow me," she says and walks away. Her cane makes a distinct clack and spring sound before fading into the music.

Jamie hesitates. Did she just say—? She bursts from the table and jogs after Eve, who has already cleared the dance floor and seems to be heading for the bathrooms. Then she takes a left and forces her way out the side doors. Jamie stops, confused, and is nearly swallowed by the crowd. She fights her way through and chases Eve out the doors.

The air is chilly and wet. Jamie's breath draws plumes of fog. A lone streetlight casts an orange shaft of light into the otherwise dark alleyway. She looks in both directions, but Eve is gone.

Jamie turns back to the doors and sees Eve leaning against the brick wall. She has a sly smile on her face. Eve releases her cane and wraps her left arm around Jamie, pulling Jamie's mouth to hers. Eve's lips are warm and soft, and her tongue is aggressive. Jamie presses Eve into the wall and wraps her in her arms.

"Hold me up," Eve whispers.

Jamie presses her chest against Eve's, pinning her to the wall, and nudges her knee below Eve's crotch.

"Like this?" she asks.

Eve smiles and nods. She leans in for another kiss. Jamie kisses Eve's neck, and Eve shivers. She strokes her breast, and Eve moans. Every touch seems to drive Eve wild. Jamie reaches her hand up Eve's shirt. Her skin is cool at first, but warms beneath Jamie's touch. Eve's nipples grow hard as soon as Jamie touches them. Jamie takes Eve's nipple between two fingers and squeezes. Eve shudders and moans.

"You like that?" Jamie asks.

"You can do it harder." Jamie does so and Eve nearly convulses with pleasure.

"I don't want to hurt you," Jamie says.

"You won't."

Jamie presses her mouth to Eve's. She presses her hand against Eve's shoulder, happy that Eve is both tall and slim, making the angle easier to navigate. Jamie keeps her knee at Eve's crotch. She coaxes Eve's tank top strap over her shoulder, exposing her left breast.

"Oh fuck," Eve moans as Jamie takes her nipple into her mouth, licking and sucking. "Yes," Eve says, bucking her hips forward, rubbing herself against Jamie's thigh. Her hips move wildly, riding Jamie's thigh. Jamie fights to hold Eve upright against the wall, pinning her like a butterfly. Jamie's jeans grow wet where Eve rides her. Eve moans loudly. Jamie takes a swift glance down the alleyway. Seeing no one, Jamie returns her gaze to Eve's breast, now glistening with saliva, and her mouth, open in pleasure.

Jamie nibbles Eve's breast, and when she grinds harder, Jamie turns the nibble into a bite. Eve nearly screams, her features twisted in pained joy. Her hips grind, getting herself off by rubbing her clit on

Jamie. Jamie uses her other hand to pinch Eve's other nipple, and the combination sends Eve over the edge. She moans, then gasps. Her face turns bright red. She trembles, bucking and writhing. Her orgasm shakes her whole body, and her eyes roll back into her head. Jamie uses all her weight to keep Eve in place. Eve's hips buck a few more times before relaxing. Her body goes slack. Jamie leans in, pressing their bodies together.

"Fuuuuck," Eve says. "That was so good."

Jamie smiles and rests her head on Eve's shoulder.

"I want another one," Eve says.

Jamie nearly laughs. "What?"

"I want to keep this going."

"Are you okay standing like this?"

"I will be if you get me to come again. One more time here, then I'm going to take you home and get horizontal."

"Yes, ma'am," Jamie says.

Eve fits her wrist back into her crutch. "I want you to finger fuck me."

"Okay," Jamie says.

"Just start slow. It'll give me some muscle twinges at first, but once I get used to it, it'll be awesome."

Jamie smiles. "You're awesome."

Eve smiles back. "What?"

"I've never been with a girl who is so direct and so nice at the same time."

"I learned early on that you need to ask for what you want if you ever expect to get it. It's true for anybody, but especially for us crips."

Jamie kisses Eve. "I want to give you what you want."

"Then saddle up."

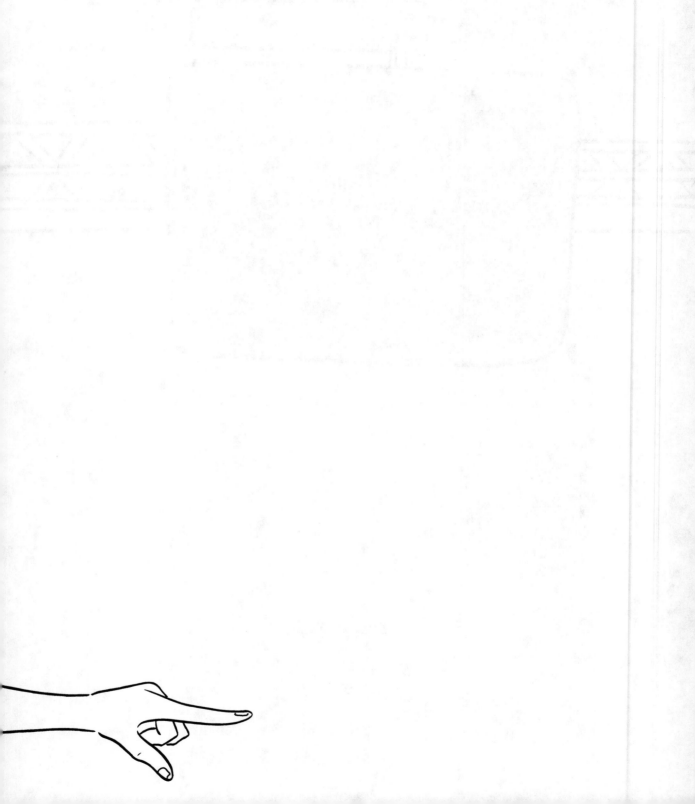

HAND SEX

Mmmmmmmm...hands.

Hands can be hard or soft, gentle or demonstrative, easy to accommodate or filling. They don't go limp if you've had one too many. And they're always there even if you forgot to pack your harness. Hands make girl sex special (other than boobs, scissoring, 69ing, and—ok fine, girl sex *is* special, and hand sex is one magical flavor of it).

The #1 thing I teach people of all genders and orientations in my workshops is to get good at using your hands during sex. As someone who has sex with people of different genders, I can say with confidence, it doesn't matter what you're packing in your panties, as long as you know how to use your hands.

Hands are great because they're dexterous and can create a wide range of different sensations: pokey, pinchy, massage-y, scratchy, rubby, tweaky, strokey, and on and on.

A lot of us who came of age in hetero relationships seem to have forgotten how to use our hands. It was as though as soon as we started having P/V sex, everything else that lead up to that just disappeared. Well, the good news is, as girls who have sex with girls, hands are still on the menu.

And, because of all the nerve endings in your fingers, and the kinds of sensations you can create, hand sex can be extraordinarily satisfying, intimate, and sensual for both partners.

HAND SEX RULES OF THUMB (HEH)

Pads Not Poke: Always approach with the pads of your fingers (instead of the tips). The difference is gentle versus pokey.

Pressure: Start off soft and increase pressure. You want her body to relax into your touch, not shirk away from it.

Pitch/Passion: Alternate finger-pad strokes and gentle scratching, or tight squeezes and gentle caresses, to create engaging sensation.

Penetrate with Permission: Don't penetrate anyone before they're ready. More on this later.

So you're making out, things are getting hot and heavy, and your fingers start... creeping... downward.

Assuming you've managed the gauntlet of her fly and/or pantyhose, your fingers should be pretty happy about now. So, congratulations, your hand is on a pussy. Most people will not have their hand on a pussy today. You are officially Ahead of the Game. Now what?

Here's a good way to start:

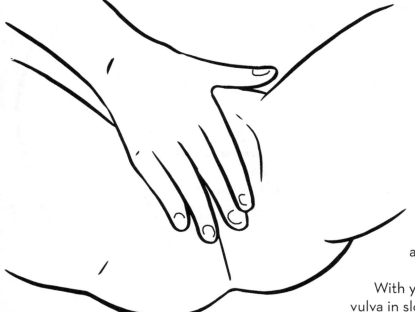

Start by cupping her vulva with the palm of your hand and applying even pressure. Your longest finger should be hugged by her lips and your fingertip is resting on her fourchette or taint. The heel of your hand should be on her mons.

At this point, it's important to keep from jabbing for her vagina. Even if she's super wet, you want to work up to that, for artistry's sake.

With your hand cupping her vulva, move her vulva in slow, even circles. What you're doing here is "waking up" her nerve endings down here, getting them ready for some yummy sensation. The cupping-with-pressure motion can also make a person feel safe and taken care of. She'll feel like she's in good hands, and that's a good thing. Sex educator and rope-expert Midori calls this the "pussy hug" and it should feel like that: a comforting, firm pressure.

(**P.S.** This is a great time to lean this book on something and use your hands to mimic this stuff on yourself. Even if you don't have a vulva, these things are good to get into your muscle memory, so give it a shot.)

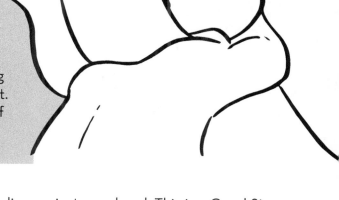

All the external techniques work just as well on non-op trans women as they do on vulva-owners. The pussy hug should still be hand position #1 and can feel super safe and delightful. The only major difference is to be careful of putting pressure on the scrotum, as it can cause discomfort. And check out the Body Shop section at the end of this chapter for girl-dick-specific moves.

If she's excited or demonstrative, she may start grinding against your hand. This is a Good Sign. If she's grinding, let her set the pace and rhythm. If she pushes her pelvis against your hand, go ahead and offer some resistance by pressing back. The pelvic mound and pelvis can handle a lot of pressure, what with the whole fucking and childbirth thing and all. If she scoots away, ease up or pause and check in. But *usually*, offering her a stable firm thing to grind on is great.

If she's not getting all humpty-humpty with you, check in by either making eye contact or listening carefully to her voice, breath, and body language.

Sometimes a well-timed, earnest "Yeah?" can be all you need for a check in. She can answer with a nod, a smile, a moan, or a word. If she's not communicating at all, you can take it back a step (by stilling your hand, making eye contact, or asking for her to give you some direction) to get the clarity you need.

If you and your sweetie are both having a good time, we can move on.

Just as with the vagina, it's not a great idea to go straight for the clit right away. You can do lots of fun things with your hands before it's time to diddle or poke:

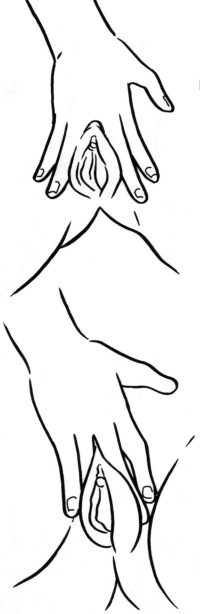

Inverted Vulcan. Start with the pussy hug, then separate your first two and second two fingers so you're making a "Live Long and Prosper" hand sign. Each set of fingers should be pressed on an outer labia. From there you can press, move your hand in a slow circle, or stroke.

Safety Scissors. From the Inverted Vulcan, bring your fingers back together, gently squeezing the inner labia and clit between your middle and ring finger. Your partner can do her Kegels which will jack off her clit, or you can vibrate your hand or continue the "mushing."

Duck face. Making a "duck face" with your fingers, pinch the outer labia together, making sure to pinch the clit and inner labia simultaneously. Similar the Safety Scissors, your partner can do Kegels to stimulate her clit shaft.

Pussy Pinch. Put well-lubricated fingertips perpendicular to her outer lips. Stroke up and down while pinching the clitoral shaft and inner lips.

Canyon Run. Like the pussy pinch, but in the valleys between the outer and inner lips. You'll often feel the crura here which can be delightful for your partner.

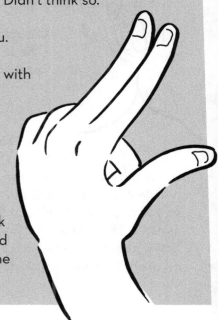

A word of warning: You don't want to move through these techniques above like they're steps in a square dance. Find something she likes and stick with it. If her energy increases, you can ramp up the speed or pressure of the moves, but switching between moves too fast can feel annoying.

Well-manicured hands are the slacks-bulge of the lesbian world. That is, they're a visible indication of sexual prowess (or at least forethought). So put your best hand forward by following these tips:

Wash your hands before you finger anyone. Or use gloves. Would you want every dollar bill, beer bottle, and cigarette you touched tonight to be shoved up your twat? Didn't think so.

Before a date, clean under your fingernails like your mama taught you.

Keep your nails trimmed and smooth. You don't have to be all butch with the super short nails, but there's a reason why lesbians earned such a reputation: Finger fucking with long nails can be challenging. If you've ever been scratched in your vagina, you'll understand. If you have femme-tastic talons, wear gloves. If you have really long nails, consider putting cotton balls in the finger tips of the gloves.

Be fingertip-aware. A lot of the techniques explained in this chapter involve your fingertips. Whenever we talk fingertip, I want you to think of the pad of your finger, the fleshy bit with the fingerprint. You should almost never go nail-tip first when dealing with the delicate flesh of the genitals.

If you and your partner want to venture further with hand stimulation, you can draw your focus to the vestibule, vaginal opening, inner lips and clitoris. Here are some things to try:

Use your middle finger to trace small circles along the slick skin of her vestibule. This will stimulate the vaginal opening, urethral opening and clitoris. If you touch the vestibule and it's not super slick, you'll want to add lubricant, either the bottled kind (see Chapter 8) or spit (only if you've negotiated this kind of fluid exchange).

Stroke the shaft of her clit. Using one finger (the middle is easiest for most people) stroke the shaft of her clit from her body down to the glans and back up. When your partner is aroused, you should be able to feel a bit of hardness to her clit shaft. You can stroke along one side, or from the top down and back up.

Clit circles. If she's good and aroused, you can give some attention to the glans of her clit. A good first move is to incorporate the glans into the circles you draw on her vestibule.

Clit stroke. You can also move the focus of the shaft stroke toward the glans. The stroke will be shorter. Try this on the side of your nose to get a feel for the motion.

The Toggle. Placing the flat of your finger pad on top of the glans, move the whole clit side to side. I think of this like those old laptop mice that were a little nub in the middle of the keyboard. But maybe you're too young for that metaphor, so you could also think of it like the joystick on the Nintendo Game Cube console. Those at least still exist on eBay. (Right?) The key with the toggle is that it doesn't generate a lot of friction on the skin of the glans (which can be ouchy). Instead, it stimulates the shaft of the clit and attached goodness by manipulating the body of the shaft itself. This is a good one to try on the tip of your nose, too. It has a similar amount of resistance as an engorged clit. Try moving the tip of your nose gently in rhythmic circles or up/down, side/side motions.

The Clit Flick. If your sweetie is good and aroused, you can try the clit flick. This is essentially creating the classic "porn-ilingus" move by flicking from the bottom up. This can be a nice feeling for some folks, especially if you use a firm, deliberate stroke and start slow-ish. This is easiest if she's not wearing pants or underwear since the best position for you involves moving your hand a bit away from her vulva. Try this move on yourself (if you don't have a clitoris, try it on the glans of your penis) and experiment with pressure and rhythm.

PENETRATION

Remember, not everyone's into penetration (pun intended), and some people may be at some times and not at others.

Permission. Asking permission to enter another person's body is polite and sexy. Ask if you can enter her in whatever kind of purred come-on she'd like. And wait until she says yes, nods, or otherwise answers in the affirmative before you go for it.

Lubrication. Remember, lubrication isn't necessarily an indicator of arousal, and a lack of lubrication doesn't mean she's not excited you're touching her. If you're going to penetrate her, you need to lube up your fingers. This could be spit (again, make sure that's negotiated) or bottled lube. Trying to grope your way inside her vagina with dry fingers is a no-no. Lube up!

Pressure. No, not peer pressure. Physical pressure. Like most genital stimulation, superficial friction is only a minor part of the pleasure. When you think of penetration, don't think of it just like jack-hammering in and out. Instead, consider how you stimulate all the good feelings hidden behind the vaginal walls. We'll talk about g-spot stimulation later in this chapter, but there's more to vaginal penetration. Explore by placing even, gentle pressure on the walls of her vagina.

One finger is usually a good start. With either your index or middle finger on your dominant hand, press the flat of your fingertip against your partner's vaginal opening. (The flat usually feels better than going fingertip/nail first.) It can be nice to leave the flat here for a bit. If your partner is really eager for penetration, this can create a fun teasing sensation. Sometimes, I like to hold my finger like this until she starts fucking my finger.

PRO-TIP: Be careful about assuming how much "fullness" your partner wants. For some people a finger can feel like enough, if not too much. Everyone has different capacity for both sensation and, well, capacity.

Ask before adding any more fingers. Most people will know what they want. And if not, you can ask to try and then be willing to "downgrade" if necessary.

With one finger inside, you may get inspired to get all innie-outie or G-spotty right away. Instead, use this opportunity to explore your partner's inner landscape. Depending on her hormones, cycle, and mood, different locations inside her vagina can feel good to stimulate. Also the specific fit of your fingers can change the sensation. Try pressing or gently stroking in multiple directions to see how she reacts.

This one's for the super geeks.
Describing directionality when dealing with bodies in space can be confusing. For instance, "up" can mean more towards the belly button, the cervix, or the anus depending on what position you and your partner are in. If you want to get REALLY good at describing where you want your partner to touch you, why not learn some scientific terms?

DORSAL: The side of the body with the spine, aka, your back. Think of a dolphin's dorsal fin.
VENTRAL: The belly.
CAUDAL: Towards the tail or ass.
CEPHALIC (seh-FAH-lick): Towards the head.
PROXIMAL: Close to the center of the body. (Think "approximate" i.e. "close.")
DISTAL: Far from the center of the body. (Think "distant") E.g. Your fingers are more distal than your shoulder.

So next time you're bedding a biologist, try telling them to "Rub the ventral surface of my vagina, as far cephalic as your fingers will reach. Oooh yeah!"

LE CUL-DE-SAC DE L'AMOUR

Unless you have really long fingers
and she has a short vaginal canal,
there's not too much risk of you
banging her cervix uncomfortably.

However, it's still good to be aware
that the cervix can change moods
drastically from one day (or hour!) to
the next. Depending on where your partner is in her
cycle, and any possible health issues, her cervix may be
very shy or very eager to play. Just like the clit, the cervix
gets more touch-friendly the more aroused the cervix's
owner is.

One way you can penetrate deeply before knocking on the
cervix's door is to put your fingers as far deep as they can
go inside of her against one of the walls. (The ventral wall is
usually easiest for people, but if she's on all fours, the dorsal
side can work, too). If your fingers can get up there far enough,
you'll notice the cervix dips a bit into the vagina. So there's a bit of a gully where the vaginal wall
meets the body of the cervix.

This part isn't quite as sensitive as the cervix, but it still is close to the uterus, so touching it can
create intense sensation anywhere on the pain to pleasure scale. If she's enjoying stimulation up
here, she may enjoy cervical stimulation, too.

You can draw circles in this gully, tracing the edge of the cervix. This will stimulate the uterus and
the attached ligaments, which can feel nice.

To stimulate the cervix directly, simply rub your finger tip across the surface. This is where gloves
become super-important. You do not want to scratch her cervix. It can create serious pain and
even bleeding, which is a pretty big buzz kill.

Using the pad of your finger, gently stroke the surface of her cervix. It may move around a bit, as
it can jump up and down with uterine and vaginal contractions.

When she's really aroused, pressing against the cervix with one or more finger pads can
feel really nice. This is usually what a woman wants when she's craving a "deep fucking"—the
manipulation of the cervix.

Proper hand hygiene is particularly important if you're having hand-sex with someone who's pregnant. Why? The os of the cervix is more dilated in pregnant people. This means bacteria can more easily get inside the uterus. And uterus infections are no joke. Wash your hands well, use gloves, and take care.

Generally, when a woman is close to ovulating, the cervix can take more sensation than usual. Cervical stimulation can induce orgasm, and for some people, a yummy sub-space kind of trance. For this kind of hand fucking, more than one finger is usually good. Two is usually easiest for the driver and receiver, but to generate that feeling of intense fullness, often three is ideal.

Again, check in before adding each finger, and let her tell you when to ramp up or ease back.

G-SPOT

The g-spot, or paraurethral sponge, has gotten a lot of attention in the past few years.

The paraurethral sponge is so called because it is spongy tissue that surrounds the urethra. During arousal, the tissue swells with blood and fluid, making the "spot" more pronounced to touch.

For most people you can't see the g-spot, but for others, if you get aroused and bear down, the area will peek into the vaginal opening.

FINDING IT

The g-spot is located about 1 1/2 to 2 inches inside the vagina on the ventral (or belly) side. The texture of it is slightly different than the rest of the vaginal walls. It has fleshy ridges much like your hard palate. Take your tongue and run it up to the roof of your mouth, where it slopes up from the teeth. That ridge-y texture is very similar to the surface of the g-spot. When it's engorged it's about the size of a ping-pong ball. Some people's g-spots get super big and full with arousal, some people's are always a bit shy. This doesn't equate to how much pleasure they can receive, though.

Like a lot of parts of the genitals, it usually doesn't feel good to touch the g-spot until you're aroused. But you shouldn't really be penetrating anyone until they're aroused anyway. When aroused, the g-spot often enjoys firm, generalized pressure and movement.

The classic g-spot move is the "come hither" technique, where you use one—or usually better, two—fingers to create a "c'mere" movement.

The Come Hither can be combined with finger fucking to create the Long Drag where your fingers go deeper on the in-stroke and press against the g-spot on the out-stroke.

Another nice technique is making a peace sign with your first two fingers and stroking the sides of the g-spot.

If in-and-out fucking isn't your partner's fave, try simply pressing firmly against the g-spot and rocking or vibrating your whole hand. This creates more of an up-and-down motion instead of an in-and-out one. The tempo can be everything from slow lovely love to vibrator-mimicking knock-your-socks off. If she's super turned on, this high-tempo hand jive can create a kind of "squishing" noise.

Navigating

G-spot stimulation for the receiver can feel like you have to pee. This is because you're stimulating a bunch of tissue around the urethra. It's normal and odds are, you won't pee. But if you're concerned, just use the bathroom before you go for any penetration. If you're *really* concerned, you can put some towels down, or play with g-spot stimulation in the shower.

Once you get into g-spot stimulation, you may be surprised with how much stimulation you can handle and enjoy. In fact, it may be hard for your partner to generate the kind of pressure you want. This is when toys can come in handy. We'll talk more about good g-spotting toys in the vibes and toys section.

Remember, it's up to you to direct your partner as to the kind of stimulation you like. So, be vocal about more or less pressure.

FLUID CHECK: EJACULATION

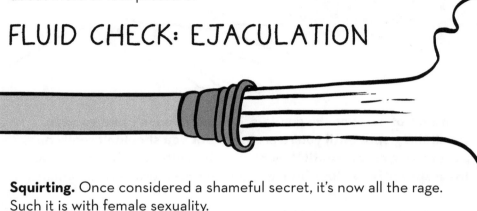

Squirting. Once considered a shameful secret, it's now all the rage. Such it is with female sexuality.

Also known as "female ejaculation" or "wet orgasm" and a ton of other cute names, squirting happens when the fluid that makes the G-spot swell exits through the urethra. It often accompanies an orgasm, but it's actually a separate process which can also happen without orgasm.

Some people do it naturally, some work hard to learn it, and some couldn't care less. Some people squirt easily and have a hard time *not* squirting when they're really aroused. Others only squirt with significant penetrative stimulation. And some never squirt.

You get to decide how much you care about your own squirt-ability.

The fluid is generated by the Skene's glands (homologous to the glands that create seminal fluid in male-assigned folks), and when it's ready, can get squirted out through the urethra, either with PC muscle contractions, or external pressure against the G-spot. The fluid often tastes and smells very alkaline. It's usually clear or milky or with a slight yellow tinge. Sometimes it smells a little bit like pee, since it comes through the same tube as urine. But, it's not pee, I promise.

The most important thing to remember is not to shame your partner if they squirt. Nothing kills the mood faster than someone shouting "Gross!" at your orgasms.

There are books and videos devoted to the subject, so if you're set on learning, scoot on over to the Appendix for recommended books. Meanwhile, take it from the expert, the person who's so adept at squirting, they're named after it!

SCENIC VIEWPOINT

High-five! Tips for Squirtastic Sex
by Jiz Lee

Whether you call it ejaculation, female ejaculation, jizz, cum, squirt, amrita (divine nectar of the goddess), or my personal favorite: "awesome sauce," names for the amazing and sometimes elusive fluid can be as varied as the words we use for our sexual acts and multi-gendered body parts. I'll alternate between the common Squirting and Ejaculation, but please substitute your own words.

1) The first rule about trying to squirt, is not trying to squirt.
This is what I call the "Anti-Goal." Like falling in love, squirting can happen when we're least expecting it. If you have never ejaculated before, but keep that goal in mind, don't be surprised if it doesn't happen. Instead of going into sex with the goal to squirt, how about just try out the different tips and actions that help folks ejaculate? No matter what happens, you'll still have a good time! So take the pressure off, and let your body guide and surprise you.

2) Foreplay, for sure!
Consider yourself a sexual athlete, and make sure to warm up before your big event! Ejaculation can be a part of the body's natural sexual response cycle. Generally summed up, the sexual response cycle is a path that starts with arousal, then sex (which of course varies from person to person, and for many it includes orgasm), and ends in resolution. You can't get to any stage without the ones leading up to it. Since ejaculation is part of the orgasm stage of the cycle, be sure not to skip the arousal stage! Of course, ejaculation isn't the end-all when it comes to satisfying sex. But if you want to improve your odds of squirting, be sure to warm up first.

3) Pee before and after sex (and don't be afraid to pee during).
Urinating before and after sex can help prevent urinary tract infections (UTIs). Even if you're not having sex but are sitting at a computer and putting it off—it's always a good idea to go if you can. It's particularly relevant in terms of ejaculation because the sensation felt before ejaculating is often described as feeling like the need to pee, so if you've already gone to the bathroom, this can help alleviate any fears of peeing on your partner or wetting the bed. That said, don't be afraid if there's a bit of urine in your ejaculate or there's a slight yellow tint or pee smell to your cum. Ejaculate is not urine, but if there's pee in your bladder there may be a trace or odor. So go beforehand, keep towels handy, and don't be afraid to get messy.

4) Be a Hot Mess While Keeping it Clean.

Keep your body clean by using gloves or washing hands with mild soap, using non-glycerine lubricant. (Silicone works well for squirting because it's waterproof and won't rinse away or be absorbed by the body.) Keep your bed/couch/floor/car/hammock clean by using towels (a stash of dark-colored towels by the bed work great for sex). You can go the extra mile with a mattress protector, which goes on the bed under the fitted sheet and will keep a mattress from retaining moisture (which can lead to mildew). If you're on the road, puppy pads will work in a pinch, and fancy waterproof blankets like Liberator's Fascinator Throe provide comfort and style.

5) Aim to Please.

Sex is so much more than in-and-out. Explore the inner ridges of the vagina and how it changes shape and lubrication based on arousal, hydration (water, water, water!), and so many other factors. You never have the same sex twice! People eroticize different sensations, even at different times in their lives, and everyone is unique in what they like. Many people find pressure (using curved fingers or hard, curved toys) just the ticket to stimulate the paraurethral gland and produce ejaculate. For others, sexual excitement and even external stimulation (such as pressure on the vulva from the base of a strap-on) can get their juices flowing. Sometimes ejaculate will gush out, other times it will form a hard stream of fluid or a sexy little trickle. Every body is different, so don't be afraid to test the waters and find what feels good!

Genderqueer porn performer Jiz Lee (The Crash Pad) is an author, philanthropist, triathlete, and self-identified "pleasure activist"... but did you know they also give great hugs? Find out more about the friendly, multifaceted porn star and their projects at JizLee.com.

There's still a lot of debate in the sex and medicine communities about why squirting is a thing and what's really going on. My favorite theory is educator and nurse Sherry Winston's. She suggests that squirting is a way to keep the urethra clean during and after sex.

My own tips for learning how to squirt:

1) **Don't be afraid to get messy.** Do it in the tub, or on top of a bunch of towels so you can feel comfortable letting loose.

2) **Explore "pushing out" while orgasming, instead of pulling in.** It's common for many people to orgasm by squeezing really tight and pulling the energy up. For me, ejaculation feels like the reversal of that energy: bearing down, opening up, and relaxing. Sex educator Tallulah Sulis (creator of the "Divine Nectar" video on ejaculation) calls it "giving birth" to your orgasm. If you can imagine (or know first hand) what childbirth feels like, you'll have a good sense of what you want to encourage your body to do.

3) **If you feel like you're going to pee, that's likely not pee.** But even if is, let loose. Get used to the feeling of pushing out and letting the fluids flow. If that idea freaks you out, don't worry, the feeling of needing to pee usually goes away after 10 seconds.

4) **G-spot stimulation, and lots of it. If you're playing alone, get yourself a curved dildo/vibrator that you can use to really work that g-spot.** If you're playing with a partner, combine something you know gets you off with intense g-spot stimulation. I like a Magic Wand on my clit with a pair of fingers working my g-spot. Your results may vary. If you don't like g-spot stimulation at all, you can try straightforward penetration or anal play to asset the pleasure.

5) **Get ready to pull out.** If you're working your goods, you'll want to remove whatever is inside your vagina just before you come. If you have anything inside you, it can block your urethral opening and prevent the ejaculate from coming out. When you're right on the edge, pull out the toy (or whatever), bear down, and orgasm. You may be surprised by a sexy flow of fluid!

Personally, I like squirting because it feels like a huge release that adds to the pleasure of my orgasms. It's also fun to have a visual representation of my pleasure, and it's definitely a turn on for my partners. But, y'know, it also makes a mess, and sometimes I'm just not in the mood. Squirting, like multiple orgasms, is as much a party trick as it is something people really enjoy. So if you want to learn, learn! But don't put too much pressure on yourself (or your girlfriend) to learn how.

ERGONOMICS & POSITIONING

As the old joke goes, it's always when she's just on the edge of cumming that your hand goes numb. And, well, the best humor is based on truth. The times I've had to clamp down and just muscle through are too numerous to count. I've had charlie horses, muscle cramps, numb tongues, legs fall asleep, neck spasms, and more, all in the service of my partner's orgasm. The things we do for love.

One of the things that make humans so damn special is how articulate our hands are. The hand is controlled by 34 muscles, and some of them are very, very small. All muscles fatigue, and the smaller they are, the faster that happens. Because of the number of muscles in your hand, they can last longer than many muscle groups (I can type longer than I can do squats, can't you?) as the muscles trade off to share the load. Nevertheless, everyone's hands get tired. No matter how fit, how dexterous, how many years you've studied the violin, your hands will fatigue.

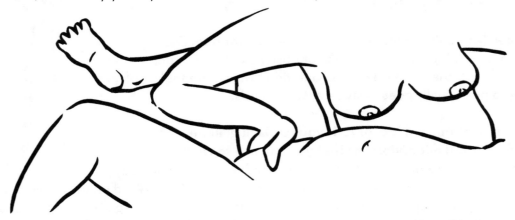

If you have chronic pain, you may be familiar with the whole dance of comfortable positioning. But even if your body is cooperative, you'll likely find yourself in a weird position more than once. It's totally normal for your muscles to get tired when you're hand – and finger-fucking. While you have many muscles in your hand and arm, those muscles are small and thus fatigue faster than, say, your hips and thighs.

The first thing you want to fix is your wrist angle. Because finger fucking often follows from vertical or horizontal making out, it can create this weird kink in your wrist.

When possible, lower your shoulder and get your whole arm closer to her pelvis. This could mean scooting down if you're lying on top of her, or kneeling or sitting if you're standing. This will immediately take some of the ouch out of the position.

The best thing you can do is put your wrist in alignment with your forearm, which can mean getting even lower. This will allow you to generate a lot more power and keep you from fatiguing as quickly. When you go for the missionary position hard-fucking, it's common to scoot all the way down so you're kneeling near her legs. Try adding some pillows or a wedge beneath her butt to adjust the angle of her pelvis. This will help you keep your wrist from kinking.

Another thing to try is bracing your wrist. You can do this with a real wrist brace, but in a pinch, you can use your other hand.

BEHOLD!

The 100% biological wrist brace:

1) Hold your dominant hand (i.e. the one you fuck with) palm up as though you're hand fucking your partner.

2) Wrap the fingers of your other hand around your wrist like so: Index and middle finger wrap around the top of your wrist crease on the back of your hand. Ring and pinky wrap around the bottom of the wrist crease.

3) Wrap your thumb around the palm side of the wrist crease. Squeeze snugly. Voila! Instant wrist brace.

The beauty of this technique is that you can switch power from one arm to the next.

If you're hand fucking and your right arm is getting sore, add the wrist brace, then use your left arm to continue fucking while you relax the muscles of your right shoulder. In a way, you're using your right hand like a sex toy while using your left arm to generate the power. When your left arm gets fatigued switch the power back to your right shoulder. This can double your endurance.

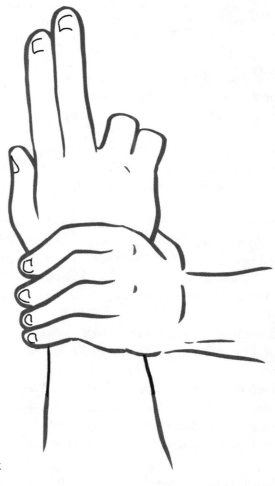

Also, try different positions. Some folks find that hand fucking from behind can be great. The navigator can relax her head on a pillow, and the driver can adjust their height to align their shoulder with the navigator's hips. Depending on the angle of entry, the driver can position their hand either palm down or palm up, whichever is most comfortable.

Big Girl Love
by Kelly Shibari

"You should do porn," he said.
"There are no fat girls in porn!" I said.

All the porn I'd ever watched starred slender women. The only fat women I'd seen in any semi-nude pose (other than in museums) were on those joke postcards you'd see at the beach. You know—those "Wish you were here" postcards with the 500lb woman in a bikini? Yeah, those.

For most of our lives, especially in the US, women are told anything over a size 6 is unhealthy, undesirable, and most definitely unsexy. It seems the "acceptable size" seems to be shrinking every year.

Being told negative messages makes you feel unsexy, which in turn messes with your ability to have awesome, fun sex. This means sex with bigger people is less about positions and technique, and more about psyche.

Stop telling yourself, "If I was only thinner, I could (fill in the blank)." It doesn't happen that way. Thinner people are not happier people. Happy people are happy. It's that simple. Real, healthy living has very little to do with a number on a pair of pants. If you're a sad or angry person, going to Hawaii on an all-expense-paid vacation isn't going to make your sadness or anger go away. You're still gonna be aggro sipping on a mai tai.

Surround yourself with positive affirmations about your size and sexuality, and things and people and tweets and posts that make you happy. If there is anything negative surrounding your self-image, get rid of it. Get rid of the haters! All they will do is eat away at you until you are completely helpless, and that sucks. Own that Block/Unfollow button! If you're happy on the inside, and working on being healthy—not skinny—you'll find that every day is more awesome. I may sound all sunshine and rainbows and guru-on-a-mountain, but it's true. And when you gain that confidence, and shun negative triggers, you'll invite a whole bunch of positivity—which is so sexy!

Confidence—not a diva attitude, nor size, hair color, or circle of "attractive" friends—is a huge attractant to the right gentle(wo)man. I'm a confident, brainy, nerdy, slightly dorky (okay, mostly dorky) chubby Asian girl who doesn't mind being naked. And you know what? Being confident, brainy, nerdy, and dorky makes sex so much fun! Trust me, size has absolutely nothing to do with it. Treat your own self with respect and pride, and you'll attract the kind of person who wants to be around all that awesome goodness.

Okay, here's the thing, we can be emotionally positive and size-accepting all we want, but we do have to agree on this: some sex positions are just plain harder for people of size. But here's the other thing: some sex positions are difficult regardless of size. Good sex is fun sex. For most people, fun sex involves positions where orgasm is possible, and that can change depending on flexibility, agility, and physiology.

Certain positions are mainstays when you're a person of size. Doggie is usually great. So is cowgirl (receiver on top). Spooning is great too. Basically, any position that allows for maximum penetration is going to be awesome when you're having sex with a larger person, and sometimes that just means you have to find a position where bellies aren't in the way. That might mean that sometimes, you're on the bed and your "top" is standing. Or you're both using toys on each other.

Anything that puts my hips above my shoulders means my boobs are in my face and I can't breathe. This might appeal to some of you, but it doesn't work for me. For some, keeping your legs up in the air for a long period of time might be exhausting. There are wedges and straps by Liberator that can definitely help with those positions, so you're able to relax and enjoy that orgasmic ride.

Everyone will have positions they prefer over others, and not all "suggested positions" will work for everyone. The best and most fun aspects of sex are experimentation and curiosity! If a position doesn't work, it might even be funny. Laughter, combined with the confidence and excitement which comes with the fact that you actually tried something new can be a huge turn on. Experimentation is the best part about fun sex, and if you're not having fun while you're having sex, then why are you even doing it?

Remember: your partner is with you because they LIKE you! They KNOW you're a person of size. It's not like they thought you were a size 2 and the minute they get you home and out of your clothes—KA-BLAMMM!—you're suddenly a size 22 and your partner runs off screaming into the night. The partner who chooses to be with you either prefers a woman of size they don't care what size you are. Either way, they like you, and your body is part of that whole package. So why deny them the sexy experience that is your fleshy awesomeness?

Performing in front of, and behind, the camera as the sexually charged figurehead for chubby Asian girls everywhere, Kelly Shibari is a stereotype-breaking tour-de-force.

HAND SEX BODY SHOP

PENETRATION AND PREGNANCY

Hygiene is especially important when penetrating pregnant people. During pregnancy, the os of the cervix dilates, allowing more things into the uterus. This can create some serious problems if you aren't using clean hands or toys. Use gloves when you're fingering pregnant people.

As for cervical stimulation during pregnancy, be careful if you're at risk for preterm labor:

> *"The activities to avoid if the pregnant woman is at increased risk for preterm labor are penetrative vaginal or anal sex that stimulates the cervix directly, nipple stimulation that causes the release of uterine-contracting hormones; semen getting on the cervix, since it contains cervix-softening prostaglandins, and any kind of clitoral stimulation, including vibrator use."* (Brill, Stephanie. The New Essential Guide to Lesbian Conception, Pregnancy, & Birth)

Fisting is generally a bad idea in the third term of pregnancy, since it's been connected to preterm labor, too. Generally, though, penetration with fingers, especially if it avoids the cervix, is fine for low-risk pregnant folks.

LOOK MA, NO CERVIX!

Some ladies don't have cervixes, either because they were surgically removed (fully or partially) or because they were never installed in the first place (as with some intersex people, trans women, or some female-assigned folks). The vagina is a cul-de-sac nonetheless, and instead of feeling a slick button at the end of it, you just feel more vagina or scar tissue at the end. Penetration can still feel deeeelightful for women without cervixes though, because the pressure still stimulates all the tissue surrounding the vaginal canal and internal clitoral structure.

The cervix, along with the ovaries and uterus, also regulate hormones, so without one, natural lubrication may be compromised. So what do you do? You know the answer! **BYOB (Bring Your Own Bottle)!**

MUFFING

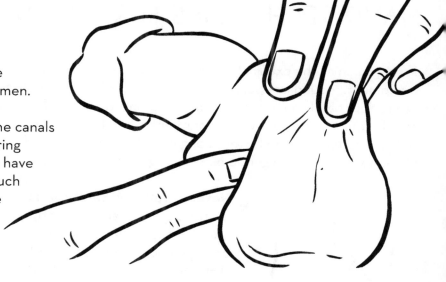

Muffing is a penetration technique enjoyed by some non-op trans women. It involves fingering (or otherwise penetrating) the inguinal canals, the canals through which the testes drop during puberty. (Female-assigned people have inguinal canals, too, they're just much smaller.) Sometimes the testes are pushed back up into the body during muffing, and sometimes they're simply moved aside to allow access to the canals.

For people without testes, this can sound kind of intense. And it can be, which is often part of the pleasure. But for many testes-having folks, it's not weird for them to move around a bit. The testes naturally rise and fall in response to stimuli (like sexual arousal, temperature, stress, etc.), and the inguinal canals, being in the pelvis as they are, are surrounded by a lot of yummy nerve tracts and erectile tissue.

Apart from the sensation-based excitement, there's also the erotic thrill that some women may have by being fingered this way. And fun enough, since most folks have not one, but two, inguinal canals, there's the option of literally doubling one's pleasure!

If your partner wants this kind of penetration, follow the same rules you would for vaginal penetration: go slow and let the receiver call the shots. Exploration with gentle pressure on the muscles and erectile tissue is usually what feels the best. Start with a gentle finger and you can, eventually, if she wants, level up to multiple fingers, small vibes, or even dildos.

While these canals are generally safe to gently explore, the spermatic cord runs through them, which contain the vas deferens. Some people enjoy vas deferens stimulation, but other people *really* don't. It's up to the vas deferens-owner to call the shots.

Post-op trans girls also have inguinal canals, but there's a little less room inside her pelvis once she has a vagina all up in there. But if she's a sexual Olympian, she could probably enjoy the mind-blowing and mystical quadruple penetration! That, however, is a topic for *at least* Girl Sex 201.

For a detailed, illustrated guide to muffing, read Mira Bellwether's brilliant and essential zine, *Fucking Trans Women*.

HAND TECHNIQUES FOR GIRL-DICK

Pretty much all the external techniques can work great for trans girls with their factory-installed equipment. Mound pressure and movement of all the tissue is great. The pussy hug is basically the same. Your hand can encompass her scrotum and clit shaft like one big package, or you can hold the shaft alone and gently tuck your fingers into her scrotum. A third option is to grab just the skin of the scrotum (not the testes) along with the shaft, and let the testes hang behind your knuckles. Once here you can do gentle massage, jiggling, or other nice sensation play.

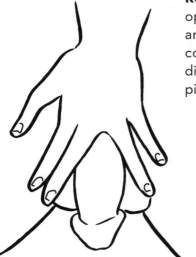

Reverse Vulcan & **Safety Scissors** can feel especially good for non-op trans girls, where her shaft is in the crux between your middle and ring fingers. If she doesn't get full erections (which is often a consequence of androgen inhibitors) pinching the base of her girl-dick can feel delightful. If she does get full erections, it'll be harder to pinch the base, but can still feel good.

If you're playing with her clit at all, you'll likely want to use lube. This is especially true if you'll be doing small, glans-related movements like **Double Clicking The Mouse**.

Remember, some girls are a-okay with all their goods, and some are fine with some parts and not with others. For instance, she might love shaft stimulation, but not like you touching her scrotum. Or hand sex might be fine but oral isn't. Or touching her all over is good as long as you touch her goods like a vulva and not a penis (e.g. small, glans-focused movements, pussy hugging and the like, not hand job grips). Get a good sense of how she relates to her body before you just start fiddlin'.

The most important thing to know about using your hands on trans clit is to treat it like you would a cis clit. Whether it's hormones or dysphoria or a mixture of both, or neither, it generally feels better to approach her goods like you would approach any girl's goods: with respect, curiosity, and a focus on her specific pleasure.

It's true that some trans girls like being touched like you would a cis guy: with a hand wrapped around and tugging the shaft. But plenty of girls don't like that. And it's always better to assume she'd rather be asked instead of just going for the kung fu grip.

Androgen inhibitors, which are commonly taken by non-op trans girls, change a lot of things about a girl's body. One of the more notable things for partners is that she usually won't get full erections.

Happily, there are a TON of awesome, fun things to do with a soft trans clit.

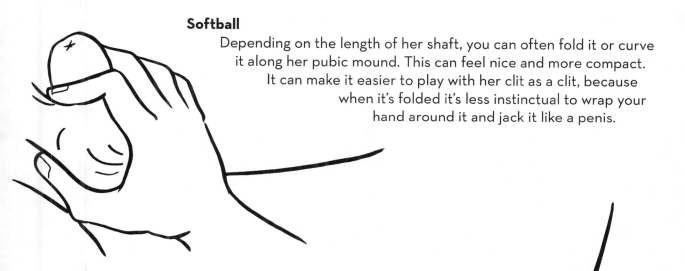

Softball
Depending on the length of her shaft, you can often fold it or curve it along her pubic mound. This can feel nice and more compact. It can make it easier to play with her clit as a clit, because when it's folded it's less instinctual to wrap your hand around it and jack it like a penis.

The Bike Seat
Non-op trans girls have an internal clitoral structure, too. It runs down below the scrotum and under the perineum. It's easy to feel when she's hard, but just as sensitive when she's not. Press the palm of your hand against her perineum and explore pressure and touch here. This is a nice place to put your hand when playing orally, too. It can feel grounding and nurturing. If she's really into feeling a solid sensation here, try placing the heel of your hand there while doing other fun things with your mouth and other hand. You can also use your fingers to stroke the edges of it, or give it a nice massage.

Alternating light strokes against the surfaces of her genitals and firm pressure can create some nice sensations. Play with using your finger tips to graze her clit, scrotum, and perineum, then adding some more massage-y moves.

The scrotum is also a delightful place to touch, if she's into it. The tissue is analogous to labial tissue, which means it's sensitive to both firm and gentle touch, and often enjoys being tugged, nibbled, and stroked. Using lubey fingers, try tracing a path from her perineum up and under her scrotum, down across the dorsal side of it, and then up and around to the caudal side to meet up with her clit.

Many people are nervous about hurting the testicles, especially if they don't have much experience with them. Here's what you need to know: what usually creates the "ouchy" with testicles is 1) the tubes getting yanked or 2) the testicles knocking together inside the scrotum. So, when you're playing with a scrotum, make sure you're only touching the skin, and you don't have the tubes in hand. Avoid jiggling or squeezing too hard, or anything that could cause the testicles to knock around inside. Instead, focus on skin pleasure, by tugging the skin, licking it, and gently stretching. Your partner may feel anxious, especially if you're new to scrotums, so always let her call the shots regarding her comfort level.

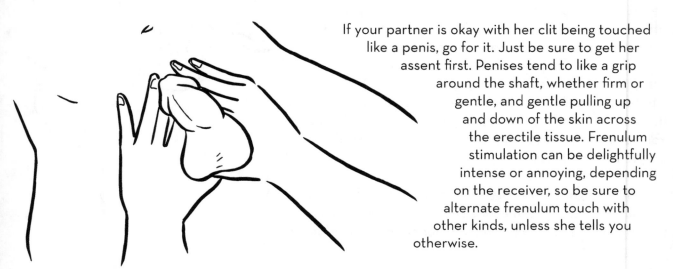

If your partner is okay with her clit being touched like a penis, go for it. Just be sure to get her assent first. Penises tend to like a grip around the shaft, whether firm or gentle, and gentle pulling up and down of the skin across the erectile tissue. Frenulum stimulation can be delightfully intense or annoying, depending on the receiver, so be sure to alternate frenulum touch with other kinds, unless she tells you otherwise.

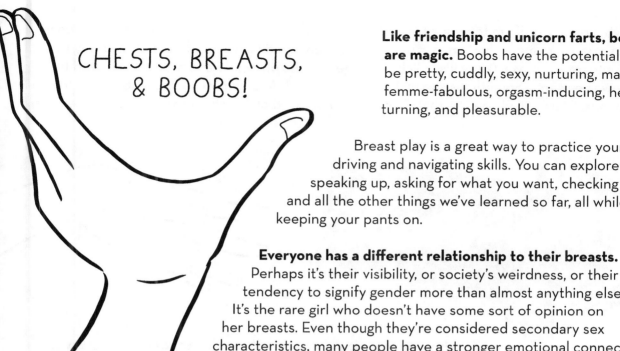

CHESTS, BREASTS, & BOOBS!

Like friendship and unicorn farts, boobs are magic. Boobs have the potential to be pretty, cuddly, sexy, nurturing, macho, femme-fabulous, orgasm-inducing, head-turning, and pleasurable.

Breast play is a great way to practice your driving and navigating skills. You can explore speaking up, asking for what you want, checking in, and all the other things we've learned so far, all while keeping your pants on.

Everyone has a different relationship to their breasts. Perhaps it's their visibility, or society's weirdness, or their tendency to signify gender more than almost anything else. It's the rare girl who doesn't have some sort of opinion on her breasts. Even though they're considered secondary sex characteristics, many people have a stronger emotional connection to their breasts than their genitals.

Likewise, when it comes to sexy time, everybody relates differently to breast stimulation. Some people can't stand it, while others can't get enough. An important and interesting fact is that all breasts have the same number of nerve endings, regardless of size. This means you may want to approach small breasts more gently than big ones, because they tend to have more densely concentrated nerve endings. Take care not to stimulate the nipples/areolae of small breasts directly unless your partner wants it.

For people with really sensitive nips, direct stimulation can be sensory overload, kind of like when you rub the same spot on your arm way too long. If this is your partner, something as simple as warm breath can be plenty, or even too much.

On the other end of the scale, some people love really intense "titty torture" in the form of clothespins, rope bondage, biting, and smacking.

I often describe nipple play to newbies as having two extra clits on my chest. Often (though not always) the way a person likes their clit stimulated is similar to the way they like their nipples played with.

Check in before you dig in. I'm always amazed at the variability of breast sensitivity among my partners. One partner likes it rough and can come from only nipple stimulation. One gets way over-stimulated by it unless she's in deep sub space. One likes it physically but it's challenging emotionally. One loves it when she's ovulating but doesn't care at all when she's not. One likes it through a binder or if I'm touching them like pecs instead of breasts. Even though I've been with all these partners more than once, it's always different. And I always check in. A nice way to do this is integrate a tease: (kissy kissy, licky licky, gentle kiss on nipple and move away). And then see how she reacts. Sometimes she makes a clear sound. And sometimes it's ambiguous. If it's ambiguous, I'll ask, "Did you like that?" or "Want more of that?" If she wants more, well, read on...

WANNA GO FOR A RIDE!?

Touching your partner's breasts through clothes can create nice tingly sensations without overstimulating the nipple. Explore full-palm stroking and gentle squeezes.

Breast kissing is dreamy for many people. It's a nice "making out, plus" move. Tugging her shirt to the side while you're necking to kiss her clavicle and cleavage can feel super sexy.

Be a tease. Explore kissing, stroking and licking her breast while pointedly avoiding the areola and nipple. If she wants direct nipple stimulation the tease can be delightfully frustrating. If she doesn't want nipple stimulation, this kind of touch can feel great on its own.

Tongue circling is the John Deere of breast play: sturdy, reliable, and gets the job done. Explore circling around the entire areola with your tongue. Try it clockwise and counter-clockwise. Mix it up with a little flick-flick or squeeze. The circle is fun to use as a tease, too, circling juuussst outside the areola until she just can't stand it anymore, then taking her whole nip in your mouth. Yum.

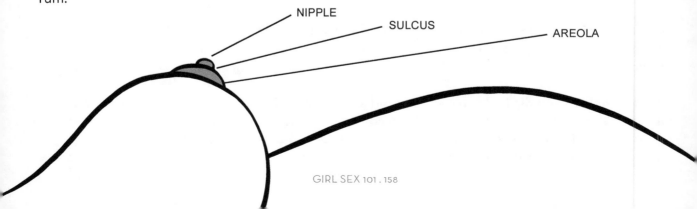

NIPPLE

SULCUS

AREOLA

Temperature play. A fun thing to do with nips is lick or suck on them, getting them nice and wet with your saliva, then blowing gently. This creates a chilly sensation that's exciting for some.

Suckling is actually a rather intense sensation. It can be great for women who aren't hyper sensitive. The cool thing is, all of us having been babies at one point (sorry for the android-erasure) we all tend to have a natural adeptness at this motion. Try gentle suction with more lip and tongue motion. If your partner likes this, you can also try taking the nipple into your mouth and rolling your tongue around it.

Flick me like you love me. One of the more "porny" moves that works for some people is the nip-flick. This is best done with a tongue, rather than a finger. Much like a clit flick, this moves taut skin with a firm tongue. Practice on your pinky fingertip to get a sense of the motion.

 PRO TIP: Flicking is one of the sensations that can be too much for super-sensitive breasts. If your partner is sensitive, try long, well-pressured licks instead of light feather touch or flicks.

Biting (gently!) Nipple biting should start exceedingly gentle. Don't overdo it or you may have a bruised nipple and/or ego. Biting can feel great for people who like their pleasure mixed with a little soupçon of pain.

PRO-TIP: I like to gauge biting preference with new partners by playing a little game. After we've verbally established that they like biting, I tell them I'm going to start biting super gently, increase my pressure, and I want them to tell me when I reach their edge. You can do this on various parts of the body, but it's especially effective on the nipple since one girl's "Yeah, girl!" is another one's "Bad dog!"

Vibes! Not just for genitals! Vibration can feel deeelightful for nipples. Try taking a tour with your favorite vibe from clit to nip and back. There are even nipple clamps that have baby vibes attached!

Symmetry is more important for bicep curls than it is for nipple play, but if you're spending a long time on one nip, switch over to the next to allow Nip #1 to recharge a bit.

The best of the rest of the breast. While the areolae tend to get all the attention, the whole breast is packed with nerve endings and can generate great sensation. Explore the crease on the underside of the breast and the area up near the armpit. If you're licking her nipple, try to switch it up occasionally by drawing your tongue across the skin of her breast, her ribcage, or her clavicle.

Nipple OH! Yes, some folks can come from nipple stimulation. Lucky bastards. If this is your partner, the general rule of thumb is the same for most of orgasm: variety, then consistency. Try different things until you land on something your partner really digs. Then keep doing that thing with a consistent, steady rhythm.

Don't forget about me. If your partner digs breast play, keep it up even after you've progressed to more genitally-focused play. If your height works out, licking on her nipples while fucking her with your hand or dildo can be a smashing combination.

Three things NEVER to do unless your partner requests it:

1) **Move the "root" of the breast.** This is a classic newbie mistake. The breasts have lots of nerve endings, yes, but most of them are on the surface, which makes stroking, kissing, and licking feel great. Twisting or kneading the whole breast seldom feels good, and can even hurt. Remember, the breasts are attached to the body, so don't try to remove them with your ardent squeeze and twist.

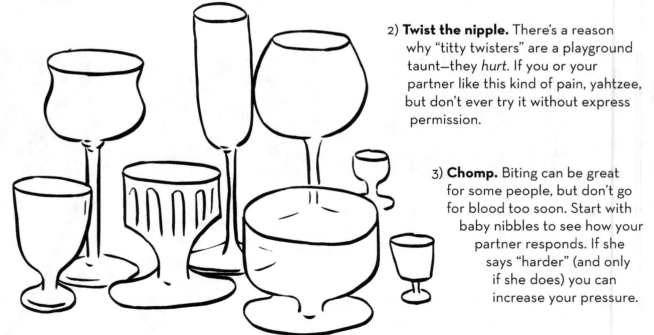

2) **Twist the nipple.** There's a reason why "titty twisters" are a playground taunt—they *hurt*. If you or your partner like this kind of pain, yahtzee, but don't ever try it without express permission.

3) **Chomp.** Biting can be great for some people, but don't go for blood too soon. Start with baby nibbles to see how your partner responds. If she says "harder" (and only if she does) you can increase your pressure.

BOOBS BODY SHOP 101

If you or your partner has had **breast augmentation** (i.e. reduction, implants, or mastectomy), sensation might be reduced or nearly eliminated. This is especially true with reduction and mastectomy, since the nipples are fully removed from the body during most versions of these surgeries. Your partner may not care about nipple touch at all, or you may need to up the sensation for it to register for her. Check in about what she likes.

Implants pose neat opportunities, because they can create a whole new range of sensation inside the breast, particularly where the implant meets the ribcage area, or where the skin is tight. If she's into it, explore moving the whole breast so that the implant moves around inside a bit. This can stimulate nerves otherwise not easily reachable.

When **trans girls first start taking hormones** they go through another puberty, so all those things cis girls experience as preteens, trans girls are experiencing for the first time. One of the most significant parts of this is breast growth and tenderness. This can be an exciting and/or weird time for some girls. Many of them will experience completely new nipple sensations and a greater capacity for pleasure. This is good news for both of you. You can play with their budding breasts just like you would anyone's, but be mindful that the tenderness can make them more easily sore, so err on the gentle side unless otherwise instructed.

The same goes for **various times on a girl's cycle.** What may be awesome one week can hurt like a mofo the next. If your partner is PMSing, take care.

Breasts can be a sore spot for a lot of **trans guys or masculine of center folks**. Much like the penis with trans women, while some people don't mind their breasts and may even derive pleasure from them, others root a lot of emotional pain there. So it's usually a good idea to steer clear unless you have a verbal confirmation one way or another.

When in doubt, refer to it as their "chest," as in "Do you like your chest touched?" If the answer is yes, ask how. Some folks are cool with their chest being stroked like it's pecs, others are excited by all sorts of nipple play and more. Making assumptions is where stuff tend to go wrong, so ask. If your partner has a hard time articulating anything about their body parts, steer clear and touch them on gender-neutral spots (aka, anything other than genitals, chest, and ass) until you get more clarity with their body.

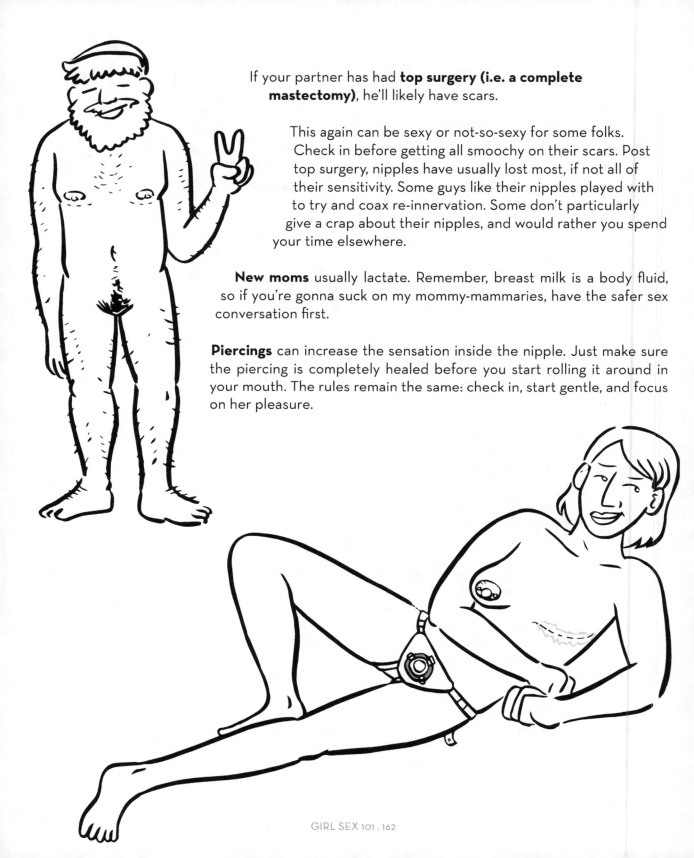

If your partner has had **top surgery (i.e. a complete mastectomy)**, he'll likely have scars.

This again can be sexy or not-so-sexy for some folks. Check in before getting all smoochy on their scars. Post top surgery, nipples have usually lost most, if not all of their sensitivity. Some guys like their nipples played with to try and coax re-innervation. Some don't particularly give a crap about their nipples, and would rather you spend your time elsewhere.

New moms usually lactate. Remember, breast milk is a body fluid, so if you're gonna suck on my mommy-mammaries, have the safer sex conversation first.

Piercings can increase the sensation inside the nipple. Just make sure the piercing is completely healed before you start rolling it around in your mouth. The rules remain the same: check in, start gentle, and focus on her pleasure.

WHAT'S YOUR RELATIONSHIP WITH YOUR BREASTS?

I'm down with my boobs (though I like my girlfriend's better!)

I bind my breasts, but they are really beautiful and I love the power of unbinding them in front of lovers.

THEY AREN'T MY IDEAL SHAPE, BUT NURSING TWO KIDS WAS ONE OF THE GREATEST PLEASURES OF MY LIFE.

LOVE THEM EVEN MORE SINCE I GOT IMPLANTS—ONE OF THE BEST DECISIONS I'VE EVER MADE!

I removed my own. I like them on others.

I love having boobs, they're great and squishy. They're also incredibly sensitive at the moment, which is fun.

I FUCKING LOVE THEM AND THINK THEY ARE DAMN NEAR PERFECTION. I'LL GLADLY PROVE IT TOO.

I love them more every day. I spent most of my life thinking they were awful/weird but then saw lots more of them and realized there's no one formula and if I could think everybody else's are beautiful then I could think mine were too.

I love and hate my breasts. They are very large and heavy making my back sore and they hurt when I try to run. I love that my sexual partners get enjoyment out of them.

Love my breasts. They're a hotbed of stimulation and I cannot get enough. If I could get two more installed just like these ones I would.

I had a breast reduction when I was 18 and it caused nerve damage so I ended up getting my nipples pierced to bring back some sensation and also lay claim to them. I love them now.

My boobs are probably the most unambiguously awesome part of my body. The rest of my body can be dysphoric or upsetting, but my boobs always feel right.

Too big and they make me buy expensive bras! But I love how it feels when they are squeezed and licked!

SOMETIMES I WANT A LOT OF ATTENTION PAID TO MY BREASTS AND OTHER TIMES NOT. MOST OF THE TIME I'M VERY HAPPY THAT PEOPLE I'VE BEEN WITH FIND MY BREASTS ATTRACTIVE.

Love/hate them. They're *huge*, and super sensitive nipples (which gets me going like WHOA. I've had a couple of orgasms from nipple play!), but they're murder on my back.

DAY 4

"This place was fucking hard to find," Layla says when Jamie opens the car door.

Jamie squints against the morning light, throws her bag in the passenger seat, and climbs in. "Oh, sorry. I thought you'd GPS it."

"We're way behind schedule."

"Schedule? What schedule?"

"Today is our longest day of driving," Layla grumbles. "It'll take almost twelve hours to get to the Bay Area." She guns the engine and swerves into the street.

"Jesus. Slow down. This is a neighborhood not the highway."

Layla fidgets as she drives, some sort of unspoken question on her lips. Jamie ignores it and focuses on her sleep-deprivation-slash-sex-hangover headache instead.

Jamie's phone beeps with a text from her ex, Sergio, who's still in her phone as Amy. She really needs to change that.

Hey. You back? I'm performing at Dada's tonight. Want to be my +1? Let me welcome you home. ;)

Jamie blushes despite herself. She texts back. *You bet. :)*

"Who was that?" Layla asks.

"Sergio."

"You mean Amy? What's she want?"

"They. We're going to hang out tonight."

Layla makes an impertinent snort. "I'm going to sleep at my friend Kurt's place in the Haight tonight," she says. "He's out of town. I'll have a whole bed to myself." Jamie stays quiet, grateful for the forthcoming evening alone in her own home. But she can sense Layla's impatience, wanting details of her night with Eve, or an invitation to stay at her apartment in Oakland.

"So are you like getting back together with Amy or—"

"Sergio. No." Jamie undoes her seatbelt and climbs into the back.

"Hey, where are you going?"

"I'm going to take a nap. Just try not to kill us."

Jamie wakes to the sunset breaking between clouds and mountains, and Layla shouting "SHIT!"

Jamie rises and looks out the front window. Smoke billows from under Olive's hood. Layla fights the steering wheel, easing Olive onto the shoulder.

"FUCK!" she screams, leaping out of the driver's seat to open the hood. More smoke pours out. Jamie climbs out the back, checking her phone for service.

"This is your fucking fault!" Layla shouts. "I wouldn't have driven so fast if I didn't have to make up time because you were getting laid!"

"Excuse me?! We added seventy-five miles onto our trip because you wanted to get laid!"

Layla fishes her cell from her pocket and searches for a tow-truck.

"Where are we?" Jamie asks.

"Some shithole named Ucky or whatever," Layla says to her phone.

"Ukiah? That's not so bad." Jamie says, standing on the running board and holding her phone in the air. "I've got some bars. Let me call a tow truck."

DAY 4

Rosie stands in the driveway to the garage, two styrofoam cups in hand. The day's heat is breaking with the slow sunset. The aguas frescas are enticing, but Carla is more enthralled with the sundress Rosie is wearing, and how the low sun makes Rosie's silhouette shine through the diaphanous fabric. Carla finishes tightening the bolt on the new battery she's just hooked up in a Honda. She straightens, places the ratchet in her pocket, and wipes her hands on her coveralls.

"Tamarind or Hibiscus?" Rosie asks.

"Jamaica," Carla says. She takes the red drink and steals a kiss. "You're sweaty."

"It's hot out here."

"Come in." Carla turns up the industrial fan and hits a red button to close the garage door. She walks to the sink and scrubs her hands clean.

Rosie leans on the hood of Carla's new project: a 1972 Dodge charger. Carla grabs a clean towel and dries her hands. She steps between Rosie's legs, nudging them apart.

"My dad had to drive all the way to Cloverdale for a tow," Carla whispers, grasping at Rosie's hips. "He won't be back for an hour." Carla's blue coveralls press against Rosie's bare thighs. Rosie's face grows hot. She looks away, her fingers finding a rough edge of bondo and picking.

"Hey," Carla says. "What's the matter?" She reaches for the edge of Rosie's skirt, and hikes it higher, exposing the tiniest bit of Rosie's white panties. She places her thigh against that spot. Rosie sighs.

"Nothing. I just wish we could see each other someplace...clean, every once in a while."

Carla pulls Rosie's face to hers. "Don't lie," she teases. "You like it dirty."

Rosie arches her back and presses her chest into Carla's. "Okay, maybe a little." She giggles.

Carla draws her palms up Rosie's hips, waist, and slides them over her breasts. She unbuttons Rosie's dress, then nudges her bra strap off her shoulder.

Rosie's chest flushes, pink under the brown of her skin. Carla leans in and kisses it, the heat meeting her lips. Rosie tastes like sweat, a mix of salty and sweet that drives Carla wild.

Carla kisses down her chest, down her belly, pulling aside Rosie's dress to bury her face in Rosie's flesh. Rosie's belly moves in and out with her deepening breath.

Carla lowers herself to her knees, trailing kisses down Rosie's abdomen. She places her mouth inches away from the gentle mound of flesh hidden by Rosie's panties. Carla runs her hands down Rosie's thighs and grips each one in her palm. She stays still, waiting. She breathes onto the white cotton.

Rosie coos, then whines, impatient. Carla smirks, knowing this dance. She traces her fingertips up Rosie's thighs, then dances them against the elastic band of her underwear.

Rosie steps her legs apart, then cocks her hips forward, bringing her groin closer to Carla's lips.

"Nah ah ah," Carla teases. "Say por favor."

Rosie pouts.

"Until you teach me how to talk dirty to you in Pomo, you're getting Spanish."

"Please..." Rosie coos.

Rosie edges her hips forward, pressing her mound against Carla's lips. "Cogeme, por favor."

"You sure?"

Rosie giggles and nods.

"Okay, baby. I can't say no to you."

Carla presses her mouth to Rosie and edges her panties down off her hips. She buries her mouth in

Rosie's vulva. Rosie bucks her hips and moans.

Rosie steps wider and leans back against the hood of the car.

"You want my fingers?" Carla asks.

Rosie nods. Carla eases one, then two fingers inside. The heat of Rosie drenches Carla's finger. Immediately Rosie starts fucking Carla's hand. Carla stands and wraps her free arm around Rosie's shoulders. She pulls her tight.

"Nah ah ah," Carla teases. "We're going to take this nice and slow."

Rosie whimpers through a smile.

Rosie slows her hips to match Carla's pace. She squeezes Carla's fingers as they pull out and relaxes when they ease back in.

"You like that, baby?" Carla whispers. The heat from Rosie's cheek warms Carla's lips. Rosie grips Carla's ass through her coveralls and squeezes.

"You want to come?" Carla asks.

Rosie nods.

"You sure?" she teases.

Rosie squeezes Carla's ass in a form of begging. "Okay, baby."

Carla lowers her right shoulder in line with Rosie's chest and increases the rhythm of her hand. She adds pressure to the front wall of Rosie's vagina as she withdraws and reinserts her fingers. Rosie holds on to Carla's back, squeezing her shoulders. She moans and screams, each exhalation carrying a sound of pleasure. Each moan makes Carla thrust harder.

Rosie lets go of Carla's shoulders and braces herself against the hood of the car, bearing down on Carla's hand.

"Good girl," Carla growls, working her fingers in Rosie, steadying her own eager rhythm.

"Just like that!" Rosie cries.

Through the garage door, Carla hears the rumbling of a truck. She turns her attention back to Rosie, whose howls bounce off the cement and steel of the space.

Rosie throws her head back and screams. Her muscles tighten around Carla's fingers, rippling, relaxing.

A truck door slams. "Lita lita!" Carla's father calls from the driveway.

"Shit!" Carla says. Rosie is still coming, but she whips herself to attention, her knees buckling beneath her as she grabs the edges of her dress to cover her bare chest.

"Abra la puerta, por favor!" her father calls. He's using his friendly business tone, but Carla hears the impatience in his voice.

"Aguanta!" Carla shouts. She throws a sandpaper block to Rosie. "Look like you're sanding something." She runs to the garage door button. "But! Don't actually sand anything." Rosie struggles to rearrange her clothes.

"Carlita!" her father shouts.

"Ahorita!" Carla yells. She hits the greasy red button and the garage door clinks to life.

The orange sunset creeps up their ankles and higher with the rising door. Rosie fixes her bra with one hand as her other hovers in circles above a bondo-ed patch of the Charger. Carla sniffs her hand and panics. She runs to the counter and shoves her hand in a tray of dirty motor oil.

Her father ducks under the garage door. Carla grabs a rag and wipes her hands.

"Sorry, I was wrist deep. Oil change."

"You should keep the door open when you're here. We want people to see us working."

Carla glances at Rosie, who stifles a giggle. "Sure, Dad."

"Hello, Rosemary," Carla's father says. "How's your brother?"

"Good. Still working at the casino. He likes the hospitality business."

"Well he's always welcome back at the garage. Lita's got her hands full around here."

Mr. Hernandez scans the garage like he's seeking the answer to some mediocre mystery. Carla clears her throat and glances at the truck to redirect his attention away from Rosemary's ill-hanging clothes and back to their waiting customers.

"Right right, we got a radiator problem with this Volvo. Think you can take care of it before closing? These two young ladies need to make it to Oakland tonight."

"You got it, Papi," Carla says.

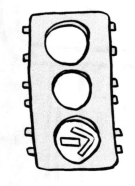

IN THE DRIVER'S SEAT

Imagine yourself in the driver's seat of a beautiful and expensive car. You're about to turn the key and put it on the road. You're a little bit nervous. After all, this isn't your car, it's worth a lot, and it's being trusted in your hands.

What's the first thing you do?

Adjust your seat? Check the mirrors? Fasten your seatbelt? Take a minute to figure out where all the gauges and switches are?

Every car is different, and this one will take a few minutes to adjust to. But soon you'll get the hang of its nuances, and you'll just drive. You won't have to run the checklists as you drive. You'll know that the steering wheel will require roughly 1.5 spins in either direction to make a turn. You'll know you use the second segment of your left middle finger to hit the turn signal. You'll gently brake when you go into a curve. You'll accelerate when you come out of it. You don't have to think of it explicitly each time. You just get a feel for it, and you drive.

When you're in the flow, driving down an open road is elegant, easy, and serene. It's a collaborative experience between the driver and the vehicle. And just as driving is a responsibility to be taken with awareness and respect, so is topping.

When you're topping, you're the Driver. The bottom is the Navigator. (It's worth noting here that "Topping" and "Bottoming" don't imply a hierarchy. You can be a dominant bottom or a submissive top. I'm using Driver & Navigator, but we could just as easily use the words "Giver" & "Receiver," "Doer" & "Do-ee," etc.)

It's her job to tell you which turns to take. It's your job to listen and drive responsibly.

PRESENCE

Most people have a hard time enjoying themselves if they're nervous. This is especially true with sex. Even if you're super experienced, there's always a small jolt of energy when you're intimate with a new person for the first time. This can certainly add to the excitement, but it can also make things like pleasure harder to wrangle.

To combat this, you don't have to put on some swaggering airs and act like you're all in control. In fact, any kind of pose can make you look like, well, a poser.

The best persona to adopt when in bed with a new person is authenticity and transparency. Speaking your mind with your sweetie will almost always endear you to her.

One of the biggest impediments to great sex is people pretending they've got all the answers. The truth is, no one has all the answers. Experts, workshops, podcasts, and guidebooks like this one, they can't tell you how to get that specific girl off in the way she likes. The individuality and multiplicity of the human experience is out of all of our scope. The best we can do is offer you ways to approach, ask, listen, and offer. The rest is a co-creation.

This is where the magic of sex happens.

So drop the facade and be real. If you're nervous, say so. If you're not sure she likes something, ask. If you need to make an adjustment to prevent a charlie horse, do it. Otherwise it'll get in the way later. Our brains just don't turn off when it's not a good time to fix something. Fix it right away and then get back to business.

 PRO-TIP: Presence also means paying attention to whether something is working for your partner or not. Don't slip into cruise control while doing a move that worked on your ex if you're not going to pay attention to whether it's working on your current.

LISTENING

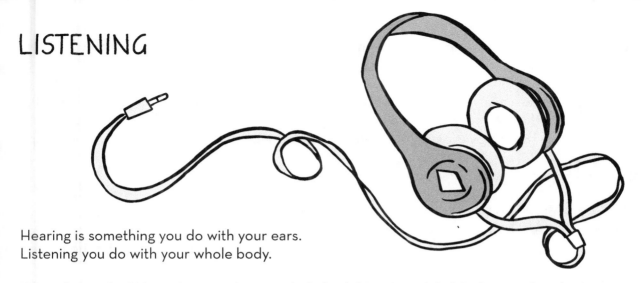

Hearing is something you do with your ears.
Listening you do with your whole body.

What does it feel like to listen with your whole body? You've probably done it already. Are you an athlete? A dancer? A musician? An artist? A martial artist? A yogini? A craftsperson?

What you're looking for is "the flow."

You may know it as the "runner's high," or "beginner's mind," or "groove." It's where your mind goes when you're trying to find the right pitch on a musical instrument, or when you're sparring with an opponent or dancing with a partner. You're standing in a river of sensation, giving equal weight to all of the input that washes over you. You're looking for the soft space in your mind where you are accepting all the stimuli without latching on to any single one of them.

Sex educator Reid Mihalko (pages 308-309) says it's like trying to make a wine glass sing. When you try to make a wine glass sing, you're tracking a lot of different things: friction, rate, pressure, etc. You track all of these at once and adjust your motions accordingly. If you're not sure what he's talking about here, put down this book and go get a wineglass. Fill it with a little bit of water, and run your moistened finger around the edge. Try to make it sing. And take note of where your mind goes while you do this.

Musicians often get this right away. It's a quality of listening not only with your ears but with your body. If you've ever played a musical instrument, you know the feeling of the vibration in your body as you seek the right pitch. You're certainly adding the stimulus, but the instrument is amplifying and altering your input and turning it into a new, co-created sound.

Your partner will do the same. You can touch her in a certain way, but her body will receive that input, and then relate to it in a specific way, and give you something back. Your job is to listen to the new sound she's giving you, and respond in turn.

You can get lost when you stay too focused on what you give rather than what you get back. Listen for what her body is actually saying, not what you expect her body to say.

Raise your hands: How many of you have been with a lover who was obviously using moves that 1) worked on one of their former partners and 2) did absolutely nothing for you? How many of you noticed that when those moves didn't work, your partner doubled-down instead of switching it up?

That's what happens when a person gets too attached to expectations.

To mix my metaphors a bit: When artists first learn how to draw, they have to learn how to draw what is really there, not what they see through the various filters of their brains. Your job as a lover is to respond to the person who is actually in front of you, not the person you think she should be.

You're allowed to use good information you've garnered from your sexual history to inform your approach. Just be malleable and receptive to the body you're touching in the moment. It's gonna be unique. And even if you're with the same woman again, her body will be slightly different next time. Our internal sensations change with our mood, our connection, our cycle, and our hormones. That's part of what makes girl sex so exciting. You're never stepping into the same river twice when you're with a woman.

There are a number of ways you want to learn to listen. Naturally you'll be better at listening in some ways and others will feel weird or challenging. The point is to practice listening in all modes.

EARS

Pay attention to her breath and vocalizations. Some people are really skilled at hiding their pleasure sounds (if this is you, go back to Chapter 1 and read how to get better at communicating with your partner). As a person gets more excited, her breath will usually quicken, become more erratic (lots of short breaths followed by big sighs, for example). Some people even hold their breath as they get more turned on. The problem with that is that depriving your blood of oxygen can make it harder to come. So if you're a breath-holder, practice taking deep breaths as you get close to orgasm, just to see how it feels. Sound helps with breath: you can't vocalize if you're not breathing.

Every woman is different in the sounds she makes. It can take a few romps with the same lady before you learn to decode her noises.

Funny story: I have a lover who gets really intense when she's in a lot of pleasure. Her face gets red and all squinched up. Her muscles tremor. She makes fists. Her sounds come out in sharp syllables. One of those syllables, I've learned, is "Na." I'll be fucking her and she'll start shouting "Na! Na! Na! Na!" which can sound a lot like "No!" I tell you, this is not the sexiest thing to hear from a girl when you think you're rocking her world. The first time this happened, I dialed back until I could do a verbal check in with her. I said, "Is this good? Are you enjoying this?"

"Hell yes!" she shouted.

"Okay, I'll keep going?"

She nodded vigorously and fell back on the pillow.

Later than night when we were having dinner, I asked her about the "No" sound. She said, "I made a 'no' sound? Weird. I loved it all."

She had no idea she made that sound. We've slept together enough by now that I've learned not to worry about that sound and know that when she needs me to stop, she's quite clear.

SKIN

Feel for sweat and heat. These are signs of increasing arousal. But there's another kind of skin-listening that is more subtle. I think of it as a vibrational feeling, or perhaps an overall kinesthetic quality of the body moving in different ways. However you feel it, you want to develop the ability to listen with the palms of your hands, your lips, your face, and the rest of you. If you're a musical person, you can think of your whole body as a piano sound board, the body of a cello, or perhaps a tuning fork. You're not only listening to her skin, you're feeling into your own and paying attention to the stimuli it's receiving. It can feel like electricity or the vibrations of a string. It can be tingly or hot or you may even have a synesthetic response like seeing colors or hearing sounds.

TUNE UP: Practice listening with your skin. Take your less dominant hand and stroke your arm with your fingertips. Slow down enough to feel each hair on your arm respond to the movement. Now, hover your hand above your arm so that it's not quite touching. Move your fingertips up and down again, and notice the sensations of air and warmth on your arm as you move.

EYES

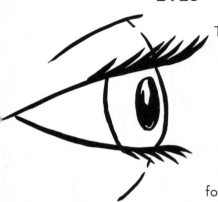

The concept of listening with your eyes can feel strange. I say listening instead of looking, because listening is a receptive sensation for most of us. We are still and let the information come into us. Listening with your eyes is the same. You're not just looking for visible signs of arousal, you're letting subtle visual cues flow into you. If you're familiar with Tai Chi, yoga, or meditation, this is often called a "soft gaze." You're letting your eyes unfocus and receive information in a softer, more holistic way. When you have that soft gaze, smaller cues like the twitch of a forehead, the flexing of toes, and the rise and fall of a rib cage all have the potential to register.

TUNE UP: Look up from this book and fixate on a spot far from you. Then, soften your gaze so that it looses some of its sharp focus. (If you wear glasses, taking them off can help.) Try to "open the aperture" of your gaze so that all the information is getting into them at once. It can feel like you're relaxing the muscles that control your eyes. Take a few deep breaths and relax into this feeling.

EMOTIONS

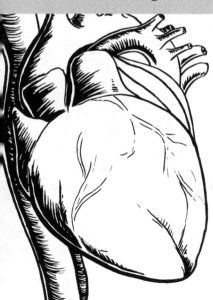

If you're a particularly empathetic person, you might find that stimuli create emotions in you. Have you ever walked into a room and had a sense of sadness? Elation? Your energy level went up or down? When you're in bed with someone, it's easy to have emotional reactions. Let the emotions tell you something. If you touch her in a certain way and your body has a visceral reaction of sadness, you may be responding to something on a more subtle level. Strong emotional shifts are a great opportunity to check in with your partner. You may be responding to something completely unknown to her. Or you may have stumbled upon an opportunity for connection, intimacy and deeper pleasure.

TUNE UP: Practice listening energetically. When you're in a room with a bunch of people (say, a cafe, or library, or restaurant), sit quietly and just listen to the room. Tune out the individual noises and let them all wash over you. Feel into the energy of the room and see what it creates in you. Does the room feel anxious? Serene? Is there an imbalance of energy somewhere?

Learning to listen in different ways is good for sex, but also for life. Many meditative and artistic practices emphasize these qualities of receptivity. When you feel anxious, try listening in a more expansive, gentle way, with your skin, eyes, ears, and heart.

WANNA GO FOR A RIDE?

As a Driver, your job isn't just to listen, but respond. So, once you've got the input, what do you do?

There are three good ways to respond to stimuli from your partner:
1) Contact Improv
2) The Conductor
3) Topping from the Bottom

CONTACT IMPROV

Contact Improv is a form of improvisational dance developed in 1972. And it's pretty much what it sounds like. The basic philosophy is to create movement inspired by your partner's movement. Quite quickly it becomes clear that neither person is initiating per se, but rather, it becomes a conversation between bodies.

Most of you have done some form of sensual contact improv before: kissing. When you kiss someone new, there's a period of adaptation where you're learning how your partner likes to be kissed. You might ease up on the tongue, or pull them closer around the shoulders. You might peck or french or be coy or be passionate. You're responding to them, and they're responding to you. When kissing is really excellent, you develop a style that works well for both of you. Sometimes you don't know who initiates the transformation—it's merely a co-created new experience.

So it is with Contact Improv sex. This could look like her bearing down on your hand, and you increasing your pressure against her to match. It could look like her holding her wrists together above her head and you grasping them with a free hand. It could look like her sitting up and you wrapping an arm around her back to hold her in that position. Contact Improv requires soft listening and presence. You want to see or feel something she gives you, and give her something back to match, amplify, or adjust.

THE CONDUCTOR

The Conductor method is more classically "top" and "bottom" oriented. This method is great when you're in Research and Development mode. Your partner can lay back and relax while you explore their body and how it responds to your touch. It's also good for shy people, pillow queens who just want you to "do" them, and folks with a submissive streak. If you and your partner get turned on by polarity, the Conductor method may end up being your favorite.

As the Conductor, you create and steer the energy, much like an orchestra's conductor. If you want to ramp up the energy, you create and guide it. If you want to bring it back down, you do that too. To be an excellent conductor, you need to have a good understanding of energy and how to manipulate it. For instance, you can increase the passion by squeezing tighter, kissing deeper, or massaging muscles with your touch. You can heighten the energy by speeding up the rhythm, moving her body in more dramatic ways, or touching her erogenous zones with more directed intention. You can cool things down by lightening your touch, slowing your rhythm, and being more "lovey dovey."

You're still listening to your partner—this is a duet, not a solo performance. But instead of tweaking small things to create a new experience, you're guiding it all and using your bodies together to create the music.

TOPPING FROM THE BOTTOM

Topping from the bottom is when the person in the position of receiving is also the one calling the shots. It can be verbal (i.e. a "bossy" bottom) or it can be more like the Conductor—initiating movement and creating opportunities for touch by moving their body in certain ways. The person who tops from the bottom is someone who knows what she wants. This can look like moving her body into a new position, initiating touch by putting her hands where you want them, or dirty talking requests and commands. (Note: "Top" and "bottom" can also refer to BDSM roles, but that's not how we're using them here.)

Remember, just because someone is topping from the bottom doesn't mean the "do-er" waives consent. Sex needs consent for both giving and receiving.

Driving is more than just knowing the components of a car. Knowing how to fix a fan belt won't teach you how to drive. And sex is more than just understanding the material science of it. You should know the parts and how they work, but you should also be willing to learn the nuances of every body you encounter.

If we expand the field of vision, look at sex as more of an equitable exchange of sensual energy, sex looks like many different, wonderful things.

All sex is a co-creation. Consent and pleasure are not one-time things, just like sex isn't a one-act thing. You want to continue checking in, asking for adjustments, and making sure everyone is having a good time.

UNDERSTANDING STONE

Stone is a term for a person who doesn't like having their genitals touched at all. It's most often heard in conjunction with "butch" but butch and stone aren't the same things. You can be stone and femme, or butch and a sissy bottom.

People choose to be stone for all sorts of reasons. Sometimes it's because of an abuse history, body dysphoria, or just a lack of interest or pleasure from that part of their body. Some people on the asexual spectrum may be stone because they don't like feeling bodily sexual stimulation even though they like giving it to other people.

The bottom line with stone is: It's not your "fault" if someone is stone. You can choose to sleep with someone who's stone if you want to, but you don't have to. If giving a person direct bodily sexual pleasure is important to you, then that's your preference and that's a-okay. However, if you really dig someone who's stone, why not try it out? Many people who are stone say they feel great satisfaction from getting their partner off. And some of those folks say it's more gratifying to give pleasure than to receive it.

THE ART OF THE TEASE

Burlesque dancers know a thing or two about being sexy. Let's look to them for some tips on orchestrating a hot experience. **There's a classic formula in the burlesque world: Tease, Present, Take Away.**

The Tease
This is when you hint and indicate at the sexy without actually showing it. This is usually how props and costumes are used. The dancer will hide parts of her body behind a fan, a scarf, a robe or a costume piece, playing like she's going to show you some more skin, but pulling back just before she gives you the goods. She's hooking you, making sure she's got your attention.

The Presentation
After teasing and coaxing you along for a while, she'll reward you with a look, often a sneak of booty or boobie. But before you get too excited...

The Take Away
She won't let you look too hard. Because she'll take the goodies away. Or she'll move your attention to a new body part that she'll tease and present in a similar way.

Then the cycle starts over again.

What can you learn from these Mistresses of Tease?

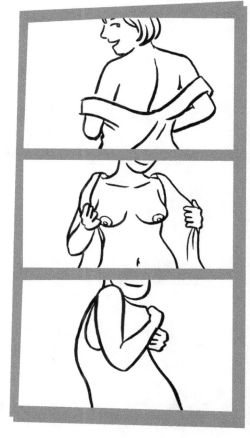

There is a lot of pleasure to be found in ramping up the excitement. It's the wrapping on a gift, the aromas from the kitchen before a meal, or the moment of eye contact before a kiss. Teasing can help make the experience even better.

You can learn to tease by not too readily giving your partner what she wants. Of course you'll give it to her...eventually. The tease can look like taking your lips on long, leisurely trip down her neck and chest before you kiss her nipple, and another long trip down her belly before you touch her clit. Or it can look like giving her soft touch before the strong grip she likes. Or turning on the vibrator so that she hears it first before you touch it to her body.

The more you get to know your partner's body, the better you'll be at teasing her. Once you know what she loves, you'll know when you can take it away and give it back to keep the energy moving.

SCENIC VIEWPOINT →

DRIVING
by Sex Nerd Sandra

I didn't know how to listen because I had never been listened to. This was what I realized the morning after some superbly mediocre strap-on sex where I had thrust away at my friend, on her request, only to witness on her face the slow dawning of, "Oh, this is no better than sleeping with a man." We were newbies and I thought I was doing it right, because I was doing it the way I had experienced it.

My experience to that point was mainly male lovers all performing what they thought sex was supposed to be: rhythmically unremarkable and angularly pornographic. In response, I would push my sexual excitement into the foreign moans and arching of some woman I'd seen on a computer screen. We had all been taught by the internet and it showed.

For all the sex books I had read, I never ran across anything on how to understand my partner. Well, I mean, I could figure out men alright but I thought pleasuring a woman was supposed to come instinctually, right?

The day after I saw my friend's face, politely serene below me as I fucked her with my strap-on something didn't feel right. "Wait. Wait! She wasn't enjoying herself much, was she? I mean, it was ok, but, wait...Oh no." The realization landed with a thud: I had been having sex with women the same way most of my partners had done to me! And what's worse is I had made fun of how bad the stereotypical guy is at sex and yet I was no better. At that moment, I declared, "This ends here."

I rejected everything I thought I knew about having sex with a woman. In my heart I knew I had never been fucked the way I wished. I felt like no one understood how to touch me. My sexual needs always seemed absurdly complicated, and different from other women's. I felt broken and undecipherable, and believed no one could ever figure me out.

I had never even verbalized it to myself, but I knew there was so much more that could be done, given, received, even in the simplest of missionary positions.

It began with me. I started to think about everything I wished for in a partner, how they would touch me, how they would enter and pause before moving upward into me, while pressing firmly with their hands. To do this, I had to listen to myself. For the first time I tapped into my inner senses, to all those subtle little nothing sensations I usually ignored.

I listened. I noticed slight twitches when I'd hear a sexy word, this loosening feeling just inside when I'd press on my opening. I'd hear my sighs when I massaged my outer labia and noted how trusting I felt when a strong forearm grabbed around my waist and pulled me in.

I started paying attention to my partner's facial expressions. As a budding sex educator, reading non-verbal signs of boredom and curiosity were important to me professionally, and luckily that skill translated to the bedroom.

I came back to bed a different person. Empathy, that ability to feel what someone is feeling, became paramount to my topping. Learning from my own senses, it has been a joy to discover I'm not so weird, not so different than other girls. I'm so glad I can give a woman what I never got myself. I never knew this thing that used to make me so sad could bring others such joy. It has helped me heal judgment toward myself and my body and has opened me to the awe of topping, of trusting and of feeling. Being a responsive, sensitive lover started with me. The person I needed so desperately to understand was myself.

Sex Nerd Sandra consensually touches the lives of millions. Born and raised in Los Angeles, the sex educator and podcaster is an avid traveler and lover of big questions.

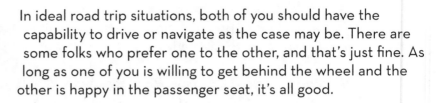

NAVIGATING

In ideal road trip situations, both of you should have the capability to drive or navigate as the case may be. There are some folks who prefer one to the other, and that's just fine. As long as one of you is willing to get behind the wheel and the other is happy in the passenger seat, it's all good.

The role of the navigator is a crucial one. You have the map. You plot the course. You call the turns.

You wouldn't expect someone to know how to get to your house if you don't give them your address, would you?

If they're new to the area, sometimes you need to give turn by turn directions.

Sometimes, it might be best to drive yourself there, and have them pay attention.

You get where I'm going with this?

To bottom is to practice the great art of receiving. According to our highly scientific (read: not at all scientific) Girl Sex 101 poll, 25% of readers identified as tops, 40% as bottoms, and 15% as switches (a switch is a mixture of both top and bottom, often changing based on the relationship and the circumstance). This doesn't surprise me at all. To receive is to be vulnerable, to be open, exposed. It can be terrifying. Which is no wonder why it's also an extremely powerful position to be in. As a receiver, the giver is in service to you and your pleasure. It is your job to navigate. It's her job to drive.

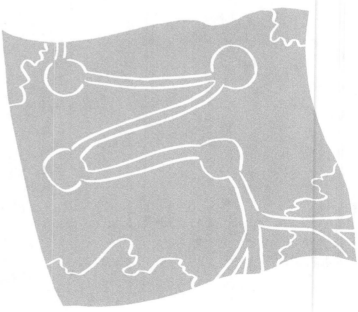

You call the turns. You monitor the surroundings. She works the pedals. Even if you're not aimed squarely at orgasm, you still get to call the shots. Even if the shot is "just do me while I lie here in blissed out silence."

PLEASURE IS IN THE BODY OF THE BEHOLDER

So how does one become a good navigator?

Know the Route
Know what gets you off, gives you yummy feelings, makes you purr, hum, or scream.

Keep Breathing
Your blood needs oxygen. Give it what it wants. If this is hard for you, practice sighing or making yummy noises.

Use Your Words
Your driver isn't a mind reader. If she whizzed past your turn, you need to let her know.

Speak in the Present
Do you know the old New England joke about giving directions? "You go straight down this highway for a few miles, then take a left where the old church used to be, drive til you get to Jimmy's house, hang a right and you're there." Helpful, right? Well...

Sometimes things that make sense for you don't make sense to your driver.
Sometimes this means you have to take their finger and place it directly on the spot you want. Sometimes this means breaking down into useful pieces that thing your ex did that you loved.

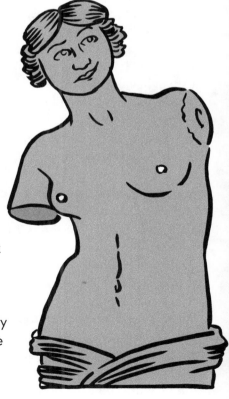

Speak Up Right Away
If something isn't good, say so. If you need to make a small adjustment, do it. It'll make it all better in the long run.

Use Your Head
Give yourself permission to indulge in your fantasy. If thinking about a certain thing really turns your crank, go ahead and think about it. Sexual fantasy gets a bad rap. We here at Girl Sex 101 think that fantasy is wonderful. Even if your thoughts are about people other than your current sweetie, or scenarios that are taboo, scary, anti-feminist or politically incorrect, you're allowed to think about those things. The only time to check yourself is when you use fantasy to disassociate. If you're retreating into your imagination to avoid the reality of what you're doing because you don't like your partner or aren't having fun, fantasizing to escape is a bad idea. Fantasy, like anything you introduce into the bedroom, should enhance the experience, not help you tolerate it.

TOBI'S TRANS-MISSION

"So How Do You Have Sex?"

It sucks getting this question, doesn't it? Queer women get it all the time from straight folks. Queer trans women and our partners also get it from other queer women. There's no one way a category of people have sex. Trans women have sex in as wide a range of ways as everyone else does. There might be some common tendencies, but everyone is different. Avoid making assumptions.

I've seen situations where folks have gotten into trouble assuming that if a woman has similar looking genitals as a cis guy, then she must want to use them the same ways a cis guy would. It can be a touchy subject. A lot of trans women experience intense dysphoria at the idea of using their genitals to penetrate a partner. Others may experience guilt or shame because they do want to have sex that way and have been told trans women shouldn't. On top of that, being on hormones can significantly change the way a trans woman's genitals respond to stimulation. It may be difficult or impossible to get erections, touch that once felt good might not anymore, and new kinds of touch might suddenly feel amazing.

So how do trans women and their partners have sex? Any way they want. If a trans lesbian and a cis lesbian have penetrative sex together, they are still lesbians. If two trans women get off together to BDSM and kinky role play, more power to them. If a couple just likes to feel each other up and grind without ever taking off their pants, that still counts as sex. If another couple chooses only to bond and create connection together through non-sexual touch, cuddling, and affection, that's just as valid as any other relationship.

Some Options for Sex You Might Not Have Thought Of

It's amazing how creative people can get when coming up with ways to have sex. Especially when so many folks are taught there is only one set of ways to have sex. A lot of times trans folks don't feel comfortable having sex in the ways we're taught. The way you like to be touched might change after starting hormones. And it's not uncommon to feel like all the options for sex just don't work. Don't get pessimistic! There's an infinite range of options. Here are a few options to get you thinking:

Muffing is penetration of the inguinal canals, that's the part of the body that testes descend from and where they get pushed back up during tucking. There's several nerve clusters in the area and gentle touch or rubbing is a very unique sensation I can't really compare to anything else. You can find it by inverting the loose "scrotal" or "labia donor tissue" on either side of the internal portion of the phallus. You can gently insert a finger, angled up and to the side. Be careful the first few times. The area may be tight and the sensation may feel alien or even alarming at first.

Grinding is rubbing your bits against your partner's, also called tribadism, humping, dry sex, or scissoring. It can be done with or without your clothes on and in several different positions. You can be lying on top or on bottom of your partner, you can press a thigh between their legs. One of my favorites is one partner sitting on the other's lap facing each other, with a Magic Wand placed between both people's bits.

Sex while tucked is somewhat self explanatory—keep on a pair of underwear to maintain a tuck but then try touching and stimulating bits through the underwear. Things can feel very different when it's all compressed. And, for women who have a hard time having sex when they or their partners can see their bits, this is a great way to remove the stress that comes along with that.

Perineum stimulation is something that a lot of trans women really enjoy. It's the area between the genitals and the anus and it can take a lot of strong pressure or stimulation. Try making a fist and firmly pressing knuckles into the area, or a knee, or a Magic Wand. Especially when done in a thrusting manner it can feel reminiscent of vaginal penetration.

CHERRIES ARE NOT THE ONLY FRUIT

Virginity is a pretty outdated concept, and a heterosexist one at that. When celesbian Suze Orman came out by saying she was a "45 Year Old Virgin" because she'd never had sex with a man, the sex-positive community let out a collective WTF?! Virginity isn't defined by penetration, and it certainly isn't defined by penises. So then, what does it mean to be a virgin at all?

There seems to be a universal joke about lesbians that no one really knows what they do (or they guess at scissoring, since it's the closest thing cis guys can imagine to P/V sex).

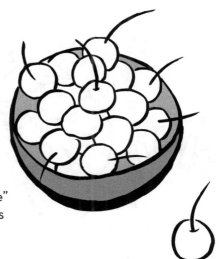

The beauty of lesbian sex (meaning girl on girl sex, in this context) is that you get to define what it is. If it feels like you had sex, you had sex. Or as comedian Reggie Watts says, "If you think you're fucking, you're probably fucking!" End of story.

"Virginity" is a shitty concept when it's used to define how "pure" a person is. But it's a fun concept when it means you have things you have yet to try. You can be choosy and adventuresome.

But sometimes it can be cumbersome too. Like when otherwise interested hotties don't want to do you because you're not experienced enough. Just like having done something a million times doesn't make you "dirty," having never done something doesn't make you naïve. The best way to deal is to offer the information to your lover or potential lover as excitement, not bad news.

There's a big emotional difference between...

And...

We're all newbies at something, and we'll all be newbies at somethings for our whole lives. There's beauty in the newness of sex. That's part of the fun. Embrace the excitement of the unknown. Give yourself permission to be new and nervous, but still willing to explore.

When you're honest about what you've done and what you haven't, you give your partner permission to be a newbie at their own things without shame.

Here's one way you can make virginity fun for you AND easy to communicate to your partner(s).

Copy the table on the next page onto a sheet of paper, or just fill it out right here.

In the "YES" column, write down things you definitely want to try.

In the "MAYBE" column, write down things you're curious about, but would need to negotiate like crazy to make work. Or things you might not be interested in but you'd be willing to explore if your partner wanted to.

In the "NO" column, write down things you definitely don't want to try.

These can be as vanilla or risqué as you want.

Here are some ideas to get you started:
- Nipple Play
- Blindfolds
- Mutual Masturbation
- Spanking
- Dildo blowjob

Put each of those examples on the list, then keep on brainstorming!

If you're partnered, do this exercise with your partner and then compare notes during a not-about-to-have-sex time. If you're single, keep these Want to Try's in mind for online dating profiles and first few dates conversations. It can be super titillating to come up with things you both want to try.

Remember, when you pop one of your own cherries, you're not really "losing" anything. You're gaining experience, insight, and a bit more understanding of the road map of your own likes and desires.

YES!

MAYBE!

NO!

THE GIRL SEX 101 ROAD TRIP CHECK LIST

When was the last time you went on a road trip? How did you prepare?

Odds are, you figured out where you wanted to go. If you brought along a friend or two, you likely made sure they wanted to go where you were headed. Maybe you planned a destination together.

☐ **A good road trip requires everyone to be on the same page** (even if that page is just "let's just drive and see where we end up").

☐ **A good road trip requires everyone feels safe about your skill behind the wheel.** It's hard to enjoy the sights if you're white knuckling from the passenger seat the whole time. Not everyone has to be able to drive, but those who choose to drive have to be safe, savvy, and skilled. Driving safe also means knowing when to pull over. If you're impaired by exhaustion, drugs or alcohol, or just burnout, you're putting everyone in a tough spot. Often it's a better choice to wait until everyone's back on top of their game before you get the ignition going again.

☐ **A good road trip requires a safe vehicle.** It doesn't have to be the prettiest car on the highway, nor the smoothest ride. But you have to feel confident in its ability to get you where you need to go. You have to take good care of it, giving it the proper fluids when necessary, and taking it in for tune-ups every so often.

☐ **A good road trip requires a certain amount of ambiance and comfort**. Music, snacks, and a comfortable ride all make the trip more fun. Whether you're in the back of a pickup, behind the wheel of a luxury car, or cruising in a noisy but sexy classic car, the right aesthetic can make all the difference.

Are you sensing a metaphor here? Sex is like a road trip. Good sex requires everyone to be in agreement on the terms of the trip, everyone to feel safe and honored while on the ride, everyone to be healthy and understand their own body's mechanics, and everyone to feel comfortable so they can relax and enjoy the ride.

DAY 4

The thump of the music rattles the walls. A doorperson wearing sequin pasties, a glittery beard, and lamé hot pants greets Jamie at the door. Inside, the bar is already two people deep, and everything smells like sugar and sweat.

Jamie tugs at the hem of her tank top, feeling both under- and over-dressed. At least she had the chance to shower, do a load of laundry, and make her bed before having to face her ex.

She gets a beer and scans the packed dance floor, finding some vaguely familiar faces. The music fades and the lights dim.

A single spotlight illuminates the stage, and the crowd hushes. A woman wearing a bikini and carrying an accordion enters, taking her place in the shadows on stage right. A skinny man in a top hat and white hot pants follows, places a chair, and sits, propping a cello between his legs. On the accordion player's cue, the band begins to play.

With the first notes, Sergio enters. They wear red sequined hot pants, a red bowtie, and black band-aids over their nipples. They grew a beard, and their mustache is waxed into little curls at the tips. They dance, and Jamie admires them—the strength of their new muscles, the emptiness of their withering breasts, but most of all, the joyful concentration on their face.

That same enthusiastic focus shines through later, when Sergio and Jamie tumble onto her freshly-made bed together. The familiar comfort of her bed and their body make her giggle and sigh.

Jamie runs her fingers across Sergio's shoulders and newly hairy chest. She buries her hands in their black curly hair. Her pale skin contrasts sharply against their rich brown. She smiles, indulging in the ease of it all. She leans down to kiss Sergio's ear.

Sergio recoils. Jamie flinches. "Are you okay?"

"I don't like my ears touched."

"Since when?"

"Just don't."

"Okay."

Sergio and Jamie return to kissing, tentatively. Sergio rolls Jamie onto her back and stretches her arms out to the side like she always liked. Sergio's thigh grinds against her groin. She bucks and runs her nails down their back. Sergio jerks away again.

"What?"

Sergio pushes to the edge of the bed. "Just don't touch me like—"

"Like I used to? Serg, I can't read your mind!"

Sergio dives under the covers, pulling the sheet over their head. "I've got a lot of feelings, okay?"

Jamie moves to leave the bed but hesitates. She's tired of confrontation, but tired of avoiding it even more. From under the covers, Sergio says, "Let's just go to sleep."

Jamie lies back and Sergio snuggles up to her, the comforter creating a thin boundary between both their bodies. Sergio fidgets for a few minutes, flips over so their butt is against Jamie, then drifts off. Jamie lies awake in the half-lit room, too keyed-up to sleep.

She slips out of bed and opens her laptop. She flips through a half-dozen of her usual websites. Closing her browser, she turns on her camera. Her blue-lit face looks back at her. Her makeup is smeared and greasy, the black eyeliner smudged like ash against her cold-looking skin. She reaches for a tissue and her water bottle. Behind the tissue box sits her vibrator. She looks back at her face on the screen, then back to the vibrator. She takes a screenshot with her eyes still on the blue plastic of her vibe.

She glances at Sergio. They're snoring.

Jamie presses the red "record" button and stares into the camera. She moistens the tissue and starts wiping away the makeup. The eyeliner smears further down her cheek, but the foundation comes with it, exposing moist pink flesh. With her free hand she moves the vibrator to her crotch and presses it to her clit, out of frame. She stares ahead. Her pussy clenches. Sergio snores on.

She feels her orgasm approach, but she strains against the noises and facial expressions, keeping her expression as still and neutral as possible. She keeps wiping away the makeup, the black smear of eyeliner and mascara fading to gray blotches on clean skin. Her orgasm seizes her brain, her eyes shift out of focus, and her exhalation trembles out her nostrils.

As the crest of pleasure breaks and dissipates, Jamie holds her gaze steady at her image on her screen. The tissue has torn and left specs of white across her cheek. She wipes once more, leaving more tufted trails along her flushed skin.

She takes a deep breath and hits the red button again to stop the recording.

She flips over to her blog, un-updated for eighteen months, the last post a stupid little paragraph about reconsidering the purpose of her art.

She chews on her lip and looks again at her recording. She sees a tense jaw and a relaxed brow. The colors: bluish light on pinkish skin, gray streaks below green eyes. It's compelling, she thinks, even though it's her own face. She presses "Play" and notices the sound of the vibe and the sound of Sergio's snoring have created a subtle, ambiguous, droning soundtrack. Her face maintains neutrality until the orgasm pitches her. Her eyes widen; she can see she's fighting a groundswell of moans and pleasured expressions. Her lips part just a bit, her pupils dilate. She swallows. She sniffs sharply through her nose, then holds her breath. Then she is frozen, the tissue held to her jaw.

She looks a little bit crazy, a little bit intense, fighting something unseen but felt.

Jamie glances at her empty blog and returns to the video, selecting "Export > Publish."

DAY 4

Layla finds the spare key under the rock in the front yard of the old Victorian. She climbs the narrow steps to the second floor and lets herself in. There's a note on the kitchen table:

Hey Layla, sorry I won't get to see you this trip. I made you a sandwich. Help yourself to anything in the kitchen that isn't labeled. There's a clean towel on my bed. My roomie Clover will likely be here. She's friendly. Call me next time you're in the Bay! – Kurt

Layla drops her bag and riffles through the fridge, finding the sandwich. She opens the baggie and starts eating before she even sits.

"Hey." A pixie-like girl stands in the hall, wearing a tank top and panties. "You're Kurt's friend?"

Layla nods.

"The lesbian?"

"Pretty much." Of course Kurt would mention that salient detail. Perv. Layla watches the girl's face move through stages of understanding. She had seen this face before. It isn't that the girl is shocked, it's that she's wondered what it means, and what it means for her, specifically. Straight girls never care. Curious girls always care a lot.

"I'm Clover," the girl says. "I live here."

"I figured," Layla says, shoving the sandwich into her mouth and talking through it. "Thanks for letting me crash."

The girl shrugs the shrug of a twenty-something in the Haight, where overnight guests are more common than foggy mornings. "Why are you in town?"

"Just passing through."

"Going to?"

"Adventure?" Layla says. "Newness. Life's been stale. I need to shake it out a little."

Clover nods, though looking as young as she does, Layla wonders if she understands at all.

"So do you have a girlfriend?" Clover asks, picking at the chipped end of the kitchen table.

Layla shakes her head, letting the girl fill the silence with her own eager awkwardness.

Clover shifts her weight to her right hip, showing off the meager curve of her waist.

"Sorry," Layla says, finally. "You seem sweet. And you're totally sexy. I just have a rule about sleeping with girls who've never been with girls before. Also hosts, though that one's more flex."

Clover responds with a long look, blinking once. "I've been with girls before."

Layla hides her mirth behind the rim of her water glass.

"I mean, if high school slumber parties count," Clover continues.

Layla chuckles openly. "Yeah," she laughs. "Those definitely count."

"I mean. Never kissed 'em. Just feeling each other up. Silly stuff."

Layla looks into Clover's earnest eyes. She takes the girl's hand, feeling like a cat with a canary. "Show me."

Clover smiles and turns down the darkened hallway, leading Layla to the room at the end. Layla smells Nag Champa and marijuana. Clover's room is illuminated with a single shawl-draped lamp.

In Clover's bed, the girls kiss and pet. Layla tugs at the edges of Clover's underwear and kisses down her belly.

"Hey," Clover says, tugging on Layla's hair. "I don't really like cunnilingus."

Layla rests her cheek on Clover's belly. "You don't like it? Or you've never had anyone do it right?"

"I—I guess I don't know."

"Would you like to figure out the difference?"

"I...Yes...But I don't know—"

"Lay back. Relax. And keep breathing," Layla says. "If you're not into it, just say so and I'll stop."

Clover nods. "Okay."

Layla works her way down Clover's spritely body to her nearly-bare vulva. She smells like marijuana and cloves. Layla inhales and smiles. She kisses her vulva. Clover tenses then relaxes.

Layla rubs her lips and tongue over Clover's vulva, enjoying the mingling of saliva and arousal. She traces her tongue in the left gully between Clover's outer lips and inner, drawing it up and over the top of her clitoral shaft and down the right side. Clover shudders and grips the sheets.

Layla presses the flat of her tongue against Clover's vaginal opening, tasting a myriad of musky sweet flavors. She pulls her tongue up and under Clover's clit, keeping her eyes on Clover's face, reading her expressions. Clover's breathing is deep, but she's draped an arm over her eyes, making it hard to know how she's feeling. Layla reads her breath and body heat, and seeing Clover's still engaged, presses on.

Layla traces her tongue across Clover's lips and clit in varying shapes, until Clover's thighs clench and she gasps. Layla repeats the same movement: a firm lick downward on the left side of Clover's clit. Clover moans.

Layla repeats the motion, increasing the intensity in stages. Clover squeezes her hands into fists and tilts her hips forward to press against Layla's face. Layla grips Clover's hips, maintaining her tongue's stroke.

Clover's breath grows deeper and more forceful. Layla places one hand underneath Clover's ass, pressing the heel of her palm into Clover's perineum.

"Hey," Clover says.

Layla stops. "You okay?"

"Do you want to do something else?"

"Huh?" Layla says, leaning onto her elbows. "I guess. If you want to."

"Yeah, we can."

"We can, or you want to?"

"Whatever," Clover says with a shrug.

Layla narrows her eyes. "Are you enjoying this?"

Clover smiles. "Yeah. Totally."

"Then what's up?"

"It's just...you've been down there for a while."

"Like, fifteen minutes," Layla says with a chuckle.

"I just don't want to, you know, make you work too hard. I don't usually come, like, at all."

"Does it feel good anyway?"

Clover nods, timid.

"Are you having fun?"

Clover smiles. "Yes."

Layla drops her chin and sighs. "Then trust me. I'm loving this. I'd happily stay down here all night. I will sleep down here after, if you let me. There is nothing I'd rather be doing than eating your pussy right now."

Clover looks as though she's about to cry. "Promise?"

Layla doesn't flinch. "I promise."

CHECKING UNDER THE HOOD

Eatin' box! Lickin' labes! Snarfing puss! Dining at the Y! Speaking beaver!

Cunnilingus is often considered the quintessential lesbian sex act and, not coincidentally, it can also be one of the most intimidating things to do. For good reasons: It's harder to detect small movements and shifts with your mouth (as opposed to your fingers), it's harder to communicate when your partner's face is far from yours, and the muscles of your tongue and face can fatigue much faster than your hands, making it challenging to "stay the course." Plus many girls consider both giving and receiving oral sex to be one of the most intimate sex acts, adding emotional hurdles to the physical ones.

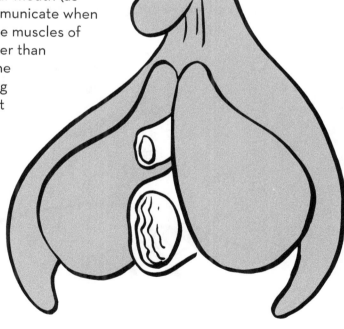

Cunnilingus integrates all of the material we've covered so far, so if you've skipped to this chapter, skip right back to the beginning and make super sure you understand anatomy, pressure, rhythm, and especially communication. And don't forget the internal clitoral structure!!! That li'l wishbone is gonna take center stage in this chapter. How? You're going to use your face, hands, tongue, and lips, to stimulate it all at once. Oh yes.

Cunnilingus is where your ability to listen to someone's body and track their energy becomes paramount.

Truth is, pussy-eating doesn't look like much when you're doing it right:

In fact, when you're doing it right, it doesn't look like much of anything at all:

This is because your face plays the stabilizing factor while your tongue goes to town. That right there is the basic philosophy of cunnilingus, yet it rarely gets the explanation it deserves.

Your face is her rock, her base, her saddle, and her support. You'll be using your face to apply pressure and give her something to hump against. You'll use your hands to asset the stimulation. Meanwhile, you'll use your tongue and lips to generate the clit-focused movements that will give her pleasure.

CUNNILINGUS RULES OF "O"

1) **Variety, then consistency.** Remember that old canard about tracing the alphabet with your tongue? This is to teach you to try a bunch of different things. But when your partner finds something she really likes, you want to KEEP DOING THAT THING. This can be challenging at first, but you'll become a heat-seeking missile when it comes to locking onto That Thing your lady likes.

2) **Offer positive affirmation.** People can feel super insecure about their bits and body, especially when someone's face is buried all up in it. So tell her how sexy she looks, smells, and tastes. Help her relax into receiving.

3) **Respect the clit.** Don't go for the clit too soon. Take your time. And once you are focused on the clit, understand you may be down there for a while. Give yourself over to the experience. It's a gift to be allowed to put your mouth on someone's genitals. Honor that gift and the person by not rushing. Indulge the experience. Practice gratitude.

Remember, most women grow up in a world that tells us our genitals are smelly, ugly, and gross. Help undo a bit of that horrible messaging by respecting your partner's whole body, including her genitals. Tell her she's beautiful (or whatever adjective would work for her) and make sure she knows you think her body is just delightful. Even if your romp is a one-time thing, it can go a long way to help undo some of the shame we women feel about ourselves.

WANNA GO FOR A RIDE!?

Like hand sex, you'll want to give attention to the whole vulva before you go straight for the clit. You want to make sure she's very aroused and ready for clit stimulation, so foreplay it up before you go for the gold.

Take the scenic route.
Take your time getting down there. Remember the classic burlesque formula: Tease, Present, Take Away. This is the Tease stage. Ease your way down to her nethers with kisses, licks, and nibbles along the way. Once you're between her legs, don't just dig in. Keep playing. Lick and kiss her labia, move to her thighs, and then back.

Get to know the landscape.
Give her whole genital area some attention. Kiss her outer lips. Nibble and suck on her inner lips. Take your tongue close to her clit or even graze it, but don't go for it just yet. Just like you don't start a movie with the protagonist's most heroic scene, direct clit stimulation needs a build-up.

Start out and work your way in.
With your tongue, trace from the base of one outer lip up and over the labial cleft to the base of another.

Tug on her outer labia with your lips.
Lick her fourchette and perineum.
Then move inward.
Tug on her inner labia with your lips.

Use your tongue to trace ovals around the base of the clit, without touching the glans.
Place the flat of your tongue on her vaginal opening. Feel the heat and taste her moisture.

French kiss her whole vulva. This is great when you're not sure what to do, when you need a break from direct tongue moves, and when you're both warming up. It's sexy, it's intimate, it feels great for both of you, and it help bring her whole vulva "online."

PRO-TIP: You know that cunnilingus symbol popular with high schoolers? The tongue between the fingers in the V-shape? It's supposed to indicate moving the lips away to eat pussy. And it's one of the best reasons not to take sex advice from high schoolers. The lips are an integral part of pussy-eating. You want to give them good loving before and during the main clit-focused event. So kiss, lick, and nibble, exciting her whole vulva before you head to the clit.

Before you go straight for the clit glans, use your tongue on the shaft and base of her clit. You might be able to feel the side of her erection with your tongue.

Don't underestimate the shaft of the clit. Like the shaft of the penis, moving the skin against the erectile tissue can feel delightful and stimulate all the good parts attached to it. In fact, many people don't like the feeling of glans stimulation at all. This is especially true for folks who tend to run more "sensitive"—the kinds of people who are super ticklish, don't like vibrators, or for whom even direct nipple stimulation can feel like too much.

Clit-shaft stimulation

Remember the "Reverse Vulcan" from Chapter 4? Try it with your lips. Shield the front of your teeth with your lips (making "toothless, missing dentures" lips), and pinch the base of her shaft with your lips. There, your partner can do Kegels to move their clit between your lips, making a jacking off type of motion. Or, with the same mouth position, you can stay still and let your partner grind against your face.

Lick up and down one side of the shaft. This works best if you place your mouth in the **Firm O Position**. See the next page!

One of my favorite techniques for clit shaft stimulation is what I call the "Tiny Blowjob" or "Teeny Beej." Remember how the clitoral hood is essentially foreskin? With the Tiny Beej, you move the hood against the shaft to create yummy sensations. Surround the shaft of the clit with your lips (this is the "ooo" sound of the word Hallelujah). Your top lip should be just above the root of the clit glans, and your bottom lip should be between the bottom of the clit and the vestibule. With lips in position, make gentle in and out motions with your head, like you're giving a tiny blowjob, or sucking on a very narrow popsicle. Keep your tongue out of the way if you don't want to stimulate her glans.

INTRODUCING
THE FIRM O POSITION

Just as in martial arts you need a strong base, so it is with oral sex. Except now we're not talking about feet and hips, but rather lips and head. Much of your cunnilingus will be served by this strong base.

1) **Open your mouth like you're going to sing a loud and proud "Aaaaahh!" sound.** Your lips should be in a wide and tall o-shape— Not a tight "Ooooooooh" but an open "Aaaaaahhh" (i.e. if you're singing "Hallelujah!" it's the last syllable, not the third one).

2) **Place your lips on her vulva.** Your top lip should be above her clit, placed in the cleft between the base of her clit shaft and her mound. If she's unshaved, your nose will be resting in her pubic hair, giving you the best kind of mustache known to (wo)man. If you can, nestle your lip up against the part just where hair starts to grow. Your nose should be nestled against her mound. Your lower lip should rest just above her vaginal opening, or a bit higher if that distance is uncomfortable for you.

3) **Lean against her, putting some pressure on your mouth, to create a sturdy connection.** Be aware this can create some fatigue in your neck muscles. We'll talk about how to deal with that in a bit.

Try this against the side of your fist to get a sense of placement. Upper lip on index finger side, lower lip on thumb web. (See *The Pinky Swear*, next page.)

The Firm O is your base for many cunnilingus techniques. It offers your partner something to hump against (i.e. your face), stimulates the clitoral legs, isolates the clit for direct stimulation, and feels grounding and secure for your partner.

THE PINKY SWEAR

**Want to practice some of the techniques in this chapter?
Here's a simple way!**

Stick out your pinky like you're drinking tea, then make a fist with your
other hand around it, leaving just the top segment exposed. This pinky
tip is your makeshift clit. You can angle your fist hand so that your chin
rests against where your thumb meets your wrist for extra realism. Just
be careful if you have long nails!

You can stick with shaft stimulation for quite a while, and some people
reach orgasm this way. If your partner is a glans type of gal, here's how
to progress.

**Maintaining the Firm O, use the flat of your tongue to press against
the glans.** Don't move it just yet. Simply press. Your partner will likely
press her clit into your tongue, which is what you want. If she pulls away, it's
probably because her clit isn't ready for that kind of stimulation. Keep playing
with her lips and thighs, or check in to see if there's something she'd like more.

If she presses against you, it means it's time to use your tongue. Again, be deliberate but subtle.
The clit is not a punching bag. Move the flat of your tongue in a way that moves the clit with it.

This means you'll keep decent pressure on it. Flicking is still not the right sensation for this stage of
things. Remember that small sensations will register big time for her. Start slow, firm, and steady. (Try
this on your pinky.) You're building tension and pleasure here.

Explore moving your tongue and the clit in a rhythmic, repetitive way. This could mean moving
it left to right to left to right to left to right. Or up and down and up and down. Or left-up diagonal
right-down diagonal left-up diagonal right-down diagonal. Or, you can try a full circle around and
around and around. Don't cycle through all of them too fast. Try one for a little while, and if she
doesn't respond with more excitement, switch to something else. Remember, this part is the "rising
action" stage of sexual pleasure. Once you get a good sense of how your partner receives pleasure,
you'll be able to explore this phase. Some people like to stay here for a looong time. It can feel like
a nice, sexy massage. So unless your partner wants an orgasm immediately, luxuriate here.

If your partner is vocal, odds are you'll hear and feel a difference between "Hey, that's nice" and
"OH MY GOD KEEP DOING THAT!"

When she arrives here, your job, my friend, is to heed your partner's cries, and *keep doing that*. When she's good and excited, you can increase the sensation on the glans of her clit. This means pulling back the hood just a touch, and here's how to do it:

Your upper lip has the "pubic 'stache," yes? Well, now you're going to take your upper lip, and curl it up and out, kinda like you're making fish lips. I think of it like Wanda from In Living Color, but that may be before your time, so maybe think of it as the girl in the "ERMAGERD" meme.

Yes, you'll look silly. But your face is buried in pussy, so I don't think anyone's going to be making fun of you.

The point of the fish lips is that you're adding a bit more tug on the shaft of her clitoris, pulling the hood back ever so slightly. Be careful not to pull too hard. A tiny bit of tension is all you need.

Making those fish lips, keep pressure on her mound with your face, and keep licking at her clit in a way she already likes, or a new direction.

 PRO-TIP: Your partner needs to be super aroused before the fish lips will feel good. Don't try it until she's grinding against your face or otherwise demonstratively revved up. A little bit makes a huge difference.

HANDS

Just because you're facedown in puss, it doesn't mean you should have idle hands.

One great thing to do with your hand is place the flat of your palm against her mound, and gently pull up toward her belly button. This will make her lips more taut, and help edge the clitoral hood back from the glans. This is a great move when she starts getting excited, especially if she's a "humper." It'll hold her stable so you don't get rodeo-bucked off, and stimulates her internal clitoral structure and concomitant erectile tissue.

 PRO-TIP: If she's really a humper, you can use your whole forearm to hold her hips down. You can still tug up at her mound, but use your whole arm instead.

You can also place the flat of your thumb against the opening of her vagina (if you've established penetration-trust already) or against her anus (ditto). Don't go inside, just give enough pressure for her to enjoy.

Okay, so you've got a hand on her mound, a hand on her vaginal or anal opening, your face pressed firmly against her vulva, and your lip curled up against the clitoral shaft. Now what?

This is when your tongue takes center stage.

GETTING OVER THE HUMP

Cunnilingus doesn't have to be about orgasm. But it sure can be fun when it is. If you want to help your partner come by eating them out, amplifying the energy while keeping consistent rhythm and pressure will be your keys to success.

Remember to pay attention to the visible and audible

signs of her increasing excitement: her vulva will swell and darken; her clit will emerge from beneath the hood; her breath with be sharper and more erratic, or deeper, or perhaps she'll hold it; her thighs, abs, vagina, hands, and ass may clench.

If she's clearly on the road to orgasm, your job is to stay the course. Whatever you're doing with your tongue, hands, and face, now is *not* the time to switch it up. Yes, it can be hard. There's an old joke in the lesbian community—it's just when she's about to come that your tongue goes numb.

For this reason, cunnilingus can cultivate a meditative state of consciousness not unlike Tai-Chi or other flow-oriented martial arts. There will be a point that your tongue will fatigue—it's natural. What makes you a black belt is 1) **your ability to continue in the flow despite fatigue** and 2) **your ability to take a breather without interrupting her pleasure experience.** Both require a mental space of focus, intention, and a bit of grace. Staying focused despite fatigue feels to me like those times in yoga when you hold that one really tough pose while your muscles jitter. What do you do? You keep breathing. You maintain a soft focus. You tap into reserves and deliver. This is especially useful when your partner is suuuuper close to orgasm but just…isn't….there….yet…

Keep breathing, keep the rhythm and focus, and be of service.

RUNNING OUT OF GAS

It may be that fatigue is more common during cunnilingus than orgasms are. Good cunnilingus requires pressure and repetitive movements that can be wearing on all sorts of bodies.

So how do you deal?

Switch it up
Swap from tongue stimulation to hand stimulation. If possible, try to recreate the same movement you were doing with your tongue with your fingers. See Chapter 4 for some finger-on-clit techniques.

Bring Backup
If your sweetie likes vibration, it may be a good idea to keep her fav on the bed. When you grow weary, turning on your buzzing buddy can save the day.

Make minor adjustments
Add pillows beneath her butt, shift from your belly to your knees, or otherwise take some of the tension out of your neck.

Remember the burlesque trick

Don't be afraid to dial it back a bit and do something else for a minute to recoup your strength before going back to the clit.

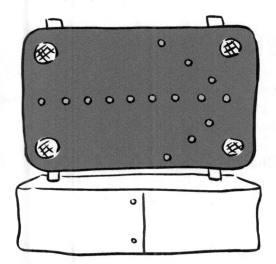

Adjust positions

If she's on her back and you're between her legs, try having her sit on your face, or even get behind her and eat her out doggie style.

There's nothing wrong with taking a breather, either.

To do so, you'll want to memorize everything you're doing (assuming she's really digging it), much like a spy in an espionage film. Where's your tongue? What's it doing? Where exactly on her clit is it doing that thing? What are your hands doing? Where are your lips? Take note of it all. Then, deliberately do something else. If you just peter out, it can be frustrating. Instead, treat it like a moment of pianissimo in an otherwise rousing symphony of sensation. Taking a moment away from direct go-for-the-gold glans stimulation can make coming back to that stimulation even more exciting. A good choice for this is the vulva-frenching. It gives your tongue a break while still providing yummy sensation to all of her bits.

POST ORGASMIC PUSS

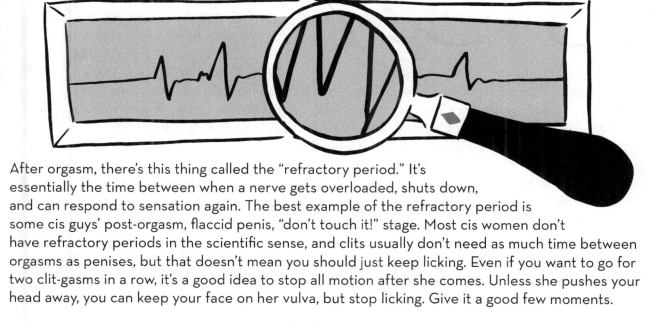

After orgasm, there's this thing called the "refractory period." It's essentially the time between when a nerve gets overloaded, shuts down, and can respond to sensation again. The best example of the refractory period is some cis guys' post-orgasm, flaccid penis, "don't touch it!" stage. Most cis women don't have refractory periods in the scientific sense, and clits usually don't need as much time between orgasms as penises, but that doesn't mean you should just keep licking. Even if you want to go for two clit-gasms in a row, it's a good idea to stop all motion after she comes. Unless she pushes your head away, you can keep your face on her vulva, but stop licking. Give it a good few moments.

Some girl-gasms can last longer than they look. Let her breath come back to normal. She'll likely shift her position after orgasm and manually relax all her remaining clenched muscles. She may flutter her eyes open. If you want to test the waters for another go-round, just give a token lick. Odds are, she'll either bear down to meet your tongue, or pull away, and you'll have your answer.

PENETRATION

Penetration rules apply equally for hand and mouth sex. Swing back to Chapter 4 if you need a refresher. But here are the basics:

Would you like a finger inside you?

1) **Check in.** It's always nice to check in before doing it while going down. A simple, sexy, "Would you like a finger inside you?" is good.

> **PRO-TIP:** Like mashed potatoes and peas, some people like mixing clit and g-spot stimulation, and some really don't. This is why it's good to check in. For some folks, if you've already jumped on the clit-train, you don't want to transfer to the g-spot train halfway through. For others, a finger at the right moment will send her shooting into the stratosphere. Check in, and don't assume.

2) **Easy, tiger.** There's a significant energy difference between cunnilingus and hand-fucking. Don't upstage yourself by getting all fancy on the inside. Stick with one or two fingers for pressure and maybe a little in-and-out, while still focusing on the clit as the main event. Flat pressure up toward her belly can help get the clitoral legs excited.

3) **Know when to hold 'em.** For some people, receiving a finger is the catapult that hurls them over the top into happy-land. If this is you or your partner, use your finger like an ace in the—er—you get it. Use it wisely and you'll both be feeling the love.

4) **Beware the splash zone.** If your sweetie's a squirter, you may be in for a face-full of jizz if you're fingering her and eating her out simultaneously. Just something to keep in mind.

BREATHING

If you're putting adequate pressure on your partner's mound, odds are you're going to have a hard time breathing. Your nose will likely be buried in her labial cleft or pubic hair, and your mouth is plenty busy at work. The challenge and key of breathing while eating box is to do it without interrupting your rhythm.

So...how not to die in a most awkward (but heroic) way?

Maybe I'm dating myself here, but I think of breathing while pussy eating as making a Ninja Turtle face. If you don't get the reference, go ahead and think I'm a weirdo, I'll still explain:

The key is to breathe through the sides of your mouth.

Try this now

Do the Pinky Swear on your hand. Don't breathe through your nose. Flick your pinky with your tongue like it's a clit. Focus on it, get into the groove. Make sweet mouth-love to your pinky. Then, when you need a breath, edge one side of your mouth out and inhale, while maintaining all the pressure and contact on the clit and mound. You won't have much room to breathe, but it's enough. Practice this without letting your clit rhythm flag.

Another option

Rock your face to the side. Maintain the clit stroke and pressure. Inhale and put pressure back on her mound. If you can get a good rhythm going, this can feel like swimming freestyle, breathing in intervals.

Finally, try the carbonation method

You know how you crack the top of a soda bottle and unscrew it juuuussst enough to let the gas escape without letting it overflow? This is how you can breathe. Press your face against the side of your hand again and get to flickin'. Make sure the seal from your mouth is nice and tight. Then ease all of your lips off just enough to breathe. You'll probably feel air rush in through the sides of your mouth and a bit around the top. Then press back in.

The neat thing about all these breath techniques is that the flow of cool air against your partner's nethers can feel really nice. Practice which one works best for you and dazzle your partner with your dedication to your clit game.

PRO TIP: Moaning isn't just about giving her positive affirmation. It also gives her sensation. When you moan, you generate vibration in the form of sound. Next time you're going down, try moaning, humming, and exploring a range of noises. You may feel silly, but it can make your partner feel goooood.

There are a few ways to find the clit even when you're flying blind.

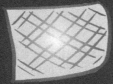

Top Down

Find the cleft in the labia. It's where the lips meet at the top of the vulva. It's usually straight down from the belly button. Sometimes there's hair, and sometimes there's not. If you stroke your finger down the cleft, the quality of the flesh will change from "normal" skin, to subtler, slicker skin. Usually no more than a few centimeters straight down from the cleft is the clit. If you reach the vaginal opening, you've gone too far.

Bottom Up

Find the opening of the vagina. It may be hotter and wetter than the rest of the vulva. The lips often fold over it so you may need to gently nudge them aside. Just north of the vaginal opening is the vestibule—a super slick tract of flesh. Go north of this until you feel what may be a small protrusion. If you've hit the labial cleft (where the big lips meet at the top), you've gone too far.

 PRO TIP: It can be easier to find the clit with your tongue than with your fingers. Try letting your tongue do the probing.

POSITIONS

The classic "missionary" style position can be hard on your neck, especially if you're putting good pressure on her vulva. You can alleviate this by wrapping your arms under her thighs and back over so your hands can touch her mound or her breasts. In this position, you can use your arms to pull her body into your face instead of having to generate all the pressure with your head and neck. It's also great because you can use your free hand to press on her mound and gently tug it upwards to tighten her lips.

Another position I like is **69ing on your side.** This is great even if you both aren't going down simultaneously. Your partner can rest their head on a pillow or your thigh while you eat them out. You can rest your head on their inner thigh and still generate good pressure with your head. Try wrapping your arm around their hip and ass and placing your finger pad on her anus, perineum, or vaginal opening. You can use this arm to pull her hips into your face to generate the Firm O pressure.

Queening. This is a fantastic position for many reasons. You as the Driver get to relax, while your partner straddles your face. This is a particularly good choice for face humpers, because they can grind against your mouth and face as hard as they want and it won't put pressure on your neck. It can be an emotionally confronting position for some people, though, especially those doing the straddling, since it feels very exposed. But some dig it for this reason, and as the "bottom" in this scenario, you get a fantastic view.

The one big drawback to this position is breath control for the Driver. Pubic hair or a fleshy mound can make it challenging to breathe through your nose. It may be a good idea for one of you to keep your mound pulled up and back from their nose to keep oxygen flowing. For big girls, you may need to hold your belly back, too. Also, be careful if the Navigator is a squirter or just gets really wet. My friend coined the term "pussy boarding" for that fear of drowning when in this position.

If you're queening, the Navigator really has all the control here, so practice safe cunnilingus by making eye contact every once in a while and getting a verbal check in. I like to use hand signals. My partner taps my thigh quickly if they need me to get off (in the non-sexual way). They give me the "okay" sign if they're all good.

One final note: Dental dams do not work well for this position. Nonconsensual suffocation isn't sexy.

Booty Beauty. Eating your partner out from behind can be superbly sexy. You'll have to reach harder with your tongue to get the clit, but that's part of the pleasure. You can do this while your partner is standing or on all fours. What makes this so sexy (and challenging for some) is that you basically have to cram your face all up in her butt crack. The position requires you put your eyes against the base of her butt cheeks, so your nose is basically penetrating her vagina, while your tongue reaches for her clit. This can feel really good for the receiver, because there's a lot of pressure on some parts that don't always get good loving, like the ass cheek-to-leg interface. It also can feel really nice on the face of the giver. I love doing this when my partner is doing mundane things, like the dishes. Dropping to my knees behind her and tugging down her undies to eat her out from behind makes housework a breeeeeze!

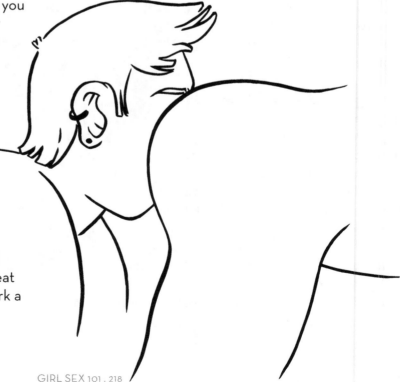

THE BOSSY BOTTOM'S CUNNILINGUS TIPS

So you're getting eaten out. Congratulations! How very nice for you.

Want to help your partner help you? Here are some tips!

1) **Be a bossy bottom.** Tell your partner what you want. Did you prefer what they were doing before better than what they're doing now? Need another pillow under your bum? Is there a thing you want them to try just to see how it feels? You know what to do! Being bossy doesn't mean being rude. It just means communicating to your partner what would make them a rock star.

2) **Lend a hand.** Many people like to press their mound when they get clit stimulation. Sometimes, though, if your partner has their hands full, it can be a challenge. Try pressing your mound or tugging up at your labia. This stretches your lips taut, which can create more pleasure, and make it easier for your sweetie to get at your goods.

3) **Hump!** Grinding your pussy against your partner's face helps stimulate your whole vulva. Humping flexes your pelvic floor muscles, which in turn stimulate your inner clitoral structure. It also lets your partner know you're liking what they're doing.

4) **Breathe!** If you forget to breathe, your body might forget to register pleasure. Take some deep breaths and relaaaaaxxx.

5) **Stop worrying about them.** This can sound selfish, and it kinda is. Too many girls worry about too many things when it comes to sex and bodies. Relax and enjoy yourself. Let your partner take care of their physical needs. You take care of you. Lay back and enjoy.

WHAT DO YOU LIKE ABOUT CUNNILINGUS?

I love the taste, the smell and the way I can get lost in the complexity of a pussy and the reactions I can get out of a woman.

I LOVE THE TASTE AND THE VIEW.

TO ME THIS IS A VERY PERSONAL ACT OF GIVING YOURSELF TO ANOTHER AND BRINGING THEM SUCH EXHILARATION AND AN INTENSE EMOTIONAL RELEASE. I ENJOY THE POWER OF GIVING THIS TO A WOMAN I LOVE.

I like feeling powerful; I like feeling someone else's face getting slippery from my juices.

I LOVE THE INTENSITY OF HAVING MY CLIT LICKED, SUCKED, AND NIBBLED GENTLY. I LOVE THE TASTE OF GENITALS, I LOVE THE FEELING OF AROUSAL IN MY PARTNER'S BODY ON MY TONGUE, AND I PARTICULARLY LOVE IT IF MY PARTNERS CUM IN MY MOUTH OR MAKE A MESS ON MY FACE, FINGERS, AND TITS.

IT FEELS LIKE MY PARTNER'S ENTIRE BODY IS DANCING AT THE TIP OF MY TONGUE, ARCHING AND REACHING AND FALLING BACK AGAIN... JUST AWESOME.

I love getting my face right in there. Tasting and exploring and learning. Feeling things on her that my fingers missed. I like not always being able to decipher what she's doing to me. The intimacy blows me away every time. It always feels special.

I LOVE giving cunnilingus. I love the taste of pussy, and those squeals of pleasure, and feeling and hearing my partner getting more turned on and out of control.

Being drenched with my partner's sweat, juices, my saliva, lube... whatever is down there, I want it on my face.

SCENIC VIEWPOINT

Cunnilingus for Straight Chicks
by Nina Hartley, R.N.

Congratulations on wanting to expand your erotic repertoire to include vulvas. Speaking as a vulva enthusiast, to say nothing of my career as a professional sex performer, I welcome you to the wonderful world of lady parts. Today's lesson is just a short guide to what can become lifelong learning, if you so desire.

If you already like penises it's helpful to realize that a penis is really nothing more than a really big clitoris. Or, a clit is just a teeny, tiny penis. No matter the external size, they're both phalluses: shaft, glans, corona, hood/foreskin and frenulum. I have several moves that I start with for most partners. After gazing upon her vulva and complimenting its appearance, I place my lip-covered upper teeth on her pubic bone, where the shaft of her clit meets the top of the cleft of her lips. This naturally places my lower jaw against the opening. Then, I just breathe naturally until she and I are breathing in sync. This moment of connection allows my brain to slow down and for our bodies to get on the same page. She'll often start subtly moving her pelvis against my face, which signals me that she's ready for the party to start.

I begin by slowly and gently sucking on her vulva. If you're stuck for how to do this have your partner suck on the web of skin between your thumb and forefinger and then just copy what she does in real time. You'll be surprised at how quickly you'll improve. It's like sucking on a penis that is not yet hard, but soon will be. Or, you can imagine how you'd give head to a cock that is only as big as the last joint of your pinky. Believe me, her clit feels as big to her as any monster, eight-inch erection feels to its owner! It's an algorithmic adjustment between transistors and microchips. While a quarter-inch move on a penis means a lot, with clits it's best to think in millimeters. The more slowly you move, the more of those 8,000 nerve endings can individually fire, adding to the pleasure.

If I lose my connection to my partner or don't know what to do next, I simply keep my teeth covered and apply pressure, leaving it up to her to supply the desired movements. Or, I suck her flesh into my mouth, pull away from her pubic bone an inch or so, and let her hump my face (keep those teeth covered!). If I'm really stuck for what to do, or she seems not to be able to go over the edge from my actions, I'll pull my face off of her and invite her to use her hands or a toy while I supply manual support if she asks for it. It's not so bad to get her most of the way there and then snuggle up next to her while she takes her clit over the goal line and into the endzone.

It takes practice, but at least the homework is fun!

Nina Hartley's motto: "One need never be unsanitary while one is being dirty, as 'sanitary' is a state of fact and 'dirty' is a state of mind," has served her well in her thirty-year career as an adult performer, free-speech advocate, sexual liberationist, educator and professional pervert.

GIRL DICK BEAN LICK!

For **post-op trans women**, the basics of cunnilingus are the same, except there's not much internal clitoral structure. This means you can focus on the glans and enjoy the labia and interior of the vagina. The labia in particular can be fun for post-op trans women, since these are made from scrotal tissue and often preserve much of their innervation.

For **non-op trans women**, use what you've learned about analogous genital structures to "map" what we talked about onto trans clit. This means you might want to focus a lot of your attention on the glans and frenulum. Many trans women say they enjoy receiving the same kind of oral stimulation as traditional cunnilingus, so explore licking, nibbling, and using your face to generate pressure just as you would with a vulva. This is quite easy if she doesn't get erections, because her clit is more malleable and easier to press against. You can press her clit against her belly to focus on the caudal side of it, especially the frenulum and corona.

For other girls, cunnilingus in the form of what looks like a blow job is actually nice. But I'd suggest not leading with that. Instead, check in with her about how she likes to be touched.

For some girls, too much glans stimulation can feel annoying. This can be especially true if she gets erections. If this is the case for your partner, try small licks about an inch down from the frenulum, on the ventral side of her clit.

Regardless, of how your partner relates to oral stimulation, it's a good idea to start small, playing with sensation instead of assuming a certain set of genitals always love a certain kind of touch.

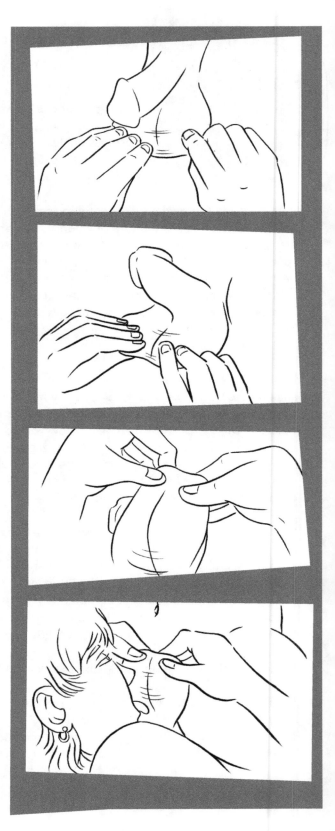

For everyone, your hand positions can be the same: a hand on her mound, gently tugging up, and a finger pad on her vaginal opening (or in this case, her perineum or anus).

Try using your hand to grasp all around her goods, with your thumb underneath her scrotum and your index finger wrapped around the base of her clit. I think of it as a **genital bouquet**. When you've got all of her goods bundled up tight together, you can play with your tongue, mouth, face, toys, or other hand.

If your girl is good with scrotal play, try what I like to call **"The Flying Squirrel."** (See previous page.)

To make the Flying Squirrel, gently grip the skin of her scrotum (being sure not to grasp the testes or tubes) and pull it over the top of her clit. The skin will stretch out and look glossy. You can then put your mouth right in the middle, pressing down against her clit through her scrotum. Then you can lick, nibble, and eat her out like whoa. This can feel super nice regardless of whether she gets erections or not. I love this technique, because it offers me the chance to really bury my face in my partner—one of my favorite parts of cunnilingus. Depending on what she likes done with her testes, you can either leave them along side her clit, or tickle or stroke them. If she likes prostate stimulation, a finger inside her anus while you're eating her out can be delightful. And if she's a fan of muffing, fingering her this way while you're going to town is also a great choice.

HOW DO YOU FEEL ABOUT ORAL SEX?

I love oral sex! There's not much I don't like, and if I don't like it in the middle of the act, I can always say no or figure out something else. I like tongue motions on my trans clit that are circular and up and down on the delta of frenulum (I learned that from *Fucking Trans Women*). Pressing my clit against my tummy, nibbling, using lips—it's all wonderful. I also like sucking. Which can be weird because it feels like when I used to think I was a boy. But at the same time, it is a little different, it still feels amazing, and it has given me orgasms more than any other sexual act.

Under some circumstances, yes. How I like it done depends on what headspace I'm in. Sometimes I enjoy getting "porn head" like one would perform on a penis. Sometimes I wear a strap-on for it, because it feels more "right." Other times, I prefer being licked and kissed and having my anatomy down there treated as a vulva.

Yes, but not for long because it's usually overstimulating (the kind that leads to pain, not rapid climax) because folks tend to focus on the tip which is also easiest to reach. It's more as if I prefer the idea that they want to. Only a handful of people have ever been able to do it well; it's not as complicated as everyone seems to try making it at first. Likewise, for me it requires someone able to go a lot deeper (to near the base) than most are capable of to reach where it's sensitive, otherwise it's like their mouth is on my elbow and all their enthusiasm is going to waste.

PREORGASMIC?

The biggest myth about preorgasmic women is that they don't enjoy sex at all since they don't orgasm. This is complete bunk. Orgasms for many people are just the icing on the cake, but the sex is still cake. Icing or no, who doesn't like cake?!

If you or your partner doesn't come, it doesn't mean cunnilingus is off the table. And even if you sometimes come but aren't feeling it at the moment, it doesn't mean anyone's broken. Enjoy the intimacy, the connection, and the embodied experience of pleasure. The hardest part about cunnilingus for most girls is getting out of their heads. If you put pressure on yourself or your partner to come like a porn star, you're going to push the pleasure further away. Instead, indulge and enjoy.

GET YER RED WINGS!

Yes, Virginia, you can eat out your partner while she's on her period. But because menstrual fluid is mostly blood, you want to make sure to be tested for and vaccinated against hepatitis, and know your partner's HIV status. If there's any doubt, you can use a dental dam, she can wear a tampon/ menstrual cup, and you can focus on external rather than internal stimulation.

Remember, these techniques are all suggestions. If your partner doesn't like any of the things I mentioned, or prefers something else, defer to them. The only real experts on personal bodily pleasure are the people who own those bodies. So ask, check in, and make choices that fit the person and the circumstance.

DAY 5

Jamie wakes to the smell of coffee and eggs and the sound of Sergio humming in the kitchen. They wear a fresh pair of briefs and nothing else.

"Good morning." Sergio smiles.

"What's all this?"

"Breakfast," they say. "And an apology. If you'd be interested, we could try again. I've missed you. I woke up thinking about eating your pussy."

Jamie giggles. "Oh man, that sounds good."

Sergio grins. "Good. Eat up, so I can too."

Jamie wolfs down the eggs. "Hey, wanna help me with a video? Two birds, one stone?"

• •

Morning sunlight streams through Jamie's bedroom window and onto her desk chair.

"Don't I need to sign something for this?" Sergio asks from their position, kneeling in front of the chair.

"It's not porn. It's art."

"What's the difference for people like us?" Sergio laughs, throaty and deep. Jamie remembers why she loved them: their exuberance.

"Okay, turn to face the chair so your back is to the camera." She turns on her camera and adjusts her position in the seat.

"My good side," Sergio jokes.

Jamie sets the camera, takes off her underwear and sits in the chair.

Sergio places themself between her legs. "Am I going to be unemployable now?" they ask from their perch.

"You're not even in the frame."

"What are you trying to see?"

"I don't know. It's an experiment."

"Ready?"

"Let's do this." She hits record. Sergio's mustache tickles her thighs, left, then right, then left, then right, closing in on her vulva. The kisses turn into licks. Sergio nibbles her outer labia from top to bottom. They place their mouth over her mound, enveloping the whole of her vulva. Sergio sighs. Jamie sighs too. She watches her mouth on the computer screen. She licks her lips as Sergio licks her other lips. Sergio kisses and rubs their face against her folds. Jamie scratches their head, a thing Sergio liked and, happily, seems to still like.

Sergio presses their mouth into her, wrapping their hand around the small of her back to pull her hips into their face. She starts to grind, and they moan. Jamie isn't sure she should use words, but she wants to say "yes!" so she does, just once, breathy and broken. Jamie struggles to keep her head centered in frame. Her mouth hangs open, and she breathes harder. Sergio holds their face still and pulls her hips against their mouth. Jamie smiles. They remember this is how she likes to come. Her orgasm imminent, she struggles against moving her head, the frame too tight to capture it.

"Fuck!" she shouts, though it sounds more like FAAAAH! She throws her head back and wraps her legs tight around Sergio's strong shoulders.

A moment of calm quiet sinks into the room. Then Sergio climbs up and kisses her sweetly. Their mustache is moist with her.

Jamie reviews the video as Sergio dresses.

"It's just your mouth," they say, peering over her shoulder.

"I was trying to draw a parallel. And maybe a little bit of metaphor."

"Huh."

Jamie sits with the video, watching all the way through. When she comes, her mouth disappears, and the camera is framed around her neck. The autofocus struggles to find its center. It pulls into focus on her pulse, a small, fluttering bulge beneath the tender flesh of her neck. Her muscles tense, but her pulse is steady and bold. Long seconds pass, layers of breath, blood, and tendon moving in a concert of pleasure on the screen.

Then Jamie's mouth drops back into frame. She offers the faintest bit of a smile before she leans forward and cuts the recording.

"Yeah," Sergio says, buttoning their shirt and rolling the sleeves into neat cuffs at their elbows. "I like it."

Jamie walks Sergio out. "You sticking around?" Sergio asks. Jamie shrugs.

"Well, I can probably help get your videos in the clubs if you want to go that route."

"Maybe," Jamie says with a smile.

'They share a peck and Sergio heads for the BART station just as Layla pulls up to the curb.

· ·

Before Layla can speak, Jamie says, "I don't want to go."

Layla groans. "How many times do I need to apologize?"

"You've been a jerk since we left Canada. Why they hell should I spend another six days with you?"

"Because..."

Jamie can see Layla searching for the right words that will put Jamie back in the passenger seat.

"Because it's more fun with you around. It feels both new and broken-in."

"More like broken."

Layla rolls her eyes. "The best part of the drive is ahead of us."

"So?"

"This is a big world, Jamie. A big state! Don't you want to just see a tiny bit of it?"

"I like being home. It's not so bad."

"Not so bad is different from awesome. Come on! We're supposed to be having an adventure. When was the last time you were in Big Sur?"

"I've never been."

"Me neither! See?!"

"I thought we were going to stay on the 101 from now on."

"Yeah, well. Adventure. Come on. Let's go climb some trees and hug some otters."

DAY 5

Olive winds along Highway 1, rolling green ranch hills to the left, endless blue ocean to the right. Slowly the hills give way to forest, the trees so high they blot out the sun above. The air smells healthy and rich. Jamie puts her head out the window like a dog and inhales.

"Henry Miller was a misogynist," Layla says over the din of rock and roll and wind through the open windows.

"And Tropic of Cancer was brilliant; Anaïs Nin was one of the sexiest literary bisexuals of all time, and I still want to see the damn bookstore."

Jamie pulls Olive into a lot covered with brown sequoia needles, parking in front of the Henry Miller Bookstore. Layla steps out and contemplates the redwoods, running her fingers over their bark. Behind the gate sits a low cabin in a small clearing. Junk sculptures dot the lawn.

Layla wanders to the amphitheater and Jamie goes inside.

The bookstore smells like a muddled mix of mold, paper, and warmth, like every bookstore should. A young man sits behind the register and smiles up from a book named The Dream of a Common Language. He asks if she needs help. Jamie shakes her head and wanders the stacks. There is one other customer in the store, a stooped man tucked into the metaphysics section.

Jamie scans the spines of the poetry section, most of them Beat-era writers, interrupted by the occasional contemporary name.

"We've got some new chapbooks in the front."

Jamie turns to see a tall brunette leaning against the shelf. She wears a white polo shirt embroidered with the words, "Libris Pistorum."

"Some good stuff. Mostly west coast queer POC. Wanna see?"

Jamie isn't really listening, too busy trying to figure out the girl's eye color, obscured by the lens-glare of her tortoise-shell glasses. Her eyes are almost green, but sparked with an undertone of brown. Jamie nods, not remembering what she agreed to. The girl turns and walks away; it takes a moment for Jamie to realize she is supposed to follow. She rushes to catch up.

The girl picks up a slim booklet held together with staples. "This chick's badass. Brutal, beautiful. You'll love it."

Jamie flips through the pages and scans one of the spare poems.

> *Cinch on my hips*
> *You inch near*
> *Fingers denting my thighs,*
> *I rise.*
> *You pull me inside.*

"Woah," Jamie says, shutting the book as though caught looking at a porn mag.

"Oh yeah," the girl says with a giggle. "She loves writing about fucking."

Jamie hands the book to the girl and turns back to the poetry section.

"I'm Sam," the girl says, holding out her hand.

"Jamie," Jamie says, taking it.

Layla enters, fiddling with her phone. "Are you getting any service here?"

Sam says, "It'll kick back in about 30 minutes further south."

"It looked like someone tweeted one of your videos, but then my service dropped," Layla says.

"Really?" Jamie feels a thrilled sort of nausea. People are actually watching her sexy videos. Strangers. On the internet.

"Videos?" Sam says.

"Experimental video things," Jamie says and waves a hand in self-dismissal.

"Sexy ones," Layla says with an arched brow.

"Layla, Sam. Sam, Layla." The girls shake hands.

"Sexy how?" Sam asks, tightening her pony tail.

Jamie's gaze wanders from the girls to the corners of the bookstore. "I film myself in limited frame engaging in...y'know."

"—Sex." Layla goads.

Sam's eyes widen. "Cool. The two of you?"

"No," Jamie rushes. Layla looks away. "Me and...other people. Though I'll have to get creative. I've exhausted all my contacts."

"She means exes," Layla says.

"I'll help!" Sam shouts and claps, startling the otherwise quiet store.

"What?" Jamie asks.

"*What?*" Layla repeats.

"I like art. Sounds fun!"

. . . .

"Are you sure you want to do this?" Jamie asks.

"Totally! It'll be cool."

Jamie lies on Sam's bed in an Airstream parked in a forest clearing. The window is open, and a cool breeze teases at the lace curtains. The air smells like air is supposed to, and Jamie feels both alert and relaxed.

"You think we have enough light?" Sam asks, adjusting the curtain.

"Yeah. It's good."

Sam looks through the camera's viewfinder. "I think you have to keep your legs like that or you won't be able to see the dildo."

"It's okay if you don't see much of it. As long as it's all you really see."

Sam laughs.

"Whatever. You'll see what I mean. Come here and lie back."

"I thought I was fucking you."

"You are, but I need to focus the camera. Be me for a sec."

Sam lies back. Her brown hair drapes the pillow. Jamie admires her body, light skin darkened by a life outdoors. Sam looks at Jamie, licks her lips, and offers a coy smile. Jamie zooms out to capture Sam's hip and thigh in the frame.

"Hold your leg up like you're getting fucked," Jamie says. Sam does, then she moves her hips and grunts in a silly, but seductive display.

Jamie laughs and adjusts. "Save it for the picture, lady. We're all set."

"Yum. Let's do this."

Jamie climbs on top of Sam, straddling her. She leans down and they kiss. Sam runs her hands across Jamie's shoulders, breasts, and waist. They grind against each other.

Sam pulls away. "Wait, aren't you supposed to be lying back?"

"In a minute. I'm enjoying this."

Sam's lips are nimble and her tongue darts. It's not what Jamie is used to, and she adapts. Sam's body is soft and strong, layers of thick muscle beneath curves, like a woman who doesn't shirk work. Jamie strokes Sam's arms and legs, feeling her thick muscle beneath her soft skin.

"Where's the harness?" Jamie asks.

"There." Sam points to the foot of the bed. Jamie slides off, and Sam slips it on, yanking the straps over her ass cheeks. "I haven't worn one of these in a million years." Jamie leans up and helps Sam adjust the straps, undoing and redoing the buckles at her waist.
"Feel good?" Jamie asks. "Secure?"

Sam bounces up and down, sending the purple, sparkly dildo flapping from her belly to her thigh. "I love this dildo! It's what my cock would look like if I were a mermaid," Sam giggles, as much to herself as for Jamie. She grabs a condom from the side table and eases it over her cock.

Jamie rolls on her back and shifts her hips onto the mark on the sheet.

"Ready?" Sam asks, moving between Jamie's legs.

"You bet."

Jamie digs through her gear bag for lube and squirts some into her hand, then slides it against Sam's shaft.

With a hand on the base, Sam eases her cock inside. Jamie sighs and smiles.

"Good?" Sam asks.

Jamie nods.

"Is this the part we're filming?" Sam says.

"Just stay right here a fuck me for a few minutes. Slowly."

Sam purrs, "My pleasure."

Sam thrusts into Jamie, slow and steady. Jamie sighs and moans sweetly. Stroking Sam's neck and shoulders, Jamie feels Sam's traps clench with each thrust. She squeezes her fingers into the muscles in counterpoint.

Sam groans with pleasure. She leans down for a kiss, and their hips shift.

Jamie rolls Sam over onto her back and eases herself down onto Sam's cock. Jamie giggles. The giggle turns into laughter. Sam's cock vibrates with Jamie's laughter, and Sam laughs in return.

"Oh my god, I so needed this!" Jamie shouts. Sam arches up to kiss her and then falls back to the pillow. Jamie grinds on Sam's cock. The dildo's head is more prominent that she's used to, but she likes it, catching the frenulum against her g-spot and grinding.

Jamie shudders. "Fuck."

"Yeah."

Sam holds Jamie around the small of her back and places her other hand against Jamie's mound, guiding her hips as they fuck.

"Fuck that feels good," Sam says, her breath heavy.

Jamie rides Sam, circling her hips. She holds her head in one hand, the other braced against Sam's forearm.

"Fuckfuckfuckfuck" Jamie repeats like a mantra with each downward thrust of her hips.

Sam pants, holding Jamie. She strokes Jamie's breast, taking a nipple between two fingers and squeezing. Jamie moans. Her moan becomes a shout and a scream. Her orgasm shakes both their bodies, the bed, and the trailer. Jamie collapses over Sam, pressing her mouth to Sam's neck.

Jamie grinds slowly, rocking their hips together. They kiss and smile.

"I have bad news," Sam says.

Jamie pulls back. "What?"

Sam nods at the camera. "I think we moved out of frame."

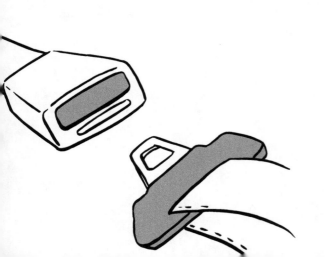

Behold, the noble strap-on, essential gear of modern lady lovers the world over. Is there anything more invigorating, more inarguably DTF than straps and a dildo? Once considered a bit "beyond" by lesbians of forgone generations, strap-ons are now more likely to be de *riguer* among the girl-fucking contingent.

GEAR UP

There are two essential parts of a strap-on:
the dildo and the harness.
Let's take a look, shall we?

DILDOS

Dildos come in a ton of different materials, shapes, colors, and sizes.

Some are realistic looking:

Some aren't:

Some *really* aren't:

Some fit in harnesses:

Some don't:

When you're looking to choose a dildo, you want to take into account a bunch of factors like:

SHAPE

Most people prefer smooth or only slightly textured dildos, especially in harnesses. Dildos with ridges or prominent curves can be challenging for harnessed fucking, even if they're fine for hand-held play. Also, pay attention to the girth of the head versus the girth of the body of the dildo. Some dildos will be smooth all the way, while others will have a promient corona (the "mushroom cap" on the head of the dildo). Some folks like smooth and some like prominent.

PRO-TIP: Prominent heads help you, the wearer, because you'll be able to feel better where the end of your dildo is based on the resistance you feel inside your partner. (G-spots often like them, too!)

You may have to clock some hours before you find a shape that really works for you. (Boo hoo!) Finally, be sure the dildo has a wide, flat base so it will fit comfortably against your body.

An often overlooked element of dildo shape is the angle of entry. Some dildos look straight, but will actually point downwards when worn. This can make missionary position hard. I love dildos with steep angles. They look weird when they're sitting on the shelf, but they're great when worn in a harness, because the steep angle actually helps the cock stick straight out from your body when worn over your pubic mound. This is great for keeping track of the tip of it when you're fucking.

REALISM

Some people build emotional or even psychic connections with their dildos. If you want a dildo to feel like it's actually your cock, you may want to look for one that represents the kind of cock you'd imagine you have. For most folks, realism means choosing a shape, color, and size that works for them. Other folks might imagine them having a unicorn horn, and that's swell, too. On the other side of things, some folks really hate the idea of a penis-analogue anywhere near them. If that's you or your partner, consider getting a non-realistic dildo, whether in a fantastical color or in a non-penis-looking shape.

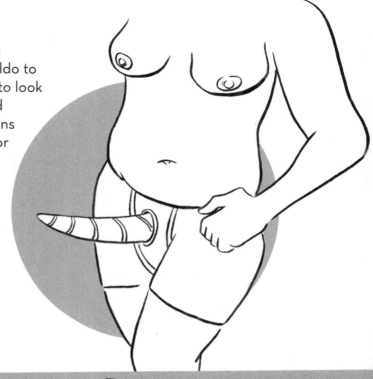

 For realistic dildos, you have the choice between "balled" and "ball-less." Balls can be great for realism purposes, plus they're great to use as a handle if you're going to use the dildo for hand sex. Balls can be bulky in certain harnesses, though, so be sure to try the combination you like best if you're shopping for both the dildo and the harness at the same time.

MATERIALS

Silicone is the queen of dildo materials. It's body safe, it can come in a huge range of colors and shapes, it's dishwasher safe and boilable (easy to clean!), and it can be squishy or firm. The downside is that it's still kind of expensive. A good silicone dong will set you back about $50. You can find cheaper ones, and more expensive too, but it's still a bit of an investment. As time goes on, the price will hopefully continue to drop.

There are other materials like **jelly rubber** which is cheap as hell, but a lot of people think is bad for your body. We sex nerds are waiting on more science on jelly's toxicity, but in the meantime we DO know for sure that jelly is porous and hard to clean. This means it can harbor some uggo bacteria. If you use a jelly dildo, you should always use a condom with it.

Allison's recommendation:
Silicone is slightly more expensive than other plastics, but for good reason. It's easy to clean, it's safe for your body, and it's durable. And now with the beauty of the internet, silicone dildos are easy to find! Don't settle for crappy, cheap, rubber jelly dildos. Instead, check out one of our Girl Sex Positive sex toy stores in the Appendix and buy something that'll last as long as your sexual explorations. And visit GirlSex101.com for a 10% off coupon from some of our favorite retailers.

Glass, metal, hard plastic, and wood dildos usually aren't designed to be worn in harnesses because they can be uncomfortable for the wearer. But some are, and they sure are pretty. Cruise on over to Chapter 8 for a breakdown of these materials.

Density/ "Squishability": Some dildos are harder than others. On the density scale, we've got glass, hard plastic, and metal on the "super hard/no squish" end of the scale. And on the other end is dual-density silicone (super squish). If you're buying a dildo to wear in a harness, err toward the softer end to help cusion the pressure against your mound.

Okay, so you've got your dildo!

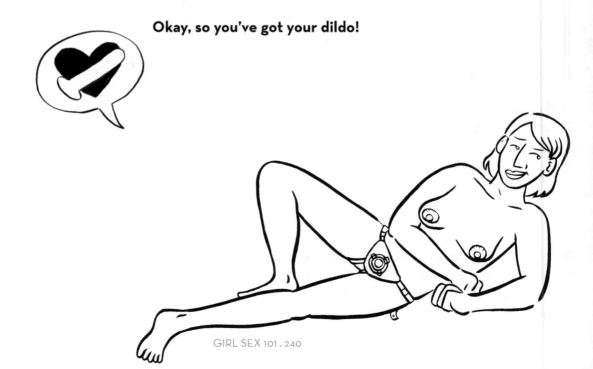

NOW, THE HARNESS

There are three main types: jock style, thong style, and underwear style.

Jock style (a.k.a. 2-strap): This is the classic shape of a harness. It's called "Jock" because there are two straps in the back that go under your butt cheeks just like a jock strap. These are great because they keep you exposed for play on your own goods. They also tend to be good for bigger girls because the straps are long and are designed to be cut down to size. Jocks are sturdy and fun for grabbing and yanking (if that's your thing).

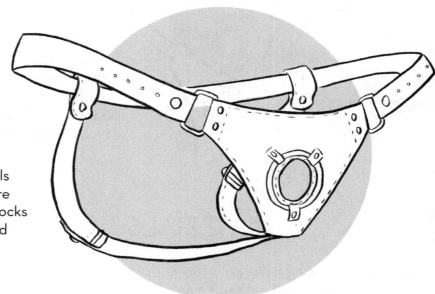

The straps can have buckle or D-rings. Sometime they rock both!

Buckles are great because they stay in place. The only bummer about them is that they can be cumbersome to slip on and off, and as the leather stretches it may move the hole.

D-rings are a breeze to slip on and off, but they can loosen during the sex. When that happens, you can just yank and tighten as you go.

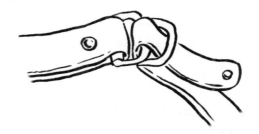

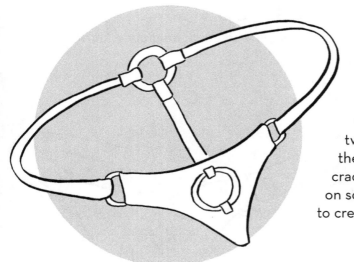

Thong styles (sometimes called a 1-strap) seem to be falling out of popularity, but they're still some folks' favorite style. The thong is exactly what it sounds like: instead of two straps that hug your ass like a jock strap, they have a single strap that goes right down your crack. People who like them say they feel securer on some ass shapes, and you can also use the strap to create sensation on your ass or vulva.

MATERIALS

Both jock and thong styles can come in a variety of materials. **Leather** is most popular, because, just like boots, over time it softens. It will also stretch a bit as you break it in. Leather is hard to clean, however, so you don't want to share your harness with anyone unless they wear underwear with it. **Vegan leather** is increasingly popular, and usually cheaper than leather. **Fabric** harnesses are easier to clean: you can just throw them in the wash. But the straps tend to stretch quicker than leather, so be sure to get a size that can be tightened a lot. Harnesses can also come in latex, rubber, pvc, or rope. Some enterprising folks have even started making harnesses out of recycled bike tire tubes.

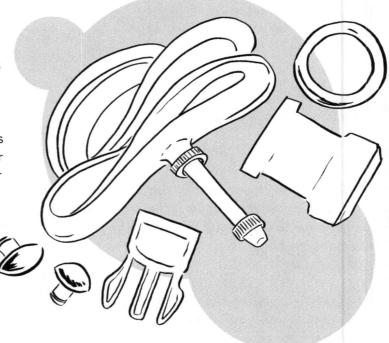

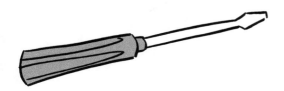

Finally, there's the **underwear** style of harness. This is a relatively new style, even though dykes have been cutting holes in briefs for years. These tend to be more structurally secure than the old MacGyvered style of things, though. RodeoH makes a pair of briefs that are most like a regular pair of underwear with a hole and cockring sewn into the front. Spare Parts is another brand that has underwear style harnesses. These feel slightly more like swimsuits than cotton briefs, and they come in a variety of styles, including a "femme-y" version with lace, ruching, and a little bow. The underwear style is super comfortable to wear under clothes, making them particularly good for packing and playing. They're also washable, meaning you can throw them right in the laundry after use. The downside is that this style of harness doesn't do well with monster dongs. That is, they tend not to have the tensile strength that a harness needs to hold a heavy dildo against your body. If you use smaller dildos, though, they can be great.

 Non-op trans girls will probably want to avoid thong harnesses because the strap can be uncomfortable on scrotums. Instead, stick with jock harnesses, because the two straps will steer clear of any dangly bits. Or, choose the underwear style that makes you feel sexiest, because it'll keep everything tucked up and tight. (Spare Parts makes a jock style harness with some extra room for your goods). If you don't get erections, place the base of the dildo on your mound to enjoy a nice internal pubic massage. If you do get an erection, you may want to tuck it up under the waist strap to keep it secure and comfortable while you're in action.

Make sure your harness can accommodate the girth of your preferred dildo(s). Most harnesses come with either permanently affixed or detachable o-rings to securely hold your dildo. O-rings come in rubber and metal. Rubber stretches, metal doesn't. Metal can often feel more secure, but can hurt the wearer if you're really going at it. Over time, metal rings can damage the dildo too if you're a particularly—ahem—ardent fucker.

If you're shopping for a strap-on with your partner, a good rule of thumb is to let the receiver choose the dildo and the giver choose the harness. This is a good starting place so you can make sure that the person who's going to be penetrated has the choice of what will feel good for her and the person wearing the harness feels secure and sexy in it. Ideally, if you have the funds, you can both choose a combo you like. This is particularly good when breakups happen, so no one feels 'stiffed' by the separation of the toys.

MATERIAL
PROS AND CONS

LEATHER

PROS
- Softens with age
- Last a long time
- Many different styles
- Strong and secure
- Can adjust

CONS
- Porous, hard to clean
- Not vegan
- 2 primary shapes: jock and thong
- Can be bulky under clothes
- Expensive
- Stretches somewhat

FABRIC

- Comfy. Easy to wear under clothes
- Butch and femme styles
- Low profile—look like undies
- Easy to wash—just throw in with the rest of the laundry
- Affordable
- Good for soft-packing, too

- Will wear out like normal underwear
- Not as strong and secure as straps
- Fixed cock rings mean certain sized dildos only

VEGAN LEATHER

- Cruelty-free
- Many different colors
- Strong and secure
- Cheaper than real leather

- Porous, hard to clean
- Doesn't soften as well as real leather

STYLE
PROS AND CONS

JOCK

PROS
- Secure
- Good for bigger booties and hips
- Some come with adjustable o-rings
- A variety of colors and materials
- Keeps your goods exposed for play
- Can adjust straps for optimal dildo placement

CONS
- Can be pricey
- Bulky
- Hard to clean

THONG

PROS
- Secure
- Good for wearer's stimulation
- Some come with adjustable o-rings
- Vertical strap allows for adjustments of dildo placement

CONS
- Tough on scrotums or big lips
- Can create too much friction on wearer's genitals
- Hard to clean

UNDER-WEAR

PROS
- Comfy
- Variety of femme and butch styles
- Easy to clean

CONS
- Not adjustable
- Limited allowed dildo girth & heft
- Not very strong

The most important thing to look for when choosing a harness is fit. You want the harness to hold your chosen dildo securely against your body. You also want the material to be okay on your skin. If you're sensitive to rubber, for instance, steer clear of that kind of harness. You also want to feel sexy in your harness. Sometimes that means the jock style that hugs your ass, or the boxer-brief style that covers you up and looks quite butch, or something else entirely.

If you're lucky enough to live near a pleasure-positive sex toy store, most of those places will let you try on their harnesses to find one that works for you. If not, try one of the online stores with a good exchange policy.

WANNA GO FOR A RIDE!?

So you're all geared up and ready for action! **Now what?**

First, put on the harness. Some people like having the base of the dildo directly over the clit, because it can aid stimulation. Others prefer putting it on their pubic mound for extra cushioning. Choose what works for you, and don't be afraid to adjust things as you go.

Get a sense for the dildo—how long it is, how heavy it is, how to, in a word, "wield" it. You may even want to try penetrating yourself with the dildo first (hand-held, of course) before you try it with a partner, just so you can get a sense of what it feels like from the receptive end.

More than any other sex act, I've seen people get totally carried away when using strap-ons. Maybe it's the thrill of wielding a cock, or the silliness of feeling a dong bounce around on your crotch for the first time. Whatever it is, it tends to make people a little bit stupid when they put one on. Just because it's exciting doesn't mean you get to forget everything you've learned so far. Remember, the vagina is a cul-de-sac, which means there's only so far you can go in. And at the end of the cul-de-sac is a cervix, which can be very touch averse at times. Most dildos are longer than most vaginas, so be aware that you probably won't be able to get all the way in. And while some people like having their cervix banged, some folks really, really don't. Start slow.

Put on a condom and use your fingers to make sure your partner's lubed up enough. If not, add some lube to your cock and the entrance to her vagina. Then, when she's ready, place the tip of your cock to the entrance to her vagina, and ease in.

If you've had penis-vagina sex before, you'll know that you sometimes need to go out and in a few times before you ease the cock all the way in. You may also know that it's totally possible to accidentally fall out.

One of the hardest things about fucking with a strap-on is the lack of biofeedback. You might feel the base of the dil on your goods, but you sure as hell can't feel the tip of it. This means you have to be extra special careful when penetrating your partner for the first time.

SETTING

Make sure you've got a cozy set up for the two of you, especially if you'll be doing a lot of experimenting of positions. A little bit of light is good here. When you're just getting used to wearing a dildo, it's easy to lose track of the tip of it. So if you have lights on, you can take a look while you thrust and get a better feeling for the length.

Also, consider the surface. Thrusting is best performed on on beds with a bit of spring. (I'm convinced that memory foam has killed more sex lives than herpes outbreaks have.) You'll want a bit of help to fight gravity, especially if you're on the bottom. Pillows are helpful to improve positioning (or get all fancy with a Liberator wedge). If she's a squirter, have some towels on hand. And keep lube and condoms within reach.

POSITIONS

It's usually easiest to start with **missionary position** or your partner on top. In missionary, you can move slower, and of course, kiss. This position is best if her hips are flexible enough to open her legs wide enough to accommodate your hips. If you're big and/or she's not too flexible, her hips may fatigue, which doesn't feel very sexy. You can fix this by having her put her ankles together and **letting her legs rest to one side**. If **she's on top**, it'll keep the dildo from migrating on you, and she'll be able to keep it in better. The downside with this is it can put a lot of pressure on the base of the dildo which can be uncomfortable for you. Also, if your dildo is longer than her vagina, her on top might be too deep for comfort. Keep your legs together so she can straddle you more comfortably. If it's hard for her to get a good rhythm, try scooting to the **edge of the bed** so she can put a foot on the floor to help with her own fight against gravity.

Doggy style is great as long as you are tall enough when you kneel behind her. If you're a bit too short, the dildo may slip out easier.

All said, keep a sense of humor and a sense of adventure, and you'll figure out a position that works for both of you. Hetero-paired couples are always making adjustments during sex, so don't think you're doing something wrong if you have to shift your body weight.

I've never had more sympathy for cis men as when I started fucking with a strap-on. If you're fucking missionary style, be prepared to do some work. You have to hold up your body weight with your arms, and generate a lot of force with your hips. It's not easy. Your wrists, elbows, and shoulders will do a lot of work. If holding yourself up on your arms is hard for you, try a position that isn't so trying on your joints, like her on top or doggy style. Also, as long as your partner is okay with it, don't be afraid to rest your body weight on top of her. Many people like the feeling of body weight on top of them when getting fucked, just be sure to ask first. Even if you're a lot bigger than your partner, odds are, you won't hurt her. My partner is 250 pounds and unless I'm already overheating, it's never a problem.

As you start fucking, going slow will also help you learn to track the biofeedback you do get from your partner. Ask her to do kegels or squeeze the dildo, and see if you can feel it. Explore how you can direct the dildo by shifting your hips or body weight. Play with thrusting and twisting your hips differently.

If your partner wants hard fucking, the best thing to do is meet half way. Generate force with your hips by thrusting, but ask her to fuck you back. This is usually easiest for both partners in doggy style, because it tends to be easy on all body types. If she's on top, bring your knees up behind her, with your feet flat on the bed/ground. When she pushes down on you, rise your hips up to meet her.

FUN THINGS TO DO WITH DILDOS

Once you've mastered the basics, try these fun modifications:

Rotate the dildo in your harness so the angle faces a new way.

Pile driver!

Standing sex!

Pack and play. Wear your harness and dil out one night and try to get your groove on by letting her hump your hard-on through your pants while you dance.

Switcheroo! Both strap it on and take turns doing each other.

SCENIC VIEWPOINT

GENDER FUCK COCK SUCK
by Tina Horn

Is there any sex act more inherently queer than the silicone dildo blowjob? Is there one that calls more upon the imagination, that huge sex organ between the ears? Nothing gets the genitals closer to the brain than oral sex. Nothing requires you more blatantly to hold contradictory ideas about gender in your head than playing with a toy that has somehow become a part of you. Sucking strap-on cock is the ultimate gender fuck.

It is difficult for some traditionalists to reckon with the presence of a phallus into their lady-on-lady intercourse; and a dick during oral sex is even more (ahem) in your face. To these people I say: have a little faith in the magic of queer sex. No: the dick is not a dick. It's a toy used by your girlfriend. On the other hand the dick is a dick is a dick, and a dick by any other name would taste as sweet shoved down your throat. So treat it like one. Reinvent the cock, whether you're trans, cis, or otherwise. Take the phallus back from the patriarchy, and lay claim to your pleasure while you're at it!

The most popular term for this act is "fauxjob," but honey there is nothing fake about looking into the eyes of a girl with your dick in her mouth.

Strap it on. Consider your cock an embodiment of your lust for your partner and feel it pulsate. Feel the straps against your hips, absorbing your history. Silicone conducts vibration, and it also conducts the movement of a mouth—the hums, the bobs, the sucks and blows. Lay back and enjoy the show. Or straddle her head and fuck her throat like you do her cunt and ass. Thick saliva forms from this kind of thing: use it as lube. If you both like it rough, then grab her hair, slap her face with your dick. Your total control of her head will blow both your minds. Or of course, you could always try a little tenderness.

Cocksuckers: enjoy having your lover in your mouth. Put on the dick sucking show. Think of the dildo as the extension of the clit, or the g spot. Show off your talented mouth; she's gonna see it more on her cock than when it's buried between her legs. You can give head to a dildo while rubbing the base on your partner's clit: this might get her off. You can fuck her cunt or her ass while her silicone dick is in your mouth: this might very possibly get her off. You can rub your drooling mouth all over her dick and then lick her pussy: she's probably gonna love that. Wrap your lips around it and for cryin' out loud, don't forget the eye contact!

Tina Horn is a writer, educator, media-maker, and professional macho slut. She produces and hosts the sexuality podcast "Why Are People Into That?!"

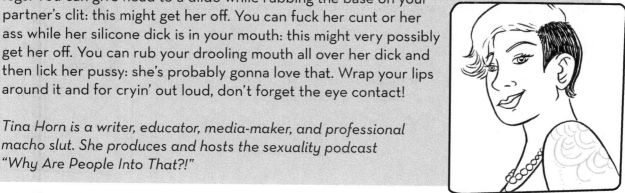

SCENIC VIEWPOINT →

FIERCE FEMME FUCKING
by Sophia St. James

My partner asked if I ever had experience with a strap-on. I didn't, but I was more than happy to learn. That partner opened my eyes to MANY exciting sexual escapades, but none as playful and multi-layered as strap-on fucking.

When I wear a strap-on, it's not a sex toy, but my cock that I control and can feel. I love being a femme, owning my feminine nature, and still being able to orgasm from using my cock. It took time to become one with my strap-on, but now it feels so right to be wearing one, as though I was born with my silicone cock. It's part of my fierce femme identity. I own the ability to give and receive pleasure with my cock. If positioned correctly, I can feel my lover's movements just as much as they can feel mine.

I even enjoy the act of putting it on. It's not an obstacle, nor distraction. It's an exhilarating foreplay moment to kiss, tease and touch my partner. I always make sure a few things are in place when I am getting ready to use my cock: I make sure the back of the cock is placed right over my vulva to help me enjoy it better. To maintain the best control over the cock, I need to make sure the straps are tight enough to hold the cock in place but not so tight the straps begin to dig in. If the harness has buckles, I only undo one side when taking off and remember where the buckle goes (I count the number of holes it takes to get the right fit).

The better I control it and the better it fits, the better it feels. If the straps aren't right, the cock isn't placed the right way, or if I don't have control of the cock (you know that feeling when your body moves back 3 inches but the cock barely moves? Yeah, that), I take a brief moment to adjust. I want both of us to enjoy ourselves. So taking a small moment of 'pleasure adjusting' can make for hours of great fun!

Strap-on fucking is a big part of my play and sex life. When it comes to my toy bag, a couple different cocks and my harness is always included. If I do strap up, it usually means we'll be playing for quite some time. I'm a primal fucker. By the time my lover and I are done, things are going to be messy. No one should look pretty after fucking.

Sophia St. James is an erotic entertainer, mother and healthcare professional who takes pride in being a body positive and sex positive fierce femme.

WHAT DO YOU LIKE ABOUT STRAP-ON SEX?

I ENJOY THE PENETRATION AND THE VOYEURISM OF IT. I CAN WATCH HER WATCHING ME FUCK OR GET FUCKED.

It's exciting to think about anatomy that can be put on just for sexy times and then removed again.

I like how my partner and I can move together.

When my hips gets going in that rocking motion, it gets me so fucking hard.

I LOVE FEELING SOMEBODY'S THIGHS CRASHING INTO MINE.

PRETENDING I HAVE A HUGE BONER AND MAKING MY PARTNER SQUIRM WITH PLEASURE.

Going hands-free, being able to look in each other's eyes, kiss, hold each other.

EVERYTHING. I LIKE THE WAY IT FEELS, I LIKE THE SUBTLE POWER PLAY, I LIKE THE WAY IT LOOKS. I LIKE GETTING ALL SWEATY....UMM...I CAN'T TALK ABOUT THIS ANYMORE LOL.

The connection and closeness. When my butch is laying on me, cock up my ass, and we're looking at each other, I could implode from the strength of the connection.

IT'S SUCH A NORMAL PART OF MY SEX LIFE THAT I DON'T EVEN REALLY CONSIDER IT A TOY. IT'S MY WIFE'S COCK. IT'S A PART OF HER. I KNOW SHE FEELS MOST COMFORTABLE ABOUT SEX WHEN SHE HAS HER COCK ON.

CONNECTION WITH PARTNER, SMOOTH PENETRATION, DEEP STIMULATION.

I LIKE HAVING MY HANDS FREE TO DO OTHER THINGS.

It fits with my gender expression during sex. I can look into my lover's eyes and pleasure them at the same time. I just really love it!

SO MANY DIFFERENT COCKS!

My wife can come from having a strap-on inside of me, and I can come that way too. It's really awesome to be able to come together that way.

I LOVE WHEN BOTH OF US ARE FUCKING WITH OUR WHOLE BODIES. I ALSO LOVE SUCKING STRAP ON COCKS AND FETISHIZING THEM.

DAY 6

Jamie edits the new video while Layla drives. She's in the render and upload phase of the project, not wanting to examine the footage too closely before posting lest she lose her nerve.

"How'd you sleep?" Jamie asks as the video renders.

"It was really fucking cold. But the stars were nice. Have fun?"

Jamie grins. "Yeah. It was nice."

Layla keeps her eyes the road and chews on her lip. "First that Portland chick, then Amy and now bookstore girl," Layla says. "You really get around."

"Uh, slut shame much? And it's Sergio." Jamie stares out the window. "We didn't have sex."

"Really?"

"Really."

Jamie returns her focus to her computer. Silent minutes pass as they sweep down Highway 1. Olive's boxiness struggles against the curves.

"So is this all?" Layla asks.

"Is what all?"

"Big Sur. I thought it was supposed to be more majest—holy cow!"

Olive curves down the road. The trees thin. They are cruising along a cliff's edge, stories above the water. The glittering sea scatters rays of light against the rock faces, a million oranges, greens and blues.

"Oh my god." Jamie flips her laptop closed. "Pull over!"

Layla pulls into an overlook lined with large rocks. Condors catch updrafts at eye level. They hang like kites, their skulls the color of the sun at dawn.

Jamie and Layla walk to the cliff's edge, mouths agape. They get high on the breeze. Layla squints at the horizon, the ocean reflecting the light of thousands of waves against her face.

"Why are you really here?" Jamie asks.

Layla doesn't move. "I want more. Of all of the good stuff. Here. With you."

Jamie and trains her gaze on the horizon. "I don't want to get back together with you."

Layla turns from the water and walks along the boulders. "Of course not. You're on a streak. Can't end it by stopping your pursuit of pussy."

"Jesus, Layla."

Layla holds up her hands like she's resisting an attack that never comes. "But whatever. It's 'art'."

"Don't mock me."

Layla leaps onto a small boulder, balancing on one foot. "Why can't you experience your sexual renaissance without recording it and sharing it with the internet?"

"Recording it is part of it. I'm interested in more than just the fucking."

Layla scoffs. "So am I."

"Right. You fucking the random airport girl was about a deep spiritual and artistic connection."

"Oh you're so above it. Your clear artistic vision raising your sex to a higher aesthetic standard than the rest of us."

"Maybe I'm just looking for a little more nuance."

"By fucking strangers."

"What are you doing? Fucking strangers, while roadtripping to nowhere just to escape your old life."

Jamie picks up a rock and chucks it off the cliffside.

"Yeah well you didn't seem to tied to your minimum wage life."

"Why do even you care? You never used to give a shit about my jobs or my projects."

"Because you're fucking everyone else! You're inviting all of your other exes into your films."

"No I'm not."

"Portland whatshername."

"Eve. We didn't film anything. And not an ex."

"But she inspired you. And Amy."

"Sergio. Her name is Sergio!"

"Hah!" Layla shouts. "You fucked it up too!"

"Shut up. They changed their pronoun, like, four months ago. I've known them for eight years. It's an honest mistake. You're just being a dick."

"You're still in love with them."

"What? I was never in love with them. We were always better as friends."

"Then why did you fuck them last night?!"

"Because I—" Jamie stops.

The realization of Jamie's lie lands on Layla's face. "Fuck you."

"Oh, what? You get to fuck everyone and I don't?"

"Fuck you for lying to me!"

"I lied because I didn't want to deal with this." Jamie reaches into the back of Olive and pulls out her duffel and backpack.

"What?"

"Your possessiveness. Your jealousy! Why do you think I broke up with you?"

"Because of Amy."

"You drove me to Amy! You always assumed we were fucking. Accused us of it! So we decided to actually start fucking, just to prove you right." Jamie walks down the shoulder of PCH, thumb out.

Layla follows. "So what, you're going to run back to her—them now?"

"No. I'm going to run back to *my home*. I'm going to make sense of my life. Without you in it."

"No."

"You brought this on yourself with your paranoia and your jealousy. Enjoy the rest of your bullshit trip." Jamie hurries down the rocky shoulder, arm out, defiant.

"Please don't go!" Layla chases Jamie, her voice cracking with tears. "Please, please don't go."

"You can't trick someone into loving you, Layla."

"I don't want that. I just want to be important to you! To be included. I don't care who you're with as long as you're with me too. "

Jamie stares. "What does that mean?"

"I want to help."

The two girls glare at each other, Jamie's eyes narrowed and Layla's full of tears. "Let me be a part of your passion."

Jamie drops her duffel to the dirt and sighs. "Christ, Layla."

DAY 6

Olive is parked in an empty parking lot in Pismo Beach. The girls organize the mess in the back. "Can you move the sleeping bag?" Jamie asks.

Layla adjusts. "Good?"

Jamie flashes a thumbs-up. "And fix that curtain."

Layla adjusts the curtain. "Yeah?"

Jamie grimaces into the viewfinder.

"What?"

"This feels like my last one."

"Way to make a girl feel special."

"This isn't romance. This is art." Jamie stares out the window at the ocean crashing onto the shore.

"Okay, regroup."

Ten minutes later the camera sits alone beneath the sunset, facing the sea. Jamie and Layla lie on their sides in the van, holding each other, naked. The wireless microphone balances on a suitcase beside them. The laptop perches on Layla's backpack.

"Just like old times," Jamie says.

"Except with more equipment," Layla says.

"Now hey, that's a great idea." Jamie says, springing up and grabbing her gear bag from below the window. "Let's play with some toys!" Jamie unzips the bag.

"Wow," Layla says, peering in. "There's so much to choose from." She reaches in and pulls out a long silicone vibrator with a g-spot curve and a nub for the clit. Then she grabs a steel butt plug, a pair of nipple clamps, and a glove made out of fake fur.

"Remind me never to take you to a buffet," Jamie says.

Layla admires her choices, then sets them aside. "Let's just start with the vibrator for now."

Jamie laughs. "Good call."

Outside, muted waves crash and clouds cast long blue shadows on the sand. The microphone picks up the friction of skin on skin, small vocalized pleasure sounds, and the moist connection of lips on lips. The equalizer on Jamie's computer screen bounces from greens to yellows.

"Ready?" Jamie whispers.

"Uh huh," Layla replies.

Jamie flips a switch. The vibrator's buzzing creates a small green wave on the equalizer. Layla's quick intake of breath makes a red spike. Her moan creates a sizzle of yellow and red.

"Inside?" Jamie whispers.

"Not yet," Layla says. "Keep it right there."

Jamie holds the vibe. Layla's grinds her hips against it. "Kiss me," she says, breathy.

Jamie leans down and presses her mouth to Layla's. For a moment it tastes familiar. Easy.

Layla reaches down and tugs up at her mound, pulling her flesh taut. Jamie increases the pressure of the vibe. Layla moans, and Jamie glances at the equalizer. A roll of yellow squares sigh along with Layla's voice.

Layla curls her hips up, putting the fingers of her free hand in Jamie's mouth. Jamie smiles and sucks on them. Layla's vocalizations come out in beats. "Ah, ah, ah..."

"Now?" Jamie asks.

Layla nods and licks her lips.

Jamie moves the vibrator to the entrance of Layla's vagina.

The buzzing mutes, now barely static behind the sounds of deep breaths and Layla's rhythmic moans. "Fuck yes!" Layla cries.

Jamie slips the vibrator all the way in and angles it up to Layla's g-spot.

"Fuuuuuck!" Layla screams.

Jamie glances at the equalizer. All red. Red. Red. Yellow. Red. Lasting as long as Layla's hearty wail. Jamie soaks in the sound, looking out the window to the ocean. She feels Layla's pulse through her pussy, echoing the crashing waves beyond.

Layla's wail becomes a moan becomes a sigh.

Jamie clicks the vibrator off and eases it out of Layla. She leans forward and kisses Layla's flushed lips. She lays her head on Layla's shoulder and places the flat of her hand against Layla's pussy. The equalizer drops down to a steady wave of green undulating with their shared breath and the waves beyond. The girls sigh together for one last swell of yellow.

And then silence.

CHAPTER 8

GEAR HEADS & LUBE JOB

TOYS & LUBE →

Just as a good mechanic knows how to use her tools, a good girl-sexer knows how to use her toys. Toys are often as integral as hands and lube to a woman's experience of sexual pleasure, so even if you're not fond of vibes or clamps or plugs, your partner might be, and you get to be of service in a wholly (hole-y?) sexy way.

VIBRATORS

Vibrators are what most people think about when they think about sex toys. And for good reason: vibrators make up 20% of all sex toy sales.

Vibrators are a great way to add pleasure to any sexy time. Whether it's buzzing off together, buzzing her off while you ride her face or whatever, vibrations are often the icing on the sexy, sexy cake.

Some girls love deep, thrummy vibrations, like a big ol' Hog. Others like whisper-light, barely there vibes. And plenty of girls like something in between. Most feminist sex toy stores have fully charged tester vibes on the shelf for you to try out. If an in-person excursion isn't an option, some online stores have great return policies where you can exchange an unused vibe if you don't like the way it thrums.

Vibrators come in a wide variety of shapes, sizes, and specialties. They can be broken down by how they're designed to be used:

Outercourse

These vibes are designed to be used on the external genitals. They're sometimes called "personal massagers," and fascinatingly enough, they can be used on your muscles as well as your goods. These are the kinds of vibes you can find on the shelves of drug stores. The Cadillac of all vibrators is the "Magic Wand." It's a well-loved toy because of its reliability and unflagging power. It's a jackhammer for your junk, and can generate vibrations through other toys. There are many knockoffs and altered versions of the Magic Wand, some with more settings or rechargable batteries. The head of most of these (where the "vibe" comes from) is porous, so you'll always want to wrap the head in a condom when using with a partner. (Learn more about materials on page 275.)

Other external vibrators look like spheres, cones, or little palm-sized discs. Some of them can be worn on your finger tip. All of these are meant to go directly on your clit, perineum, or any outer bits that would like some stimulation. They can be used in conjunction with penetrative toys or not. It's up to you where and how you want to enjoy them.

Internal "Wand" style and G-Spotters

These are vibes that often look like dildos: long and cylindrical. Some are smooth and straight, and others will have a curve or angle for g-spot and/or prostate stimulation. Some—like the Rabbit—have external bits too, for "dual" sensation. The controls for wand type vibes are usually near the base.

They come in a huge range of materials, styles, and prices, from the super low end to the crazy fancy high end. Because of their versatility, this is the most popular kind of vibe you'll find, and it's where much of the innovation in sex-toy engineering is happening.

Wand style vibes can be waterproof, rechargeable, Bluetooth controlled, customizable with memorized vibration patterns, touch-responsive, ultra-quiet, and more. If you're shopping for your very first vibe, it may be good to start with a cheaper, simple wand with some g-spot curve just to see what kind of stimulation you like, since these can be used both internally and externally.

Bullet Style

These vibes look like eggs or bullets, often attached to a battery pack with a cord. Some don't have a cord, but rather an on/off button on one end. The ones with cords can be used both externally and internally. Those without need to stay on the outside of your body. Some strap-on harnesses have small pockets in the part that goes over your pussy designed to hold a bullet. Bullets tend to be on the weaker side, which can be great for folks who prefer hummingbirds to jackhammers. They're also little and quiet, which make them great for travel and throwing in your safer sex kit.

Novelty

If you can imagine it, it's probably been turned into a vibrator. Everything from dolphins to lollipops to, yes, Barack Obama, has been molded and fitted with a mechanical vibrating mechanism.

You can certainly buy these toys for the fun factor, just be aware that you may also want a toy that delivers the O's, or at least the "Aahs," so don't let cute decide the day.

WANNA GO FOR A RIDE!?

The most utilitarian way to use a vibrator is for clitoral stimulation, either on its own or in addition to other kinds of pleasure. But there are some other fun things to try:

Put on a show
Using a vibrator to masturbate in front of your partner can be thrilling for both of you. She gets to see you in your pleasure without having to do anything but enjoy the show.

Double duty
Sometimes when my partner and I are too tired to fuck, we like to masturbate together, which helps us feel connected without having to stay up past our bed time. This is particularly effective if both of you have different things—and vibrators—you like. One of the more challenging things about queer female sex is that simultaneous orgasm often isn't easy to come by. But with vibrators, you can sometimes make it happen.

Rocket Ride
The head of the Magic Wand is big enough that often you can both ride it at the same time. Either in Yab-Yum position or Missionary, wedge that puppy between your crotches and get groovin. Be aware that there's a good possibility for fluid exchange here, so have the Safer Sex talk (page 309) before you go for it.

Insta-vibe

Use a vibrator on an insertable toy. This works particularly well on toys with flared, broad bases. Some materials, like silicone, conduct vibration quite nicely, turning your favorite dildo into your favorite vibrating dildo.

Double-insta-vibe

If you have a double-ended dildo, you can place the vibe on the space between your two bodies while you're fucking. It can create a yummy shared sensation, making you feel more connected than just silicone by itself can.

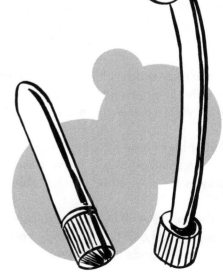

 If you're a trans girl who likes using your girl-dick for penetrative play, try placing the vibe on your shaft while you're penetrating your partner. Experiment with different kinds of vibes. The Magic Wand is easy to wield, but it can be super intense. Your results may vary.

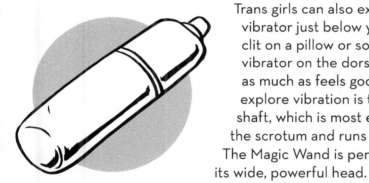

Trans girls can also experiment with putting the vibrator just below your glans. Or you might enjoy placing your clit on a pillow or some other cushy thing, then placing the vibrator on the dorsal side of the shaft and pressing down as much as feels good. Another good place to explore vibration is the internal part of the shaft, which is most easily accessed behind the scrotum and runs along your perineum. The Magic Wand is perfect for this because of its wide, powerful head.

Go on tour

Try placing the vibe on other parts of your body like your perineum, your anus, your mound, or your vaginal opening. Depending on how strong the vibration is, it can create nice sensations even if it's not directly on your clit.

Be a clit tease

Using a vibe is one of the easiest ways to be a total clit tease. You can hold the vibe against your partner until she's just on the edge, then take it away. It can be fun (for both of you) to watch her squirm.

ANAL TOYS

WHAT WHAT (CAN I PUT) IN THE BUTT?

Anal toys come in three main flavors: Plugs, Dildos, and Beads.

The number one thing you need to know about toys in your butt is they need to have a FLARED BASE. Say it with me now: F-L-A-R-E-D B-A-S-E.

That means the bottom should look like this:

NOT this:

A flared base is essential to keep you from losing a toy up your butt. Remember, the vagina is a cul-de-sac, but the anus is a loooong stretch of open road. Especially if you're playing alone, you need to make sure lubey fingers aren't going to create an awkward ER visit.

If you're playing with a partner, make sure the toy has either a flared base or a long and easy-to-grip handle. The muscles in your anus are strong and hungry. Don't give them something to munch on long after you're done playing.

Butt plugs come in various sizes, shapes, and materials. The most common shape is conical, easing from a small point to a larger base. These are great to learn with, because you can penetrate your ass only as far as you feel comfortable.

Other plugs look more like bulbs with a handle. These can be nice, because you can wear them for longer, and keep them in while you enjoy other kinds of play. Some of the coolest kinds of plugs have decorative ends like crystals or even (my personal favorite) TAILS!

We've already covered dildos, and there's nothing different between ass dildos and vaginal ones. Again, just make sure any dildo you put in your ass has a good handle or a flared base so it doesn't go on an colonic field trip.

Beads are exactly what they sound like, a series of often increasingly girthy beads attached by a cord or silicone. These are great because they allow you to play with the muscles of the highly sensitive anal sphincter.

The best kinds of beads are molded from one piece of silicone. This makes them easier to clean. The old school version with cord and separate beads aren't great, because they can harbor bacteria easier. FUN Factory and other great companies make cute, comfortable, and sexy beads. Find more info in the appendix.

WANNA GO FOR A RIDE!?

Anal sex in porn is all showy with the in and out. While you may indeed like this sensation, it's more likely you'll enjoy small movements, at least to start. There are plenty of nerve endings for you to enjoy yourself without the theatrics. Plugs are good because you can place them inside and then just keep them there, either squeezing against it, or gently tugging it against your anus.

The key for all anal penetration is START SLOW.

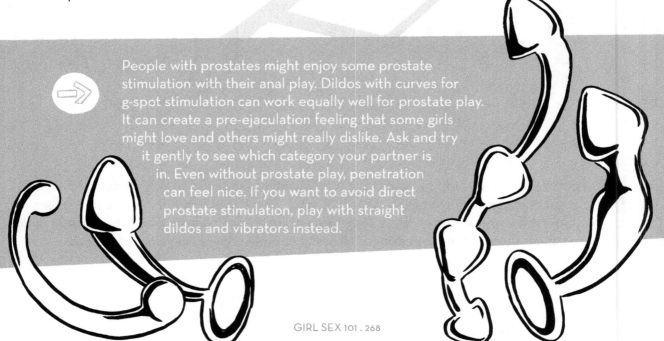

Most of us are well-practiced at keeping our ass tight and closed, for useful and generally appreciated reasons. We're not nearly as good at relaxing on command. Learning to relax these muscles is often the first step of all anal sex. It can take some practice and time, but the reward is vast. Remember to breathe and use **copious amounts of lube**.

When you first practice receiving anal penetration, let the toy (or hand or whatever) rest inside first. Entering can be the most stimulating and challenging part, so take it easy. This is your chance to practice relaxing. It's kind of like breathing, but with your ass: Inhale and squeeze. Exhale and relax.

Once your toy (or whatever) is as inside as you want it, practice squeezing your anal muscles around it. Squeeze and relax. Squeeze and relax. Then give a gentle back and forth. Like with vaginal penetration, the point is not to generate a lot of friction on the sphincter. Instead, explore tugging out just enough to give the internal sphincter a nice massage. Experiment with rocking and grinding—not fucking—motions.

Generally small in-and-out can be very satisfying. If you or your partner wants more in-and-out, you can definitely work up to it. Make sure you have lube on hand to reapply if necessary.

And as always, let the receiver (whether you or your partner) dictate the speed and depth.

People with prostates might enjoy some prostate stimulation with their anal play. Dildos with curves for g-spot stimulation can work equally well for prostate play. It can create a pre-ejaculation feeling that some girls might love and others might really dislike. Ask and try it gently to see which category your partner is in. Even without prostate play, penetration can feel nice. If you want to avoid direct prostate stimulation, play with straight dildos and vibrators instead.

Anal Sex Rules of Thumb

1) **Start slow.** The ass is sensitive. Many of us have uber-tight anal sphincters. Combine those things, and even a little bit of massage can feel like a lot of sensation. The slower you go, the faster you get there.

2) **Flared base! Flared base! Flared base!**

3) **LUBE and LOTS of it.** Your ass doesn't self-lubricate like vaginas do. So you'll need a lot of lube for any sort of anal penetration. Use lots, and use often. Don't be afraid to reapply. What often feels like muscle tightness is exacerbated by friction. Check out the next part of this chapter for advice on lube.

4) **Practice good hygiene.** There are a lot of bacteria that belong in your butt but not anywhere else. Don't penetrate a mouth or vagina with anything that's been in a butt. Vagina to ass? Great. Vagina to Mouth to Ass? Splendid! Ass to vagina? No no no!

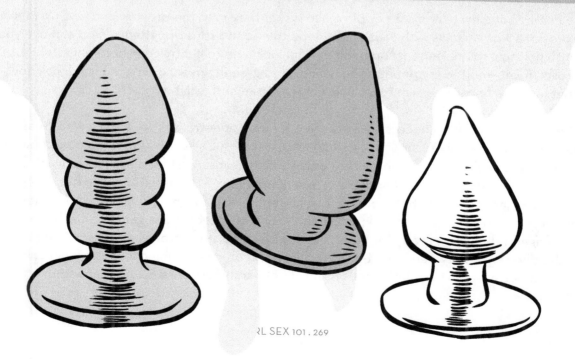

SCENIC VIEWPOINT

ANAL FOR GIRL SEX
by Tristan Taormino

People think that girl sex is all about pussy, pussy, pussy. BUT WHAT ABOUT THE BUTT? Our asses are magical, often under-explored erogenous zones, full of super sensitive nerve endings, forbidden fantasies, and plenty of orgasmic potential. So, take a deep breath, grab a bottle of lube, and meet me at the back door—we're going to talk about safe and pleasurable anal sex.

How do you know if a woman likes anal play? a) She sends you an Anal Bouquet—a tasteful arrangement of roses accompanied by a card that reads "Do My Ass;" b) During enthusiastic cunnilingus when your tongue wanders to her taint, she moans louder, bucks harder; c) You ask her. It may feel like a scary proposition, but talking about anal pleasure will give each of you an opportunity to express your desires, fears, and explore any questions either of you have.

In general, an ass scout is always prepared. If you're worried what you or your partner might run into along the way, take a soapy bath or shower beforehand and go to the bathroom. To get sparkly clean, give yourself a plain water enema at least two hours before you start. It can prevent a messy situation and give you more confidence. (But remember, there are no guarantees, so keep the baby wipes close and your sense of humor even closer.) Speaking of hygiene, a finger or toy should never go directly from ass to pussy. Bacteria from your butt can wreak havoc on your vagina.

The number one mistake most people make is that they rush the process and end up in trouble. Approach a woman's ass with caution, a gentle touch, and tons of patience. You can use your mouth first to explore her anal opening, taking your time to gently coax her sphincter muscles to relax. If you want to try penetration, you might agree in advance on a realistic goal: how about just one finger or a slim toy, plus a great orgasm and call it a night?

Lube isn't just nice, it's a necessary ingredient for anal penetration. Try a thick water-based lube that's the consistency of hair gel or a silicone lube (careful: silicone lube isn't compatible with silicone sex toys). Make sure fingers are butt-friendly (short, well-filed nails are a must!), and use dental dams, gloves, and condoms on toys to prevent STI transmission. To begin, lube up your index finger and touch the pad of it to her anus. Wait for the opening to relax, then slip your finger inside just to the first knuckle and stay there. Let the ass get used to the feeling of your finger. When she's ready for more, begin with some slow strokes. Clitoral stimulation can be the difference between I-don't-get-the-allure and oh-my-fucking-god. Your tongue, her hand, or—even better—a powerful vibrator on the clit can transform anal sex into an intense, full-body experience.

I recommend toys made of non-porous materials like glass, metal, or silicone, which warms to body temperature and can be easily cleaned. Back in the day, anal beads were hard plastic beads on a nylon string. Thankfully, the sex toy industry has evolved, and now the safest, best anal bead toys are made of one continuous piece of material with 5-10 "beads" spaced out along the length of the toy; sometimes the beads are the same size and others get bigger as you move from the end toward the base; beginners should aim for beads similar in size to peanut M&Ms. The idea here is that you coat each bead in lube, and slide them in the ass one at a time. For each bead, the ass relaxes, the bead goes in, and the muscles close around it. Once you have a portion or the entire length of beads in your ass, you can pull the toy out all at once, creating an entirely different sensation!

When you think about anal toys, a butt plug may be the first thing that pops into your head; if you love the feeling of fullness or pressure that comes with having something in your ass—without any in-and-out movement—then consider popping a butt plug in your ass. A classic butt plug shape is the teardrop: tapered at the top, pear-shaped at the widest part, with a slim neck (for the sphincters to close around) above a round/oval flared base. Some butt plugs have a thick mushroom cap-shaped head and a neck that's narrower than the head (but not as narrow as on the teardrop style) that leads to the base. Unless the plug is super slim, you always want to warm up with a finger or two first.

Butt plugs are great for solo play or partner sex, whether you use them on their own or as tools to work your way up to a bigger toy or strap-on anal sex. Try this: slide in a well-lubed plug, then get into a 69 position. As you go down on each other, your arousal builds and the plug-wearer's ass gets used to the feeling of fullness: win-win!

If you crave more thrusting action, any dildo can be used for anal penetration as long as it has a flared base. A slim, smooth dildo (like Tantus Silk) or one without a very bulbous head (like Vixen Creations' Mistress) is a good choice for beginners. Everything you've read about strap-on sex applies to butt sex, with a few caveats: a soft, flexible dildo is best to help you navigate the rectum, which is curved—another reason to approach it with care. If a dildo has a pronounced curve, you should always aim the curved end toward the front of the receiver's body to indirectly stimulate the G-spot. After warming up, place the dildo head at the opening and use your hand to guide it. Have your partner bear down slightly to help the sphincters relax for initial insertion. Penetrating someone's ass while wearing a strap-on is a learned skill, so give yourself some time to get the hang of it.

Tristan Taormino is the author of The Ultimate Guide to Anal Sex for Women and seven other books on sex and relationships. She is the host of Sex Out Loud, a weekly radio show/podcast.

ANAL! LOVE IT? LOATHE IT?

Loathe it in real life.
In fantasy it's a real turn on.

Gotta be in the right mood.

Love giving it, but
don't enjoy receiving
it as much as I enjoy
vaginal penetration.

OFF LIMITS.

ANAL PLAY IS MY FAVORITE KIND OF PLAY.

*Rimming and external stimulation are amazing,
but I don't like being penetrated anally. Happy
to play with partner's butts however they wish!*

Jury's still out.

I enjoy a bit of anal play, but
not much more than a finger
or smaller sized butt plug.

I like the act of submitting,
and breaking the taboo,
but physically don't get
much from the sensation.

Receiving anal sex is second only to
vibrators in my sexual repertoire.
Apparently all the nerves are in
my ass instead of my vagina.

**MY GIRLFRIEND LIKES ANAL SIMULATION, SO
I ALSO ENJOY GIVING PRETTY REGULARLY.
IT OFFERS GREAT POTENTIAL TO TAUNT
HER ABOUT HOW DIRTY A GIRL SHE IS,
SINCE SHE LIKES TO HEAR THAT.**

I want anal sex more than
anything but I have to be very
careful with it as it can trigger
strong panic reactions in me
if I become overwhelmed.

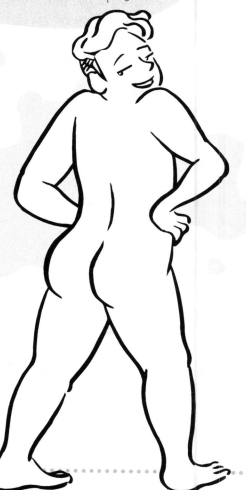

TOY MATERIALS

Stainless Steel

Steel toys are pretty special. They're beautiful, body safe, and easy to clean. Njoy is the leader of the market here. The down side is that steel is as pricey as it is pretty. But if you're down to invest in a basically indestructible piece of shiny sexy pleasure, these toys are great. One of my favorite things about steel is how it responds to temperature. You can make it chilly or warm it up depending on your mood. The weight of these toys can be nice, too.

As we said in the Strap-On chapter, **Silicone** is the queen of dildo materials. It's body safe, it can come in a huge range of colors and shapes, it's easy to clean, and it can be squishy or firm. Silicone is so moldable that it's used to make a lot of different kinds of toys, from insertable vibes to cock rings to anal beads. Some companies are making silicone cheaper by mixing it with other things. The best way to avoid this is by buying from only companies you trust, often those which manufacture in America, where the standards for materials are higher. Check out the Appendix for a list of trusted toy companies and resellers.

Glass/Pyrex

This is another material, like steel, that makes for some very pretty toys. It holds lube really well, so you usually only need a little for a nice and slippery ride. Pyrex is nonporous and dishwasher safe, so it's easy to clean. It's most commonly found in butt plug and dildo shapes. Lucite and acrylic have a similar look to Pyrex, and are more durable than glass, but you can't boil them to clean them.

Hard Plastic

This material is falling out of favor, but it's still easy to find. Hard plastic is good because it's cheap and usually nonporous. You can clean these with soap and water, but don't boil plastic.

Wood

Though some people wrinkle their noses at the thought of wooden toys, these are some of the prettiest and most unique toys on the market. The real deal are made of polished wood and coated with a non-toxic and non-porous sealant, preserving the lovely look of wood while being body safe. Wood has the added bonus of being nice to touch (no chilly steel on your bits) and hard without being uncomfortably so.

There are many toys still made with jelly rubber, especially cock rings and vibrators. But you have other options, so use those other options. I try not to make blanket assertions when talking about sex, but you're going to get one anyway: you don't want jelly rubber in your body. Avoid it.

Nipple clamps

Nipple clamps look like little alligator clips, and are designed to stimulate the nipples without having to use your hands. They come in a variety of styles, but steel tends to be the most popular. Sometimes they're connected with a chain for easy dual-stimulation, and sometimes they have little jewels or vibrators attached. Obviously, nipple clamps are great for people who like nipple play. Clamps can be gentle or super pinchy depending on the style. Some can be adjusted to provide different amounts of pressure.

HOW TO BUY SEX TOYS

First, it's important to find a body-safe, sex-positive retailer. Check out the Appendix for our suggestions.

Don't be afraid to ask for what you want. Sex toy store employees generally have a passion and joy for connecting people with toys that make them feel good. They are, in many ways, the sexual booksellers of your dreams, matching a passionate person with a passion-delivery vehicle. You can make their job easier by being direct and unabashed.

I like anal penetration with heavy vibration and hate the color pink. Where's my aisle?!

If you don't know what exactly you want, think about sensation. Do you want clitoral stimulation? Or deep penetration? Do you want to explore anal or vaginal or both? Do you want to learn how to squirt? Or do you want something easy to use with a partner? Start with the seeds of desire, and you'll be able to head in the right direction.

Be a Noob. There's a first time for everything. Even experts have their first times. Pretending you know everything is a terrible way to learn anything new.

Ask questions.

Google wantonly.

Try new things.

Invest in the good stuff. You get what you pay for. And professional tools create professional results. Once you know what kind of sensations you want, save your pennies and get a good reliable toy from an ethical, quality company.

 If you're afraid of throwing away big money on a toy you don't like, you can get the cheap-o version of a style of toy you're curious about and once you know you dig the feeling, toss the old toy and buy the nice version of that style. No, it's not great for the environment, and no it might not be great for your body, but you can at least take a toy for a test drive first.

Don't let your eyes be bigger than your stomach (or vagina). Sex toy stores are buffets for your genitals. Don't overindulge—or in this case, buy a toy you can't actually handle. Start modest and then progress to the fist-sized triple penetrator with kung-fu grip.

I bought my first vibrator from one of those strip-mall sex stores in rural Ohio. There wasn't much to choose from; the store sold mostly porn and cheap lingerie. Even as a precocious 18-year-old sex geek, I had no clue what I was doing or looking for. I chose a silver-painted wand that reminded me of the Terminator films. It cost $12 and lasted about a year before becoming a dullish looking paperweight. You, my dear readers, are blessed with the Internet and no shortage of options, even if the only sex toy store in your grasp exists on the web. Check out the appendix, log on, and start getting excited.

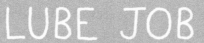

LUBE JOB

Like an engine needs oil, sex needs lubrication. Lubrication helps ease friction so skin can move against skin in sexy and pleasurable ways. Lube can come in a variety of forms: sweat, spit, vaginal fluid, etc. In this chapter, we're going to talk about the bottled kind.

Of all the parts of the genital system, the only thing that naturally lubricates is the vagina. Surgically-installed vaginas can self-lubricate, but generally not nearly as much as factory-installed ones. Regardless of how you got your vag, bottled lube is your friend.

 A healthy vagina always has a little bit of moisture. Regular, unaroused vaginas vary in their moisture by a number of factors, such as:

- How much water you drink
- How much alcohol and caffeine you drink
- Where you are in your monthly cycle
- Ambient temperature
- Exercise
- How old you are (menopause often dramatically shifts the amount of natural lubricant a person makes)
- The kind of clothes you're wearing
- The amount of pubic hair you have
- How recently you bathed
- Hormone levels (especially testosterone)
- Stress levels
- Marijuana or antihistamine use

 During arousal, the amount of natural lubrication generated by the vagina usually increases. This can be a lot or a little depending on the above factors and also:

- Duration of foreplay
- Kind of foreplay
- Mental versus physical arousal. (Some people can "think" themselves wet. Others need direct genital stimulation before the flood gates open.)

Long thought to be the #1 indicator of arousal state (kind of an analogue to a penis's erection), the unfortunate reality is that while arousal and wetness do correlate a little, it's not nearly as cut and dry (pun not intended) as we've been taught. A person can be dry as the Mojave and really turned on. Or they can be wet as the Pacific and ambivalent.

When it comes to sexy time, the important thing to keep in mind is just because you or your partner isn't gushing from go, doesn't mean things are going south. That's what words are for. Lubrication helps increase sensation and reduce friction. A good driver always keeps lube nearby, for her pleasure and your peace of mind.

There are three basic types of lubricants: Silicone-based, Water-based, and Oil.

WATER-BASED LUBE is the most popular. It's cheap, easy to find, good for toys, and generally okay for most bodies. Sometimes these lubes (especially the cheap ones) contain parabens, which can cause mild sensitivities in some people (usually swelling or itchiness). Try to get paraben-free if possible. Propylene Glycol is often an additive to cheaper lubes and can irritate tissue. Recent studies show Prop Glycol may increase HIV transmission. One downside to water-based lubes is that the body absorbs water, so if you're fooling around for a while, you may need to reapply. This is especially true for butt sex, since the anus is such an absorbent organ. Water-based lube also rinses away easily, so it's not great for shower sex, but it makes for easy cleanup. It comes in some different consistencies like gel, liquid, and creme.

SILICONE is an increasingly popular lube. It's a large-moleculed polymer, which means it doesn't get absorbed by the body, so it stays slippery forever. I'm going to repeat that: It stays slippery for-ever. This means you'll stay lube-y until you wash with soap and water. This can make for some weird squishy feelings the day after sex. It's inert and won't hurt you, but it can feel a little weird for some folks. It's also great for shower sex, because it doesn't rinse away easily, but BE CAREFUL, because it can make the shower floor or whatever super slick, and that's dangerous.

It's also *not* good for silicone toys. Silicone toys and silicone lube don't like each other. Actually, it's the opposite—they like each other way too much. The silicone in the lube and the silicone in the toy will bond, making the toy degrade over time and get a weird tacky texture. No good for a toy you may have just dropped $70 on. If you want to play with toys, wrap them in condoms, or just switch to a water-based lube.

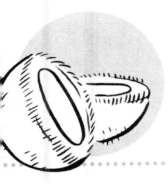

FOOD-GRADE OIL is great for non-barrier sex (that is, sex without gloves, condoms or dams). Coconut oil is the paragon of food oils. This is because it stays slippery, has a really yummy taste and smell (your goods will smell like a piña colada!) and is generally safe for people who don't have specific food allergies. However, oil will degrade latex, so you can't use it with latex gloves, condoms, or dams. Only use food-grade oils on your bits. No mineral oils or petroleum jellies! If you wouldn't want it in your mouth, don't put it in your twat.

A FEW MORE WARNINGS:

GLYCERIN is a relative of sugar and is often found in water-based lubes. Sugar and vaginas are mortal enemies. Don't use glycerin in your vagina unless you want to risk a gnarly yeast infection*. You can use glycerin for anal sex, or for analingus or blowjobs, since it tastes, well, sugary. But no glycerin in vaginas, no glycerin in vaginas, no glycerin in vaginas!

When you're buying lube, avoid stuff that comes in tubs (that you have to scoop out with your hands). Especially if you're not monogamously partnered. Tubs are a typical container for coconut oil and similar things. Go for pump bottles (easy with one hand), squeeze bottles (easy to transport), or individual packets (sometimes hard to open, but handy in a pinch). If you do go with a tub, use a spoon, not your fingers. This will reduce risk for contaminating the lube with your juices (especially true if the coconut oil is going back in the pantry afterwards!).

Also, learn to read labels and find retailers you can trust. Most feminist sex toy stores have policies around carrying body-safe products, and most of these stores have online shops, so if you're not near one, you can call or visit online and get good info. Many lubes come in packet form, too, so you can try before you invest in a 20-gallon tub of the stuff. (See the Appendix for Girl Sex 101-approved online retailers).

---

* Though it's widely speculated, there aren't any studies supporting the belief that glycerin itself causes yeast infections, If you love a glycerin lube and it doesn't hurt you, go ahead and use it. Otherwise, avoid it.

How To Read Lube Labels
by Sarah Mueller, The Smitten Kitten

When hunting for the perfect lubricant it can help to understand what packaging and ingredients mean for you! Here are some tried & true tips for lubricant lovers of discerning taste:

First, know that packaging on lubricant is there to sell products. In most cases if a lube is marketed to a specific gender or type of sexual act, that's a selling point, but not a rule! If you can pronounce everything on the label, or there is a short ingredients list, that's usually a good sign.

Also, check the fine print and ingredient list. For example, if using organic products is important to you, look closely. Many lubes with "organic(s)" on the label contain some organic ingredients, but are not 100% organic. Often, the water in water-based lubricants is difficult to certify as organic, so some lubricant manufacturers use "natural" to describe organic ingredients that are not certified.

Buying lube from a trusted retailer that makes sex education and pleasure their focus can simplify things; retailers like this can typically provide you with customer reviews along with informed answers to any questions you may have, plus they've already done all the research for you!

Next, really read the ingredients list, keeping a look out for some potential red flags:

Glycerin (aka Glycerol or glycerine) is a common ingredient in lubricants and should be avoided by people with sensitive skin, or who plan on putting their lubricant inside of a vagina. Glycerin is a sugar alcohol that can upset the vaginal pH and exacerbate yeast infections, or, in high concentrations, cause damage to mucous membranes. More often than not it just feels sticky or tacky. Glycerin can be plant- or animal-based, although animal-based glycerins are extremely uncommon in skin care products.

Petroleum-based oils, or synthetic oils, should be avoided in lubricants being used for any sort of penetrative play, as they are not cleaned out of the body naturally as fast as water-based products and can promote the breeding of bacteria inside of the body.

Parabens, ingredients that are used as preservatives, can mimic estrogen and act as endocrine (hormone) disruptors. The most common parabens in lubricants are Methylparaben and Propylparaben, and these are typically only found in water-based or hybrid lubricants.

Propylene Glycol, often added to lubricants to aid in water retention and absorption, can cause irritation on sensitive skin, and some studies have indicated continuous exposure to propylene glycol can lead to a propylene glycol allergy.

Vitamin E Additives (aka Tocopheryl Acetate) are generally good for your skin, unless you have severe soy or gluten allergies. Vitamin E additives are often derived from either wheat germ oil or soy oil, and lubricants with these ingredients may contain trace amounts of soy or gluten.

Grapefruit Seed Extract (a.k.a. Citrus Seed Extract or Citrus Grandis): Often marketed as a natural anti-microbial, this is generally considered safe in small amounts; however they're poorly regulated and have been found to contain synthetic contaminants which may cause skin irritation, especially on sensitive skin and mucous membranes.

Diazolidinyl Urea is an antimicrobial preservative that functions as a formaldehyde releaser and should not be used for penetration or against a mucous membrane. Continuous use of products containing diazolidinyl urea may lead to an allergy to this ingredient.

Benzocaine is used as a numbing agent, and a similar ingredient, Benzoic acid, produces a milder sensation and can be found in stimulating products. Using a numbing lube is never recommended; if your body is experiencing pain you should listen!

Most lubricants are vegan, but if this is critical to you, take a closer look at your label. Many oil-based lubes contain beeswax or a derivative wax that may not be vegan. Glycerin and urea can be plant– or animal-based, which might not necessarily be information made available on the packaging. Also, if you want to be sure your lubricant hasn't been tested on animals, you may have to do some extra research. Very few lubricants include testing information on their labels, and any lubricants that have FDA approval have most likely been tested on animals at some point in their production.

If you or anyone who may come in contact with your lubricant has allergies or skin sensitivities, always read an ingredient list thoroughly. Even the most pure or organic lubes may contain an allergen!

*Sarah Mueller is a sex educator at The Smitten Kitten,
a progressive sex toy store in Minneapolis, MN.*

LUBE RULES OF THE ROAD

SILICONE
- Stays slippery forever
- Generally-body safe
- Don't use directly on silicone toys

WATER
- Safe for toys
- Will lose its lube-iness. Usually have to reapply or revive with a little water
- Sometimes loaded with other gunk, so learn to read labels...

  GLYCERIN
  - Sweet-tasting
  - Stays lubey longer
  - Not to be used in or near vaginas

FOOD-GRADE OIL
- Safe for most bodies
- Edible and slippery
- Not to be used with latex

WANNA GO FOR A RIDE!?

So you're getting all sexy and you're wondering....
when to bring up the lube?

Here are some options:
- Have it on the bedside table so your partner knows it's there.
- As soon as things move to genital stimulation, ask if your partner would like some lube.
- As soon as you want lube for your own body, ask for it.
- If you don't have lube handy (bad girl!), use your own spit on your body, and let your partner use her own on hers. This is especially important if you two haven't had your safer sex talk yet or if you haven't been tested in a while.

Everyone has different preferences for different kinds of lubes. Some people like flavors and some don't. Some like oil and some prefer water-based. It's all good as long as you know what you like and how to use it. And it's a good idea to have a selection on hand in case your partner is feeling one way or another.

And remember, there is NO SHAME in needing or wanting extra lubrication. Not generating natural lube doesn't make you less of a woman, and not making your partner soak the sheets doesn't make you less of a lover. Lube, like toys, music, and a comfy bed, is just part of a good time. So lube up and get that engine revving.

SANTA BARBARA

DAY 6

Layla and Jamie sit at a picnic table outside a taqueria, munching on shrimp burritos. "Oh California burritos, I missed you so," Layla singsongs.

Jamie smiles and sips from her beer. Layla smiles back. For a moment it feels like it used to in the best moments of their relationship. "Let's get married," Layla says, mouth half-full.

Jamie snorts. "Are you saying this because you love me or because you want citizenship?"

Layla swallows and sips from her beer, scrutinizing Jamie. "Both."

"I know that look," Jamie says. "It's your way of contemplating the future."

Layla shrugs and takes a swig from her beer. "You know me too well."

"Do you really think we could stand being married to each other?"

"Our relationship was great!" Layla says.

"Until it wasn't. Then it suuuuuucked."

Layla reluctantly acknowledges the comment with a half shrug, then turns her attention back to her burrito. To the west, the sound of traffic mixed with the sound of the ocean creates a steady, inseparable drone. "I dunno. You're fun to adventure with."

"I'm alright," Jamie says. "But you're a shark. You can only breathe when you're moving."

"You're a clown fish. You like your space."

"My own little anemone to call home." Jamie laughs.

Layla takes a hearty bite and nods. "Let's get a hotel tonight."

"I can't afford that."

"I can. It's fine. Let's treat ourselves to a shower and cable TV and clean sheets."

"Hmmm," Jamie says, chewing. "Sounds romantic."

Layla grins. "If we're not careful..."

· ·

In the hotel, both girls sit in their underwear on the bed, attention on their computers. Layla's curiosity piques each time Jamie's laptop beeps with emails delayed by their detour off the grid.

"Anything good?" Layla asks.

Jamie scrolls. "A mix of pointless ads and job postings. Sergio says they're blushing at the comments on the video and that it looks amazing."

Layla bites back a snarky response.

"Then there's a final one with the subject, Permission to Gush?"

"Another ex?"

"No, I don't know this person." Jamie says. "Can I read this to you?"

"Go for it."

"Hi Jamie, I hope this doesn't sound weird, but I've been enjoying your videos quite a lot. I'm new to the whole 'lesbian scene thing' and am pretty shy in general. Your videos are beautiful and communicate something about sex that's hard to get from porn. I feel like I'm learning about sex in a completely different way through your videos. I hope you'll keep posting. It's fun for me to learn while watching you from the cozy blue light of my laptop at home. I love your newest video, with the sexy sounds superimposed over the shot of the ocean. I shared this one on my video networking site.

I hope that's alright. It's getting a lot of great feedback. Thought you might want to check it out. That said—and here's where I know I sound weird—I'd really love to take you to out for coffee when you're in LA, which, if your estimates are correct, is this Saturday. I promise I'm not a weirdo. Well, I'm a weirdo, but a lovable one. Anyway, maybe let me buy you a coffee and show you around town? Best, Angela Borgesse"

"Borgesse?" Layla asks.

"Like Jorge Luis? The playwright?"

"Or like Cyborg?" Layla says.

Jamie falls silent as she re-reads the email.

"Is it weird?" Layla asks.

Jamie shakes her head. "If anything's weird, it's how flattered I feel. I kinda got in my mind that my art was all bullshit. Even if it is bullshit, it's nice to know that someone out there likes it."

"You going to meeting her?" Layla asks.

Jamie reads aloud as she types. "Hi Angela. Thanks for your email. I will be in LA tomorrow. Let's get coffee. Why not? Anything for a fan. Winky face."

"You're not going to put her in one of your videos, are you?"

Jamie turns her laptop to face Layla, displaying a page of Google results. "Maybe. She's cute."

"Slut."

"Whatever, jerk." Jamie playfully pushes Layla. They wrestle and kiss. Jamie rubs Layla's breasts and kisses her neck. Layla's wet already, wanting it quick and hard.

Layla pushes back into Jamie, gripping handfuls of her flesh. Their legs intertwine, and they grind on each other's thighs. Jamie flings Layla onto her back.

Layla moans, then says, "Wait." She reaches to her laptop. "Gotta put this out of the line of fire," she says, giggling.

Layla starts clamping her computer shut then stops to read. Jamie moves down Layla's body, pulling her underwear aside and kissing her labia.

Layla opens her legs and clicks the email.

Hey Layla, This is a weird thing to have to write, but...

Jamie runs her tongue against Layla's opening, gliding up to her clit. Layla moans, her focus pulled in two directions.

...I found a spot on my vulva this morning. I have herpes, but I wasn't having an outbreak when we hooked up, so I didn't think it was a big deal...

Jamie rubs her tongue against Layla's clit and cups her hands around her ass.

...I'm on suppressive therapy, which reduces my likelihood of transmission, but you may want to get tested soon. Thanks again for a nice night. Best, Clover.

Layla moves her computer to the floor and lies back. "Shit," she groans.

Jamie presses harder, moving Layla's clit in tight, thrilling circles.

Layla squeezes her pc muscles, sending chills of pleasure throughout her body. "Fuck, that feels good," she says. "Fuck, yes."

Jamie eases her finger into Layla's vagina and strokes.

"Mmmmmm...wait."

"Huh?" Jamie asks.

"Stop."

"You're so close," Jamie says.

"Yeah, I know. But stop."

Jamie pulls back and eases up to her elbows.

Layla reaches for her laptop. "You should read this email."

VENTURA

SEX GEEK

DAY 7

Layla listens to dubstep through one earbud. She taps the steering wheel with the beat. The sun is just starting to set. She squints as it drops into the top of the windshield. The highway climbs over a golden hill and the speedometer slows to 55. The van rumbles up the rise.

Layla fumbles for her sunglasses and tosses them on. The road is overwhelmed by the orange glare of the sun. She focuses on the white dashed lane markings to avoid running off the road. Jamie's forehead is pressed against the window. Her skull rocks on the glass with each bump in the road.

The road takes a turn south, and the sun ducks behind a hilltop. Layla's vision adjusts, and she sees a figure on the side of the road just as the rumble strip on the shoulder jars her to lucidity. Jamie wakes, shouting. Layla swerves the back into the lane. Jamie shouts again as the van narrowly avoids grazing the man's shoulder.

Layla slams on the brakes and eases onto the shoulder.

"Jeez!" Jamie shouts one more time.

"Are you okay?" Layla asks.

Jamie takes a deep breath and nods.

Layla looks in her rearview mirror and sees the man wave. She gets out of the van.

"Sorry!" she shouts.

The man walks to her, blond hair and glasses accompanying a big goatee-d grin. He wears a shirt emblazoned with the words SEX GEEK. He waves away her concerns. "I'm fine. All limbs intact."

Jamie slides out from the passenger seat, jumpy and blurry eyed.

Layla smiles. "Where you headed?"

"I ran out of gas about a mile back. I need to make it to LA by seven."

"That's where we're going."

Jamie shoots Layla a look. Layla ignores her. "I'm Layla," she says, holding out her hand.

The man grasps her hand and shakes it. "Reid," he says.

"What's in LA?" Layla asks.

"I'm teaching a workshop in West Hollywood," he says.

"Are you gay?" Layla asks.

"Layla!" Jamie scolds.

"Sorry. But are you gay?"

The man smiles. "Occasionally."

"Cool. Do you need a ride to a gas station?"

He looks a little surprised. "That would be great."

Jamie snatches the keys from Layla's hand. "I'll drive."

Five minutes later Olive is back on the road.

"So, sex geek," Layla says, turning in her seat. "What does that mean?"

Reid perches on a suitcase in the back. "I'm a sex educator. I travel around the country teaching people about sex and relationships."

Jamie glances in the rearview mirror. "Like what?"

Reid shrugs, "Oral sex, open relationships, threesomes."

Jamie makes a face and a small sound of disgust.

"Don't mind her," Layla says. "She's feeling prudish today because she's afraid she got herpes last night."

"Oh," Reid says. "You want to talk about it?"

"Jeez, Layla!" Jamie shouts. "It's because this jerk had sex with someone who didn't disclose in advance."

"And then we had sex two days later," Layla says, gesturing to Jamie.

"You didn't talk about safer sex?" Reid asks.

Layla turns back to face front. She fiddles with the frayed edge of her shorts. "It's so awkward."

Reid smiles at Jamie through the rearview mirror and Jamie returns it, weakly.

"Would you like to hear my Safer Sex Elevator Speech?"

Layla makes a face. "N'aw, dude. We're not those types of queers."

"I'm not hitting on you," Reid says. "If you can't talk about this stuff with people you don't want to screw, how can you do it with people you do?"

SAFER SEX

The good news is, all said, girl sex is a fairly safe endeavor. You probably won't get pregnant from it, and because of the limited fluid exchange of a lot of girl sex, exposure to sexually transmitted infections (STIs) can be easily mitigated. But, just as with anatomy and labels, being in the know is sexy. Even sexier is when you can talk about this stuff with your current and future sex partners.

Here's what you're going to learn in this chapter:

1) The different kinds of STIs (often called "STDs" for "sexually transmitted *diseases*") and how they're transmitted.

2) What risks certain acts have. Just like visiting a certain country or playing a certain sport, it's just a good idea to know what to expect, even if worst case scenarios are unlikely.

3) What you can do to mitigate risks.

4) How to determine your status and when to get tested.

5) How to figure out your boundaries and protocols.

6) How to communicate your status and boundaries.

All together, I'm calling this **Girl Sex Risk Assessment**.

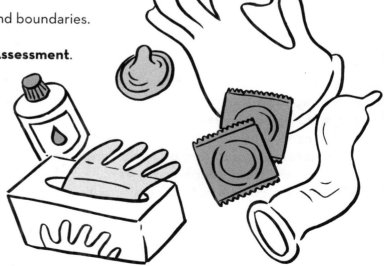

WHAT ARE STIs?
HOW ARE THEY TRANSMITTED?

Sexually Transmitted Infections are viruses and bacterial infections that can be transmitted through sexual contact. While sex is a good way to transmit all sorts of things (like the common cold, for instance), STIs are usually only or most likely transmitted via sexual contact. Some STIs are transmitted through blood, some through genital fluids (precum, semen, vaginal secretions, and female ejaculate), some through saliva, some through breast milk, and some through skin/skin contact.

These are the main ones:

HIV

HIV should be on your radar if you enjoy blood play, or unprotected Penis/Vagina or Penis/Anus sex. But despite all the horror stories, HIV is easy to avoid if you play responsibly. That means use a barrier (either an internal or external condom) for P/V or P/A sex. Don't share needles (this goes for heroin or speed AND piercing play or at-home tattoos).

Use gloves if you have a partner who's tested positive, and use a dental dam or condom for oral sex. The rate of transmission is low for oral sex, but it's often better to go overboard with protection than freak out the next morning.

If you think you've been exposed, visit your local clinic or hospital and ask for a PEP (post-exposure prophylactic), which can help protect you from contracting the virus, even if it made its way into your body.

HPV

This is what your doctor is testing for with a Pap smear. Some strains (about 15 of the 120-plus varieties of the virus) can lead to cervical or other genital cancers, though most cancers are caused by only 2 strains. A different 2 strains cause 90% of genital warts. And the rest are often inert: either just hanging out but not causing symptoms or discomfort, or eventually fought off by your immune system. There's a vaccine called Gardasil that protects against the cervical cancer one for people who fit a certain profile. Ask your doctor about it.

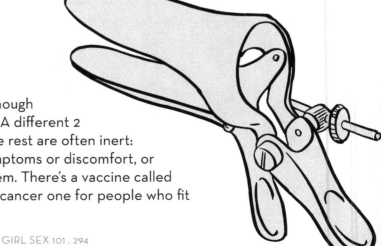

Annoyingly, there's not a whole lot of decisive information about transmission. As of 2014, male-assigned people can't even get tested for it (though in some places they can get the vaccine). It sucks. But here's what we do know: women who have unprotected penis/vagina sex are at a greater risk. Get the vaccine if you can, get a PAP smear every so often, and talk to your sex partners about it.

The best precautions are to avoid direct genital/genital contact and don't penetrate yourself with anything that penetrated your partner unless you wash it well and/or switch out the barrier (this includes fingering yourself if you just fingered her. Wash your hands or put on a glove if you're going to do that).

HEPATITIS

Hepatitis is an inflammation of the liver. Hep A, B, & C all have similar symptoms though they're caused by different viruses. Hep A is spread by ingesting feces (as can happen with unprotected rimming), Hep B by ingesting infected blood or other body fluid (like semen or vaginal fluid) and Hep C is transmitted by ingesting blood. Hep A & B have vaccines, and many people now are vaccinated while quite young. Hep C doesn't have a vaccine yet. The key to avoiding or managing Hepatitis is knowing your status and knowing the status of your partners. When in doubt, use barriers for all oral sex, as well as genital/genital contact.

Menstrual fluid is about half blood. This means it can put you at risk for Hep C. Be especially cautious of eating out your partner while it's her Shark Week. Want to go to town even when it's a-flowin'? Use barriers, get tested, and get vaccinated.

HERPES

If you think you don't have herpes, you're probably wrong. It's estimated that about 1 in 4 American women have HSV-2 (most commonly associated with genital herpes), and 58% of all Americans have HSV-1 (most often oral) herpes. Most people are asymptomatic, which means they'll never have an outbreak, and they'll never really know they have the virus. Like warts (the kinds you get on your fingers, not your goods), the virus just hangs out in your body not doing much until you're sick, stressed, or otherwise immunosuppressed.

While this may freak you out, the good news is herpes is really a dermatological problem. It can cause potentially embarrassing and/or painful cold sores (a.k.a "fever blisters") on your lips or on your genitals, but it's not going to kill you, and it may not even cause discomfort. Unless you're planning on giving birth when you're having an outbreak, it's not something to be super concerned about. Most doctors don't test for it unless you get an outbreak, and when you get a standard STI panel at a clinic, the test usually isn't included.

Herpes is spread via skin to skin contact, like kissing (hence its prevalence), and it's most easily transmitted 2 weeks before sores appear. The best approach: 1) Avoid direct contact with anyone's sores. 2) Ask your partner if they get cold sores at all. 3) Take care of your body and keep your immune system in good shape. 4) Use barriers for oral sex.

CHLAMYDIA, GONORRHEA, & SYPHILLIS
These are bacterial infections that are treated with antibiotics. There's some recent info about a antibiotic-resistant strain of gonorrhea, so again, it's better never to catch it rather than have to deal with treating it. But as of this writing it's still totally treatable.

You can get these from fluid exchange, like oral sex or direct genital/genital contact. You can protect yourself by using barriers for oral sex and genital/genital sex.

TRICHOMONIASIS is a parasite that is transmitted via sexual contact and causes 3.7 million infections each year. It's likewise treated with antibiotics. Symptoms are rarer in male-assigned folks, so they can often be carriers without knowing it. As always, get tested regularly and use barriers to reduce your risk.

HOW CAN I PREVENT CATCHING AN STI?

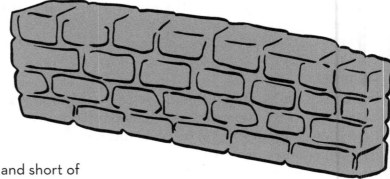

Using barriers minimizes fluid exchange, and short of abstinence, it's one of the best ways to mitigate your risk. Typical barriers are gloves, dental dams, and condoms. These come in both latex and nitrile. Check in with your partner if they have latex allergies before you use a barrier.

Gloves

Gloves are great for hand sex. They protect your partner from long or sharp fingernails, hold onto lube better, and cover up any small cuts you might have. They also make sex easier because you can touch yourself with the same hand simply by removing or replacing the glove. They come in latex and nitrile, and an assortment of colors to avoid that "dentist" feel. Good times.

External Condoms

Not just for peens! You can also use an external condom on a dildo or vibrator, which keeps them cleaner (especially for porous toys). And yes you can use them on penises, too.

Internal Condoms

Often called the "female condom," this is a larger, looser condom that goes inside the receiver. The edge of the internal condom hangs outside the body, so they actually do a better job of covering more skin than regular condoms, making them a good option for preventing skin-transmitted STIs like HPV. You can put one in up to 6 hours ahead of any sexy time and leave it in until you're ready to remove it. It works in in both vaginas and anuses, to double your pleasure.

Dental Dams

Dental dams are thin pieces of latex or nitrile that act as a barrier for cunnilingus or analingus. To use one, just lay it flat against your partner's vulva so it covers the whole thing, hold it in place, and go to town. If you don't know how to use a dental dam, you're not alone. Dental dam use isn't very common, but that doesn't mean you shouldn't know how to use one.

Want to use a barrier for cunnilingus or analingus but don't have a dental dam lying around?
Use a condom!

Here's how to make a dental dam from any ol' condom.
Materials: Condom & Sharp Scissors

Step 1:
Cut the tip off the condom, and cut the ring off the base, creating a cylinder.

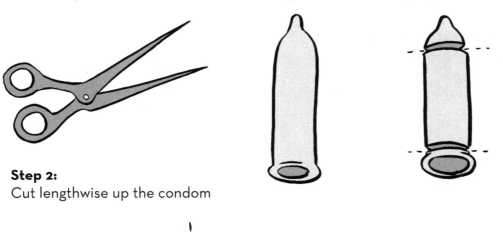

Step 2:
Cut lengthwise up the condom

Step 3:
Unroll and enjoy!

HINT:
You can also use plastic wrap! Kitchen queens unite!

All of this info is great, but it doesn't mean much unless you know your status. The only way to really know what's going on down there is if you get tested. Many STIs don't cause symptoms until they've progressed, and these are the kinds of things you want to nip in the bud. Your normal primary care physician or gynecologist can usually administer the tests. Just say you want an STD screening/panel. Insurance usually covers it unless you want a test that isn't usually covered (like herpes blood test if you've never had an outbreak).

Getting tested can be nerve-wracking, especially if you don't know what to expect. I've been getting tested regularly since I was eighteen and I still get nervous when I wait for my results, even if I haven't engaged in any risky behavior. Know that it's normal to be nervous. But what's more important is learning your status. Blissful ignorance doesn't last long. Most STIs are easily treatable and manageable, but only if you catch them early.

What does an STI test look like?

A complete STI test usually looks like a
   1) blood draw
   2) an oral swab
   3) a urine test and
   4) a Pap smear (for cervix-owners)

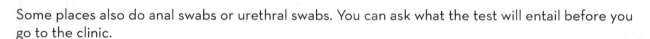

Some places also do anal swabs or urethral swabs. You can ask what the test will entail before you go to the clinic.

Many clinics around the U.S. have drop-in screenings. Most of these places have anonymous or confidential services (if your state allows it), as well as treatment and education programs. Some of these programs administer questionnaires along with the test. This is because many of these programs are grant funded, and require statistical reporting as part of their funding terms. You're always allowed to ask if there's a questionnaire and how they use the data they collect. To find the free and cheap testing centers near you visit hivtest.cdc.gov or call your local LGBT center.

Some results are available immediately, as with Rapid HIV tests. Sometimes your samples have to be sent away for testing, and you can get the results by phone or coming back to the clinic. Any reputable clinic will give you all the info you need to get your results and ensure your privacy. You can also get tested by your regular doctor. Just ask for a full STI panel.

When should I get tested?

Get tested as soon as you start being sexually active. Then, get tested about 2 weeks after each new partner or after any risky encounters (e.g. un-barrier-ed sex, disclosure of an STI by a partner). Get tested right away if you have any odd symptoms, or every six to eight months if you're otherwise healthy.

What if I haven't been tested & there's this hottie..?

A good rule of thumb if you don't know your status is behave as though you *do* have STIs. That is, use barriers, discuss protocols, and tell your partner you don't know your status.

I tested positive! Now what?

If you test positive for an STI, your doctor or clinician will give you treatment options. This can look like medication, a "wait and see" approach, or maintenance tips. As a responsible sex-haver, you should contact anyone you've had sexual contact with to let them know your status. Stigma and silence are what allow STIs to spread. So let your partners know what's up so they can take care of their bodies and partners, too.

WHAT IS A SAFER SEX PROTOCOL? HOW DO I DETERMINE MINE?

Safer Sex Protocol is what you need to feel both emotionally and physically safe in bed. These protocols are different for everyone and often change based on your relationship status, your partner's needs and disclosures, your general sense of health and wellbeing, and your preferred modes of sexual play.

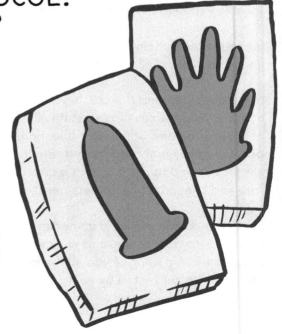

The key to being happy with your protocols is that they're in alignment with your sense of safety and integrity. For instance, if the mere idea of herpes squicks you out, it's probably a good idea for you to avoid kissing anyone who hasn't been tested for herpes. Or you could be okay with hand sex or toys for a one-night stand, but you only have oral sex with people you're serious about.

Your protocol can look like:

- Certain acts are reserved for a certain depth or duration of a relationship.

- Requirements for your partner's testing status.

- A "getting to know you" period before you get naked with anyone.

- Choosing partners whom you trust deeply.

- Choosing partners who have a solid ability to have safer sex conversations.

- ...Or more. It's up to you. It's your body. Treat it with the respect it deserves.

WHAT ARE YOUR SAFER SEX PROTOCOLS?

Birth control pills, external condoms, internal condoms.

Condoms, dental dams, gloves. Know the risk factors of different acts. Cover toys.

MONOGAMY.

I DON'T HAVE SEX WHEN I HAVE A HERPES BREAKOUT.

I've been in a committed relationship for two years. We got tested at the beginning of our relationship, and now we get tested as part of a regular annual doctor checkup.

Condoms, latex gloves, open discussion before things get heated.

No sex until a STI screening. Until the results are back, just kissing, massage, masturbation.

Condoms, dental dams, gloves. Know the risk factors of different acts. Cover toys.

TALKING, GETTING TESTED REGULARLY, NOT SHARING TOYS. NOT HAVING DRUNKEN HOOK-UPS WITH STRANGERS ANYMORE!

Fluid bonded with my husband. Condom usage for anyone with a penis/penis-like toy. Dental dams with my trans woman partner (by her other partner's request, not mine). Before anything other than kissing and cuddling happen, risk factors are always discussed, as well as STI history and testing protocols.

We have to have discussed things beforehand: consent, safe words, fluid bonding.

Phew! Okay. That was a lot of information. Which is all well and good, but how do you talk about this stuff? Communication is the point, right? Read on...

EMOTIONAL SAFETY VS. PHYSICAL SAFETY

Physical safety is fairly straightforward: preservation of your physical health and bodily integrity.

Emotional safety can be more nebulous: preservation of your emotional integrity and mental health.

You can engage in play that's physically safe, but is emotionally edgy (cheating, for instance, or exploring kink).

Similarly, you might feel emotionally safe (perhaps in a monogamous partnership) but your physical safety is compromised if your partner has an undiagnosed STI.

Knowing the difference between physical and emotional safety is key to negotiating safer sex boundaries. And for sex to be good and consensual, you need to be able to get both your physical and emotional safety needs met. If you don't know that a protocol need you have is really an emotional safety thing, not a physical one, it can be hard to communicate with your partner(s) why you need something.

How do you figure out your emotional needs? Consider your emotional situation. Are you partnered? Single? Seeking a partner? Playing the field? A sex partner doesn't have to be the mirror image of your emotional needs, but they need to be able to hear where you're coming from and support you in it.

The bottom line is, your boundaries are your own. You get to decide what makes you feel safe. You can have übersafe sex by using gloves, condoms, and dental dams, and not kissing. Or you can trust in your partners to get tested and report their status to you and not use any barriers at all. It's your body, and it's your choice. You get to define your boundaries, and you can negotiate them with your partners if you want. But don't feel bad about any of them. As long as you've thought it through, they're yours and they're fine.

When it comes to physical safer sex protocols, here are some common options:

Barriers for everything and no kissing
The safest safe sex you can have while still touching another person's body. You use gloves for hand sex, dental dams for oral, and condoms for penetration with toys/dildos. No fluid exchange at all because you won't be kissing.

Barriers for everything but kissing
Same as above but with kissing. This exposes you to herpes and possibly gonorrhea of the throat.

Barriers for oral sex
This can help prevent gonorrhea of the throat, HPV, and genital herpes transmission.

Barriers for toys
Barriers for toys are great if you're going to share toys with your partner during sex. Switching out a barrier will help prevent transmission of things via genital/genital contact.

Barriers for genital/genital contact (scissoring or P/V[A] sex)
Scissoring and P/V(A) sex are the least safe girl sex acts, because they involve direct genital/genital contact. If you have penetrative sex with an attached cock, barriers (either internal or external condoms) will help prevent pregnancy. Using barriers for P/V and scissoring will also reduce risk of STI transmission.

No barriers
People in monogamous or closed relationships often choose no barriers. This can be done safely if you're both STI-free and don't have sex with other people. Others who choose to have sex without barriers may do so by having a conversation with their partners about their status. This works best when you trust your partners to get tested regularly (especially after having sex with new people) and you get tested regularly, and both of you can communicate your statuses. If you have P/V sex, though, you're still going to have to figure out contraception.

TOBI'S TRANS-MISSION

PREGNANCY RISK: DON'T IGNORE IT, DON'T PANIC

I get the sense that a common experience for cis queer women with terrible school sex education classes is basically, "Wow, pregnancy sounds terrible and could ruin my life, good thing I don't have to pay attention because none of my partners will ever get me pregnant." Then if you date a trans woman later on, suddenly all those scare tactics comes flooding back but without any of the information you didn't pay attention to (or weren't given).

If that's you, here's what you need to know: sperm is not magic. It doesn't fly through clothing. It doesn't invisibly hide under your fingernails and get you pregnant when you go to the bathroom later. Keep in mind trans women often have complicated emotional relationships to semen too. If you freak out about pregnancy when you get some cum on your fingers, that might make her feel shitty about herself. Instead get yourself some information so you don't have to panic about little things that really won't get you pregnant.

That said, I've known some couples who go overboard in the other direction and assume that being on hormones means that pregnancy can't happen. It certainly makes it harder, especially for trans women who don't ejaculate anymore, but it's still a good idea to use barriers. It's rare, but I know a couple or two that got pregnant that way. And, of course, barriers are a good idea anyway because of STIs.

 If you're going to be use a girl-dick for penetration, you run the risk of spreading HPV. Currently, there's no HPV test for male-assigned people, which means you could be a carrier and not know it. Plus, the HPV vaccine is usually only given to female-assigned folks. So use condoms if you're going to be penetrating anyone with your genitals.

KITS

Just like every driver needs a toolkit, every sex-haver needs a safer sex kit. What you put in it and what it looks like is up to you.

Kit Essentials
- Condoms
- Lube (Multiple varieties to suit the scene. See Chapter 8 for details.)
- Gloves (latex and nitrile)
- Dental Dams
- Mouthwash
- Hand sanitizer (just don't confuse it for the lube!)
- Baby wipes (antibacterial is good for cleaning toys, hands, and face after sex or if you're sharing toys, but rinse it off before using the toy again)

Recommended
- A vibrator or two (very gentlemanly thing to offer should she need or want one. I usually carry a small bullet type and a Magic Wand or other heavy-duty toy)
- Spare batteries and/or charger for the vibes
- Gum/breath mints
- Tissues
- Harness/dildo (should strap-on sex be on the menu)
- A spare pair of underwear
- Travel toothbrush
- Kink gear
- Ear plugs & eye mask—in case of kinky scenes and/or sleepovers
- Make-up (you never know when you'll want a touch-up)

This bag should be portable, or you can have one at-home version and one slimmed-down version for travel. At the very least, lube, condoms, and gloves are a good thing to keep on you. I keep little cosmetic bags with these essentials in all my bags. My main kit is a gold satin knitting bag. It's perfect because these bags are designed to hold long knitting needles, so they're a great length for dildos and vibrators!

My partner's kit is a mini-duffle, and I've seen purses, totebags, cargo belts, briefcases, and more used to store and haul safer sex goodies. I suggest choosing a bag that's stylish and suits you, so you'll be more inclined to take it with you places. Sometimes if I'm going out for a night on the town, I'll toss the bag in my car, just in case. Even if I don't use it (and lez be honest, it's more often than not) I feel better knowing I have it.

SAFER SEX ELEVATOR SPEECH
by Reid Mihalko

Many people find it difficult to have a Safer Sex conversation. I used to worry, like most people do. What if it ruins the moment? What if they don't want to sleep with me afterwards? What if they think I'm a slut because I brought it up?

These "what ifs," combined with the fact that we don't know what to say or how to say it, leave most people taking the "let's let it happen organically" route: saving it for the last possible moment (awkward!) or, worse, passing it up all together and crossing your fingers while you uncross your legs.

Be the change you want to see in the bedroom. *Speak up!*

Most people learned how to pleasure themselves in silence. We explored our growing bodies behind locked bathroom doors, or hiding beneath the covers with the lights out. We uttered nary a peep during our reconnaissance missions lest we be discovered and shamed. We basically trained ourselves to be sex mimes!

This mime-like silence weaves itself through our love lives, making it harder to speak up about safer sex or the kinds of pleasure we like. If you can't speak up about it, you can't ask for it, which means you might never get to try it in the first place! Break the mime habit and speak up!

It's harder to speak up when you don't know what to say.

In high school, I had a semester of drivers' ed, and an entire class just to learn typing, but I never learned how to talk about safer sex! High school would have been a great time for me to practice getting comfortable reciting my STI statuses, instead of telling the classroom how "lovely, dark and deep" Robert Frost's woods were. Add the anxiety of having sexual desires, wanting to "do it right," our culture's sex-negativity, and a hefty dose of slut shaming ("Nice boys and girls don't talk about sex! Only sluts and whores negotiate sex!"), and no wonder no one wants to be the first to open up their mouth.

By sharing your Safer Sex Elevator Speech not only do you break the ice and model that it's okay to talk about sex, you also model a direct and easy way for your partner to share back. Whatever they tell you in the next 2-3 minutes speaks volumes!

By initiating the safer sex conversation, you create the perfect assessment opportunity to figure out where others are in their sexual and relationship development, if they have ever thought about safer sex conversations or gotten tested, what they like and don't like in the bedroom, their relationship status, and their ability to use their words! These are great things to know so that you can adjust your needs and expectations accordingly. Better to do this before you get naked than leave it to the last second, isn't it?

Here is the "script" I use for my Safer Sex Elevator Speech. Write down your answers for each and then try it out on yourself in the mirror or on a friend or a lover.

Reid's Safer Sex Elevator Speech

1) When were you last tested for STDs, what did you get tested for, and what were the results?

2) What is your current relationship status and what, if any, relationship agreements do you have that the other person should know about?

3) What are your Safer Sex Protocols and needs?

3.5) Optional: Quick rundown of any risky sexual things you've done since you were last tested.

4) One or two things that you know you like sexually (or might want to do with this person).

5) One thing you know you don't like sexually (or that you aren't up for today).

Last step: Then ask the other person, *"AND HOW ABOUT YOU?"*

"And how about you?" speaks volumes...

You will alleviate many of your love life woes simply by upgrading whom you sleep with, and you will know how to upgrade those people when you see how well they respond to your speech. If you scare a potential sexy-time prospect away by initiating a conversation on safer sex needs, that just means they're not playing at your level. They did you a favor. You want to be knockin' boots with the awesome people who are more likely to be taking their own sexual health into account (and yours by extension). Make your sexual orientation "awesome sexual," and pick the Einsteins, Hepburns and Bruce Lees of the sex and relationship world. These people will probably bring less drama into your life and bedroom!

So the next time you find yourself with 2 minutes to spare and a hottie next to you, consider turning to them and asking them if they'd like to hear you practice your Safer Sex Elevator Speech!

Sex and relationship expert Reid Mihalko of www.ReidAboutSex.com helps adults create more self-esteem, self-confidence and greater health in their relationships and sex lives using an inspiring mixture of humor and knowledge.

DAY 8

Jamie fidgets with her video camera. The cafe is filled with people hunched over laptops and lattes. A weird part of her wants to film her first meeting with Angela. Another part of her is just looking for something to do to distract her from her nerves. Bells jingle and the door opens. A girl walks through. Jamie recognizes Angela from her website's "About" page but looks away. Jamie looks up again, and Angela catches her gaze. Angela smiles, but a tiny, nervous furrow forms between her brows. Angela giggles as she approaches. Jamie stands and knocks the table with her knees. Angela giggles again and stretches out her hand, using the other to tuck a stray strawberry-blond hair behind her ear.

Jamie takes Angela's hand and smiles. They both take a breath together.

"It's nice to meet you," Angela says, still grinning nervously. "This is so weird."

Jamie nods and laughs. "Yeah, but the coffee's good."

Angela nods, hangs her jacket on the chair, and walks to the counter just as another patron does the same. Angela ends up behind him and stops awkwardly. She glances Jamie's way, too close to ignore her, but too far to continue the conversation. They both pretend to ignore each other. Angela is tall and lean. The LA sun slanting through the windows makes the red in her hair glow. Her nervous energy makes her look younger than she probably is. She seems to have a hard time standing still, which Jamie finds weirdly charming. She doesn't wear much makeup—her whole style is a kind of H&M office-wear chic. Nothing like what Jamie usually goes for. And yet...

"Want a warm up?" Angela asks from the counter.

"Huh?" Jamie says.

"Refill? You need more coffee?"

Jamie shakes her head, and Angela returns to the table with a mug.

"I love this place," she says, scooting her chair to the table. "They still use ceramic."

"It's a novelty," Jamie says. "But they still use mugs at that place on Beverly, too."

"Oh, you've lived here?"

Jamie shakes her head. "I dated a girl down here for a few months. She worked a lot, so I got to know many of LA's fine coffee shops."

"They are impressive, in quantity if nothing else."

"Quality, too. I'm kind of picky about cafes. This is a good one."

"I'm glad it pleases you."

Jamie grins and takes a sip. Angela does too. "I thought about moving here then," Jamie says. "I was in Portland at the time. Before that, Seattle. I've been sort of working my way down the coast."

"Like the road trip."

Jamie raises her eyebrows. "Huh, I didn't really think about that."

"I was born in Alaska," Angela says. "But I grew up here. Sherman Oaks, just over the hills."

"What do you do now?"

Angela giggles again, a blush coming to her cheeks. "I code for a video sharing social media site." Jamie doesn't know why this would be embarrassing, but Angela blushes and fidgets nonetheless.

"It's weird when being online is your job," Angela says. "It feels hard meeting people in real life."

"To be fair, we met online. We're only getting to know each other in real life."

"Even harder," Angela says. Jamie notices Angela has dimples. She's never cared about dimples before, but on Angela they're adorable.

"I feel like I knew you already. Your videos say a lot."

Now it's Jamie's turn to blush. "I feel like a poser."

"They don't feel true to you?"

"No, they feel incredibly true, which is why I feel like a poser. Like I've hit a nerve in myself I didn't know could register sensation."

"I think that means you're an artist."

"That word. It's always been something I wanted, but not something I felt like I could claim for myself."

Angela reaches into her purse and pulls out a yellow pencil. "Bow your head," she says.

Jamie makes a face. "What?"

"Bow your head. I'm going to knight you."

Jamie laughs and lowers her head. Angela touches the pencil tip to Jamie's shoulder.

"Jamie!" Angela says with playful pomp. "—what's your middle name?"

"Elizabeth."

"Jamie Elizabeth Cross! By the power invested in me by copious amounts of caffeine, adrenaline, and a variety of competing hormones, I dub thee A Real Artist worthy of making things that speak to you and to others, and to share them with the world for they—and you—are beautiful and worthy." She taps the pencil on Jamie's other shoulder, then ceremoniously presents it for Jamie to take. "Use it with intention and integrity."

"It is my honor, your highness." Jamie smiles and takes the pencil.

Two hours later, the sun is setting, and they are both wired on caffeine.

"I feel like I didn't think this through," Angela says.

"Weren't expecting me to be such dazzling company?" Jamie smiles. Angela blushes.

"Cocktail?" Jamie asks. "Take the edge off?"

Angela shakes her head. "Nah. Wanna walk? There's a great record store this way. And a big-ass movie theater. And—well—what used to be a bookstore, so maybe not that." They walk.

"So, 'Borgesse'? Is that Italian?"

Angela half-smiles, looking at the sidewalk. "I guess this is as good a time as ever to tell you."

"Witness protection program?" Jamie jokes.

"It's kind of a sci-fi thing, like cyborg. I gave it to myself, both the last name and the first."

"So you're an angel cyborg?"

Angela laughs. "That's what I'm going for. A bit divine, a bit super human, a bit scientifically acquired..."

"Which means?"

"You didn't Google me, did you?"

"Er...just your pictures." Jamie blushes. "That sounds creepier than I intended."

Angela giggles. "No. It's fine. It just means I get to tell you to your face that I'm trans."

Jamie stops. So does Angela.

"This is the part where you shrewdly analyze my presentation."

"No." Jamie shakes her head. "Just integrating."

The orange glow of the streetlamps cast Angela's face in harsh shadow. This new piece of information changes nothing and yet slightly more than nothing.

Angela looks away. Her shyness makes Jamie bold. "Can I touch you?" she asks.

Angela nods, staring at her feet. Jamie raises her hand to Angela's cheek and strokes her hair behind her ear. "You are lovely."

Angela meets Jamie's gaze and grins. "Lovely," Jamie repeats.

They keep walking, wandering the city, no particular destination in mind. When their feet get sore and everything but the bars and cinemas are closed, they see a movie, a midnight double feature. In the theater, reading subtitles, Jamie grasps Angela's hand. Angela squeezes, sending tingles like tiny shocks up Jamie's arm. In the warm, white screen-glow, Jamie sees Angela smile.

"**I'm talking about a little truth-in-packaging here. To be perfectly frank, you don't quite look like yourself. And if you walk around looking like someone other than who you are, you could end up getting the wrong job, the wrong friends, who knows what-all. You could end up with somebody else's life.**"

This is one of my favorite quotes from one of my favorite books, Michael Cunningham's *A Home at the End of the World*. I read the book right after college, when I was living in LA and miserable about so many things, among which were my sex life and my gender presentation.

I put the book down, picked up some scissors, tied my long peroxide-blond hair into a braid, and cut it off. I stood in front of the mirror, braid in hand, and sighed in relief. Then I marched to my closet, grabbed a sports bra, a baggy plaid shirt, and an ACE bandage. I bound my breasts, tucked a sock into my underwear, put on my baggy clothes, and went for a walk down Sunset Boulevard.

I don't remember if anyone stared. I didn't care.

I walked with a wide, long stride, and felt invincible.

Since that night, I've refused to listen to anyone who tries to tell me how I should look. I've worn my hair any way I felt, got the tattoos I wanted, wore clothes that made me feel sexy and strong, whether femme or butch or both or neither.

Making those choices changed my life. Some people think these things are shallow. I think they're essential. We present ourselves to the world every day, both in real life and online. And people respond to us based on those presentations. So if you have the "wrong" haircut, clothes, friends, job, and so on, you may indeed end up living a life you didn't choose for yourself. Why not make small changes to be as *you* as possible?

Like masturbation, the best way to figure out what you like is by trying a bunch of different things.

Step 1: Self-exploration

This often starts as a solitary intellectual exercise ("What would it feel like to wear this leather corset?") or an emotional one ("Oh god, I want to wear that leather corset!"). This phase can last a long time—sometimes even a lifetime! Popularly, we tend to think of people who have a solo exploratory practice as fetishists of some type, but often it's that folks are in the nascent stages of a full-fledged identity.

Step 2: Public experimentation

When you've tried on your identity in solitude, it's common to want to present it to the world. Sometimes this is in controlled environments: queer clubs, among friends, costume parties only, etc. Sometimes it's in tiny increments, like fingernail polish, a certain kind of underwear, etc. Or sometimes you'll come crashing out of the closet like so many drag kings and queens I knew in college. How you do it is up to you. When we present something to the world that we feel is really true for us, the stakes feel much higher. Positive feedback can feel extremely good here. And negative feedback can be devastating. What can keep negative feedback from destroying your ego is tying your presentation to an indefatigable truth. It's the part of you that is un-fuck-with-able. It's the part of you that says, "Fuck all y'all, I'm FABULOUS." No matter how meek we are in real life, we all have that part of us somewhere. It's your job to find out where that piece is and nurture it.

If you get shamed by your friends for being you, it's probably time for some new friends.

After my big gender-coming out in LA, I realized my job at the time was thoroughly demeaning—I was constantly exotified and objectified for my sexuality and gender presentation. So, I quit. Some friends made fun of me, some didn't. The friends who thought it was hot and awesome when I went out to an LA club in full boy drag were the ones who stuck around. I don't miss any of the ones who didn't stay.

Step 3: Identification/Integration

Sometimes this kind of experimentation is just dress up or play. But sometimes we strike identity gold. When that happens, do what gold miners do, and follow that vein. Explore the cultural signifiers and identities immediately around that thing you love and see what else fits.

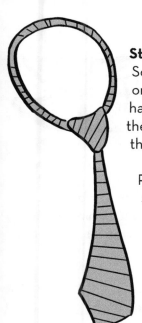

For instance, If you find yourself fascinated by sharp suits, suspenders, and tie tacks, you may want to check out dapper dandy culture, steampunk, or other things related to high-end menswear and the culture around it.

If you put on a feather boa and feel luscious, maybe you'll want to check out burlesque, femme culture, drag, stripping, or more things where a boa is a common accessory.

Read books by people who have similar identities you're curious about. Hang out with other folks who are into what you're into. Find or build chat rooms for people who like what you like. Find events that cater to your kind of thing. Drag culture has this in spades, so does trans culture. Femmes are finding their collective voices, and butches are having some intense conversations about masculinity, identity, family, and fashion. Find your people and make friends.

Step 4: Know that all of this can and will change.

When people discover something that really speaks to them, most tend to cling to it hard. We can feel threatened if people question it, or offended if people don't understand it. We can insist that "This is the real me and it always has been and always will be forever and ever and ever!" And maybe it will be. But maybe it won't. There are people who vacillate from straight to gay and back their whole life without ever considering they might be bi/pan. Some people, when they realize their transness, will go full tilt to the other end of the gender scale without stopping to think "What kind of woman/man/person do I want to be?"

The sad fact is, many people treat themselves worse than the world ever will. You have to give yourself the permission to keep exploring, even if something new enters your life that feels contradictory to everything else you've been before. That's life. And it's great, if you give yourself permission to believe it's so.

And now I'll leave you with another quote from *A Home at the End of the World*, **"I was not ladylike, nor was I manly. I was something else altogether. There were so many different ways to be beautiful."**

COMING OUT

There are as many ways to come out as there are things to come out as (hint: more than a bunch). If you're considering playing in a more public way, you're going to have to think about coming out. Coming out can be simple or complicated, safe or scary, depending on your circumstances.

Here are some steps to consider if you're going to bust out of the closet:

1) **Make sure you're in a safe environment.** Do you live at home? Are you afraid you might get kicked out or disowned? Have a Plan B. Figure out if you have a sympathetic friend with nice parents, or a relative who cares. If you live in a place that's dangerous, start making plans to get out. Maybe that's working hard for a little while and scraping together enough cash to move. Maybe that's working hard to get a scholarship to go to a college out of town. The circumstances may never be perfect, but take steps you can control to make sure you're coming out into a space that can handle it.

2) **Decide who you want to tell.** It can be everyone, some folks, or no one but yourself. You decide for you. Remember, it's still legal in many states for companies to fire you for your sexuality, so make sure you're protected if you want to come out at work. Don't be too surprised if you get resistance from people in your life you weren't expecting.

3) **Give yourself permission to be clumsy or confused.** The first time I walked into a lesbian bar alone, I was terrified. I had already been having sex with women for years at that point, but for some reason that was a big, confusing moment. I couldn't talk to anyone but the bartender, and she was so pretty I had a hard time putting a sentence together. But whatever. 10 years, tons of hairstyles, and even more hot, shared, girl orgasms later, I'm happy as a clam and queer as a 3 dollar bill. A little humiliation never hurt anyone. You'll be fine, too.

4) **Change can be scary.** Most people don't handle new information well. Give people their space to be shocked or confused. But don't take shitty treatment from anyone. If you need space from a person, or if they need space from you, while they process, take that space. As long as they don't get violent with you, it's natural for them to react to their shock or confusion with anger, frustration, denial, or all sorts of negative emotions. Sometimes you just need to let people soak in the new for a while. This may mean they try distancing themselves from you. That sucks, but it can be very helpful. To the degree you can, let people take the space they need to adjust to the new information, and often they'll come back when they're ready.

5) **Don't let anyone tell you who you are.** We queers love policing each other. It's called infighting, and we do it well. But your journey is your own. If someone tells you you're not gay enough, or trans enough, or kinky enough, or whatever, you can tell them they're not cool enough to hang out with you. You can be a dyke who sleeps with men, or a trans girl who likes her penis, or a straight girl who loves eating pussy, or a monogamous slut or whatever. Anyone who tells you otherwise can go ahead and fuck off.

6) **Celebrate yourself.** It's one of the worst-kept secrets in the world: being queer is AWESOME. Yes, society shits on us all the time, but here's the thing: you get to have awesome sex with awesome people and dress however you want and genderfuck and dance all night and make out with the people you've always fantasized about, and choose your own family and say "I do!" or "I don't!" and raise socially conscious babies or not, and stay friends with your exes, and move to big cities and make hilarious wonderful friends, and move to small towns and create little queer utopias, and a million other things that queers get to do. Sometimes it sucks, it's true. But you live in a time that is changing for the better. The pace is slower than we'd like, but we're going in the right direction. Love yourself. Practice self-care. Celebrate your community. Support each other. Have fun.

COMING OUT!

Came out at 16, 17, 24 as bisexual, a crossdresser, and a trans woman.

MY ORIENTATION IS HARD TO EXPLAIN AND DOESN'T HAVE A HUGE IMPACT ON MY LIFE, SO I DON'T TALK ABOUT IT A WHOLE LOT.

CAME OUT AS TRANSGENDER AT 26. CAME OUT AS LESBIAN AT 29.

I've come out as bisexual, then pansexual, polyamorous, genderqueer. For a while I thought I might be some flavor of asexual but that turned out not to be right.

Coming out never stops. I came out again this morning to the repairman after I got sick of him referring to my husband.

Two big coming out experiences for me, so far. At age 13, I came out as bisexual. I am now 28 and just beginning to come out as trans (FTM).

First time was 15 and just to some friends, but I lived in a smallish rather bible belt town and promptly got beat up. So I crept back into the closet behind last year's winter coat and stayed there til I moved away at 19.

I spent most of my life heavily repressed. It took about a month between me accepting my feelings and coming out to my husband.

I first came out to my parents when I was 11 years old quite accidentally. My father came home early from work and found me with my girlfriend in a very compromising position. It prompted a two-family discussion and ultimately the end of my first relationship by force. My parents still do not accept my identity 20 years later.

I am pretty open about my sexual orientation with anyone I talk to at length, so in a way I'm always coming out. I haven't posted it on Facebook or had any kind of large scale ceremonious coming out, but I am considering it.

I NEVER REALLY NEEDED TO FORMALLY "COME OUT" AS ANYTHING. MY FRIENDS AND FAMILY JUST KIND OF KNEW.

I am a lesbian. I don't feel its necessary to make any statements. When I meet someone new I don't do anything different and when I introduce my girlfriend, there is typically no issue. If someone asks I tell the truth but I do not advertise nor make a point of pointing out my orientation. Straight people don't so I don't either.

I was 30 when I came out. I missed SO much. If only I could have been ou in my 20s...

I'VE COME OUT MORE TIMES THAN I CAN COUNT. AS A MULTI-RACIAL QUEER, KINKY, POLY, HIGH FEMME THAT EASILY PASSES FOR A STRAIGHT, WHITE, MAINSTREAM, MARRIED WOMAN I COME OUT OVER AND OVER AND OVER AGAIN. I AM FORCED TO FIGHT FOR MY PLACE IN THE SUBCULTURES THAT FEED MY SOUL JUST AS OFTEN AS I BEND THE BOUNDARIES AND ALTER THE PERCEPTIONS OF WHAT IT MEANS TO BE QUEER, KINKY, POLY, OR A POC THAT ARE HELD DEAR BY THE PEOPLE IN THE MAINSTREAM.

I TRIED COMING OUT IN HIGH SCHOOL TO MY BEST FRIEND BUT I WAS REJECTED (AND HURT AND SCARED), SO I WENT BACK TO THINKING THAT I WAS GOING TO CHOOSE TO BE STRAIGHT. I CAME OUT TO MYSELF AS QUEER WHEN I WAS 22. THEN TO MY 1ST HUSBAND AFTER WE HAD BEEN TOGETHER FOR TEN YEARS. THEN TO MY BEST FRIEND WHEN I WAS 25 AND WE STARTED HAVING A SEXUAL RELATIONSHIP. THEN I CAME OUT AS POLY, BECAUSE I WAS HAVING A RELATIONSHIP WITH BOTH MY HUSBAND AND THAT GIRLFRIEND. THEN, YEARS LATER, I MET A WOMAN I FELL IN LOVE WITH. I CAME OUT TO MY KIDS AS 'GAY.' ONCE MY PARTNER WAS INCORPORATED INTO MY LIFE, I CAME OUT TO THE REST OF THE FAMILY AS QUEER/POLY. THEN AFTER A YEAR AND A HALF OF DATING HER I CAME OUT AS GAY TO WORK PEOPLE. I HAVE SINCE DIVORCED MY SECOND HUSBAND, AND I CONTINUE TO IDENTIFY AS BISEXUAL, BUT I COME OUT SELECTIVELY AS BI, SO AS TO AVOID AWKWARD CONVERSATIONS ABOUT MY CHOICE OF MONOGAMY (OR NON-MONOGAMY).

I first came out as bi based on romantic attractions to men and women. Then a year or so later as lesbian, because my sexual interest was only in women. Now, I realize that it's a bit more complex than that, as my sexuality is pretty much, "I like everyone, but am not sexually, and very rarely romantically attracted to cismen," so I just say "queer." I continue to come out as queer to new people who meet me in the context of my FTM partner and assume I'm straight.

SCENIC VIEWPOINT

Some Advice About Identity
by Julia Serano

While some people may complain that identity labels "box us in," these labels also have the potential to set us free. The first time that I called myself trans, or queer, or a woman, or lesbian, or femme, or bisexual—on each of these occasions, it allowed me to see myself in a new light. Embracing these labels seemed to give me permission to explore novel ideas and experiences that had not seemed possible for me before. In each case, I learned many important things about myself in the process.

I might call myself a writer, a Californian, a biologist, a guitar player, an agnostic, or a cancer survivor. None of these labels sums me up as a whole person, but each offers a small bit of insight into who I am and what I've experienced.

In most cases, when we use identity labels to describe ourselves, nobody challenges us. If I call myself a "cat person," nobody is going to expect me to only hang out with other cat people, or question my identity if I just so happen to adopt a dog. But things are different when it comes to labels that describe our genders and sexualities. Because these matters are highly policed in our society, we are likely to come across people who will question our identities. Some might insist that we are not "real women," or "real lesbians," or "really queer," and so on.

Others might deny that what we identify as even exists—for instance, when people assume that we're "really straight," but merely confused about our sexualities or genders. When they do this, it erases who we are. It may make us rightfully angry and frustrated.

At this point in time, I identify as a bisexual femme-tomboy transsexual woman. Femme-tomboy refers to my gender expression—I am feminine in some ways but tomboyish in others. Bisexual refers to my sexual orientation—I use it because it is the most commonly used and understood term for people who are attracted to members of more than one sex or gender. Woman refers to my gender identity—the fact that I identify and live as a woman. Transsexual refers to the fact that my identified gender is different from the one I was assigned at birth.

Because I've had people deny my identity in the past, I try not to question other people's identities—even in cases where they use an identity label that I am not familiar with. I remind myself that they know themselves better than I do. And as long as their identity doesn't erase or make assumptions about other people's identities, no one is negatively affected.

If someone describes themselves using an identity label that you have never heard of before, it is usually okay to ask them what that label means. But if you act as though you are suspicious of their identity, or if you ask a lot of highly personal or intrusive questions about it, they may be offended or feel put off by you.

Some identity labels are broader than others. For example, I also describe myself as queer (an umbrella term for all sexual and gender minorities) and transgender or trans (umbrella terms for all people who transgress gender norms). Broader labels can be useful for activism (there is strength in numbers!), although sometimes certain subgroups may feel like their issues are drowned out within larger umbrella movements.

Often, people who share the same gender or sexual orientation, identity, expression, or experience will choose different identity labels to describe themselves. One person may prefer lesbian while another prefers the term dyke. One may prefer the label bisexual while another prefers the term pansexual. There is no one "right" word—people may choose one label over another for personal, generational, regional, or political reasons. Also, some identity labels may come and go, or change meanings over time.

Usually when we don't like a particular identity label, it's not the word itself that we dislike, but rather the stereotypes that people project onto that label. When people say "queer" or "lesbian" or "dyke" or "bisexual" or "pansexual" or "transgender" or "genderqueer" or "femme" or "butch" or what have you, sometimes it conjures up certain less-than-flattering images in our heads. Sometimes these negative stereotypes come from straight mainstream culture, but they can also come from within our own queer communities too.

Rather than condemn a particular identity or label, it is often more constructive to challenge the stereotypes associated with it. We can do this by recognizing and emphasizing the fact that people who share a particular identity may differ from one another in countless ways. And just because some individuals within a group may seem to fit a particular stereotype, that doesn't mean the stereotype holds true for other members of that group. Most of us hate being stereotyped—we should keep that in mind before we try to stereotype others.

Occasionally, we may come to question or even modify some aspect of our identity. Sometimes this occurs in response to us learning about new identities and ways of being. Or we may experience internal shifts in our desires or interests. Or some combination thereof. This is normal—all people grow and inevitably change over time.

Having experienced shifts in my identity on several occasions over the course of my life, I'll be the first to admit that it can be quite scary. It is difficult to question a part of ourselves that we have come to take for granted. It can also be scary for the people closest to us—our partners, close friends, and family—as they may worry that the person that we have been up to that point may suddenly disappear. I always tell myself (as well as those close to me) that such shifts are more like part of a gradual evolution process than an abrupt and dramatic change. We remain the same person, it's just that we've opened up a new door in our lives. I always give myself permission to explore that new path, but I also give myself permission to return if I don't like what I find on the other side. It is okay for us to change our minds. And no decision that we make about our identity needs to be permanent.

Julia Serano is the author of two books, 2007's Whipping Girl: A Transsexual Woman on Sexism and the Scapegoating of Femininity and 2013's Excluded: Making Feminist and Queer Movements More Inclusive. She makes indie-pop music under the moniker *soft vowel sounds*, and lives with her partner, cat, and four parrots in Oakland, CA. juliaserano.com

BUT WHAT DOES THAT MAKE ME?!

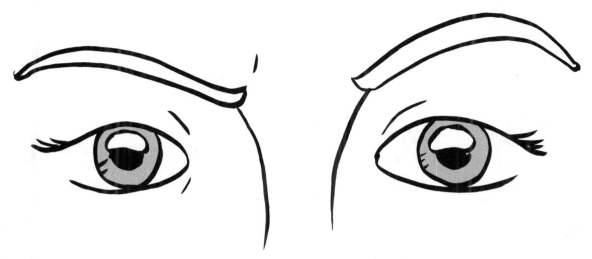

Let's imagine you're a heterosexual cisgender woman in a monogamous relationship with a man. Then, one day, seemingly out of the blue, your partner comes out as a trans woman. You love this person. You want to stay together. So, are you now a lesbian?

Now let's imagine you're a lesbian, your identity and community hard-earned. And then your partner comes out as a trans guy. Do you become straight? Does your partner passing as a hetero man erase your powerfully-claimed lesbian identity?

What if you live as a straight man, only to realize well into adulthood that you're a trans woman? Are you now a lesbian?

And what if, after taking hormones and living as a heterosexual trans man for a long time, you start being curious about other men? Are you bi? Curious? Gay? Confused?

These scenarios happen all the time. It can be a fun theoretical experiment when we talk about it in generalities. But it can be much harder when it happens to you or your partner.

The challenging thing about sexual and gender identity is that they don't just affect you, but the people you're in (or seeking) relationships with. Gender identity is intrinsic—it doesn't usually change even if your context does. Sexual orientation, however, is usually defined in relation to gender identity. According to popular definitions, a man who likes only women is straight, for instance. But a woman who likes only women is a lesbian.

In this way, Sexual Orientation = Gender Identity x Gendered Attraction. If you transition your gender, you may also unintentionally move from straight to gay or vice versa, even though nothing about your attractions have changed, because orientation is contingent.

This phenomenon—of sexual identity being dependent on gender identity—creates big conundrums. There's no easy way to answer these questions, and (in my opinion) that's part of their beauty.

BUT BUT BUT THIS IS MY WORD!

Words like "straight," "gay," "lesbian," and others often fail when confronted with the staggering multiplicity and complexity of human life. In fact, it means that you as a human being are bigger and more complex than any simple words can define. Fancy that! Sexuality is a complex and mercurial thing. Trying to lash it down to any sort of ontological meaning is an exercise in futility.

It's normal to be attached to our words. Often we have to fight hard to stake a claim to them in the first place. It sucks when they're taken from us without our consent.

But it's also important to remember that our language is a faulty, frail thing.

So most of us—if not all of us—are doing the best with a faulty system.

My overarching advice? Follow love. Trust your inner sense of rightness. If you love someone who wants to change a fundamental part of who they are or how the world perceives them, you can choose whether you want to stand by them. But you'll likely be best served by following a choice that leads to more love not less.

Remember: **you define your identity. It doesn't define you.** You have control over how you want to interpret a word or discard it. If a word works for a while and then stops working as well, you can change it. If the words you use change meaning based on your context (where you are, who you're talking to, etc) you can choose to change your words or be explicit with your choice.

If following your inner sense of rightness takes you down a gender path that frightens you, you get to choose how far you travel. As long as you head toward rightness and love, you'll likely make the right steps, or at least you'll be able to tell where the right steps are.

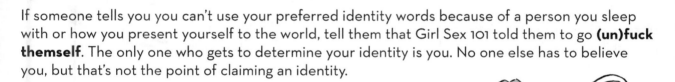

Years ago I heard a caller on Dan Savage's Savage Love podcast who was worried. She and her girlfriend were lesbians, but they both had been jonesin' for boy meat. They didn't know what that made them, and were worried they weren't the women they thought they were. I called in to respond with my own story: I was a lesbian who had been fucking a man and it didn't change my identity. A third woman called in to take me to task saying lesbians aren't allowed to fuck men, because it invalidated their lesbianism. Dan's advice to all of us: **"Anyone is allowed to identify however they want. And you're allowed to not believe them."**

If someone tells you you can't use your preferred identity words because of a person you sleep with or how you present yourself to the world, tell them that Girl Sex 101 told them to go **(un)fuck themself**. The only one who gets to determine your identity is you. No one else has to believe you, but that's not the point of claiming an identity.

If someone comes out to you as something, it's pretty simple:

Don't be a dick about it. If your mega butch brother or femmey-femme sister come out as trans, or your ex girlfriend who ate pussy like a pro comes out as a cis-dude loving het, you may not feel inclined to believe them. So-fucking-what? Do you love them? Do you want to see them happy? Do you support them in their life's journey even if it isn't a life you would choose for yourself? Good. So say those things and keep your critiques to yourself. No one needs more bullies in their lives. If you love them, treat them like it. Because...

Your (negative) opinion is irrelevant. You expressing disbelief or disgust at a person's chosen identity ain't gonna change anything. Even worse, acting like a gatekeeper to an identity is only going to make it feel like the cool kids' table. Instead...

Show them love and support. Thank them for trusting you with the information. Ask how you can support them. Coming out can be scary. And most people don't just do it willy nilly. So, be grateful they felt safe enough to tell you.

BORN THIS WAY—KINDA

For a long time, gay-rights advocates banged the "Born This Way" drum, saying we can't choose who we love; we're born this way. We're normal. We're Just Like You™. And that's true...a lot of the time. But it's not the whole story.

Some folks aren't born gay, queer, trans, or whatever. They don't know as soon as they're old enough to hold a softball bat that they're different. Some folks do actually *choose* to transition their gender or pursue a relationship with someone of the same gender.

The fact that these things are choices doesn't make them wrong. In fact, it can be noble and brave to choose something that's commonly denigrated. For some folks, choice means losing privilege or a step into uncharted territory. Some people risk losing family, friends, jobs, children, and community, all because of a conscious choice.

Your personal narrative doesn't have to be an unbroken timeline of certainty to be valid. In fact, there's often much truth to be found in the endless vacillations of identity and community. If you suddenly find yourself in love with someone of the same gender, or questioning your own gender identity, it doesn't mean you've been "living a lie" up until that point. You're normal, just like everyone else.

FALLING FOR SOMEONE WHO ISN'T YOUR TYPE

ALL THE TIME. My identity seems to be getting simpler as it is more defined. I am a genderqueer femme who LOVES queers, especially queer kinksters.

I REMEMBER THE FIRST TIME I WAS SEXUALLY ATTRACTED TO A MAN! IT CONFUSED ME SO VERY MUCH, AS I HAD COMPLETELY COME OUT AS A DEDICATED LESBIAN. I DID A LOT OF REASSESSING OF MY IDENTITY AND MY PREFERENCES AFTER THAT.

I SMASHED A LOT OF FATPHOBIA WITH A SWEET BEAR LOVER A FEW YEARS AGO.

I'm dating a trans woman, and dating her has made me reasses my own identity and change it from bisexual to queer.

When I started having sex again in my 30's it was with boys which, having identified as a lesbian for so long, really threw me for a loop. Then I discovered the queer community and that identity felt like home.

MY ATTRACTION TO MY CURRENT PARTNER HAS CAUSED ME TO COMPLETELY REASSESS MY TASTES AND TAKE A HARD LOOK AT MY IDENTITY. I MET MY PARTNER BEFORE HE WAS OUT AS A TRANS MAN, AND I'VE BEEN WITH HIM THROUGH HIS TRANSITION. I'M STILL REALLY ATTRACTED TO HIM NOW THAT HE IS PRESENTING FULLY AS A MAN, HAS MORE BODY HAIR AND A LOW VOICE, AND NO LONGER HAS BREASTS. I SPENT A LOT OF TIME WONDERING WHETHER I'D SECRETLY BEEN ATTRACTED TO MEN THIS WHOLE TIME (I HAVEN'T), AND WHETHER I COULD LEGITIMATELY CALL MYSELF A LESBIAN ANYMORE (I CAN IN SOME SITUATIONS BUT NOT OTHERS), AND THE WHOLE THING HAS CAUSED ME TO PUT MUCH LESS STOCK IN TRYING TO FIT MY IDENTITY INTO TIDY BOXES.

Sex work has thrown any solid ideas I had about my tastes and identity into permanent question, and I love that. I've had amazing sex with people I never would have imagined I'd find attractive!

SCENIC VIEWPOINT

Your identity is yours!
But you might not even need one
by Carol Queen

Once I was giving a talk to a group of students in a Queer Studies class, discussing what it was like in The Olden Days of the 1970s. Back then, I was a GLBT activist, but our community had a lot of trouble, actually, with the B and the T parts. I myself was B, that is, bisexual, and I had to put up with people telling me I was confused, women who wouldn't go out with me because they were already imagining me leaving them for a man, and nonsense like that.

In this talk, I used a phrase like, "...whether they identified as gay, a dyke, straight, or bi, or as just sexual, or as nothing at all..."

One of the students shot her hand in the air. "You mean," she asked, "that you don't *have* to have a sexual identity?" She looked shocked, and a little elated around the edges.

You know what? You don't. We've made Western culture, including our sex and gender culture, really dependent on the idea of binaries: two (and only two) possibilities that are opposites. Gay and straight: opposites. What does that even mean? Men and women are not opposites! And this business of binary-fying everything means that people who don't really feel either/or often feel left out of community, or worse: shamed or harassed for who they are, not just by straight people, but by the people they hope will create a safe place for them. Not to mention be their girlfriends or whatever. We all have a sexuality, even if it's asexuality; but there are way more possible versions of us as sexual people than identity words to choose from.

Plus, according to these silly rules, there are so many ways to be a queer wrong. How can that be? If we start out as an alternative to the norm, how exactly is there only one way to do or be alternative? Plenty of heterosexuals are unlike other heterosexuals, hence they too are living some version of an alternative life. This can be the case in so many ways: open or closed relationships, interest in kinky sex or just vanilla (don't let anyone tell you that's an insult, either—vanilla is a delicious flavor whether or not you put fancy [or kinky] toppings on it)...the list of diversity goes on.

Bottom line is: We don't want who we are to result in us not fitting in, so too often we either suppress parts of ourselves (don't! Think of all the fun/life/joy/sex/adventure/**you** you'll miss if you don't follow your desires and interests) or we look for specialized communities to embrace us as is. The latter is a good option, if you can find that special place for vegan monogamish lesbian ex-Catholic Buddhists who eroticize playing all the roles in the Rocky Horror Picture Show. But if you can't fill up a whole commune (or, even better, small town) with people just like you, how about looking at it this way?:

Be part of the personal and erotic diversity that is us: us queer girls, us lesBlans, us women-loving women, us fierce femmes and butches, us people who'd rather not be pinned down to one or another identity, us humans. Don't ever EVER let anyone tell you this community or world would be better off without you. Desire what you desire. Learn about it and learn to talk about it. Help make more space for the next bunch who come out, whether there will be a word then to describe them, or whether they'll choose not to choose.

Carol Queen is a pleasure activist who writes, speaks and teaches about sexuality. She co-founded the Center for Sex & Culture and works at Good Vibrations.

PREFERENCES & TASTE

Preference is a guiding force in dating. We need some way to filter through all the humans in the world to find the ones we actually might want to fall in love with and/or fuck. So we make discernments and judgments. We filter through all the stimuli to identify qualities we actually want in our beds. Internet dating is based on this. So is small talk.

Sometimes if you're filling out one of those online dating profiles, it can feel weird to answer some of the questions.

Some of us might be afraid of saying the wrong thing, accidentally filtering out a winner, or offending someone.

You are allowed to have preferences.

In fact, **I *ENCOURAGE* you to have preferences**. If your only criterion for potential mates is a pulse, you may find yourself overwhelmed by terrible prospects. You're not doing anyone favors when you cast too wide a net. Because, odds are, you *do* have preferences, you're just scared to choose, or you don't want to believe you're a judgmental person.

Preferences save everyone heartache. If you HATE that your sweetie isn't a vegan, and they hate that you hate that about them, no one's happy. If you avoided speaking up at the beginning of the relationship because you weren't honest with yourself about how important veganism is to you—guess what? *You're* the jerk in the scenario. Have your preferences, and be willing to stick with them, and you'll date people who thrill you instead of make you grind your teeth in an herbivoracious rage.

In fact, **the more specific you are, the better.** This may seem counter-intuitive. Especially if you're a queer, it's easy to think that there's only one-in-a-million for us. Maybe. But probably not. There are an estimated 5.5 *million* lesbian and bisexual women in America alone. Let's assume you're looking for only one person. Your odds are pretty good. Be specific. You can always make exceptions later.

Preferences don't have to be an all-or-nothing deal. **Know the difference between deal-breakers and wiggle room**. If my preference is to date an English speaker, there might be some wiggle room at how adept they are at the language. Some English ability may be enough to avoid my deal-breaking mode. Wiggle room gives you the opportunity to be flexible, as long as it's something you want to be flexible about.

Your preferences don't have to be PC. In fact, many of them may not be. You are allowed to have preferences that violate workplace-hiring laws. If you don't want to date skinny people, kinky people, polyamorous people, fat people, straight people, white people, black people, college grads, high-school-dropouts, yoga teachers, parents, coffee-drinkers, drug-users, or dog-lovers, you don't have to. And you shouldn't feel obligated to, just to prove something to someone. Let those people be the skinny, kinky, GED-wieldin', coffee addicts of someone *else's* dreams.

All that said, you need to know that **your preferences are not immune to critique**. If someone calls you on only dating tall Latina math nerds, saying "it's just a preference" doesn't give you any moral high ground. This is especially true if you espouse one set of morals to your friends, but practice another. Sooner or later someone might call you on it, and that's their right.

This goes for genitals, too. You can prefer people who are packing one set of goods, but remember genitals ≠ gender. If you only like people with vulvas, remember that some trans women AND trans guys have vulvas. If you say you only like people with vulvas as a way of weeding men or trans women out of your dating pool, you're not doing a very good job of it, and you may be acting shady at the same time.

Because, **you should be willing to examine your preferences.** Like much of life, we make a lot of assumptions. It's how we survive. But when it comes to dating and sex, we often let these assumptions run the show. We might let one bad experience make that mean something about a whole type of person.

If you're choosing away from a certain kind of person because of a history of abuse or pain, you're allowed to do that. But know that it's not fair to anyone, especially yourself, to avoid a whole group of people because of something someone else did to you. If you find yourself cutting a certain kind of person from your friend or dating pool in this way, it's worth examining. Maybe in therapy, or maybe just with your community. But either way, it's a gift you can give yourself to deconstruct the pain of your past and give yourself new opportunities for love and connection in the future.

As Jeanette Winterson said, "It is right to trust our feelings, but right to test them, too. If they are what we say they are, they will stand the test, if not we will at least be less insincere." (*Art Objects*, 1995)

Even if your preferences aren't rooted in pain, it's worth deconstructing them. You might find that what you thought was a deal-breaker wasn't such a big deal at all. This is especially true if any of your preferences could fall under any of the – isms, i.e. racism, ageism, classism, ableism, etc. Odds are, if your preferences nestle comfortably within any – ism, it's because you're letting stereotypes rule your sex life. If you think high school dropouts can't talk philosophy or disabled people make bad dance partners, you've got a lot more living to do, and a lot more opportunities for connection than you think.

Most of all, **give yourself permission to follow love**, even if it's not wrapped up in the kind of package you thought you wanted. You deserve love, you deserve pleasure, and you deserve to be seen for the great human you are. And so does everyone else.

MY COMING OUT STORY

I'm going to share something vulnerable with you. I'm afraid you might judge me for it, or call me a fraud. I'm afraid you're going to lose respect for me. And I'm afraid you're going to think I'm a bad person. I'd like you to find this story useful, or even illuminating. It taught me how to deconstruct my own preferences and find love.

I'm going to share with you my own—abridged—coming out story.

It starts off pretty standard: I always had crushes on my friends, boys and girls both, but mostly girls. I thought it was totally normal to think about kissing your besties in junior high. It was only when I was dating my high school sweetheart did I learn I wasn't "normal." He told me I was weird, it was wrong, and of course most people can't love people of the same gender; love, he said, didn't work that way. Luckily I didn't believe him. In college I came out as bisexual, had my first girlfriends, gave away my girl-ginity, and was living happy and free. After graduation, I moved to Los Angeles and realized that I really wasn't interested in men at all. Even though I was physically attracted to guys every once in a while, I found so many of them to be such jerks, I wrote all men off completely.

I came out as a lesbian.

About 6 years later, at the LGBT center where I worked, I met a man. A cis man. A big, burly, goofy blond cis man. Even when I dated guys, I didn't date guys who looked or behaved like him. For a few days after our meeting, I was conflicted. I knew he liked me, but my chosen label told me that I didn't date people like him. I didn't date men. I didn't *like* men. I was a lesbian. My preference was for people unlike him.

But I couldn't stop thinking—not just about him—but about the potential of him. I took a long bike ride to clear my head and ended up at a burger joint. I was the only one there except for three dudes in the corner. They were drunk and boisterous, and I could hear every horrifyingly misogynistic thing they were saying. On the ride home, I had a strange realization. I didn't hate men. I hated the patriarchy. I hated entitled douchebags. I hated misogynistic jerks. The blond man who wooed me wasn't one of these guys. He was one of the good ones. I decided to take a chance and fall in love with a man for the first time.

Seven years later, we're still dizzily, happily partnered.

I'm not sharing this story to convince you to like dudes or dick or blonds or anything. I want to impress on you the value of deconstructing your preferences to figure out what really matters to you. For me, it wasn't that I didn't like men, it was that I didn't like douchey heterosexist misogynists. Had I grouped a good person with those jerks, I would have missed out on being with a great love of my life.

Deconstruct your preferences, find out what's really underneath, and choose for or away from that. You may be surprised with the results.

SCENIC VIEWPOINT

LESBIAN SEEKING TRANS
by Ignacio Rivera aka Papí Coxxx

Desiring, loving or fucking a trans person doesn't change who you are unless you want it to. You are the only person who can identify you. So, if you're a lesbian or a queer woman, there you will stay, unless you decide different. No one else can do that, no matter how hard they may try. I have sex with lesbians but I'm not one. Years ago I was, but I've come to identify as transgender, and more specifically, gender queer or gender non-conforming queer. Trans identity and experience is as immense as lesbianism and queer identity, so think about that when you find yourself about to sex it up with a trans person.

Gender can be understood in three parts:
1) Gender Identity: How we see ourselves
2) Gender Expression: How we express ourselves, and
3) Gender Attribution: How the world sees us.

Our gender identity has little to do with surgery or hormones. Although those things can bring us closer to how we view ourselves, those need not be present for us to understand who we are. All three components play into whom we have sex with, how we have sex, and in some cases, what we deny ourselves. For instance, butches aren't supposed to get fucked, femmes are "pillow queens," trans men don't want to be touched, trans women only get fucked, femme lesbians only date butch women, trans femmes only date straight men and trans masculine folks don't date each other. What a load of crap! We all know that we cannot fit into neat little packages. Stepping outside of gender attribution can be liberating but scary. We want our identities validated and we want to be true to our desires. Sometimes society's gender stereotyping limits the vastness of our sexual expressions. Don't generalize.

I'm a trans identified switch. I like to fuck and be fucked. I desire and play with people of different genders, sexual orientations and sexual identies. My sexual activities and appetite change frequently. Sexual moods or desires shift depending on comfort level, who we're with, where sex is happening and sometimes what kind of day we've had. I want my fuck experiences based not on assumptions but fact. Assumptions are only right half the time so don't take that gamble. Make every experience with other lesbians, queer women and or trans people unique. You'll be more satisfied for it.

Here are some things to know about some trans people and our bodies:

As trans people, we are constantly aware of our bodies, how others see us and how we want to realize ourselves. When it comes to sex, the first thing I always like to convey to a sex buddy is what I call the parts of my body. It's a total mood killer when someone calls my junk a cunt or pussy. That's not what I call it. I know some trans guys who call their genitals pussy and I know some trans women who call their bits a dick. I also know trans feminine and masculine folks who would never use those terms to describe their anatomy. I usually tell people my pronoun and about my body right away. I also like it when people ask upfront.

It can be challenging to express ourselves sexually when our bodies don't match how we feel inside. We may have disassociation with the genitals we were born with. Other trans people are able to share their bodies while in their evolution. The sex you have with a trans person can be "traditional" and/or "creative." You both get to decide what this looks like for you. This is all part of the negotiation.

Negotiating is like foreplay. It can be a conversation, flirting, a play-by-play while it's happening, fantasy sharing or physically directing someone's hands to where I want them to be on my body. Negotiating ahead of time decreases the likelihood of mis-gendering, and increases the chances of a good time. Every trans person and experience is different. Don't generalize. Approach, flirt, negotiate and discover the sexual possibilities.

Remember (not in any particular order)
1) Ask pronoun
2) Ask what they call their body (genitals)
3) Ask about sex roles (top/bottom/switch)
4) What they're into? / What they'd like to try?
5) Do's and Don'ts

If you're not sure how to ask:
• Use gender-neutral words for body parts until the person tells you.
• Role model by sharing your own pronoun, body words and sex roles.

You may help them feel more comfortable communicating their own boundaries and words.

Ignacio Rivera aka Papí Coxxx, who prefers the gender-neutral pronoun "they," is very queer and wonderfully gender fluid. They organize, write, perform and educate on race, gender and sexuality.

INTEGRITY

Integrity has two useful and relevant definitions for Girl Sex 101.

in·teg·ri·ty
[in-teg-ri-tee]

1) adherence to moral and ethical principles; soundness of moral character; honesty.
2) the state of being whole, entire, or undiminished.

1) Adherence to moral and ethical principles; soundness of moral character; honesty.
   A person with sexual integrity:
   • Honors agreements.
   • Speaks up when necessary.
   • Respects their body and the bodies of their partner(s).
   • Comes clean when necessary.
   • Does not tolerate abuse, hatred, or bigotry.
   • Respects the privacy of others.
   • Acknowledges that one's own boundaries may not be the same as another person's.
   • Honors their identity, and the identities of their community members and partner(s).

2) The state of being whole, entire, or undiminished.
   A person with sexual integrity also:
   • Examines their own desires and proclivities.
   • Investigates their fears, concerns, and hangups.
   • Questions their assumptions, about others and themself.
   • Tends to their physical health, as well as their emotional and spiritual health.
   • Seeks partnership and peermanship with people with integrity, who support their wholeness of being.
   • Considers their sexuality to be an intrinsic part of their humanity, and gives it the same respect and consideration as spirituality, intellect, and emotional wellbeing.

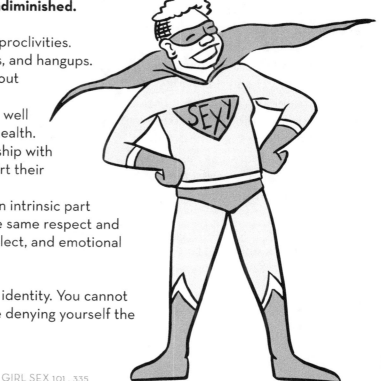

Integrity, by definition, encompasses one's identity. You cannot be a whole and undiminished person while denying yourself the wholeness of your experience.

If you want to have sexual integrity, you must be honest to yourself and the people you have sex with. You must be willing to engage in safer sex conversations. You will not impede on another person's self-expression, even if it doesn't fit your ideal.

The cool thing about sexual integrity is it gives you a reputation—the good kind. As I mentioned before, lesbian and queer communities are small and incestuous. If you're dating or sleeping around, odds are, the people you sleep with are going to talk. You can influence what they say by having integrity. If you violate a boundary, or intentionally misgender someone, or are a bully, that's going to get around. Do you want to be known as the chick who bullied someone into doing something they didn't want to do in bed? Or do you want to be the chick who rocked someone's world, understood when someone needed to use their safeword, and checked in about relationship agreements before getting naked?

Don't be a sexual bully. Women have it hard enough in this world when it comes to sex. You can be the respite, the kindness, the sexual superhero who listens, cares, and behaves like a standup lady.

DYKE DRAMA 101

Yes, it's going to happen. But, no, it doesn't have to. Back in my younger days, there was a weird allegiance girls had to dyke drama. I couldn't go to my favorite lesbian bar without warring groups of girls breaking out into fights and shutting down the dance floor. I couldn't hang out with friends without the conversation eroding into gossip about who cheated on whom with an ex. It was as if drama—more than our haircuts, tattoos, girlfriends or hand sex skills—indicated a true dyke.

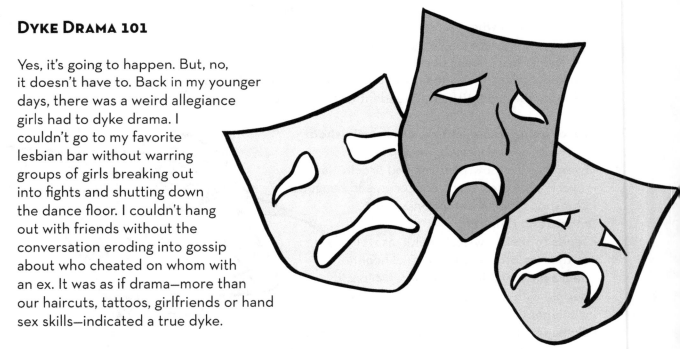

Ugh, I'm so glad those days are over. Dyke drama is a pernicious byproduct of girls who are unwilling to talk to each other about important things. It's totally unfair, and immature, but it's tradition, so...

No way.

Dyke drama happens when we let problems fester instead of talking it out. It is, at its worst, a queer, adult manifestation of the Mean Girl syndrome. It often involves your whole community, and requires gossip, choosing sides, and passive aggression. In other words: bullshit.

In my opinion, dyke drama happens when people are afraid to speak up. Queer women's communities are small. We are afraid to confront our problems in communal space, and we don't want things to get ugly in front of other folks.

Most people say they don't want drama in their lives, but few people do the work to prevent it.

So, how do you deal with Dyke Drama?

1) **Don't start it.** I know, famous last words. But I bet half the time you have the opportunity to stop it before it starts, but you don't. Commit to speaking up like a grown-up instead of complaining to your friends.

2) **Don't gossip.** I know it's hard. We love this kind of lascivious stuff, even if it involves people we love and respect. But shutting gossip down is always better than a hurt friend come to you in tears asking, "What did they say about me?"

If someone comes to you with gossip, ask them, "Were you there?" If they weren't, don't let them keep going with it. Or ask them, "Why are you telling me this?" If they don't have a good answer beyond the exciting gossip, shut it down.

The primary difference between Gossip and Venting is that gossip doesn't directly involve the person talking. For instance:

This...

....is gossip.

And this...

....is venting.

If you're in the position of being the compassionate listener in these conversations, you should put a stop to gossip and check in to make sure that venting is really just venting (as opposed to trying to bolster the armies on either side).

If it's gossip—that is, it has to do with people who aren't involved in the conversation—the best thing you can do to avoid the dyke drama is stop the conversation. Yes, I know this can be hard. Do it anyway.

 If you're curious beyond salaciousness: That is, if you have a real, compelling, non-gossip-oriented reason to know what happened, talk to a person who was involved in the conversation. You'll be 100% more likely to hear a more accurate version of the truth.

Vent with care. Don't just spill all over someone. Who likes having a stream of invectives thrown at their face without knowing why? If you need to vent to a friend, ask them if you can vent. They have the right to say yes or no. If they're a yes, get it out, but don't keep digging to find more anger. Get the anger out, then try to start processing or get your mind off it for a bit. If they say no, respect the no, and then try to find another way to vent.

Don't feed the trolls. In this case, the trolls may indeed be your friends. What this means is, don't add fuel to the fire. If someone is venting at you, make sure it's venting and not gossip, and don't throw your pile of hate onto the bonfire.

Try practice conversations. A practice conversation is where you practice sharing what you need to share with a neutral party before you take it to the person who you're having issues with. It helps you get some of the bad juju out beforehand, and helps you articulate the real cause of your concerns without being a rage monster.

Remember Reid Mihalko's "Difficult Conversation Formula"? That's a great formula for having conversations with someone who's causing drama in your or your community's life.

I'm going to reprint it here for you so you remember:

REIDABOUTSEX'S
DIFFICULT CONVERSATION
FORMULA

1) I have something to tell you.

2) Here's what I'm afraid will happen when I tell you...

3) Here's what I want to have happen...

4) Here's what I have to tell you...

USE IT!

Look inward. If dyke drama seems to be everywhere you go, you might want to take a look at yourself. You may indeed be the common denominator. Some people like being the center of drama because it makes them feel important, others because it's how they grew up and it feels normal. The good news is, if you're the one starting and stirring it, you can be the one to put down the spoon. Go to therapy, apologize to those you need to apologize to, and make a promise to yourself to be the bigger person.

If there is a concern for safety, treat it as such. If there's a threat of abuse, get the information you need to be able to act. But get it from a party directly involved. Don't trust gossip when it comes to abuse. If you're worried that one person is a source of not only drama, but physical or emotional harm, talk to your community about removing that person from the fold, and possibly working with the person directly affected to press charges or get counseling.

Dyke Drama is not status quo. It's not like the weather—just a thing you have to put up with. It is a human creation that is both generated and fed by people making bad choices. You can put a stop to it by being the bigger woman.

THE GIRL SEX 101 GUIDE
TO SEXUAL INTEGRITY

1) **Know & Share Your STI Status.** Practice Reid's Safer Sex Elevator Speech (page 315) and USE IT. Get tested. Have the conversation before you're grinding your bits on anybody.

2) **Know Your Intentions.** Many of us have pasts full of awkward or ill-communicated hookups, flirtations, and sleepovers. My first three years out of college, I broke hearts simply by not considering the other person's feelings. I was, in a word, a jerk. If you're looking to make out at a club, or get drunk and fool around in the bathroom, or seeking certain kinds of friends or community, or looking for a longer-term playmate, cool. It doesn't matter what you're into, as long as you communicate those intentions to possible playmates.

3) **Respect Yourself.** You are responsible for your choices. Your job is to make choices you can feel good about. "Good" here doesn't mean morally superior or even, let's say, *constructive* choices. What it means is you make choices with a clear enough head to know when your choice is your own and when it's not. When it's not is when there's addiction, coercion, or nonconsent involved. In those instances, I recommend seeking help, in the form of therapists, lawyers, friends or trusted community members. But you're allowed to make sexual choices that are edgy, risky, or scary. Get the risk-assessment formula (page 301) ingrained in your head. Some of you will already have it instinctually, and some of you will have to learn and practice it. The bottom line: get on a working relationship with your self-esteem. Learn to trust your instincts. Honor your emotions. Listen to your conscience (instead of your shame).

4) **Respect your partner(s).** Respect a person's intentions, identity, and proclivities. If a cutie drops a bomb (like a kink that skeeves you out or an aspect of their identity that you weren't expecting), your reaction is yours. People are into all sorts of things and they have all sorts of arrangements. If you're flirting and they share something you're not into, you can either negotiate based on that information, or you can politely say "thanks, but I'm not interested." Trust yourself to know you, and trust others to know themselves. No judgments, no shame.

5) **You Are Allowed to Change Your Mind.**
A yes can become a no. A maybe can become a
yes. You are allowed, and encouraged, to change
your mind. Remember when we talked about how
important it is to check in with a lover? Well, it's
even more important to check in with yourself.

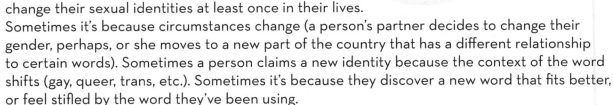

6) **You Are Allowed to Change your Label.** A lesbian
can become bisexual. A bisexual can become
queer. A queer can become straight. Most people
change their sexual identities at least once in their lives.
Sometimes it's because circumstances change (a person's partner decides to change their
gender, perhaps, or she moves to a new part of the country that has a different relationship
to certain words). Sometimes a person claims a new identity because the context of the word
shifts (gay, queer, trans, etc.). Sometimes it's because they discover a new word that fits better,
or feel stifled by the word they've been using.

Sometimes changing your identity is a really healthy choice. Sometimes doing it twelve times
is the right thing to do for you. Your parents might roll their eyes, but your identity isn't about
them, or anyone. It's how you relate to yourself. So, choose words that fit.

Me? I've come out roughly four times now: as bisexual, then lesbian, then queer, then
nonmonogamous. And I've still got a lot of living left to do. Identities are living things. In the
'90s, no one called themselves "cis." In the '80s, "queer" was mainly a slur. Who
knows what new identities will blossom in the future?

7) **Identity is flexible, unless it's not.** Don't let your identity
or your partner's identity shame you. Likewise, if
you're flexible or experimenting with your gender or
identity, that doesn't mean your potential playmate
is. Suggesting that anyone is "just going through
a phase" or "doing it wrong" is condescending.
Likewise suggesting a straight girl just "hasn't
been with the right woman yet" or a monogamous
person is a tool of the patriarchy or a trans dude
has internalized misogyny or whatever, is bullshit.

8) **No Shame in Your Game.** Don't let people shame
you for your identity. Don't shame others for
theirs. Most importantly, don't shame yourself for
what you want.

THE GIRL SEX 101
SEXUAL INTEGRITY CHECKLIST

- [ ] Understand consent, remembering that it is ongoing, instantly revocable, and required from all parties.

- [ ] Memorize and use the Safer Sex Elevator Speech.

- [ ] Know how to use a variety of safer sex barriers and risk-mitigation techniques.

- [ ] Honor emotional and relationship agreements.

- [ ] Check in regularly and whenever there is a question about participation and enthusiasm.

- [ ] Ask for preferences regarding pronouns, body part names, No Zones, and preferred practices.

- [ ] Communicate boundaries.

- [ ] Respect the identities of my partners and peers.

- [ ] Support friends through their own sexual and gender journeys.

- [ ] Don't stir drama.

DAY 9

Jamie wakes to the smell of coffee. Their host, Maria Teresa, stands over stove in a sarong and slippers. Her long brown hair is tied into a knot on top of her head. Somehow she's even more fit and feral looking than back in college, a look aided by the heavy plugs in her earlobes and bright orange phoenix tattoo stretching across her back. "Coffee's fresh," she says. Jamie kisses her cheek in greeting. Layla sits at the dining table, drinking juice and reading the New Yorker. "MaTe was telling me about a retreat center in Joshua Tree that hires folks under the table."

Jamie fills her mug and joins Layla at the table. "Cool. What kind of retreat?"

"Silent meditation, yoga, that kind of thing," MaTe says, serving up scrambled tofu and adding a sprig of grapes to each of their plates. "Cool people. Tons of queers. I did a summer there."

"We could head there after San Diego," Layla says, waggling her brows.

"We?"

"Why not?"

"I have an interview on Wednesday," Jamie says.

"For a job you don't want," Layla replies.

"Which will give me money I need."

"To do what you really want to be doing instead, which you could do anyway."

Jamie snarls and spears tofu on her fork.

"Why not figure out a way to make money from your art?" MaTe offers.

"The eternal question," Jamie says, mouth full.

"LA is filled with people making money from their art. That's how I got into the business."

"You're a yoga teacher," Layla says.

"Yeah, on-set for the rich and famous. I don't do this shit for fifteen dollars an hour anymore. And neither should you," MaTe says, gesturing at Jamie with her fork. The three women eat, and the conversation moves on to other topics, catching each other up on the years since college graduation.

After breakfast, MaTe throws two surfboards on top of the car and packs some lunches. Jamie and Layla get to be passengers for the first time in two weeks.

• •

Jamie sits on the beach blanket, watching MaTe teach Layla how to surf. She pulls out her camera and records. Not an art video this time. Today it's more a diary, a memory, a presencing in place. Jamie watches through the viewfinder, placing a layer of distance between her and Layla. Her cell phone vibrates with a message from Angela. *For the record, I really wanted to kiss you last night.*

Jamie smiles. *Likewise :)* she responds.

I just need to take things super slow these days. I hope you won't leave town without me being able to kiss you goodbye.

Jamie contemplates the waves, the beach, the trees, her friends, and her camera. *Not a chance*, she types. Layla runs up the beach, panting and pink. "Whew, that's hard work."

"You looked good," Jamie says.

"I even stood up once!" Layla laughs. She digs through the cooler for a bottle of water.

MaTe lays her board on the sand. "You doing okay all alone up here?"

Jamie nods. "Just processing."

"I'd expect nothing less from a queer," MaTe says. "What about?"

"My life? Facing some big decisions. Not sure how to proceed."

MaTe grabs the sandwiches from the cooler and tosses one to Jamie. "Start with food. Always start with food."

LOS ANGELES

DAY 9

The whole ride back to MaTe's place, Layla bites the inside of her cheek. In the backseat, Jamie is texting. Her new crush, no doubt. Layla feels sick. She rests her head on the window.

Back at the house, Jamie and Layla unload the surfboards from the roof of MaTe's car.

"I'm thinking of heading to San Diego after rush hour," Layla says. "Aaron's gonna meet us after his dinner gig."

"Why don't you go on without me," Jamie says. "Your brother never really liked me anyway."

"You mean end it here? You wanna stay in LA?"

Jamie nods. "For a day or two."

"Ditching the interview, then?"

"Guess so. Angela wanted to take me to some open studios this weekend. I'm digging the scenery."

"Ah. I know what that means."

Jamie shrugs. "Feels right."

Layla looks away and nods.

Inside the house, Jamie goes to nap in the guest room. Layla opens the last beer and scoots onto the hammock in the backyard. A freshly showered MaTe approaches.

"Permission to come aboard?"

"Granted," Layla says, weakly.

MaTe eases onto the hammock and offers her chest for Layla's head. Layla cuddles up and squeezes back tears.

"She break your heart again?"

Layla half-shrugs and wipes a tear from her cheek.

"Can I make an observation?" MaTe asks.

"Sure."

"I love Jamie. She's a wonderful human and a good friend. But you two are traveling different highways."

Layla soaks in the statement. "I just like having her in my passenger seat."

"Not if you're heading to different destinations. What do you want to do in the next three years?"

"Like a list?"

"Hit me."

Layla stares at the sky and lets her mind ride the innumerable possibilities. "Surf in Ibiza. Ride a camel in Egypt. Practice Japanese in Kyoto. Pick grapes in Umbria. Learn how to salsa in Argentina..."

"And what does Jamie want to do?"

"Make art and stay put."

MaTe squeezes Layla and says, "Ta-daa."

Layla lets a few more tears roll down her cheeks. "But I love her."

"Good. Love her. But don't try making her into the girlfriend you want. She's not your copilot. This world is filled with amazing, sexy women who will beg you to stamp their passports. Go find them."

MaTe kisses Layla's forehead. Layla smiles.

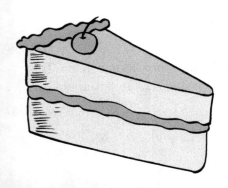

**Sometimes sex has unintended consequences, and I don't mean babies. I'm talking about the L word.
No, the other L word.**

Do you need love for sex? That's up to you. Some people think that sex is a fun exchange of energy, and it shouldn't be any more tied to love than sharing a nice dinner, dancing, or having connected conversation with someone. Love isn't always on the menu when you're sharing sweaty times with another hottie.

Other folks believe that monogamous, devoted love is a prerequisite to sex. And others don't think love is a prereq, but it makes the sex better.

I have my opinions, and you'll have yours. The key is to not use your own yardstick to measure other people's worth. Both slut-shaming and calling women "frigid" comes from placing your own values on others. You do you, and let other people decide for themselves what they want.

For the moment, let's assume you want to have fun, fulfilling sex but avoid falling in love. I'm going to use the reclaimed version of the word "slut" to describe that. Usually this usage of slut means a person who enjoys sex. Plain and simple. It's used as a big "fuck you" to the paternalistic jackholes who shame women like it's their job. Because most people enjoy sex. Yay.

SLUT PROTOCOL

In the following context, I'm using slut to describe a person who has sex for pleasure outside of a monogamous relationship.

So how do you be an effective slut? Is it possible to share orgasms without sharing your heart? I think so, but it's not as easy as just willing it to be so. **There are some rules:**

1) **Know yourself.** Are you the kind of person who gets gaga over anyone you kiss? Is cunnilingus the ultimate intimate act? Do you just love falling in love? Do you have an addictive personality? Love highs are real. That cascade of love hormones is like cocaine for your brain—literally! Know yourself and choose accordingly. You might just not have the kind of personality that can handle sluttery.

2) **Hang out with other sluts.** If after every romp your friends ask "Is she the one?!!" that's going to put a lot of pressure on you. Hang out with people who get it.

3) **Sleep with other sluts.** If after orgasm your sex partner asks, "Am I the one?!" you're doing it wrong. If you want to sleep around, but you're doing it with people who want monogamy, you're the jerk. Don't be that person. Sleep with other sluts.

4) **Public/group sex helps.** Playing at orgies, play parties, or dungeon parties is a great way to have a good time without getting into the one-on-one habit.

5) **Once (a week) is enough.** If you only see each other once a week, and you only see each other for sex (as opposed to date-like things) you can help avoid the oxytocin spiral. KISSS: Keep It Seldom and Simple, Slut.

6) **Diversify.** If you're relying on one person to meet all of your emotional and physical needs, you're in the danger zone. Diversify your community, and source your needs from multiple people. That may mean you have a cuddle buddy, an action movie buddy, a go-out-dancing buddy, a bath time buddy, and a couple fuck buddies. This helps you reduce the hormonal hit you get from one person and spreads out the yummy feelings of connection and love over multiple different people.

RELATIONSHIP PROTOCOL

Okay, so being easy is easy. What if you DO want love? Good on you! Love is grand, a many splendored thing, and yadda yadda yadda. **So how do you find the love AND sex partner of your dreams?**

1) **Know what you want.** Be specific. Not everything has to be a dealbreaker, but if you have no standards, guess what? You're going to find someone who drives you nuts.

2) **Stick to your guns.** Remember what I said about preferences back on page 331? Consider this a gentle reminder: the only exceptions you should make to your rules are POWERFUL ones. Don't think, "I'm so lonely, I'll relax my stance on Israel and Palestine. It'll be fine." Take it from me: *it won't be fine*. It won't make you happy, and you might end up with someone who stokes your rage more than your lust.

3) **Honor chemistry.** Have you ever dated someone who was "perfect" in every way but didn't get you wet? How did that work out for you? *Exactly.* Dating someone who doesn't rev your engine is putting an expiration date on your relationship. No matter how much you like a person, you can't fake attraction. True, there are many important components to a relationship and sex is only one of them. But if sex is important to you, treat it that way. Prioritize it.

4) **Be transparent.** If you want a relationship, say so. Put it in your dating profile. Tell your besties you're looking for love. Declare powerfully your intention, and you might find the pair-bonding hotties of your dreams start gravitating toward you.

5) **Don't be a missionary.** Don't waste your time trying to convert anyone. If you meet Ms. Perfect Except She's Not Ready For A Relationship, you'll be pulling out your hair in no time. Same goes for Ms. Amazing But Is Super Straight. Date people who want what you want. The life you want is worth it.

LI-LI-LI-BIDO!

Asymmetrical desire. It happens to everyone. You are, after all, an individual, and your partner is too.

Libido is affected by a lot of things: medications, self-esteem, emotions, life events, monthly cycles and hormones, stress, access to orgasm, and more. It's totally normal for you or your partner to want more or less sex because of any of these things, or anything else. Nothing and no one is broken.

If you and your partner are finding yourselves in mismatched states, here are some tips:

1) **You ebb, I flow.** Is this a phase? Or is it a permanent state of things? Look at the evidence. Did one of you just...
- give birth?
- start a new medication?
- deal with some trauma?
- have a medical procedure?
- get fired?
- get promoted?
- start therapy?
- start her period?
- start hormones?
- start menopause?

If you can draw a straight line between your shift in libido and a significant life situation, odds are it's a phase.

2) **Expand the possibilities of sex.** Sometimes you don't want sex, but do want an orgasm. Or sometimes you want to feel sexy and/or connected without having "the sex." Sometimes if I'm horny when my partner isn't, I'll masturbate while they hold me, or vice versa. Sometimes nonsexual intimate touch (like a nice backrub or shared bath) is enough to satisfy a need for connection.

3) **Examine your priorities.** It's possible that this isn't about mismatched libidos but mismatched priorities. Your partner may find it more important to share non-sexual quality time than to have sex.

4) **Take stock of the health of your relationship.** Are you two going through a big shift? Did you recently have a fight? Some people have sex to ensure everything is okay, like bonobos. Sex can help seal emotional bonds and repair any wonky dynamics. Others have sex only when things are okay, like pandas. They need all the circumstances to be healthy before they wanna bone. If you're going through a rough patch, it's possible one of you is a bonobo and the other is a panda.

5) **Consider your options.** If you're dating someone with a vastly different sexual expression than you, you have some work to do. This might mean renegotiating the boundaries of your relationship, whether to allow for kink, cyber sex, or real-life sex with other people. If you think this may be a good solution for you, check out the list of books in the Appendix relating to open relationships.
Denial, patience, or subverting your own desires are all doomed tactics. You may buy yourself some time, but you're not going to miraculously wake up in the right relationship one day. Eventually, lying to yourself about your sex life or waiting for your partner to change is going to wear you down, breeding resentment or anger.

6) **Neither of you are wrong.** You may have noticed that our society is pretty fucked up when it comes to sex. On one hand, if you want it a lot, you're considered greedy, selfish, slutty, and degenerate. On the other hand, if you don't want it very much, you're frigid, withholding, and cruel. Neither of these stereotypes is accurate. Life changes can affect our libidos, but there's usually some sort of baseline. That baseline can be high for some social, sexual people, and really low for others.

Unfortunately, our society tends to side with the partner who wants sex less and shames the partner who wants it more. If you're the higher libido in the relationship, you may have to deal with friends and family telling you to suck it up and deal with a sexless partnership.

If it's just a phase, give it some time. But locking a partner out of sex can often be a precursor to locking them out of your heart. If your partner is denying you sex for a reason you can't understand, you need to start talking to each other. You may need to bring in professionals in the form of sex therapists, couples counselors, or others.

Libido is not a constant through life, but sexual value systems often are. If you or your partner values sex more, odds are, that's not going to change overnight. You should have a real conversation about shared intentions for sex and sensuality in your relationship, ideally before you get in too deep.

A BIT ABOUT ASEXUALITY

Asexual people are finally starting to have a voice in society. They have community, advocacy, unique identities, and individual relationship styles. In short, people are starting to acknowledge that asexual people exist.

Asexuality is generally described as indifference to sex. It's not low libido, though some asexuals may have this too. The difference is that folks with low libido usually experience sexual attraction and desire, but lack enthusiasm to fulfill on those attractions. Meanwhile, asexuals usually have little or no desire at all. Some asexuals are actively repulsed by sex. Others don't have big feelings about it in either direction.

If you're a sexual person, asexuality can be hard to understand. It can seem almost like not feeling hunger. Meanwhile, for asexuals, it's just a real fact of life. The most popular way asexuals try to describe their experience to sexually-inclined people is with a cake metaphor:
Let's say a bunch of your friends are eating cake. "Here! Have some cake!" They shout. You shrug. "No thanks. I don't really like cake."

"Everyone likes cake!" They're enthusiastic. They love cake. They want you to be as happy as they are. "It's good for you! Cake is great for society! It's important that everyone enjoys cake!"

You don't necessarily disagree with them. You just don't like cake. It does nothing for you. Maybe you're more of a flan person.

"What's wrong with you?!"

"IS IT THE CAKE? DID THE CAKE DO ANYTHING TO YOU?"

"WERE YOU HURT BY CAKE AS A CHILD?"

"You just haven't found the right person to eat cake with yet!"

Can you see where this is going? Everyone has different desires when it comes to sex. Some people want a lot of it. Some people can take or leave it. No one is broken, damaged, or evil. We just have different interests.

There are gradations to asexuality. It's not a completely cake vs. no-cake situation. There are Grey A people who have a super low interest in sex but aren't completely against the idea. There are Demi-sexuals who can experience sexual attraction, but usually only to specific individuals when a significant emotional bond is formed. Or they may masturbate but don't desire sex with others. There are Sensual Asexuals who dig cuddling, smooching, and sensual touch, but don't want sexual touch or energy. And there are Romantic Asexuals who dig all the sweet lovey stuff of relationships but don't want sex.

And there are more labels and versions of it. (Check out the Appendix if you want to learn more about asexuality and its many variations.) If you're asexual, it's a good idea to disclose to your partners or potential partners early on the in the relationship. Many people take it personally and assume the worst when their sweetie doesn't want to jump their bones. If you have a significantly lower interest in sex in general, that's a good thing for your partner to know before things get too serious. There are plenty of people who have healthy relationships that encompass disparate sexual self-expressions. Just because one of you has a greater interest in sex than the other doesn't mean whatever relationship you want to create is doomed. But you have to talk about it, so everyone can be on the same page.

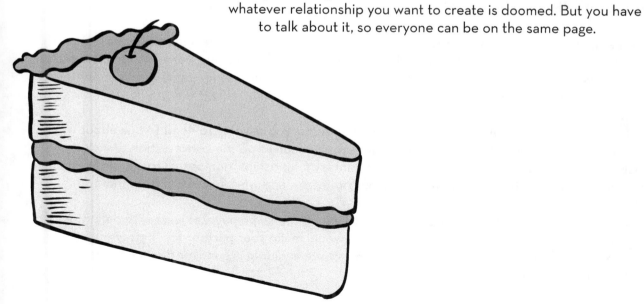

SEXUAL SELF-Expression

Before you get too serious with someone, it's good to talk about sexual expression. How often do you like to have sex? How long can you go without before you start getting cranky? Is monogamous sex a requirement? How about playing with other people together? Watching porn together? Exploring kink or BDSM? Playing sensually or sexually with others?

If you're seeing someone who you think may be relationship-worthy, these questions are worth asking. The honeymoon phase can occlude all sorts of things, because you're having all of the sex and all of the fun. But what happens when that new relationship energy wears off? How much and what kind of sex will feel adequate and connected for you and your partner?

You need to be able to be honest with one another, respect one another's sovereignty through consent and identity. Good love helps you co-create joy and pleasure, just like sex does.

MONOGAMY: ONE PARNTER, MANY DEFINITIONS

If you want a monogamous relationship, it's a good idea to get clear about what monogamy means for you. Does it mean no porn? No cyber sex? No intimate friendships? No kissing? No sensual excitement with others?

Sex is a range, and so is relationship expression. Your monogamy may be another's cheating, and vice versa. As you may have noticed reading through this book, using any word as shorthand often doesn't give you the information you need. One person's "lesbian, mono, trans, vanilla" is another's "queer, single, fluid, kinky."

So if you want a monogamous relationship with someone, you're going to need to talk about what that means. When you're in a good groove with someone, open up the conversation to include what monogamy means to you. Consider porn, fantasy, friendships, non-sexual touch, and more. Think about what might make you angry, jealous or unsafe, and work backward from there.

If you're designing a relationship, it's important to get on the same page, at least with definitions if not self-expressions. Get perfectly clear on what would make your partner feel betrayed. If it's a goal post far different from your own, you can negotiate a middle ground, or decide if pursuing a relationship together even makes sense.

SLUT-SHAMING

Slut-shaming is criticizing or devaluing a person because they have sex. It's a technique for controlling women's sexuality using shame. Rarely does it actually condemn any specific act or style of sex. Instead, it's a catchall tool for telling a woman she's bad, immoral, or worthless. Women in monogamous heterosexual marriages get slut-shamed, celibate women get slut-shamed, prostitutes get slut-shamed, and lesbians get slut-shamed.

Slut-shaming can be explicit: "You're such a slut!"

And implicit: "You just met her!"

It can be disguised as concern: "Aren't you afraid you're going to catch something?"

Or envy: "Wow, I wish I could bed hop as much as you do."

It can apply to desires: "Why would you let someone choke you?"

Or presentation: "Do you really want to wear that?"

It's easy to spot it when it comes from politicians, police, and parents. It's harder to recognize when it comes from friends. But, odds are, if you're a girl, you've been slut-shamed by someone in your community.

We live in a sex negative culture. The messages we get are shaming, cruel, victim-blaming and disproportionately focused on women and our bodies. We're supposed to be consumable, sexy objects, while at the same time preserving the image of women as incorruptible, pure, and virginal. Meanwhile, our society is still entrenched in the belief that the only kind of legitimate sex is between married, heterosexual, cisgender couples.

It is—literally—impossible to win.

The thing to remember is that you're allowed to seek and have the sex you want. You are allowed to choose your partners, choose to be celibate, choose to be slutty, choose to be monogamous, and choose to have sex solo or in groups. You get to have consensual sex when you want, as often as you want, with whomever you want. That is your right as a human in this world, regardless of what any preacher or politician says.

The preachers and politicians know what they're doing when they slut-shame. But your friends probably don't. This is because society is on their side. Even if you're a sex-positive, progressively-minded person, it's often easier to judge people for their sexual preferences than it is to accept them without bias.

In fact, you may be the one doing the shaming. Perhaps you read something in this book that made you wince. Maybe you thought, "How could anyone *like* that?" This, as innocuous as may sound, is a form of slut-shaming. Have you ever been out to eat with a friend and grimaced at the food they ordered? That's what slut shaming is like, except with sex. I've caught myself slut-shaming people—even my partner—wondering how someone can do a certain kind of porn, or enjoy a certain kind of kink, or have sex with a certain number of people all in one day. This stuff goes deep, and is often invisible. It takes work to excise slut-shaming from your life.

Here's how to defeat slut-shaming:

1) **Don't accept slut-shaming from your community.** If your friends talk smack about you or other people because of the sex they like to have, call it out and shut it down.

2) **Practice catching yourself when you start slut-shaming.** If you judge someone—whether silently or publicly—for expressing their sexuality, pay attention to the story you're telling in your head. Is it that you're envious? Or that you're repeating a shaming message you've been told by people whose opinions don't really matter? If you hear yourself saying "I could never do that!" or "Feminists don't..." or any "icky" responses to your friend's sharing, you may be slut-shaming.

3) **Eradicate shaming words from your vocabulary.** If you hear yourself calling someone "loose," "desperate," "a whore," "easy," or "slut," in a way that isn't reclaimed, quit it. Women have enough judgment in this world as it is. Don't be a woman who's denigrating other women for choosing to have the kind of sex they want.

4) **Broaden your horizons.** If you're skeeved out by a kink or practice that people genuinely enjoy, it might behoove you to do some research, whether in person or with our friend Mr. Google. Find out why people enjoy it, and you might have a new appreciation for your friends and the wide world of sexuality.

5) **Be an ally.** Remember that women are pitted against each other in our society. Be a good feminist by refusing to partake in the infighting.

SEX VS. MAKING LOVE

Sometimes, when faced with a naked woman in our bed, we can get a little...flustered. There's so much to track, contemplate, and listen to. It can be overwhelming and terrifying. We can get so caught up in the mechanics that we forget about the magic and beauty of making love.

We all relate to the phrase "making love" differently. When I was a kid I thought it was the grossest. Now, well, I'm a bit more of a softie.

To me, the difference is akin to the difference between a good dinner and a four course meal made with love. Both are nourishing and healthy, but one encourages you to slow down and savor that much more.

HOW ARE LOVE & SEX CONNECTED FOR YOU?

Sex has something extra to it with someone you love, but sex can still be good without it.

Sex is something I do when I'm bored. Love is an ongoing act of political dissidence.

WITHOUT SOME SORT OF ROMANTIC ATTACHMENT, I DON'T GET WHAT I NEED FROM SEXUAL INTIMACY.

I cannot have sex without love but I can love without sex.

Love and sex are two different things that intersect in many ways.

THEY'RE USUALLY TOTALLY SEPARATE FOR ME. I HAVE A REALLY HARD TIME WITH EMOTIONAL INTIMACY, BUT I FIND PHYSICAL INTIMACY REALLY EASY.

Sex can be a wonderful way to express your love to someone. However, a person doesn't have to be in love to have good sex or sex at all. Sometimes sex is just for comfort and release. Other times it's all about enjoying making your love melt at your touch.

Sex is an expression of love, every time. The love is always different, and could even be celebrating something other than the two (or more) of us. But it's always an expression of love and gratitude for these bodies and earth and awareness.

Regardless of how you relate to the terms, every so often it's helpful to remember to take some breaths and slooooow doooown. Slowing down your tempo will help you track sensations, listen closer to your lover's body, and savor the experience.

There's plenty of room for clothes-ripping passion, but remember how important it is to nourish your bodies with slow, deliberate sensations.

This often becomes an issue in long term relationships where you know what gets your partner off, and you can do it fairly quickly. It's a "rote" kind of sex that turns everything into shorthand. That can be fine every once in a while (not everyone can spend hours in the sack every day) but sometimes it's good to forgo the Cliffs Notes and indulge in the poetry of the whole book.

It can also be a problem when you're new to the relationship, and you're so stuck in your head with the "Am I doing this right? Does she like this? Does she like me?!" anxiety monologue that you forget to savor the experience.

If you catch yourself checking out of your partner's body because you're stuck in your head, take a deep breath and center. Take note of the sensations, scents, and visuals of the experience. Pay attention to your partner's body. Feel her skin with your hands, and her breath with your cheek. Remember to savor the magic.

LONG-TERM LOVE & LUST

Lesbian bed death is an exaggeration. Every relationship, regardless of the genders of the participants, will go through sexual ebbs and flows. That's normal. The important part is to respect whatever importance sex has for you in the relationship, and strive to get everyone's needs met. Here's how:

1) **Respect each other's autonomy.** Just because you're partnered doesn't mean you're the same person. Each of you will have your own tastes, proclivities, desires, and kinks. Lesbians especially have a rep for merging our identities with our partners and losing our own in the process.

2) **Respect each other's privacy.** Everyone is entitled to their own inner world, which includes fantasy, imagination, and desires. If your partner doesn't want to share everything they're thinking while you two fuck, that's fine. Whatever gets you off is yours. Of course, this shouldn't compromise the integrity of your relationship, and if either of you are checking out more than being present, you may need to have a conversation about that. But barring that, you and your partner both are allowed to keep your secrets secret.

As long as no relationship boundaries are being violated, privacy means you can have real world things that you can keep secret too. This can mean porn habits, casual flirtation with a coworker, or cybersex or whatever. If you don't know if you're violating a relationship agreement, it's probably because you haven't had the conversation with your partner. Perhaps that's a sign you should schedule that conversation, hmmmmm?

3) **Respect each other's bodies.** You're entitled to your privacy, but that ends when your privacy encroaches on your partner's consent. If you've tested positive for anything, or have had sex outside the relationship (whether ethically or cheating) that could expose you to anything, your partner deserves to know. Trust me, STIs are the worst "sorry I cheated on you" gift ever.

4) **Allow space for exploration.** Sex columnist Dan Savage came up with the perfect way to describe this: GGG, which means Good, Giving, and Game. If your partner is curious about something that doesn't turn your crank, aspire to be GGG: Respect their interests, examine how you might be able to help/participate, and be game to try it if they want. This doesn't mean you'll always be excited about everything they want, but being GGG means you'll honor your relationship above whatever squick you have and at least investigate their desire.

5) **Play!** Lifelong learning is the key to maintaining a sharp mind. And lifelong play is the secret to maintaining a healthy sex life. Odds are, as you age, your ideas of what is sexy, fun, and arousing will change. This is a good thing. It means you're learning and growing.

SEX IS AN EXTRAORDINARY WORLD.

ANGELA'S

DAY 9

Olive idles outside Angela's apartment. Layla unloads Jamie's bags.

"I'm glad you're sticking around stateside for a bit," Jamie says, "even if it is on the lam."

"You know me. Always gotta find a way to rebel."

"Have fun at the retreat, eating vegan and...vegan girls." Jamie grins. "You know they smell worse—"

Layla smiles. "But taste better."

The two grin at their old joke. "Say hi to your brother for me," Jamie says.

"Will do." Layla says. She gestures to Angela's building. "Don't order a U-Haul too soon."

"Nah. Taking it slow."

Layla smiles. "Sorry if I came on too strong. Nostalgia and hormones..."

"Helluva drug," Jamie says. "You're going to do great. You always do."

"Do I?"

Jamie pulls Layla into a tight, loving squeeze. "I can't wait to hear about all the trouble you get into."

"As long as I can get out of it again."

Jamie pulls away and holds Layla by the shoulders. "I love you," she says.

"I love you, too," Layla replies. They share a sweet kiss and Layla lets one last tear escape.

Jamie stands on the sidewalk and watches Layla drive away into the night.

Up the single staircase, Angela waits in her doorframe. Her posture is casual, but Jamie can read the nervousness on her face. Jamie smiles, finding her awkwardness endearing. Inside Angela's apartment, Jamie drops her bags and takes a look around. Angela blushes.

"Can I have that kiss now?" Jamie asks.

Angela nods and tucks a stray lock of hair behind her ear.

"Oh wait. First, I may have been exposed to herpes the other day. Yet to be confirmed. Just wanted to say that. Because it's nice to do."

Angela giggles. "Thanks for letting me know. That's not a problem. I still want you to kiss me."

"Noted." Jamie smiles. She grasps Angela's chin and coaxes her closer. Angela licks her lips. The kiss is tight and awkward, then relaxes into pleasant, sizzling softness.

They separate and smile.

"When I said really slow," Angela says, "I may have been overstating."

Jamie chuckles.

"I just haven't been with anyone since I started hormones, which was...a while ago. I feel like a virgin."

"That's all right."

"I still want to go slow, but I want to do it—"

"Naked?" They laugh together.

"We'll talk through it," Jamie says. "We'll learn as we go. No rush, and no agenda. Just two girls enjoying each other's company."

"That sounds wonderful."

"Good. Now c'mon," Jamie says, offering her arm for Angela to grasp. "Let's go for a ride."

ALLISON MOON

Allison Moon is the author of the sex memoir *Bad Dyke*, the Tales of the Pack series of novels about lesbian werewolves, and *Girl Sex 101*. She was a 2011 Lambda Literary Emerging LGBT Authors Fellow.

Allison has presented her workshops—on strap-on sex, cunnlingus, polyamory, sexual self-expression, erotica writing, and more—to thousands of people around the US and Canada. She has a degree in neuroscience from Oberlin College.
She lives in Oakland with a sun bear and a very large squid.

Learn more about her at AlliedMoon.com or follow her on Twitter @HeyAllieMoon

KD DIAMOND

KD DIAMOND has spent the last decade drawing, sketching, and doodling all manner of things, but specifically things related to sex. She's illustrated nine erotic how-to books, including *The Ultimate Guide to Kink*, *Playing Well With Others*, *The Ultimate Guide to Prostate Pleasure*, and *Partners in Pleasure*, and isn't planning on stopping anytime soon. Her comic art has been featured in various papers and magazines, and in the anthology *Gender Outlaws: The Next Generation*. She also illustrated and designed *Backwards Day*, a gender-non-conforming children's book by S. Bear Bergman, and serves as the art director for Bergman's Flamingo Rampant imprint. Additionally, Diamond is the founder and editor of *Salacious*, a queer feminist anti-racist porno mag. Since 2010, Salacious has released four compilations of dirty comics, erotica, and photography.

By day, Diamond braves Times Square crowds to draw cute things for an off-Broadway theater. By night, when she's not drawing anatomically accurate pictures of vulvas, she loves to teach people how to take really, really good care of their leather boots.

She lives in New York City with a magical time wizard.

Her art and contact info live at katiediamond.com.

FURTHER READING

Books & Zines

Ecstasy is Necessary by Barbara Carellas has a special way of exalting pleasure. If you want to explore ways of cultivating more juicy pleasure in your life, in bed and out, check out this book.

The Ethical Slut by Dossie Easton & Janet Hardy. This book is considered the bible of non-monogamy, written by two radical queers. Excellent reading even if you're not sure you want an open relationship.

Exhibitionism for the Shy by Carol Queen. Great advice for coming out of your lusty shell!

Fucking Trans Women by Mira Bellwether. The zine all about hot sex with and between trans women.

The Gender Book by Mel Reiff Hill & Jay Mays. A cute, short comic book all about gender. Fun to read and informative.

Lesbian Polyfidelity by Celeste West. Still radical after all these years. If you're curious about how some queer women build communities and families outside the covential paradigm, this is a cool book to check out.

My Gender Workbook by Kate Bornstein. Kate Bornstein is the fairy queermother of a whole generation of trans and gender queer folks. My Gender Workbook is an excellent introduction to gender and can help you get to know your own.

Not Your Mother's Meatloaf. A sex ed comic book that covers a lot of ground.

*Oh Joy Sex Toy & Girl F*ck* by Erica Moen. Like comics? Like sex stuff? Erica Moen's the gal for you.

She Comes First by Ian Kerner. Heteronormative as can be, but a truly excellent cunnilingus guide nonetheless.

The Ultimate Guide to Orgasm for Women: How to Become Orgasmic for a Lifetime by Mikaya Heart and Violet Blue

The Ultimate Guide to Pregnancy for Lesbians by Rachel Pepper Self-explanatory, no?

The Ultimate Guide to Sex and Disability by Cory Silverberg & A terrific exploration of the many ways different bodies can feel and give pleasure.

Whipping Girl: A Transsexual Woman on Sexism and the Scapegoating of Femininity by Julia Serano A groundbreaking and essential book from a trans woman exploring gender, sexuality, and the politics inherent in both.

The Whole Lesbian Sex Book: A Passionate Guide for All of Us by Felice Newman. This big, comprehensive book covers a huge amount of ground. It works particularly as a reference book, because of its thorough index. Flip through and explore.

Woman: An Intimate Geography by Natalie Angier Excited by anatomy? Check this one out.

Women's Anatomy of Arousal by Sherri Winston. If you're curious about the mechanics of "female" anatomy, this is a terrific read that explores the various glands, veins, and muscles that make up the vulva and more.

Porn & Edu-porn

If you want to see some of the techniques in this book in action here are some places to do it:

Pink & White: queer, feminist porn. Their online series, the Crash Pad has featured some of the authors found in this book, including Ignacio Rivera, Tina Horn, Jiz Lee, Sophia St. James, Tobi Hill Meyer, and Nina Hartley. CrashPadSeries.com

GoodDykePorn.com

Tristan Taormino's "Expert Guides": including titles about orgasm, female ejaculation, and anal. Taormino is the mama of feminist porn. PuckerUp.com

Websites

Autostraddle.com: a culture blog all about queer women

CuddleParty.com: Need help with your communication skills? This is a live workshop that will turn you in a self-advocating blackbelt!

GirlSex101.com of course!

Scarleteen.com: Great, free sex-ed for all genders

Stores

East Coast

Babeland – New York City – babeland.com

The Center for Sexual Pleasure and Health – Providence, Rhode Island – thecsph.org

Good Vibrations – Boston, MA – goodvibes.com

Oh My – Northampton, MA

Please – Brooklyn, NY – pleasenewyork.com

The Pleasure Chest – New York City thepleasurechest.com

Purple Passion – New York City – purplepassion.com

Sugar – Baltimore, MD – sugartheshop.com

Midwest

A Woman's Touch – Madison, WI sexualityresources.com

Early to Bed – Chicago, IL early2bed.com

The Pleasure Chest – Chicago, IL thepleasurechest.com

Tulip Toy Gallery – Chicago, IL – mytulip.com

Smitten Kitten – Minneapolis, MN smittenkittenonline.com

Tool Shed – Milwaukee, WI – toolshedtoys.com

Southwest

Self Serve – Albuquerque, NM – selfservetoys.com

Q Toys – Austin, TX – qtoysaustin.com

West Coast

As You Like It – Eugene, OR - asyoulikeitshop.com

Babeland – Seattle, WA – babeland.com

Feelmore 510 – Oakland, CA – feelmore510.com

Good Vibrations – San Francisco Bay Area (multiple locations), Boston, MA – goodvibes.com

Pure Pleasure – Santa Cruz, CA – purepleasureshop.com

She Bop – Portland, OR sheboptheshop.com

Canada

The Art of Loving – Vancouver, BC – artofloving.ca

Good for Her – Toronto, ON – goodforher.com

Venus Envy – Halifax, NS & Ottawa, ON – venusenvy.ca

Womyn's Ware – Vancouver, BC womynsware.com

CONTRIBUTOR BIOS

Megan Andelloux is the founder and director of The Center for Sexual Pleasure and Health, a 501c3 organization dedicated to reducing sexual shame through education, in Pawtucket, RI. She is an in-demand lecturer at universities and medical institutions nationwide, having delivered programs at more than 170 institutions of higher education and 50 medical establishments since 2009. She is a nationally certified Sexuality Educator through The American Association of Sexuality Educators, Counselors and Therapists, a board certified Sexologist through The American College of Sexologists, an appointed Fellow within the International Society for the Study of Women's Sexual Health and an Adjunct Instructor in the Brown University Medical School and the Brown University Pediatrics Residency Program. Contact Megan at megan@thecsph.org and follow her on Twitter: @HiOhMegan.

Claudia Astorino is an intersex activist living in NYC and pursuing her Ph.D. in the sciences. Claudia is the Associate Director of Organization Intersex International's USA chapter (OII-USA) – the only global advocacy group for individuals born with atypical sex characteristics, with branches on 6 continents. Claudia is the coordinator of the Annual Intersex Awareness Day (IAD) events in NYC, and has led workshops and lectures on intersex issues at New York University (NYC), Bluestockings Books (NYC), Green Chimneys (NYC), UC Davis, McDaniel College (MD), and The Wooden Shoe Books (Philadelphia). She currently writes about intersex issues on her personal blog, Full-Frontal Activism: Intersex and Awesome (http://fullfrontalactivism.blogspot.com), and Autostraddle.com, with several upcoming projects. Contact Claudia at full.frontal.activism@gmail.com and follow her on Twitter @intersexgrrrl.

Sandra Daugherty a.k.a. Sex Nerd Sandra punches sexual shame in the face! Brimming with book smarts and street smarts, the professional sex nerd's methodology includes heavy doses of physical comedy, playful curiosity and emotional honesty. Listen her podcast at SexNerdSandra.com

Still in high demand as an on-screen talent in X-rated features, **Nina Hartley** also co-produces her own line of instructional videos, Nina Hartley's Guides, the market-leader in adult sex-education-video programming, currently in its thirty-eighth installment. She lectures on campuses across the country and has contributed extensively to anthologies regarding sex and feminism. Her publishing credits include "Sex Work: Writings by Women in the Sex Industry," "Whores and Other Feminists," "Tricks and Treats: Sex Workers Write About Their Clients," and "The Feminist Porn Book." She currently writes advice columns for the magazine Hustler's Taboo. Ms. Hartley is the author of "Nina Hartley's Guide to Total Sex," a comprehensive book based on her video Guide series, for Avery, a division of Penguin Group. Further information about Nina Hartley can be found at www.nina.com.

Tina Horn (@TinaHornsAss) is a writer, educator, media-maker, and professional macho slut. She produces and hosts the sexuality podcast "Why Are People Into That?!" (whyarepeopleintothat. com / @intothatpodcast). She holds an MFA in Creative Nonfiction Writing from Sarah Lawrence. She is the author of a book about sex work called *Love Not Given Lightly* and an upcoming book about sexting. She has read from her zines and given workshops on spanking, dirty talk and sex worker rights at such venues as Red Umbrella Diaries, Perverts Put Out, Lesbian Sex Mafia, IMsL, and the Feminist Porn Conference. She once sold a golden dildo to Beyonce. Born in Northern California, Tina now lives in Manhattan with a very sweet bear.

Doing porn can often lead to writing and talking about sex. Take **Jiz Lee**, for example. Shortly after performing in The Crash Pad, the genderqueer porn performer took to blogging their adventures in queer sex and soon after found themself published in The Feminist Porn Book, Erika Moen's Oh Joy Sex Toy, and writing about squirt in GirlSex 101. What will they get into next? Find out at JizLee.com.

In 2010 **Tobi Hill-Meyer** made her film making debut, winning an Award for Emerging Filmmaker of the year and being named #3 in Velvet Park Media's list of the 25 Most Significant Queer Women of 2010. She is a multiracial trans woman with over a decade experience working with feminist and LGBTQ organizations on a local, state, and federal level, having served on several boards and offering support as a strategic consultant. Since receiving her degree in Sociology and Women and Gender Studies, Tobi has turned her focus to media analysis and productions. Most of her work can be found at www.HandbasketProductions.com or www.DoingitOnline.com

Reid Mihalko, creator of ReidAboutSex.com and SexGeekSummerCamp.com, has affectionately been called "America's favorite sex geek" and the "Tom Hanks of sex education." Reid helps adults and college students create more self-esteem, self-confidence and greater health in their relationships and sex lives using an inspiring mixture of humor and knowledge. Reid's workshops and college lectures have been attended by close to 50,000 men and women. He has appeared in media such as Oprah's Our America With Lisa Ling on OWN, the Emmy award-winning talk show Montel, Dr. Phil's The Doctors on CBS, Bravo's Miss Advised, Fox News, in Newsweek, Seventeen, GQ, The Washington Post, and in thirteen countries and at least seven languages.

Sarah Mueller is a sex educator at The Smitten Kitten, a progressive sex toy store in Minneapolis, MN. Along with education and sales, Sarah coordinates sex positive art shows at Smitten Kitten with local artists and kinky crafters, manages inventory, helps with website maintenance, and has previously written for Smitten Kitten's educational blog and participated in their Sex & Coffee Podcast. Aside from Macalester College's weekly newspaper, in which Sarah wrote the weekly sex advice column for 2 and a half years, Girl Sex 101 if her first real publication, and she's looking forward to being published in the first issue of the Nu Project Magazine. With a focus on personal empowerment, body positivity, and sex positivity Sarah hopes to continue to use her sex-nerdery to pursue pleasure based sex education, and she firmly believes the right lube can change a (sex) life. Contact her at sarah@smittenkittenonline.com or follow her on Instagram @sarahemueller.

Dr. Carol Queen [www.carolqueen.com, @CarolQueen] is a noted writer and cultural sexologist whose work has been widely published, she's written or edited several books, including Real Live Nude Girl: Chronicles of Sex-Positive Culture, PoMoSexuals, and Exhibitionism for the Shy. She has been speaking publicly about sexuality for over 30 years. She has addressed many conferences; she frequently speaks to college as well as general and specialized audiences. Queen co-founded the Center for Sex & Culture [www.sexandculture.org] in San Francisco and is staff sexologist and Company Historian at Good Vibrations, the women-founded sex shop, where she has worked since 1990.

Ignacio Rivera aka Papí Coxxx, who prefers the gender-neutral pronoun "they," is a trans, gender queer, Two-Spirit, Black-Boricua-Taíno. Ignacio is an activist, filmmaker, kinky-sex-positive sex educator, sex worker, and performance artist. They blog about, among many other things, sex and gender on "What they said" and is the founder of Poly Patao Productions.

Julia Serano is the author of two books, 2007's Whipping Girl: A Transsexual Woman on Sexism and the Scapegoating of Femininity and 2013's Excluded: Making Feminist and Queer Movements More Inclusive. She makes indie-pop music under the moniker *soft vowel sounds*, and lives with her partner, cat, and four parrots in Oakland, CA. juliaserano.com

With a background in design and construction in mainstream film and television production, to performing in front of the camera as the sexually charged figurehead for chubby Asian girls everywhere, **Kelly Shibari** is a stereotype-breaking tour-de-force. Never one to shy away from challenges, Kelly is a a true ground-breaker by making a name for herself by continually doing what people tell her can't be done, and usually being the first in her niche to do so.

Sophia St. James has been an erotic entertainer since 1996. She has traveled performing and educating the public on self confidence, self worth, and the art of sensuality no matter their outer appearance. She started SSJ Entertainment in 2010 and won her first Feminist Porn Award with her directional debut of 'Twisted Getaway'. Sophia is also a mother and healthcare professional who takes pride in being a body positive and sex positive fierce femme.
For more details on Sophia, visit her website at http://www.sophiastjames.com.

Tristan Taormino is an award-winning writer, editor, sex educator, college lecturer, feminist pornographer, and host of Sex Out Loud, a weekly radio show/podcast. She is the editor of 25 anthologies and author of eight books, including The Ultimate Guide to Anal Sex for Women.

Illustrations on pages 90 and 94 reprinted courtesy of Tristan Taormino.

ACKNOWLEDGEMENTS

Huge thanks to Justin Alves, my pinch hitter for life, who stepped in during the witching hours of this project and helped me get it all done, and done well. You are a Prince.

Another huge thanks to the Family Dinnerettes, who wined, dined, and timed me. I would have lost my mind after long, long work upon work hours if it weren't for you.

– kd

I'd like to thank:
- The Center for Sexual Pleasure and Health in Rhode Island for fact-checking and existing
- Andy Izenson for offering notes on consent
- Carol Queen for editing and proofing the non-fiction
- Alyc Helms for editing the fiction
- David Higgins for introducing me to the idea of Attraction vs. Chemistry
- Reid Mihalko for letting me steal some of his best jokes
- The fantastic Trans Girl Brain Trust for answering super initimate questions in service of this book: Amy Dentata (amydentata.com), Autumn Nicole Bradley (lifeinneon.com), Dee, & Tobi Hill-Meyer
- All of the contributors and survey respondents who shared their passions and expertise

To kd, for our topless cross-country video chat sessions, sparked with moments of pure brilliance in the bathtub.

Most of all, thanks to my queer community both near and far. Everything I know, I learned from you. Thank you for your compassion, your patience, your brains, and your butt-slappin' sexiness.

– Allison

A huge thank you to all of our Kickstarter supporters. This book would not have been able to happen without you. A particularly robust Girl Sex thanks goes out to these supporters who backed at the Tune Up Level and above. You rock!

Aaron P. Churchill
Abigail Bunyan
Adam Israel &
   Andrea G Redman
AGC
Aida Manduley
Aidan Sullivan
Áine Richards
Alex Dulude
Allison Shaffer
Amanda Morgan
Amy Kirby
Amy Sutedja
Andrew Siegler
Angela Prendergast
Ann M. Sasala
Annamarie Stockwell
Anonymous
Apurva
Ash Miller
Barbara Carignan
Ben, Kim, & Micaela
Beth Papagolos
BG
Blythe Baldwin &
   Gina Ferrante
Boobs Ruddock
Brandon Kitchens
Brenda Schwerdt
Brian Schantz
Camilla Chaplin
Candace Adams
Candice Mackinnon
Cas Thomas
Cassandra Dahl
Caterina Poh
Charles and
   Jessica Payseur
Charley Connnolly
Chris Burlingame
Christina Warner
Claudio Bottaccini
Cowboi Jen
D Roy Mitchell IV
Danielle
Dara
Darcy Murphy

Debbie Millman
Delia Gable
Dharma Kelleher
Diego Vazquez Jr
DnA
Drew Cordes
Edmund Charles
   Davis-Quinn
Ellie Hail
Emily Conger
Emily Millay Haddad
Emily Legere
Erica Rand
Erin Easley
Fizbin
Forth Sadler
Fred Brown
Fureigh
Gabriel Seah
Glo Schindler
gnumpen
Guido Alexander Sanchez
Heather Powers
Helen Corkin
Holly Krajacich
Hugh Patterson
Hunter Riley
Isabelle Testoni
Jae & Laurie Coleman
Jay Parry
Jean Franzblau
Jeanie McAlpine
Jeff "JJ" Peterson
Jemma Rea
Jenn Harris
Jennifer Pickens
Jennifer Pina
Jennifer Wortman
Jenny Blacker
Jessica J. Eckstein
JM & Talia
Joanna Kahn
Joanna F.N. Eyles
Joe, Tam, and
   Kat Tortuga
Jordan Mendelson
Joslin Chidester

Joy Antoinette
JTT
Jude Schell
Julie Schottman
Julie Wesler-Buck
K C del Castillo
K Zimolzak
K. Morrell
Kate T
Kay Seitz
Kayla Potter
Keiko Lane
Kelsea J. Wilhelm
Kerkyra Brock
Kimmy Bunni
Kitty Harding
Kristen Gilbert
Kristin M. Block
Kristina A.C. Orlandi
Lacey Stewart
Lauren E Clair
Leishycat
Lily Seville
Lisa Jakobsen &
   Hanna Miller
Livia Iacolare
lorgle
Lydia Howchin
Mabby & Sara Howard
The MacDylans
Mallory Lass
Marcia Silk
Maria-Katrina Lehtinen
Marisa Grippo &
   Maggie Laigaie
Matteo Rossi
Megan M. Hetzel
MegaZone
Melissa Marie
Mia Nutick
Michael Mullen
Mickey
Missy Dugan
Mistress Kara
   and her kitten
Monica Majewski
morgan

Morgan L. Bornstein
Natey Martin
Nicholas Larzalere
Nick Elliott
Nico
Nivair H. Gabriel
Noah 'bibulb' Ramon
Olha
Olivia Desormeaux
Pam
Pauline Driscoll
Rachel Gold
Rosie Radcliffe
Sally Rose
Sam Orchard
Sarah Bruce
Sarah Langlais
Sarah Maple
Sean R. Reeves
Shannon Bolger
Stephanie Coulson
Susan Rizzo
T.R. Fullhart
t'Sade
TaAnna
Tarna
ThatMissQuin
The Lady Kay
Tina Marie
Trevor Sexton
Vanessa Wayling
verybookish
Victoria Robinson
Viviane
Waxmonkey
Whitney Moses